Culture NL Ltd

7 779751 48

KT-479-282

OF
BLOOD
AND
BONE

By Nora Roberts

By Nora Roberts
Trilogies and Quartets

THE BORN IN TRILOGY
BORN IN FIRE
BORN IN ICE
BORN IN SHAME

THE BRIDE QUARTET
VISION IN WHITE
BED OF ROSES
SAVOUR THE MOMENT
HAPPY EVER AFTER

THE KEY TRILOGY
KEY OF LIGHT
KEY OF KNOWLEDGE
KEY OF VALOUR

THE IRISH TRILOGY
JEWELS OF THE SUN
TEARS OF THE MOON
HEART OF THE SEA

THREE SISTERS ISLAND TRILOGY
DANCE UPON THE AIR
HEAVEN AND EARTH
FACE THE FIRE

THE INN AT BOONSBORO TRILOGY
THE NEXT ALWAYS
THE LAST BOYFRIEND
THE PERFECT HOPE

THE SIGN OF SEVEN TRILOGY
BLOOD BROTHERS
THE HOLLOW
THE PAGAN STONE

CHESAPEAKE BAY QUARTET
SEA SWEPT
RISING TIDES
INNER HARBOUR
CHESAPEAKE BLUE

IN THE GARDEN TRILOGY
BLUE DAHLIA
BLACK ROSE
RED LILY

THE CIRCLE TRILOGY
MORRIGAN'S CROSS
DANCE OF THE GODS
VALLEY OF SILENCE

THE DREAM TRILOGY
DARING TO DREAM
HOLDING THE DREAM
FINDING THE DREAM

THE COUSINS O'DWYER TRILOGY
DARK WITCH
SHADOW SPELL
BLOOD MAGICK

THE GUARDIANS TRILOGY
STARS OF FORTUNE
BAY OF SIGHS
ISLAND OF GLASS

eBooks by Nora Roberts

CORDINA'S ROYAL FAMILY
AFFAIRE ROYALE
COMMAND PERFORMANCE
THE PLAYBOY PRINCE
CORDINA'S CROWN JEWEL

THE DONOVAN LEGACY
CAPTIVATED
ENTRANCED
CHARMED
ENCHANTED

THE O'HURLEYS
THE LAST HONEST WOMAN
DANCE TO THE PIPER
SKIN DEEP
WITHOUT A TRACE

NIGHT TALES
NIGHT SHIFT
NIGHT SHADOW
NIGHTSHADE
NIGHT SMOKE
NIGHT SHIELD

THE MACGREGORS
THE WINNING HAND
THE PERFECT NEIGHBOR
ALL THE POSSIBILITIES
ONE MAN'S ART
TEMPTING FATE
PLAYING THE ODDS
THE MACGREGOR BRIDES
THE MACGREGOR GROOMS
REBELLION/IN FROM THE COLD
FOR NOW, FOREVER

THE CALHOUNS
SUZANNA'S SURRENDER
MEGAN'S MATE
COURTING CATHERINE
A MAN FOR AMANDA
FOR THE LOVE OF LILAH

IRISH LEGACY
IRISH ROSE
IRISH REBEL
IRISH THOROUGHBRED

BEST LAID PLANS
LOVING JACK
LAWLESS

SUMMER LOVE
BOUNDARY LINES
DUAL IMAGE
FIRST IMPRESSIONS
THE LAW IS A LADY
LOCAL HERO
THIS MAGIC MOMENT
THE NAME OF THE GAME
PARTNERS
TEMPTATION
THE WELCOMING
OPPOSITES ATTRACT
TIME WAS
TIMES CHANGE
GABRIEL'S ANGEL
HOLIDAY WISHES
THE HEART'S VICTORY
THE RIGHT PATH

RULES OF THE GAME
SEARCH FOR LOVE
BLITHE IMAGES
FROM THIS DAY
SONG OF THE WEST
ISLAND OF FLOWERS
HER MOTHER'S KEEPER
UNTAMED
SULLIVAN'S WOMAN
LESS OF A STRANGER
REFLECTIONS
DANCE OF DREAMS
STORM WARNING
ONCE MORE WITH FEELING
ENDINGS AND BEGINNINGS
TONIGHT AS ALWAYS
A MATTER OF CHOICE

Nora Roberts also writes the In Death series using the pseudonym J. D. Robb

NORA ROBERTS

OF BLOOD AND BONE

piatkus

PIATKUS

First published in Great Britain in 2018 by Piatkus

1 3 5 7 9 10 8 6 4 2

Copyright © 2018 by Nora Roberts

The moral right of the author has been asserted.

*All characters and events in this publication, other than those
clearly in the public domain, are fictitious and any resemblance
to real persons, living or dead, is purely coincidental.*

All rights reserved.
No part of this publication may be reproduced, stored in a
retrieval system, or transmitted, in any form or by any means, without
the prior permission in writing of the publisher, nor be otherwise circulated
in any form of binding or cover other than that in which it is published
and without a similar condition including this condition
being imposed on the subsequent purchaser.

A CIP catalogue record for this book
is available from the British Library.

ISBN: 978-0-349-41497-3 (hardback)
ISBN: 978-0-349-41498-0 (trade paperback)

Printed and bound by CPI Group (UK) Ltd, Croydon, CR0 4YY

Papers used by Piatkus are from well-managed forests
and other responsible sources.

MIX
Paper from
responsible sources
FSC® C104740

Piatkus
An imprint of
Little, Brown Book Group
Carmelite House
50 Victoria Embankment
London EC4Y 0DZ

An Hachette UK Company
www.hachette.co.uk

www.littlebrown.co.uk

For Kayla, who's growing up smart and strong

THE CHOICE

So nigh is grandeur to our dust,
So near is God to man,
When Duty whispers low, *Thou must*,
The youth replies, *I can*.

—Ralph Waldo Emerson

PROLOGUE

They said a virus ended the world. But it was magick, black as moonless midnight. The virus was its weapon, a barrage of arrows winging, silenced bullets striking, a jagged blade slicing. And yet the innocent—the touch of a hand, a mother's good-night kiss—spread the Doom, bringing sudden, painful, ugly death to billions.

Many who survived that first shocking strike died by their own hand or by another's as the thorny vines of madness, grief, and fear strangled the world. Still others, unable to find shelter, food, clean water, medications, simply withered and died waiting for help and hope that never came.

The spine of technology cracked, bringing the dark, the silence. Governments toppled from their perches of power.

The Doom gave no quarter to democracy, to dictators, to parliaments or kingdoms. It fed on presidents and peasants with equal greed.

Out of the dark, lights dimmed for millennia flickered and woke.

The rise of magicks, white and black, sprang from the chaos. Awakened powers offered a choice between good and evil, light and dark.

Some would always choose the dark.

Uncannys shared what was left of the world with man. And those—man and magickals—who embraced the dark struck, turning great cities into rubble, hunting those who hid from them or fought against them to destroy, to enslave, to bask in blood even as bodies littered the ground.

Panicked governments ordered their militaries to sweep up survivors, to "contain" Uncannys. So a child who had discovered her wings might find herself restrained on a table in a lab, in the name of science.

Madmen claimed God in their vicious righteousness, stirring fear and hate to build their own armies to purge what was "other." Magick, they preached, came from the devil's hand, and any who possessed it were demons to be sent back to hell.

Raiders cruised the ruined cities, the highways, and the back roads to burn and kill because they enjoyed it. Man would always find ways to wreak cruelty on man.

In a world so broken, who would stop them?

There were murmurs in the light, rumblings in the dark, that reached the ears of men—of a warrior to come. She, daughter of the Tuatha de Danann, would remain hidden until she took up her sword and shield. Until she, The One, led light against the dark.

But months became years, and the world remained broken. Hunts and raids and sweeps continued.

Some hid, skittering out at night to scavenge or steal enough to survive another day. Some chose to take to the roads in an endless migration to nowhere. Others took to the woods to hunt, to the fields to plant. Some formed communities that ebbed and flowed as they struggled to live in a world where a handful of salt was more precious than gold.

And some, like those who found and formed New Hope, rebuilt.

When the world ended, Arlys Reid had reported it from the New York anchor desk she'd inherited. She'd watched the city burn around her, and in the end had chosen to tell the truth to all who could still hear her and escape.

She'd seen death up close, had killed to survive.

She'd seen the nightmares and the wonders.

She, along with a handful of people, including three infants, found the deserted rural town they had christened New Hope. And there they made their stand.

Now, in Year Four, New Hope was home to more than three hundred, had a mayor and town council, a police force, two schools— one for magickal training and education—a community garden and kitchen, two farms, one with a mill for flour and grain, a medical clinic—with a small dentistry—a library, an armory, and a militia.

They had doctors, healers, herbalists, weavers, sewing circles, plumbers, mechanics, carpenters, cooks. Some of them had made their living on those skills in the old world. Most studied and learned them in the new.

They had armed security posted around the clock. And though it remained on a volunteer basis, most all residents participated in combat and weapons training.

The New Hope Massacre, in their first year, remained a raw scar on their hearts and minds. That scar, and the graves of the dead, led to the forming of the militia and to the rescue parties who risked their lives to save others.

Arlys stood on the sidewalk, looking at New Hope, and saw why it mattered. Why all of it mattered. More than surviving, as it had been for those first horrible months, more even than building, as it had been for the months that followed.

It was living, and it was, like the town, hope.

It mattered, she thought now, that Laurel—elf—came out to

sweep the porch of the building where she lived on a cool spring morning. Up the street, Bill Anderson polished the glass on his shop window, and inside the shelves held dozens and dozens of useful things for easy bartering.

Fred, the young intern who'd faced the horrors of the underground out of New York with Arlys, would be busy in the community garden. Fred, with her magick wings and endless optimism, lived every day with hope.

Rachel—doctor and good, good friend—stepped out to open the doors of the clinic and wave.

"Where's the baby?" Arlys called out.

"Sleeping—unless Jonah's picked him up again when my back was turned. The man's bedazzled."

"As a daddy should be. Isn't today your six-week checkup, Doc? Big day for you."

"This doctor's already given her patient the all clear, but Ray's going to formalize it. Big day for you, too. How do you feel?"

"Great. Excited. A little nervous."

"I'll be tuning in—and I want to see you in here when you're done."

"I'll be there." As she spoke, Arlys laid a hand on the mountain of her belly. "This baby's got to be about cooked. Much longer, I won't even be able to waddle."

"We'll check it out. Good morning, Clarice," Rachel said as the first patient of the day came up the walk. "Come right on in. Good luck, Arlys. We'll be listening."

Arlys started to waddle—really, what other word was there—and stopped when she heard her name called.

She waited for Will Anderson—her childhood neighbor, current town deputy, and, as it turned out, the love of her life.

He laid a hand over hers on her belly, kissed her. "Walk you to work?"

"Sure."

He linked fingers with her as they walked to where he'd lived during his first months in the community. "Okay with you if I hang around and watch?"

"If you want, but I don't know how long it's going to take to set up. Chuck's optimistic, but—"

"If Chuck says we can do this, we can."

As her belly pinged with nerves, she let out a breath. "I've got to go with you there."

Chuck had been her primary source during the Doom, a hacker and IT genius who now ruled over what technology they had. In the basement, of course. The man was a confirmed basement dweller.

"I want to see you at work," Will added.

"What do you call what I do at home with the *New Hope Bulletin*?"

"Work, and a boon to the community. But we're talking live broadcast, baby. It's what you're meant to do."

"I know some people are worried about the risk, about drawing attention here. The wrong kind of attention."

"It's worth it. And Chuck not only knows what he's doing, but we'll have the magickal shields going. If you can reach one person out there, you can reach a hundred. If you can reach a hundred, who knows. A lot of people still don't know what the hell's going on, where to get help, supplies, medicine. This matters, Arlys."

It mattered, a great deal to her, when he risked his life on a rescue.

"I was just thinking about what matters." She paused outside the house, turned to him. "You're top of the list."

They circled around to the back of the house to the basement door.

Inside, what had been a large family room now stood as a computer geek's wet dream—if he dreamed of cobbling together components, cables, hard drives, motherboards, gutting ancient computers, reconfiguring desktops and laptops, hanging various screens.

She figured Chuck did.

He sat at one of the keyboards in a hoodie and cargo pants, a backward ball cap on hair recently bleached white courtesy of the community beautician. He'd gone bright red on his pointed little beard.

In the theme of bright red, Fred's curls bounced as she popped up from where she'd been sitting with three four-year-olds and an array of toys.

"Here's the talent! I'm production manager, gofer, and assistant camera."

"I thought I was the gofer." Katie, mother of three, kept an eye on them from the arm of the sagging sofa Arlys knew Chuck often slept on.

"Co-gofer, and supervisor of the power boosters."

Katie looked at her twins, Duncan and Antonia. "They're excited. I just hope they—and everybody—know what we're doing."

"We make it go for Arlys and Chuck," Duncan said, grinning at his mom. "Me and Tonia."

"Push!" Tonia giggled, lifting a hand. Duncan pressed his palm against hers. Light glowed.

"Not yet."

Hannah, blond and rosy against the twins' dark hair, got up. She patted her mother's leg, as if in comfort, then walked to Arlys. "When's the baby come out?"

"Soon. I hope."

"Can I watch?"

"Ah . . ."

On a laugh, Katie rose to swing Hannah up and kiss her. "She probably would."

"I don't know about that, kiddo." Chuck swiveled around in his chair. "But you're about to watch history, and the debut of New Hope Broadcasting."

"We're up?"

He grinned at Arlys, gave her a finger salute. "We're up. Definitely up with some help from our boosters."

The twins jumped up, eyes alight.

"Not yet, not yet." This time Arlys held them off. "I need to look over my notes, and . . . things. I need a few minutes."

"We're not going anywhere," Chuck told her.

"Okay, um, just give me a few."

Rattled when she hadn't expected to be, she walked back outside with her folder of notes. Fred walked out behind her.

"You shouldn't be nervous."

"Oh Jesus, Fred."

"I mean it. You're so good at it. You were always good at it."

"I got the desk in New York because everybody died."

"You got the desk when you did because of that," Fred corrected. "You'd have gotten it anyway, later, but anyway."

Stepping closer, Fred put her hands on Arlys's shoulders. "Do you remember what you did that last day?"

"I still have nightmares about it."

"What you did," Fred continued, "when Bob held a gun on you, on live TV. You held on. And what you did when he killed himself right there, right there sitting next to you? You held on, and more. You looked straight into the camera and you told the truth. You did it without notes, without the teleprompter. Because it's what you do. You tell people the truth. That's what you're going to do now."

"I don't know why I'm so nervous about this."

"Maybe hormones?"

Rubbing her belly, Arlys laughed. "Maybe. Hemorrhoids, heartburn, and hormones. Having a baby's an adventure."

"I can't wait to have my adventures." On a sigh, Fred looked over the back garden. "I want a zillion babies."

Arlys hoped she'd get through having this one—and soon.

But right now, she had a job to do.

"Okay. Okay. How do I look?"

"Amazing. But today, I'm also your makeup artist. I'm going to powder you for the camera and do your lipstick, then you're going to be great."

"I love you, Fred. I really do."

"Aw. I love you back, I really do."

She let Fred powder and paint, did a few tongue twisters, sipped some water, did some yoga breathing.

When she came back in from the bathroom, she saw her father-in-law on the sofa surrounded by the children. He had a way of drawing them.

"Bill, who's minding the store?"

"Closed it for an hour. I want to see my girl live and in person. Your folks would be proud of you. Your mom, dad, Theo, they'd be proud."

"Consider this your anchor desk." Chuck tapped a chair in front of one of his many tables. "You're going to face this camera. I've got the angle. What we're doing here, boys and girls, is a fu—a freaking simulcast. We got the ham radio, the live-streaming, and the cable TV going. I'll be monitoring you and doing what I do over there. But pay no attention to the man behind the curtain. It's your show, Arlys."

"All right." She sat, adjusted. Opening her folder, she took out the photo of her last Christmas with her family. She propped it against a keyboard. "I'm ready when you are."

"Fred's going to give you the countdown. Okay, kids, let's make it boom."

"Don't say 'boom'!" Katie threw up her hands. "You have no idea."

"We make it go." Tonia wiggled her butt in delight. "We make it push, Duncan."

"Push." He grinned at his sister, they linked hands. Light shimmered through their fingers.

"That's what I'm talking about!" Chuck dashed from monitor to monitor, adjusted, let out a whoop. "That's what I'm saying. We're a go, and I mean *go*."

"Arlys." Fred moved behind the camera. "In five, four . . ."

She used her fingers to finish the countdown, and with a brilliant smile swept the last one forward.

"Good morning, this is Arlys Reid. I don't know how many can hear me, or see me, but if you're receiving this, pass the word. We'll continue to broadcast as often as possible, to give you information, to give you truth, to report. To let you know, wherever you are, you're not alone."

She took another breath, pressed her hands to her belly.

"Four years after the Doom, sources confirm Washington, D.C., remains unstable. Martial law remains in effect through the metropolitan area while gangs known as Raiders and the Dark Uncanny continue to attack. Resistance forces broke through security at a containment center in Arlington, Virginia. According to eyewitness accounts, more than thirty people were liberated."

She spoke for forty-two minutes. Reporting of the bombings in Houston, the Purity Warrior attack on a community in Greenbelt, Maryland, fires set, homes raided.

But she ended with stories of humanity, courage, and kindness. The mobile medical clinic that used wagons and horses to reach remote camps, shelters for the displaced, rescues, and food banks.

"Stay safe," she said, "but remember, it isn't enough to stay safe. Live, work, gather together. If you have a story, if you have news, if you're searching for a loved one and can get word to me, I'll report it. You're not alone. This is Arlys Reid for New Hope Broadcasting."

"And we're clear." Chuck stood up, pumped his fists. "Fucking A."

"Fucking A," Duncan echoed.

"Oops." Roaring with laughter as Katie just closed her eyes, Chuck jumped over to Duncan and Tonia, held out his fist. "Hey, totally awesome, kids. Fist bump. Come on! Fist bump."

Their heads tipped together as they both lifted their tiny fists, knocked them against his.

His sparked. "Whoa!" He danced around a little, blowing on his knuckles. "Major power surge. I *love* it."

Fred blinked at tears. "It was you-know-what A, and awesome."

Will bent over, kissed the top of Arlys's head. "You stagger me," he told her.

"It felt . . . right. Once I got over the hump, it just felt right. How long was I on?"

"Forty-two awesome minutes."

"Forty-two." She swiveled in her chair. "I shouldn't have kept the twins at it so long. I'm so sorry, Katie, I just lost track."

"They were fine. I kept track," Katie assured her. "They're going to need a nice long nap." She glanced toward Hannah, curled up and sleeping in Bill's lap. "Like their sister. You look like you could use one. That had to take a lot out of you. You look a little pale."

"Actually, I think about five minutes in, I think I started having contractions. Maybe actually before that. I thought it was nerves."

"You—what? Now?"

Arlys gripped Will's hand. "I'm pretty sure we should go see Rachel. And I think it's— Okay!"

She braced one hand on the table, and squeezed Will's hand— bone against bone—with the other.

"Breathe," Katie ordered, hurrying over to lay a hand on Arlys's rock-hard belly, and began to rub in circles. "Breathe through it— you took the classes."

"Classes my ass. It doesn't hurt like this in classes."

"Breathe through it," Katie said again, calmly. "You just did the first New Hope simulcast while in labor. You can breathe through a contraction."

"It's easing off. It's easing."

"Thank you, Jesus," Will muttered and flexed his aching fingers. "Ow."

"Believe me, that's not even close to ow." Arlys blew out a strong breath. "I really want Rachel."

"Me, too." Will levered her up. "Let's take it slow though. Dad?"

"I'm having a grandchild."

Katie lifted Hannah from his lap. "Go with them."

"I'm having a grandchild," Bill repeated.

"Fred?" Arlys looked back. "Aren't you coming?"

"Really? I can? Oh, oh boy! I'll run over and tell Rachel. Oh boy! Chuck."

"Oh, no, thanks. I'll pass. No offense, Arlys, but, uh-uh."

"None taken."

"We're having a baby!" Fred spread her wings and flew out the basement door.

Duncan walked to the door to watch them all go. "He wants to come out."

Katie shifted Hannah. "He?"

"Uh-huh." Tonia walked over to stay with Duncan. "What's he doing in there?"

"That's another story," Katie told her. "Come on, kids, time to go home. Good work, Chuck."

"Best job ever."

Over the next eight hours Arlys learned a number of things. The first, and most urgent for several of those, was that contractions got a lot harder and lasted a hell of a lot longer as labor progressed.

She learned, not with any surprise, that Fred was a cheerful and tireless co-coach. And Will—no surprise, either—was a rock.

She got reports—a fine distraction—that her broadcast had reached at least the twenty miles out where Kim and Poe had traveled with a laptop on battery.

She sure as *fuck* learned why they called it labor.

At one point she dissolved into tears and had Will wrapping his arms around her. "It's almost over, baby. It's almost over."

"Not that, not that. Lana. I thought of Lana. Oh God, Will, oh God, to have to do this alone. Without Max, without Rachel, without us. To be alone and doing this."

"I don't believe she was alone." Fred stroked a hand down Arlys's arm. "I really, really don't. On the night—I could feel it. A lot of us could. The birth of The One. She wasn't alone, Arlys. I know it."

"Promise?"

"Cross my heart."

"Okay. Okay." When Will brushed her tears away, she managed a smile. "Almost over?"

"He's not wrong. Time to push," Rachel told her. "Will, support her back. Next contraction, push. Let's get this baby into the world."

She pushed, panted, pushed, panted, and eight hours after she made broadcast history, Arlys brought her son into the world that was.

She learned something more. Love could come like a bolt of light.

"Look at him! Look at him." Exhaustion fell away in stupefied love as the baby cried and wiggled in her arms. "Oh, Will, look at him."

"He's beautiful, you're beautiful. God, I love you."

Stepping back, Rachel rolled her aching shoulders. "Will, do you want to cut the cord?"

"I . . ." He took the scissors from Rachel, then turned to his father, saw the tears on his cheeks.

He'd lost grandchildren in the Doom. A daughter, a wife, babies.

"I think Granddad should. How about it?"

Bill swiped fingers under his glasses. "I'm honored. I'm a grandfather."

As he cut the cord, Fred swept the room with rainbows. "I'm an aunt, right? An honorary aunt."

"Yes, you are." Arlys couldn't take her eyes off the baby. "You, Rachel, Katie. The New Hope originals."

"His color's excellent." Rachel took a good visual study. "I'm going to need to take my nephew in a minute. Clean him up for you, weigh and measure him."

"In a minute. Hello, Theo." Arlys pressed a kiss to the baby's brow. "Theo William Anderson. We're going to make the world a better place for you. We're going to do all we can do to make it a better place. I swear it."

She traced Theo's face with her finger—so tiny, so sweet, so hers.

This is life, she thought. This is hope.

This is the reason for both.

She would work and fight every day to keep the promise she made to her son.

Holding him close, she thought again of Lana, of the child Lana had carried.

Of The One who was promised.

CHAPTER ONE

On the farm where she'd been born, Fallon Swift learned how to plant and grow and harvest, to respect and use the land. She learned how to move through fields and forests, silent as a shadow, to hunt and fish. To respect the game, and take no more than needed, to take none at all for sport.

She learned to prepare food grown or taken from the land in her mother's kitchen or over a campfire.

She learned food was more than eggs fresh from the henhouse or a well-grilled trout. Food meant survival.

She learned to sew—though she disliked the time spent sitting still plying a needle. She learned how to tan leather, far from her favorite lesson, and could, if given no choice, spin yarn. Clothes, she learned, weren't simply something to wear. They protected the body, like a weapon.

She respected weapons, and had learned from a young age how to clean a gun, sharpen a knife, string a bow.

She learned how to build, with hammer and saw, to keep the fences in repair, to make repairs on the old farmhouse she loved as much as the woods.

A strong fence, a sound wall, a roof that held back the rain offered more than a happy home. They, too, meant survival.

And, though she often simply knew, she learned magicks. How to light the flame with a breath, how to cast a circle, how to heal a small wound with the light inside her, how to look, and how to see.

She learned, though she often simply knew, magick was more than a gift to be treasured, a craft to be honed, a weapon to be used with great care.

It was, and would be, survival.

Even with food, with shelter, with clothing and weapons, even with magicks, not all had survived. Not all would in the times to come.

She learned of a world that had existed before her birth. A world crowded with people, a world of huge cities with towering buildings where people had lived and worked. In that world people had traveled routinely by air and sea and road and track. Some had even traveled into space, and to the moon that hung in the sky.

Her mother had lived in a great city, in the City of New York. Fallon knew from the stories told, from the books she devoured, it had been a place full of people and noise and light and dark.

A wonder of a place to her, one she vowed to see someday.

She imagined it often at night when she lay awake watching the faeries dance outside her window.

There had been war in that world, and bigotry and cruelty, just as there was now. She knew of the wars that had been from the books, from the stories. And she knew of the wars that were still raging from visitors who stopped at the farm.

Her father had been a soldier once. He had taught her to fight—with her hands, her feet, her mind. She learned how to read maps and how to make them, and imagined following them one day on the journeys she knew, had always known, she would take.

She had no attachment, as her parents did, to the world that had been before the Doom had killed so many. Billions, it was said. Many remembered when those great cities fell to the burning, the mad things, the dark magicks. The cruelty and greed of men still swam in the minds and the blood of those who'd lived through it.

When she caught glimpses of tomorrows, she knew there would be more burning, more blood, more death. And she would be part of it. So she often lay awake at night, cuddling her teddy bear, a gift from a man she'd yet to meet.

If those tomorrows weighed too heavy, she sometimes slipped out of the house while her parents and siblings slept, to sit outside while the little faeries flickered like fireflies. Where she could smell the earth, the crops, the animals.

Most often she slept the quiet and innocent sleep of a child with loving parents and three annoying little brothers, a healthy child with a questing mind and an active body.

Sometimes she dreamed of her sire, the man her mother had lived with in New York, the man she'd loved. The man, Fallon knew, who had died so she would live.

He'd been a writer, a leader, a great hero. She bore his name, just as she bore the name of the man who brought her into the world, who raised her, who taught her. Fallon for Max Fallon, her sire. Swift for Simon Swift, her father.

Two names, Fallon thought, equally important. Just as her mother wore two rings, one from each man she'd loved.

And though she loved her father as deeply and truly as any child could love, she wondered about the man who'd given her the color of her eyes and hair who, along with her mother, had passed powers to her with their mating.

She read his books—all books were gifts—and studied the photo of him on the back of them.

Once, when she was only six, she'd curled up in the library with one of Max Fallon's books. Though she couldn't understand all the words, she liked that it was about a wizard, one who used magicks and brains to fight against evil forces.

When her father came in, a stab of guilt had her trying to hide the book. Her dad had no magicks, but he had a lot of brains.

He'd plucked her and the book up, then sat to hold her on his lap. She loved how he smelled of the farm—the earth, the animals, the growing things.

Sometimes she wished she had eyes like his that changed from sort of green to sort of gold or just mixed those colors together. When she wished it, she felt guilty about Max.

"It's a good book."

"You read it?"

"Yeah. My mom really liked to read. It's why she and my dad made this room for books. You don't have to hide anything from me, baby. Not anything."

"Because you're my daddy." She turned into him, pressed her face to his heart. *Beat, beat, beat.* "You're my daddy."

"I'm your daddy. But I wouldn't have gotten the chance to be if it wasn't for Max Fallon." He turned the book over so they could both look at the picture of the dark, handsome man with strong gray eyes. "I wouldn't have my most beautiful girl if he hadn't loved your mom, and she hadn't loved him. If they hadn't made you. If he hadn't loved her and you enough, been brave enough, to give his life to protect you. I'm real grateful to him, Fallon. I owe him everything."

"Mama loves you, Daddy."

"Yeah, she does. I'm a lucky guy. She loves me, and she loves you, and Colin and Travis."

"And the new baby that's coming."

"Yeah."

"It's not a girl." This on a huge, sorrowful sigh.

"Is that so?"

"She has a boy in her, again. Why can't she make a sister for me? Why does she always make brothers?"

She heard the laugh in his chest as he cuddled her. "Actually, that's supposed to be my job. I guess it's the way it goes."

He stroked her long black hair as he spoke. "And I guess that means you'll just have to go on being my favorite girl. Have you told your mom it's a boy?"

"She doesn't want to know which kind. She likes the wondering."

"Then I won't tell her, either." Simon kissed the top of her head. "Our secret."

"Daddy?"

"Hmm?"

"I can't read all the words. Some are too hard."

"Well, why don't I read the first chapter to you before we go back to chores?"

He shifted her so she could curl up, then opened the book, turned to page one, and began.

She hadn't known *The Wizard King* had been Max Fallon's first novel—or perhaps some part of her had. But she would remember, forever, that her father had read it to her, chapter by chapter, every night before bed.

So she learned. She learned about goodness from her father, generosity from her mother. She learned about love and light and respect from the home and family and life given to her.

She learned of war and hardship and grief from travelers, many wounded, who came to the farm or to the village nearby.

She had lessons on politics, and found them annoying, as people talked too much, did too little. And what good were politics when reports claimed the government—such a vague word to her—had begun to rebuild in the third year after the Doom, only to fall again before the end of Year Five?

Now, in the twelfth year, the capital of the United States—which didn't seem united to Fallon, then or now—remained a war zone. Factions of the Raiders, groups of the Dark Uncanny, and those faithful to the cult of the Purity Warriors battled for power, for land, for the smell of blood. Against each other, it seemed, and against those who sought to rule or govern.

Even though Fallon wanted peace, wanted to build, to grow, she understood the need, the duty to fight to protect and defend. More than once she'd seen her father arm himself and leave the farm to help protect a neighbor, to help defend the village. More than once she'd seen his eyes when he'd come home again, and had known there'd been blood, there'd been death.

She'd been raised to fight, to defend, as had her brothers. Even as the farm basked in summer, as the crops ripened and fruit hung heavy, as the woods ran thick with game, bitter battles raged beyond the fields and hills of home.

And her time, her childhood, she knew, was counting down like the ticks of a clock.

She was The One.

On days when her brothers deviled her—why had she been plagued with brothers?—when her mother understood *nothing* and her father expected too darn much, she wanted that countdown to hurry.

Other times she raged. Why should she have no choice? No choice? She wanted to hunt and fish, to ride her horse, to run in the woods with her dogs. Even with her brothers.

And often she grieved for what something beyond her, something beyond her parents, demanded she become. Grieved at the thought of leaving her family, her home.

She grew tall and strong, and the light within her burned bright. The thought of her thirteenth birthday filled her with dread.

She stewed about it—about all that was unfair in her world, all that was unfair in the world outside—as she helped her mother prepare the evening meal.

"We're going to get a storm tonight, I can feel it." Lana pushed at the butterscotch-blond hair she'd bundled on top of her head before cooking. "But it's a perfect evening for eating outside. Go ahead and drain those potatoes I've got parboiling."

Fallon sulked over to the stove. "Why do you always have to do the cooking?"

Lana gently shook a covered bowl. Inside slices of peppers fresh from the garden marinated. "Your dad's grilling tonight," she reminded Fallon.

"You made everything first." With that stuck in her craw, Fallon dumped chunks of potatoes into the colander in the sink. "Why doesn't Dad or Colin or Travis make it all?"

"They help, just like you. Ethan, too—he's learning. But to answer the point of your question: I like to cook. I enjoy making food, especially for my family."

"What if I don't?" Fallon whirled around, a tall, long-limbed girl currently all stormy-gray eyes and defiant scowl. "What if I just don't want to cook? Why do I have to do things I don't want to do?"

"Because we all do. Lucky for you, on next week's rotation you move from under chef to cleanup. I need you to season those potatoes for the grill basket. I already chopped the herbs."

"Fine, great." She knew the drill. Olive oil, herbs, salt, pepper.

Just as she knew they had the oil and spices because her mother and a witch from a neighboring farm had culled out three acres, and had cast a spell to turn it into the tropics. They'd planted olive trees, *Piper nigrum* for pepper, coffee beans, banana trees. Figs, dates.

Her dad had worked with others to construct olive presses for the oils, dryers for the fruits.

Everyone worked together, everyone benefited. She *knew* that.

And still.

"Why don't you go ahead and take those out, tell your dad to start the chicken?"

Leading with her foul mood, Fallon stomped out of the house. Lana watched her daughter, her own summer-blue eyes clouding. She thought: More than one storm's coming.

They ate at the big outdoor table her father had built, using colorful plates, with bright blue napkins and wildflowers in little pots.

Her mother believed in setting a pretty table. She let Ethan light the candles with his breath because it always made him laugh. Fallon plopped down beside Ethan. She didn't consider him as much a pain in her butt as Colin or Travis.

Then again, he was only six. He'd get there.

Simon, his mop of brown hair streaked from the sun, took his seat, smiled at Lana. "It looks great, babe."

Lana lifted her wine, made from their own grapes. "Credit to the grill master. We're grateful," she added, with a glance at her daughter, "for the food grown and made by our own hands. We hope for the day when no one goes hungry."

"I'm hungry now!" Colin announced.

"Then be grateful there's food on the table." Lana set a drumstick— his favorite—on his plate.

"I helped Dad with the grill," he claimed as he added potatoes, vegetables, an ear of just-shucked corn to his plate. "So I shouldn't have to do the dishes."

"That's not going to fly, son." Simon filled Travis's plate as Lana did Ethan's.

Colin waved his drumstick in the air before biting in. He had his father's eyes, that hazel that blurred gold and green, hair a few shades darker than his mother's going bright from the summer sun. As usual, it stood up in tufts that refused taming.

"I picked the corn."

Travis, already eating steadily, elbowed Colin. "We picked it."

"Irrelement."

"*Vant*," Simon corrected. "*Irrelevant*—and it's not."

"I picked *most* of the corn. It should count."

"Instead of worrying about the dishes—which you will do—maybe you should eat the corn," Lana suggested as she helped Ethan butter his ear.

"In a free society, everybody has a vote."

"Too bad you don't live in one." Simon gave Colin a poke in the ribs that had Colin flashing a toothy grin.

"The corn is good!" Ethan, though he'd lost a couple of baby teeth, bit his way enthusiastically down the ear. He had his mother's blue eyes, her pretty blond hair, and the sunniest of dispositions.

"Maybe I'll run for president." Colin, never one to be deterred, pushed forward. "I'll be president of the Swift Family Farm and Co-operative. Then the village. I'll name it Colinville and never wash dishes again."

"Nobody'd vote for you." Travis, nearly close enough in looks to be Colin's twin, snickered.

"I'll vote for you, Colin!"

"What if I ran for president, too?" Travis asked Ethan.

"I'd vote for both of you. And Fallon."

"Leave me out of it," Fallon rebuked, poking at the food on her plate.

"You can only vote for one person," Travis pointed out.

"Why?"

"Because."

" 'Because' is dumb."

"This whole conversation is dumb." Fallon flicked a hand in the air. "You can't be president because, even if there were any real structure of government, you're not old enough or smart enough."

"I'm as smart as you," Colin tossed back, "and I'll get older. I can be president if I want. I can be anything I want."

"In your dreams," Travis added with a smirk.

It earned him a kick under the table, which he returned.

"A president is a leader, and a leader leads."

When Fallon surged to her feet, Simon started to speak, to shut things down, but caught Lana's eye.

"You don't know anything about being a leader."

"You don't know anything about anything," Colin shot back.

"I know a leader doesn't go around naming places after himself. I know a leader has to be responsible for people, make sure they have food and shelter, has to decide who goes to war, who lives and dies. I know a leader has to fight, maybe even kill."

As she raged, shimmers of light sparked around her in angry red.

"A leader's who everybody looks to for answers, even when there aren't any. Who everyone blames when things go wrong. A leader's the one who has to do the dirty work, even if it's the damn dishes."

She stalked away, trailing that angry light into the house. Slamming the door behind her.

"Why does she get to act like a brat?" Colin demanded. "Why does she get to be mean?"

Ethan, tears swirling in his eyes, turned to his mother. "Is Fallon mad at us?"

"No, baby, she's just mad. We're going to give her a little time alone, okay?" She looked over at Simon. "She just needs some space. She'll apologize, Colin."

He only shrugged. "I can be president if I want. She's not the boss of the world."

Lana's heart tore a little. "Did I mention I made peach pie for dessert?" Pie, she knew, was a no-fail way to turn her boys' moods around. "That is, for anyone who clears his plate."

"I know a good way to work off that pie." In tune with Lana, Simon went back to his meal. "A little basketball."

Since he'd created a half court on the side of the barn, basketball had become one of his boys' favorite pastimes.

"I wanna be on your team, Daddy!"

Simon grinned at Ethan, gave him a wink. "We'll wipe the court with them, champ."

"No way." Colin dived back into the meal. "Travis and I will crush."

Travis looked at his mother, held her gaze a long moment.

He knows, Lana thought. And so did Colin, even if anger and insult blocked it away.

Their sister wasn't the boss of the world, but she carried the weight of it on her shoulders.

Fallon's temper burned out in a spate of self-pity tears. She flung herself on her bed to shed them—the bed her father had built to replicate one she'd seen in an old magazine. Eventually the tears died away into headachy sulks.

It wasn't fair, nothing was fair. And Colin started it. He always started something with his big, stupid ideas. Probably because he didn't have any magicks. Probably because he was jealous.

He could have her magicks, then he could go off with some stranger to learn how to be the savior of the whole stupid world.

She just wanted to be normal. Like the girls in the village, at the other farms. Like anyone.

She heard the shouts, the laughter through her open window, tried to ignore it. But she rose, looked out.

The sky held blue on that long, late summer day, but like her mother, she felt a storm coming.

She saw her father, with Ethan perched on his shoulders, walking toward the barn. The older boys already raced around the curve of blacktop in the basketball shoes their father had scavenged.

She didn't want to smile when her dad nipped the ball from Colin, held it up for Ethan, then walked Ethan to the basket so he could drop the ball through the hoop.

She didn't want to smile.

The older boys looked like Dad, Ethan looked like Mom.

And she looked like the man on the back of a book.

That alone often cut more than she thought she could stand.

She heard the soft knock on her door, then her mother came in. "I thought you might be hungry. You barely touched your dinner."

Shame began to push through the sulks. Fallon only shook her head.

"Later then." Lana set the plate on the dresser Simon had built. "You know how to warm it up when you're ready."

Fallon shook her head again, but this time tears spilled. Lana simply walked to her, drew her in.

"I'm sorry."

"I know."

"I spoiled everything."

"You didn't."

"I wanted to."

Lana kissed Fallon's cheek. "I know, but you didn't. You'll apologize to your brothers, but right now, you can hear they're happy. Nothing's spoiled."

"I don't look like them, or you, or Dad."

Lana ran a hand down Fallon's long black ponytail, then eased back to look into those familiar gray eyes.

"I've told you about the night you were born. It's always been one of your favorite stories." As she spoke, she guided Fallon to the bed, sat on the side of it with her. "I've never told you about the night you were conceived."

"I . . ." Heat rose to her cheeks. She knew what *conceived* meant, and how it happened. "That's— It's weird."

"You're almost thirteen, and even if we hadn't already talked about all of this, you live on a farm. You know where babies come from and how they get there."

"But it's weird when it's your mom."

"A little weird," Lana allowed, "so I'll ease you into it. We lived in Chelsea. That's a neighborhood in New York. I loved it. There was a sweet little bakery across the street, a good deli on the corner. Pretty shops close by, lovely old buildings. We had a loft—I moved into Max's loft. I loved that, too. There were big windows facing the street. You could see the world rush by. Shelves full of books. The kitchen wasn't nearly as big as the one here at home, but it was completely up-to-date. We often had dinner parties with friends.

"I worked at a good restaurant, and had some vague plans about opening my own one day."

"You're the best cook."

"Not a lot of competition for that now." Lana tucked an arm around Fallon's waist. "I came home from work, and we had some wine, some really good wine, and made love. And after, only minutes after, something just burst inside me. Such light, such glory, such . . . I can't explain the feeling, even now. It took my breath, in the most beautiful way. Max felt it, too. We joked about it a little. He got a candle. My gift had been so small that even lighting a candle was hit-and-miss, and only hit after a lot of effort."

"Really? But you—"

"Changed, Fallon. Opened, that night. I lit the candle with barely a thought. It rose in me, the new power. As it did in Max, in all of us who had magicks inside. But for me, what I had inside was you.

That moment, that burst, that glory, that light was you. I wouldn't know for weeks, but it was you. You sparked inside me that night. I came to know, and some you showed me while still inside me, that you aren't just special to me, to Max, to Simon, but to all."

"I don't want to go away." Fallon buried her face in Lana's shoulder. "I don't want to be The One."

"Then say no. It's your choice, Fallon. You can't be forced, and I'd never allow anyone to force you. Your father would never allow it."

She knew this, too. They'd told her, always, it would be her decision. But . . . "You wouldn't be disappointed in me? Ashamed of me?"

"No." Lana pulled Fallon close, held her tight. "No, no, never." How many nights had she raged and grieved over what would be asked of this child? This *child*. Her child. "You're my heart," Lana comforted. "I'm proud of you every day. I'm proud of you, your mind, your heart, your light. Oh God, it burns so bright. And I'd take that light from you without hesitation to spare you from making the choice. From having to make it."

"He died to save me. My birth father."

"Not just because of what you might be. Because he loved you. Fallon, you and I? We're the luckiest women. We've been loved by two amazing men, two courageous men. Whatever you decide, they and I will love you."

Fallon held on, comforted, eased. Then felt . . . She drew carefully back. "There's more. I can feel it. I can feel there's more, things you haven't told me."

"I told you about New Hope, and—"

"Who's Eric?"

Lana jerked back. "Don't do that. You know the rule about pushing into another mind."

"I didn't. I swear. I just saw it. Felt it. There's more," Fallon said, and now her voice trembled. "More you're not telling me because you're worried. You're afraid for me, I can feel it. But if you don't tell me everything, how will I know what to do?"

Lana rose, walked to the window. She looked out at her boys, at her man, at the two old dogs, Harper and Lee, sleeping in the sun. At the two young dogs running around the boys. At the farm, the home she treasured. At the life she'd built. Dark always pushed against the light, she thought with some bitterness.

Magick always demanded a price.

She'd kept things from her child, from the brightest of lights because she feared. Because she wanted her family together, at home. Safe.

"I kept things from you because, under it all, I wanted you to say no. I told you about the attack when we lived in the house in the mountains."

"Two who were with you turned. They were Dark Uncanny, but you didn't know until they tried to kill you. To kill me. You and Max and the others fought, and thought you'd destroyed them."

"Yes, but we hadn't."

"They attacked again in New Hope. They came for me, and to save you, to save me, Max sacrificed himself. You ran like he told you to do. You ran because they'd come back again, and you had to protect me. You were alone a long time, and they hunted you. And you found the farm, you found Dad."

Fallon took a breath. "Was this Eric one of them? One of the dark?"

"Yes. He and the woman he was with, the woman I think helped turn him away from the light. They wanted to kill me, to kill you. They killed Max. Eric is Max's brother."

"His brother?" Shock ran straight through her. Brothers, she thought, horrified, however irritating, were *brothers*. They were family. "My uncle. My blood."

"Eric chose to betray that blood, chose to kill his own brother. Chose the dark."

"He chose," Fallon murmured. After another breath, she squared her shoulders. "You need to tell me all of it. You can't leave anything out. Will you tell me?"

"Yes." Lana pressed her fingers to her eyes. She already knew, looking into those familiar gray eyes, what choice her child would make. "Yes, I'll tell you everything."

CHAPTER TWO

Fallon apologized. Colin shrugged it off, but since she knew from experience he held a grudge, she prepared for retaliation. With her birthday—and the choice—only weeks away, she preferred thinking about her brother's revenge.

That was normal, that was family.

And she preferred the calculation in his eyes to the worry she often saw in her mother's, her father's.

She helped cut hay and wheat, harvest fruit and vegetables. Daily chores helped keep her steady. She didn't complain about the kitchen work—or only muttered about it in her head. The end of summer and the coming of fall meant hours of making jams and jellies, canning that fruit and those vegetables for the winter to come.

A winter she dreaded.

When she could, she escaped, using her free time to ride the fields and the woods on her beloved horse, Grace. Named for the pirate queen Fallon had long admired.

She might ride to the stream just to sit and think—her baited hook in the water was an afterthought. If she brought home fish to eat or to barter, so much the better. But the hour or two of solitude fed her young, anxious soul.

She might practice little magicks there—calling the butterflies, making the fish jump, spinning little funnels of air with her fingers.

On a hot day of bold sun and stingy breezes that seemed to claim summer would never end, she sat in her favorite spot. Because she wanted to read, her fishing pole hung magickally suspended over the stream.

She could make the fish bite the bait, but such powers—she'd been taught—were only to be used to feed real hunger.

Birds called now and again. She heard an occasional rustle in the understory. If she hadn't been deep in her book, she would have tested herself to identify the sounds. Deer, rabbit, squirrel, fox, bear. And more rarely, man.

But she enjoyed letting herself slide into a story—a really scary one—about a young boy with a gift, with a shining (a light), trapped in an old hotel with evil.

She didn't pay attention to the plop of the water, even when it repeated. Not when the bushes shaped like animals outside the evil hotel moved, not when they threatened the boy.

But the gurgling voice got her attention.

Her heart, already racing from the story, gave one hard *thud* as she heard her name whispered in that watery voice. And the water in the stream rippled.

Cautiously, she set the book aside and rose, one hand on the knife in her belt.

"What magick is this?" she murmured.

Was it a sign? Was it something dark come to call?

Her name came again, and the water seemed to shudder, to writhe.

Butterflies that had danced along the water's edge swarmed away in a buttercup-colored cloud.

And the air went silent as a grave.

Well, she wasn't a little boy in a book, she reminded herself, stepping closer to the edge of the stream.

"I'm Fallon Swift," she called out over the beat of blood in her ears. "Who are you? What do you want?"

"I have no name. I am all names."

"What do you want?"

A single finger of water rose up from the rippling stream. It only took her a second to recognize which finger, and the meaning. But it was a second too late.

They hit her from behind, three against one. She face-planted in the water, then surfaced to the sounds of her brothers' hilarity.

After she swiped her dripping hair out of her eyes, she found the bottom with her feet, stood.

"It took three of you, and an ambush."

"'Who are you?'" Colin repeated in a quaking voice. "'What do you want?' You should've seen your face!"

"Nice to see how you accept apologies."

"You deserved it. Now we're even."

Maybe she had deserved it, and she had to give him credit for biding his time, enlisting his brothers. Even more, she had to admire the complexity and creativity of the trick.

But.

She considered her options, the humiliation if she failed, and decided to take the risk.

She'd been practicing.

While her brothers laughed and did their victory dance, she spoke to her horse, mind to mind. Moving forward, Grace head-butted Colin into the water.

"Hey!" Shorter than Fallon, he tread water, managed to find his footing. "No fair."

"Neither is three against one."

Mad with laughter, Ethan jumped in. "I wanna swim, too."

"What the heck." Travis toed off his shoes, cannonballed in.

While the boys splashed and dunked each other, Fallon rolled over to float. This time she spoke mind to mind with Travis.

This was your work.

Yeah.

I apologized.

Yeah, but he needed this. And it was fun.

He turned his head, smiled at her.

Plus, it's a hot day.

The middle finger was rude.

But funny.

She couldn't hold back her own smirk. *But funny. I need a few minutes alone with Colin.*

Jeez, it's just water.

Not about that. Even steven. I just need a few minutes.

His gaze sharpened on hers. He saw, he knew, as he usually did. He started to speak out loud, then turned away. Only nodded.

She waded out of the stream, climbed out. After whisking her hands down her body to dry off, she stowed her book, her rod.

"We have to get back," she called out.

She ignored the whining—mostly Ethan's—gave a come-ahead gesture. "We've got to help with dinner, start the evening chores."

Travis climbed out; Fallon dried him off.

"Thanks."

She had to crouch down to help Ethan out.

"It's funny to swim in your clothes."

She poked him lightly in the nose. "It wouldn't be so funny if you had to walk home in wet, squeaky shoes."

She dried them, then his pants, then the faded Under Armour shirt she knew had once been scavenged for Colin.

After taking up Grace's reins, she turned to Colin.

"Come on." He waved a hand at her. "You paid me back for paying you back."

"I'll dry you off if you give me your word you're not going to pay me back for paying you back."

He hesitated for a minute, then just grinned. "I had a good one I'm working on, but I can save it until the next time you're a bitchy bitch. Probably won't take long."

She stuck out her hand. "But this round's done."

"Done."

They shook on it.

Dry again, he glanced around. "Why'd they take off?"

"I told Travis I needed to talk to you."

Suspicion and retaliation gleamed in his eyes. "We said done and shook."

"Not about that." She began to walk, the horse plodding lazily behind. "It's almost my birthday."

"Yeah, yeah."

"My thirteenth birthday."

"So?" With a shrug he found a stick to bang on trees as they walked. "You're probably going to start kissing boys and putting bows in your hair. Dopey."

"I'll have to leave."

"And you're going to get to drive the truck. I could drive the truck. I don't see why you get to do everything first."

"Colin, I won't be here to drive the truck. I'll have to go."

"Go where?"

She saw the knowledge flash over his face. Her parents hadn't held the story of Mallick, of The One, of two years of training away from home a secret.

Furious denial immediately followed knowledge. "That's bullshit. You're not going anywhere. That's just a bullshit story."

He liked to swear, Fallon thought idly. He swore at every opportunity out of their parents' hearing.

"It's not. And when he comes, I'll have to go with him."

"I said bullshit." Furious, red-faced with it, Colin heaved the stick away. "I don't care who this weird guy is, he's not going to make you go. We'll stop him. I'll stop him."

"He won't make me. He can't make me. But I have to go with him."

"You *want* to go." Bitter now. So young, so bitter now. "You want to go off and pretend you're some big-deal Savior. Pretend you're The One who's going to save the world. Just more bullshit."

He shoved her, hard.

"You're not so damn special, and there's nothing wrong with the stupid world. Look at it!"

He flung out his hands to the thick woods, the dappled sunlight, the verdant peace of late summer.

"This isn't the world, just our part of it, and even that may be threatened."

It rose up in her, rose so fast, so hot, it left her breathless. "You look at it. See the world."

She lifted her hands, flung them apart like whipping open a curtain.

A battle raged, dark and bloody. Buildings in rubble, others aflame. Bodies, torn and mangled, lay across . . . sidewalks, she realized. Streets and sidewalks of a city, a once great city.

Gunfire ripped across the still woods, and screams followed. Lightning struck, black and red, exploding chasms where more fell.

Some flew on wings that slashed through flesh. Some flew on wings that tried to shield.

Uncannys, dark and light, people, good and evil, waging war over the blood of those already fallen.

"Stop it." Colin gripped her arm as she stood, transfixed. "Stop it, stop it."

He sobbed the last, got through.

Shaking, she whipped the curtain closed again.

"How did you do that? How did you do that?"

"I don't know." Queasy now, dizzy with it, Fallon slid down to sit on the path. "I don't know. I feel sick."

He yanked her canteen out of her saddlebag and, crouching, pushed it at her.

"Drink some water. Drink it and maybe put your head between your knees."

She sipped, shut her eyes. "I see it in my head sometimes. When I sleep mostly. Like that, or other places. It's always fighting and dying and burning. Sometimes I see people in cages, or on tables, strapped down on tables. And worse, even worse."

She capped the canteen. "I'm okay now. I don't know how I did that. I don't know enough."

He helped her to her feet, put the canteen away for her. "Where was that place?"

"I'm not sure. I think it was Washington, D.C., but I don't even know why I think that. I don't know enough. It's why I have to go. I have to learn more, I have to, and I'm afraid. I'm so scared. They want to kill me, they tried to kill me and Mom. They killed my birth father. They'll find me sooner or later. They could come here and find me. If anything happened to Mom and Dad, to you and Travis and Ethan . . ."

She turned to her horse, pressed her face to Grace's neck.

"I have to go and learn how to stop them or it won't ever stop."

Awkwardly, Colin patted her back. "I'll go with you."

"You can't."

"Just try to stop me." The bullheaded bravery, the sincerity and innocence of it, sprang back. "You think because I can't do stupid tricks and all that crap I can't fight? I'm going with you, you jerk."

It touched her, she didn't know if she could ever tell him how much, that at her lowest point, he stood up for her. "It's not because of magick." And, even at so young an age, she understood basic tactics. "It's not because you wouldn't fight."

She wiped at tears, turned, saw he'd shed tears of his own.

"You have to stay because you have to be president."

"What the fuck?" Even with his newfound love of swearing, Colin reserved the Big F for his most important cursing.

"It's like this." Steadier, she began to walk again. "Mom and Dad are like the king and queen, right? They rule. But they don't know everything that goes on. They'll know about the stream today unless you guys swore Ethan to secrecy. If he's not sworn, he'll blab."

"Damn it."

"So they'll know, but that's okay. Nobody's mad about it. But they don't know everything, and the oldest—that's going to be you—has to be in charge, too. You have to be president and look out for Travis and Ethan, and Mom and Dad, too. I need to know everybody's going to be okay. Please. It's a hard job. You have to make sure everybody's okay, everybody does their chores and lessons. And you can't be too bossy about it or it doesn't work."

He hip-bumped her as they walked. "You're bossy."

"I could be bossier. Lots. Please, Colin."

They stopped at the rise where so long before their mother had first looked down at the farm, first felt hope again.

"I can be president," he mumbled. "I already told you I could."

"Okay."

She draped an arm over his shoulders, and for a few moments they looked down at home.

Ethan fed the dogs, the old and the young. Travis walked along a row in the garden, filling a basket with green beans. Their father, head shielded by a cap, walked back from a near field with one of the horses, and their mother straightened from her work in the herb bed to wave at him.

She'd take this picture with her, Fallon thought. This and others, wherever she had to go. Whatever she had to do.

Day after day, night after night, Lana watched her children with a kind of wonder. Before the Doom, she'd never given more than a passing thought to having children—someday. She'd enjoyed the life she'd lived, the urban glint of it, with a man she'd loved and admired.

She'd dabbled in magicks mostly for the fun, and her powers had been barely whispers in any case. Or so she'd believed.

Her work satisfied her, so ambitions for more had been, like children, a passing thought for someday.

She'd lived with a writer whose books had found a solid niche. Max had taken the Craft more seriously than she had, and his powers had been more overt—but still, in those days a pale shadow of what would come.

Their love had still held the bright shine of the new and exciting, and the future—if she looked beyond a day or two—had seemed limitless.

Then the world ended. Everything she'd taken for granted, gone in smoke and blood and the screams of circling crows. With the life that sparked inside her that night in January, another world began.

In those months between that winter night and the bold summer day she'd first seen the farm, she'd changed into someone the contented urban woman wouldn't have recognized. Changed, she knew, not just with the child growing inside her, not just with the rise of her own powers, but fundamentally.

Just as the hungry, desperate, grieving woman Simon found raiding his henhouse for an egg had changed into the woman who lay sleepless in her husband's arms on a cool autumn night listening to the incessant hooting of an owl.

This woman had learned to love not only for days and weeks and months, but for years. She had planted fields, hunted game, embraced her power. She'd given birth to four children in the bed she shared with the man who'd helped her bring them into the world.

Their world.

But she knew the world beyond this farm, this haven. She'd lived in it, fought in it, survived it. Escaped from it.

And now, after all the loss, the gains, the grief and the joy, she faced sending her firstborn into that blood and smoke.

Simon stroked her back. "We can say no."

She nuzzled a little closer. "Reading my mind now?"

"It's not hard when we're on the same page. She's just a kid, Lana. Yeah, it was important for us to be straight and honest with her from the jump, not to wait and just spring all this on her, but she's still just a kid. We sit her down, make sure she knows we've got her back on this. She doesn't have to go."

"We never lied to her, or kept secrets. And still, I think she'd have known even if we had. It's in her, Simon. I felt it when I carried her. I feel it now."

"Remember that time, her first spring? We were working in the garden. We had her napping in the shade under the old apple tree with Harper and Lee. We looked over when we heard her laughing and there must've been a couple hundred butterflies and—"

"Faeries, those little lights." At the pretty memory, Lana could smile. "All dancing around her. She called them."

"She couldn't even walk yet. I know she's not a baby anymore, but, Jesus, she's only twelve years old."

Thirteen, Lana thought. In only days now.

Absently she twisted the chain that held the medal of Michael the Archangel, which he wore around his neck. "She's decided to go."

"You don't know that."

She only spread her hand over his heart.

Under her palm, Simon's heart tore a little. He lifted his hand to take hers.

They'd promised each other to stand united when the day came, and, whatever choice she made, to stand with Fallon.

"I guess that explains why she hasn't been fighting with the boys. Has she talked to you about it?"

"No, not with words. I know she was born for what's about to begin. I know it with all I am. And I hate it." She turned her face into his throat. "She's our baby, Simon. I hate it."

"We can find a way to stop it, stop her."

Lana shook her head, burrowed deeper. "It's beyond us, Simon. It always has been. Even if we could, what happens when the boys grow up, when they need a life beyond this farm? Do we keep them here forever, like treasures caught in amber? We've been able to give them the life we have, to keep them safe, because of Fallon. Because we were given this time."

"Time's up, I get it. I know how to defend what's mine, Lana."

"You proved that to me before I was yours. But we can't fight this. I'm yours." She lifted her head to look at him, laid a hand on his cheek. "As Fallon's yours, as the boys are. I'm not strong enough, we're not strong enough, to face this without you. We have to let her go." A tear spilled out. "Help me let her go."

He shifted, sat up, gathered her close so she could weep a little. "Here's what I know for sure. She's smart and she's strong and, hell, she's fucking wily on top of it."

Lana managed a watery laugh. "She is. She really is."

"Between us, we've taught her everything we know, and she already had a pretty big leg up there, too. It's two years."

He squeezed his eyes shut as his heart tore a little more. "Time's going to go fast, and she's going to be fine. It's like wizard boarding school, only she already knows more than Harry Potter."

She sighed now, comforted. "Simon."

"What do you say we make the rounds?"

"Yeah." Lana dashed away tears, shook back her hair. "That's a good idea."

She thought of the house, that square, sturdy house she'd seen from the rise. How he'd opened it to her and the child she'd carried.

They'd added to it over the years—the man could build. They'd opened a wall in the living room to add space for necessities like sewing, spinning, weaving. They'd added sheep to their stock. They'd added space to the kitchen for canning, preserving. And a second greenhouse for growing through the winter.

And while they'd built, she thought as she wrapped herself in a robe, they'd filled the bedrooms with babies. That tangible proof of love and hope, those precious lights.

Together they'd built a family, and kept it safe—within that amber, she admitted. Together, they'd given their girl the best foundation they knew how to give.

Now together they walked first to the room Travis and Ethan shared. Moonlight streamed through the windows onto the bunk beds Simon had built.

Travis sprawled belly down on the top bunk, one arm flung over the edge and the soft cotton blanket she'd bartered for with two jars of pickles, made from her own cucumbers, knotted around his feet.

Though it would end up there again, she moved into the room to spread the blanket over him.

On the lower bunk Ethan slept in a cheerful puppy pile with the two young dogs, Scout and Jem. He smiled in his sleep.

"He'd have half the animals on the farm in bed with him if he could get away with it," Simon whispered.

"Piglets," she said, making him laugh.

"I still don't know how he got those three piglets past both of us."

"He has such a kind heart. And this one." Gently, she lifted Travis's arm back onto the bed. "He loves his pranks, but he sees so much, knows so much."

"He's a damn good farmer."

She smiled, stepped back. "Like his daddy."

After one last look, they backed out and walked over to Colin's room.

Curled on his side, he had one hand clutched on his blanket as if someone might try to steal it from him while he slept.

His odd assortment of found items filled a wooden box on his dresser or stood on his windowsill and on the shelves Simon had hung for him.

Interesting pebbles or stones, some green glass smoothed and polished by time in the stream, a clump of dried moss, a quarter, a few pennies, a broken pocketknife, an old bottle cap, the dented top of a thermos, and so on.

"Nobody scavenges better," Simon commented.

"It's his gift, seeing the potential for treasure. I know sometimes he resents not having the abilities like the others, but he has that curious mind."

"And plenty of ego. Colinville."

Smiling, she bent to kiss Colin's cheek. "President Swift of Colinville doesn't smell like a little boy anymore. Travis and Ethan still have that wild, innocent scent. Now, with him, there's a hint of gym locker. Healthy and male."

She turned, slid into Simon's arms. "I wonder if Colinville will ever have gym lockers."

"Since his first act as chief executive will be the construction of a basketball court, gym lockers follow."

She tipped her face up to his. "You're so good for me."

He kissed her, lingered. "You know what we should do?"

"Didn't we already do that?"

"Bears repeating. But I was thinking, we should get John Pike to come over with that old film camera he's got, and take a family portrait. He's got that darkroom set up, and the last I heard he still has the supplies."

"And you have to barter your left leg for a photo."

"I can talk him down from that. Trust me."

"I always have, and I'd love to have a photo."

They left Colin sleeping, walked down to Fallon's room.

Faeries flickered outside her window as they often did. She slept facing them with one hand resting on the pink teddy bear.

Mallick's other gifts, the candle, the crystal, stood on the dresser with *The Wizard King*. Moving closer, Lana saw Fallon held a little wooden horse in her other hand.

"You made that for her first Christmas." She turned into him again. "You want the photo for her, so she can take it with her."

"John can make two. She's so damn pretty, isn't she? Sometimes I look at her, and it just stops my heart. And I think, all I really want is to be able to scare off the boys that'll come around, at least until I figure one's good enough for her. Like when she's thirty or forty. Maybe fifty. I'd like to be able to bitch at her how she's wearing too much makeup or her skirt's too short or—"

Lana squeezed hard. "You've given her everything a father could and should." She eased back, cupping his face because she saw pain in his eyes. "The night she was born. Into your hands. Into yours, Simon. She'll always reach for your hands."

Breathing out, she took his hand now. "She'll come back to us. I couldn't let her go if I didn't know that. She'll come back to us."

But for how long, and what happened between, what happened after, she couldn't see.

CHAPTER THREE

On Fallon's thirteenth birthday, the woods splashed vibrant against the sky. Fruit not yet harvested hung heavy on the branches of the apple and pear trees. Grapes grew in fat, glossy clusters on the vine.

The garden spread autumn color with pumpkins, squash, zucchini, plump cabbages, rows of kale and turnips.

The air held warm, but cool nights warned the first frost would come, and soon.

Simon put the boys on apple-picking duty, as it gave them an excuse to climb the trees. As she had the best hand for it, he had Fallon harvesting grapes for jellies, wine, eating, and drying. He knew Lana had already baked the spice cake—Fallon's favorite—and now worked the garden, gathering more of the harvest while he stacked firewood for the winter to come.

And everyone pretended it was just an ordinary day because they could do nothing else.

He listened to his boys laughing, the low hum of the chickens, the deeper hum from the beehive. He felt the sweat dampen his back, the fatigue of muscles as he hauled another log to the splitter.

Somewhere in the woods, a woodpecker drummed manically. The dogs ignored the beat as well as the deer that roamed along the ridge as they slept in a flood of sun.

Situation normal, he thought, all fucked up.

Once, he'd chosen a soldier's life, and he'd learned the cost of war. He'd given up that life and come home to the farm when his mother was diagnosed with cancer. He'd learned a great deal about love, sacrifice, and a woman's strength.

She'd beaten the cancer, only to fall to the virus. So he'd buried both his parents within days of each other, and had learned the pain of real loss.

He'd chosen to stay, to farm, and learned what he and others could do to make a life even while the world shifted out from under them. And what others could and would do to bring more death, more destruction.

More than once over the years, he'd helped a neighbor fight off those others. And he'd buried friends as well as enemies.

He'd seen crows circling in the distance, beyond their quiet acres. He'd seen the lightning flash black.

Now his daughter would go beyond him, into that dark and dangerous world. And he, a man, a solider, a father, was helpless to stop it.

He looked over at her, his long, lanky, lovely girl. The sun glinted on the dark braid down her back. She wore one of his mother's old gardening hats, a wide-brimmed straw. The faded blue shirt had been his mother's, too, and showed that his girl had sprouted what Lana called booblets.

He didn't like to think about it.

He'd bartered for the jeans—on the baggy side, as she was so slim—and the sturdy brown boots.

He wanted to hold her there, just like that. Standing in the little vineyard, a bunch of ripe purple grapes in her hand, her face lifted up to the sun.

With his eyes still on her, he hauled up the split wood to add to the stack. He saw her stiffen, watched her turn slowly, her face blank—a mask of control no one so young should wear.

She set the grapes in her basket, slid the clippers into the sheath on her belt, and began to walk down the terraced rows of the vineyard.

Everything went silent. The laughter of the boys, the hum of bees and chickens. The dogs didn't bark. Simon felt for a moment, one long, breaking moment, the world stopped breathing.

His did.

Mallick stood at the edge of the farm road, holding the reins of his horse. The same horse he'd ridden thirteen years before, Simon would swear it. He looked the same as well, not a day older, the dark hair waving down, the white streak in his beard.

Lana stood in the garden, one hand pressed to her heart, the other fisted at her side.

Simon dropped the wood on the ground, rushed forward.

"Dad." Her voice steady, her eyes dry, Fallon stopped to reach for his arm.

Until she had, he didn't realize he had a hand on the gun in his belt.

"You should get Ethan," she told him. "He's crying."

"Baby."

"I'm okay. I need you to help me do this. Please, please, Daddy, help me do this."

The mask slipped; his daughter's eyes pleaded with him. "Go to your mom first. I'll get the boys."

So she went to her mother, took Lana's hand. Together they walked to Mallick.

"Lady," he said, "the years sit well on you, and on this land."

"A choice, you said. You can't make her go."

"Mom."

Already grieving, Lana rounded on Fallon. "I'm your mother. I decide. You're not old enough to make a choice like this. You don't know what's out there. You don't—"

She broke off when Fallon's arms came around her, when Fallon spoke in her head.

I know what you know. I've seen what you've seen. I've dreamed what you've dreamed. Help me do this. Help me be strong like you. Let me go so I can be what you helped make me. Let me go so I can come back.

Fallon drew back, but kept her mother's hand as she faced Mallick.

"Have you chosen, Fallon Swift?"

"Will they be safe while I'm gone? I won't leave my family unless I know they'll be safe."

"No harm comes to them while you train with me."

"If it does, you'll pay for it."

He nodded. "Understood. Simon Swift." Absently he patted one of the dogs who sniffed at him as Simon led the boys up. Mallick scanned the boys, the grim-faced Colin, the cool-eyed Travis, Ethan, who knuckled away tears. "You've made fine sons. May I water my horse while you say good-bye?"

"Now? But she hasn't had her cake or her gifts. I—I have to help her pack."

"Mom. I'm packed. I'm ready. I'll go get my things."

Saying nothing, Simon gestured Mallick to the water trough by the barn.

"I . . . I need to pack some food. She needs to have her cake."

Lana escaped into the house.

"Go get your presents for your sister," Simon told the boys. He crossed to Mallick. "Where are you taking her?"

"Not as far as you fear, not as near as you might wish. I can't tell you more, for her safety."

"And how do we know she's safe?"

"You know duty, and she's my duty. Believe me, I would lay my life down for her. Not for love, as you would, but for duty that's as strong in me. She is my purpose, my hope, my duty. I will not fail her."

"You know duty," Simon repeated. "Believe me, if harm comes to her, I will hunt you down whoever and whatever you are. And wherever you are, I will find you and I will kill you."

"If harm comes to her, Simon Swift, I will already be dead. And what is left of the world will wish for the same fate. In two years she'll come back to you, and you'll see what you helped her become."

"Two years from now, if she's not back safe, I'll come for you."

He strode away, stopping short when Fallon came out with a small duffel bag. "I need to saddle Grace."

"I'll do it." Travis rushed out. "I'll do it. I made you this."

He offered her a leather sheath for her knife, one with symbols carefully burned into the leather.

"They're magick symbols to keep the blade sharp and clean, and to help it strike true."

"It's really beautiful, Travis. You . . . must've worked on it a long time."

"I know you have to go." When his voice thickened, he swallowed. "I know you're afraid, but you'll come back."

"Yes. I'll come back."

"You'll be different, but you'll come back. I'll bring Grace."

She started to speak to her father, struggled for what she wanted to say. Colin and Ethan came out and spared her.

"I don't want you to go." Ethan flung his arms around her legs. "Don't go away."

"I have to, for a while, and I need you to do something for me."
She opened her bag, took out the pink bear. "I need you to take care
of her, okay? She really needs to be snuggled at night."

"You should take her with you."

"She doesn't want to go. She wants to stay here. Will you take care
of her until I get home?"

"I won't let anything happen to her. I made you this. Well, mostly
Dad made it, but I helped, and I said make a flower, and I painted
it. It's a birthday flower."

She took the little wooden tulip painted bright and inexpertly pink
and green. "It's really pretty. Thanks, Ethan."

She crouched to tuck it into her bag, then unbuckled her knife
sheath to replace it with her new one.

"I did this." Colin shoved a little box at her.

From inside, she lifted out a small wind chime. Thin white stones,
pieces of smooth colored glass hung from fishing wire attached to
an old metal hook.

"It's beautiful."

"It's stupid, but—"

"It's beautiful."

She saw tears in him, barely held back, and hugged him hard.
"You're the president now," she whispered. "Don't forget."

When her mother came out, Fallon saw the signs of weeping even
through the glamour.

"There's some of your cake, and bread from this morning, some
meat and cheese, and . . . Well, here's Travis with Grace. I'll put this
in your saddlebag."

"I'll do it." Colin took the food pack, and the duffel.

"It's so fast," Lana murmured. "It's all too fast."

Afraid she'd lose her nerve, Fallon bent down, hugged Ethan.
"Take care of the bear, and don't let the big guys push you around."

She straightened, turned to Travis, held tight. "Don't even think about moving into my room."

Then to Colin. "Try not to be such a big jerk."

"You're the jerk."

"Try not to screw up too much while I'm gone."

She stepped back, turned to her mother. "Mom."

"This is from your dad and me."

Fallon reached for the chain that held what she knew was her father's wedding ring and her dad's St. Michael's medal. Tears and love flooded her throat.

"I'll always wear it." She slipped the chain around her neck. "Always. Mom." She fell into her mother's embrace. "I love you. I love you so much."

"I love you. I'll think of you every day, and count the days off until you're home again. Shine bright, my baby, and I'll know. Send me a sign," Lana whispered.

"I will."

Fighting tears, she turned into her father's arms. "Daddy. I love you."

"If you need me. Listen." He cupped her face, lifted it. "If you need me, call for me. I'll hear you. I'll come to you. I'll find a way."

"I'm not afraid because I have you. I'm not afraid because you love me. I'll come home." She pressed her cheek to his. "I swear it."

She grabbed the reins, launched into the saddle. "My fifteenth birthday, don't forget. I want presents."

She set Grace into a trot. Mallick, already mounted, rode up to her, gestured south.

She turned, one more look, saw her family standing together, close, touching, in front of the house where she'd been born.

Colin straightened his shoulders, sent her a snappy salute that made her lips curve, her eyes blur.

She lifted her hand into a wave, then turned her eyes south and urged Grace into a gallop.

Mallick let her set the pace. He could give her free rein for a few miles, see how long it took for her to steady herself. And his sturdy old bay could handle the run.

They passed another farm, smaller than the Swifts', where a woman and a skinny boy dug for potatoes. They paused in their work, and in the few seconds it took to thunder by, Mallick felt a wave of longing from the boy.

For the girl, and for what the boy saw as freedom.

They galloped on, past a scatter of abandoned houses with lawns gone back to meadows. A few sheep grazed on the rock-pocked hills, and their elderly shepherdess stood on a mound with an old-fashioned crook in one hand and a rifle slung over her back.

The image of her, gray hair under a worn cap, the rough gray rocks pushing out of the green, the white sheep mindlessly cropping, brought him a quick, unexpected tug of nostalgia.

When Fallon slowed to a trot, then a walk—more for her horse's sake than her own, Mallick concluded—she turned for the first time to look at him directly.

"I want to know where we're going."

"A day's ride and a bit more, to a place where you'll train and learn and grow."

"Why are you the one to train me?"

"That is a question I can't answer. Why are you The One? We are what we are."

"Who gave you the authority?"

"This you'll learn. Who is the shepherdess?"

"Her name's Molly Crane."

"And what is her power?"

If she wondered how he knew old Molly had power, she didn't ask. "Shapeshifter."

"How many sheep was she tending?"

Fallon answered first with an annoyed shrug. "Maybe ten."

"'Maybe'?"

"I didn't count them."

"You have eyes. How many did you see?"

"I don't know."

"You didn't look, so didn't see. Fourteen. One stood behind a rock, and the pregnant ewe carries two."

Grief and nerves fought a bitter war in her belly. Her sharp, slapping tone to an adult would have earned her a rebuke at home.

But she wasn't home now.

"What difference does it make?"

"Another time you may see the enemy. How will you know their number? One may hide behind a rock, another may conceal two others."

Angry, aching, she sneered at him. "The next time I have to fight sheep, I'll be sure to get the full count."

Mallick gestured east. Far over the rolling hills, crows circled. "They know the waiting time is done. You'll be hunted, from this day until the end."

"I'm not afraid of crows."

"Be afraid of what rules them. Fear can be a weapon just as courage. Without fear there is no prudence. Without prudence there is recklessness. With recklessness, defeat."

"What rules them?"

"You'll learn."

With that, he urged his horse up a rise and into the trees.

The air cooled, and though she'd never traveled this far from home, the scents of the forest had a comforting familiarity. She passed some time watching for tracks, identifying the deer, a lone bear, a coyote, and a pair of raccoons that had passed over the rough trail.

They crossed a narrow stream where water bubbled and spilled over rocks. A wild turkey called as they veered east.

"How many deer were in the shadows by the stream?" she demanded, adding a cool stare when he turned his head to study her. "What if they were enemies? Would you know their number?"

"Four does and two yearlings."

"What's the difference in the yearlings?"

Amused, Mallick answered, "One is a young buck, the other a doe."

"Besides that."

Now his eyebrows lifted. "I cannot tell you."

"One has a sore left front leg. He's favoring it. Didn't you see the tracks? Isn't it good tactics to know if your enemy's injured?"

"You have a good eye for tracking. If your aim is as keen, we'll eat well this winter."

"My aim's true. My father taught me." She lifted her hand to the chain around her neck, found comfort there. "I can still go home. I can change my mind and go home."

"Yes. You could live out your life there and never truly become. And the world would bleed around you until even what you love drowns."

She hated, hated, *hated* knowing—somehow knowing—he spoke absolute truth.

"Why do I have to be The One? Everybody's Savior? I didn't screw everything up, so why am I supposed to fix it?"

"Mae gennych atebion y tu mewn i chi."

"What? What language is that?"

"I said the answers are inside you."

"That's just the same as saying I'll learn. It's not an answer." However much she wanted to dismiss him, curiosity poked at her. "What language is it?"

"Welsh."

"Is that where you're from? Wales?" With the question she tried to form a map in her head, place it exactly. She loved maps.

"Yes. Do you know where that is in the world?"

"It's in what was Great Britain, with England on one side and the Irish Sea on the other."

"Very good. Your geography skills are accurate even if your language skills are poor."

"Why would my parents teach me Welsh? They don't *know* Welsh. And anyway, it's not like I'm going to just drop down over there."

Fueled by anger, aching, and now insulted for her family, her words shot out like barbs. "And they taught me plenty, me and my brothers. How to read and write and *think*. We learned science and math and history, how to read maps, how to draw them. Maybe we couldn't go to the school in the village very often because Raiders and Dark Uncannys could come too close. My dad fought them to help protect our neighbors, and he and Mom taught us how to fight, too."

"They taught you much, and they taught you of the light and of the earth. And a most important lesson. They taught you loyalty. You learned it well."

"You don't learn it. You are or you aren't."

He smiled at her. "However we might disagree, know I am loyal to you."

"Because you have to be, and that's different."

"You're right," Mallick said after a long moment. "But my loyalty remains."

She rode a few miles, stewing, until the questions just pushed out of her.

"Why did you leave Wales?"

"I was called."

Her sigh, long and derisive, said everything about being thirteen and dealing with an adult.

"If I ask who called you, you're just going to say 'you'll learn.'"

"And you will. I was young, like you, and like you I wondered why such hard things were asked of me. Know I understand what it is to leave home and family."

"Do you have kids?"

"I've never been given that gift."

"You brought me the teddy bear."

"It was kind of you to give it to your young brother, to leave that piece of yourself in his care."

She shoved that aside, as it brought Ethan and his tears to her mind.

"You brought me the candle and the crystal ball. They're not toys like the bear. Only I can light the candle. Sometimes I do. It never melts away."

"It was made for you."

"Did you make it?"

"Yes."

"My mother said I'd be the only one to see into the crystal, but I've never seen anything when I look."

"You will."

"Where did you get it?"

"I made it for you. The bear I bought for you before even your mother knew you existed. The woman at the shop told me it was a happy gift for a baby girl."

It occurred to her, as they rode, that she'd never had a longer conversation with anyone outside of family. While it didn't make her feel any warmer toward him, she did find it interesting.

"What are you going to teach me?" she demanded. "For two years? My father taught me how to shoot—a gun and a bow. He taught me hand-to-hand. He was a soldier. He was a captain in the army. And my mother taught me about magicks. She's a witch, a powerful witch."

"Then you have a good foundation for more."

She stopped her horse. "Do you hear that?"

"Yes."

"It's engines. More than one."

"There's a road, not far, and some travel on it. So we make our route through the trees, over the hills. You're not yet ready for battle."

The sounds receded, until only the forest spoke.

"Who taught you?"

"His name was Bran. A difficult taskmaster."

"Will I meet him?"

"He's no longer with us."

"Did he die in the Doom?"

His duty was to teach, to train, he thought, and he would fulfill it. But who could know the girl had so many questions in her?

"No, he passed from this world to the next long before. But while I was with him he taught me many things. I traveled to many lands with him."

Because she could, Fallon took Grace for a little jump over a fallen tree. "Before the Doom people traveled all over the world, in planes. I've seen two planes and a chopper—the smaller plane with blades on the top. My mother put a shield over the farm in case people in planes were the ones looking for Uncannys to lock them away. Or worse, Dark Uncannys. So we could see the planes, but they couldn't see us. Have you ever flown in a plane?"

"I have, and I didn't enjoy it."

"I think it would be wonderful." She tipped her head up, looked at the pieces of sky through the canopy of burnished leaves. "I'd like to see other lands. Some have beaches of white sand and blue water, and others are covered in ice. And the great cities with buildings tall as mountains, and mountains taller than the tallest building, and deserts and oceans and jungles."

"The world has many wonders."

He turned his horse through an opening in the trees and into a small clearing. A cabin sat sheltered under trees with a slope-roofed lean-to attached.

"You said a day's ride."

"And so it will be. We stop here only for the night."

"We've still got more than an hour before dusk."

"The horses need rest, to be tended and fed. And so do I."

Mallick dismounted, led his horse to the lean-to. Reluctantly, Fallon followed suit. She noted the shelter had fresh bedding, grooming supplies, a tub of grain. Mallick handed her a bucket.

"There's a creek just to the east. The horses need to be watered."

"What is this place?"

"A place to break our journey." When she said nothing, simply stood, he loosened the cinches, hefted off his saddle.

"A hunting cabin, what would have been a weekend or holiday sort of place. It belonged to a man who worked as a plumber and enjoyed coming here with his friends. He was immune, so survived the Doom only to be taken in one of the sweeps and confined to a government facility, where he died."

"You knew him?"

"No, but there was enough of his energy left here, where he had many happy times, for me to know of him. The horses need water."

She took the bucket, walked no more than ten yards east to a bright and cheerfully winding creek. For a moment, she studied the woods—this new place. The hemlock and oak, the old pines and young poplars. For all she knew, Mallick would ask her how many trees in the stupid forest. Or how many rapid taps from the woodpecker, how many feathers on the cardinal.

She filled the bucket, walked back to dump water in the trough. It took another two trips, and by then Mallick had removed both saddles and was toweling off his gelding.

"What's his name?" she asked as she got a clean towel to rub down her own horse.

"He's Gwydion, named for a powerful wizard and warrior."

"She's Grace, for the pirate queen. The lean-to is much newer than the cabin."

"I built it only a few months ago."

"It looks sound," she said, picking out Grace's hooves.

With the horses fed and watered, Mallick took up his own light pack. Fallon shouldered her heavier duffel and the food her mother had packed.

The cabin, a square and squat structure, included a narrow front porch up one short step.

Beside the step, in a pool of pebbles, stood a rough stone figure. Female, Fallon judged.

Mallick paused to open his water flask, and trickled some water over the pebbles.

"In tribute and respect for the goddess."

"Does she protect or bless?"

"She may do both, at her whim. She is Ernmas." He sighed a little when Fallon only frowned. "She is a mother goddess, she is of the Tuatha de Danann, as you are. You are of her blood and bone, Fallon Swift. Do you know nothing of your ancestors?"

"We had some books on mythology, mostly like the Romans and Greeks. You don't seriously expect me to believe I'm related to some goddess? Because, you know, *mythology*."

"Your ignorance does you no credit." He walked onto the porch, flicked a hand at the door. It opened with a rush of wind. "Do you think power—the light, the dark—has no source? Has no history or purpose? You owe what you are to all who came before you. To their bounty and their battles, their cruelty and their compassion." He shook his head. "That the fate of the world rests with a girl who knows so little."

As he walked inside, Fallon rolled her eyes behind his back. She looked down at the goddess. "How am I supposed to know what I don't know?"

Insulted—she was *not* ignorant—she stomped in behind Mallick.

Inside, the main area consisted of one open room with a fireplace on the north wall and a kitchen in the back—windows east, she noted, to overlook the creek, and catch the sunrise.

A big—and ugly to her eye—couch in some sort of black-and-brown plaid faced the TV over the fireplace. They had a TV at the farm, and once a week they had movie night with the DVDs.

She loved DVDs almost as much as maps, as both took you to other places, other worlds.

Two chairs, that same plaid, a table with a lamp with a black bear climbing a black tree for a base, an overhead light fashioned from some sort of cart or wagon wheel and a round wooden table with four wooden chairs filled the space in what she considered a really ugly way.

She took the food pack to the counter covered in a muddled gray over white, set it down.

"Your room for the night is on the left. Start the fire, then put away your things."

He wasn't the only one who could show off, she thought. She turned away, tossed a glance at the logs in the stone fireplace. They burst into flame.

"I'm not stupid."

"Ignorant," he corrected. "I've heard the expression 'you can't fix stupid.' It may be true. But ignorance can be educated. Put your bag in your room, then you'll need to bring in more firewood before dark. There's plenty out the back of the house."

"And what are you going to do?"

"I'm going to have a glass of wine before we share what your mother kindly provided."

When she stalked away, he looked at the fire, the bright, hot light of it, and smiled.

CHAPTER FOUR

Pure stubbornness mated to insult tempted her to lock herself in the dumb room with its two sets of bunk beds—covered in plaid again, this time red and black. But she was hungry, and she had to pee.

So she'd pee, and she'd eat, but she didn't have to be friendly. She didn't see why she had to be polite, either. He'd called her stupid— oh, excuse me, *ignorant*. Just because he was old didn't mean she had to be polite to somebody who called her ignorant.

A bathroom stood directly across from her room. She did lock herself in there.

She tested for running water by turning the handle on the faucet over the wall-hung sink, and was almost disappointed when it ran. She supposed Mallick had seen to that, so she had no reason to test her powers there.

The toilet rocked a little, but served its purpose.

She took a moment to study her face in the mirror over the sink.

She hadn't slept well the night before—or the night before that, she admitted. It showed in the shadows under her eyes, a paleness to her cheeks.

Though she didn't care about looking pretty, she did care—a lot—about looking strong. So she did a light glamour.

Not ignorant, she told herself, and not weak.

She strode out, sailed straight by Mallick as he sat near the fire with his glass of wine. She didn't slam the door on her way out for wood, but shut it with a solid *snap*.

As dusk fell, a soft gray sliding through the trees, the air carried a sharper chill. And the smell of the smoke, of the galloping fall.

The firewood would be welcome, she thought, but she wanted a walk first, wanted to stretch muscles tight after the hours in the saddle.

She checked on the horses first, found them already dozing. Still, she rested her cheek against Grace's for the comfort of home. And when Mallick's horse looked at her with kind, wise eyes, Fallon stroked him—and thought he deserved a nicer rider.

She let them go back to dozing and walked along the edge of the winding creek.

Glancing up, she saw the deer stand built on the thick oak, and found it amusing to watch five deer graze their way down the sloping land through the trees.

What would it be like, she wondered, to just keep walking? Like the deer. Just walk and live in the woods. To wander as long and far as she liked, with no thought but to her own needs.

No one to tell her what to do, she imagined, or when and how to do it. No one to expect so much of her when she just wanted to be.

She leaned on the tree, pressed her cheek to its rough bark. Felt its heartbeat. Closing her eyes, she felt the heartbeat of the deer across the little creek and the pulse of the water, the earth.

All the things that lived and thrived around her, and were not man, she felt their life inside her. In her mind's eye she saw the bird winging overhead, its heartbeat small and quick, small and quick. And the owl deeper in the woods, slumbering until night fell and hunting began.

She squeezed her eyes tighter because she understood she didn't just want to walk away, to live forever in the woods. She wanted to feel her mother's heartbeat, her father's, her brothers'. And they were too far away.

"It's just the first day," she admonished herself. "I can get through one day. I can change my mind, anytime I want. I can go home tomorrow if I want."

Comforted by that, she opened her eyes again, and turned to walk back to the cabin.

The sun burned through the trees to the west, flamed over the hills with a light that she felt, like the heartbeats, inside her.

Watching that fire of the day's end, she walked back, and brought in a load of firewood.

A teenager, even one descended from gods, knew how to sulk. Fallon ate the food Mallick set out, but she ate in silence. She took a small slice of her birthday cake because she wanted to feel her family close. But it only made her sad, only made her accept that they weren't close, and wouldn't be for two long years.

If Mallick had made any attempt to cheer her, that sadness would have lashed out as bright fury. Maybe he knew, as he offered no conversation or small talk through the simple meal.

When he told her to see to the dishes, she didn't argue. She repacked the food, washed the plates, ordered the kitchen, while he sat by the fire reading.

Despite her innate curiosity, she didn't ask about the book, but actually locked herself in the bedroom and added a charm to the lock, simply out of pique.

Though it invariably brought her comfort, she refused to take the candle out of her pack and light it simply because it had come from him. In her mind, in that moment, Mallick and Mallick alone held responsibility for her misery.

Instead, she huddled under the blankets with *The Wizard King*, illuminating pages as she read. But the familiar words only added more sadness.

She set the book aside, lay in the dark wishing she'd taken the time to hunt through the cabin for something else to read. Old magazines and newspapers never failed to fascinate her. She didn't expect to sleep, fully anticipated brooding through the night. Even looked forward to it.

And dropped off before she felt sleep sliding over her, not waking even when the moonlight shifted through the windows or the faeries came to dance outside the glass.

She woke at the trembling edge of dawn. Her first reaction was embarrassment that she'd slept so long and so well. Then she remembered what her mother called heart-sleep. That sleep a wounded heart needed to help it heal.

She rubbed the ring and medal between her fingers. As she lay quiet, just a few more minutes, she imagined her dad getting up for the day, going down to make the coffee from the beans harvested from the tropics. And her mom coming down to start breakfast.

Everybody up, stock to feed, eggs to gather.

Chores to do, lessons to take, the smell of fresh bread baking. Maybe a trip to the village or the neighboring farms to barter. Free time to read or ride or play.

Where would she be as her family went through the day?

But she, a child of the farm, rose, put on her boots. She added wood to the fire gone to embers and went out to tend to the horses.

She watched the sun rise, as she'd watched it fall.

When she went back in, Mallick had two mugs of strong tea on the counter and fried eggs with bacon in a skillet over the fire, camp-style.

"Good morning," he said. "We'll leave after our breakfast."

"All right." She took the tea—stronger than she liked and more than a little bitter without the honey she preferred.

She wished she'd thought to bring some honey. But she sat with it, and when Mallick put a plate in front of her and sat with her, she ate.

Some of her resentment for him had faded with sleep, but over and above that, she'd grown bored with silence.

"You have no woman or children."

"I don't."

"Is it because you prefer men?"

"No." He continued to eat as he spoke. "My duty, my purpose has been my mate."

"Why would I care, or the gods care, or whatever care if you had a woman, or a man, by your side or in your bed?"

His gaze shifted to hers, held. "What was asked of me, what I vowed, was unswerving loyalty to The One. A mate, a lover, should also have loyalty. And those loyalties might come to odds."

She dismissed that reasoning. "My parents are loyal to each other, and still are loyal to their children. All of us."

"That is love, even more than duty or a vow taken. And love is more powerful."

"You've never loved anybody?"

"There was a girl once, with lively eyes and hair like fire. I can't say if I felt love, but I felt longing. My heart would pound if I caught sight of her, and if she should smile at me? I was the wealthiest boy in the land. I knew if I ever felt the touch of her hand on my cheek, even just that, I would die happy and fulfilled."

Fallon snorted out a laugh. "Nobody dies from love."

"Oh, but they do, from where love may lead them or what it may ask of them. And so I never felt her hand on my cheek. I made my choice."

"Maybe you did love her because you were a boy, and now you're old, but you remember her." She ate the last of her eggs. "How old are you?"

Mallick sat back, looked her directly in the eyes. "I was born on the third day of the third month in the year six hundred and seventy-one."

"Come on." Out of habit, she started to reach for his plate to clear it. "If you don't want to tell me, just—"

He clamped a hand on her arm. "I was born to a witch, sired by a solider whose own mother had elfin blood. I have little memory of him, as he died in battle when I was barely weaned. I was her only son and, like your mother, she wept when I was called. I had ten years when I left her. And ten more while I trained and studied and traveled. Ten more to practice, to live in solitude.

"Then I slept as the years passed and the world changed, and magicks hid or died as those who held them were persecuted or reviled, or ignored. Until the night I awoke to the sound of a single drop of blood striking the first shield, of the shudder of it cracking beneath the sacrifice. And my time began again as yours would come."

She believed him, and belief made her heart hammer. "You're saying you're immortal."

"No. No. I bleed. My life will come to its end as any man's. But I was asked to train and serve and defend The One, she who would take up the sword and shield, she who would bring the light and restore the balance. I said yes. I took a vow. I made this choice. I will never break that vow. I will never betray you."

He rose, cleared the plates himself.

"What's the first shield and how did it crack under a drop of blood? How many are there? Where are they? How did—"

"You'll learn. For now, gather your things and saddle the horses. I'll deal with the dishes."

"Give me one answer," she demanded. "One damn answer."

"Ask the right question."

She hesitated, then asked what she realized weighed heaviest. "What if I'm not good enough? What if I'm just not good enough or smart enough to do all of this?"

"Then I would have failed. I don't intend to fail. Don't dawdle. We have a long ride ahead."

She rode a full hour in silence. Not sulking silence, but thinking silence. She knew some faeries could live more than a hundred years. Like old Lilian at home, who claimed to be a hundred and twenty. Elves could have long lives, too, and children of mixed magicks . . . there hadn't been enough time since the Doom to know for sure.

But she'd never heard of anyone who'd lived for more than a thousand years. He'd said he'd slept, she remembered. Like hibernation?

And if it was all a choice, why had he been called all the way back to train somebody born more than fifteen hundred years later?

It was really confusing. Not understanding wasn't ignorance, she assured herself. It was just not understanding.

They rode through woods, across fields, over roads. Some of the roads still had cars abandoned on them. She saw hills and houses, even a few people, and what she realized was a village, larger than the one she knew, with buildings and the places where they'd once sold gas for cars and food to travelers.

Though for the most part, Mallick stayed off those roads, away from buildings, she'd spot them in the distance.

And wonder.

She'd studied maps and globes and the atlas. She'd seen DVDs that showed a world, showed lives, that seemed so distant and different and exotic.

But the world, once you were out in it, she realized, was so much bigger than anything imagined.

It just went on and on. She couldn't believe it had ever been filled, that cars had streamed along those wide roads she knew had been called highways.

It seemed like make-believe, like the movies on the TV.

"Did you see it?" she asked. "When it was full of people and cars and planes?"

"Yes. And though I had looked in the crystal, though I'd been shown, it was a wonder."

"Is it really a choice, could I have really said no?"

"It's always a choice. I won't betray you, and I won't lie to you."

"Then if you were called so long ago—before there were cars and planes, before the world was so full—how could that happen a zillion years before I was even born?"

"Powers greater than mine, greater than even yours will be, foresaw what might be. It's the nature of people, magickal and not, to wish for peace and march to war. It's the nature of those with darkness in them, more than the light, to plot for war, to covet power. If the dark had failed that night and the shield remained whole, I might have slept another millennium, and The One would not yet be born. But at some point in time, it would happen."

"Did you dream?"

He smiled a little. "I lived lifetimes in dreams. And I learned, even as I slept, of the world and its changes."

"That doesn't seem very restful."

He let out a laugh, rich, full, unexpected. "It wasn't," he told her. "No, it wasn't restful."

Together they crossed a fallow field at a brisk canter, then rode up a steep slope to a blacktopped road.

"How much farther?"

"Another two hours. The rain will come at nightfall, but we'll be there long before."

"Sooner—for the rain," Fallon said.

He gave her a slow, haughty glance. "Is that so?"

"We're riding southeast, and the wind's coming from the east, bringing the rain with it. Unless we change directions, we'll have the rain at least an hour before nightfall if we're traveling this way another two hours at this pace."

She glanced at him with a shrug. "Farmers know the weather. The rest is just math."

He said, "Hmph," and continued to ride.

"Somebody's—"

She broke off when he threw up a hand, as he heard the engines, too. He cursed himself for taking this stretch of the road—to save some time—with little to no cover on either side.

Even as he considered options—the first to lead her in a gallop back over the field—three motorcycles topped the rise of the road, barreled down it.

"If I tell you to go, ride and ride fast, back over the field. I'll find you."

Something in her quivered; something in her steeled. "There are six of them, and one of you."

"There is only one of you in all the world. Do as I say. Do not speak to them, and if I say go, ride."

They rode two to a bike, Fallon noted. Three with sidearms, three with long guns. Four men, two women.

All Raiders, she concluded, with the skull symbols painted on the bikes.

The one in the lead swung his bike across the road so that she and

Mallick stopped the horses. He wore a bandanna covered in skulls around his brown hair, a pendant of another around his neck.

He'd groomed his beard into two long tails.

The woman behind him bore the slash of a scar over her left cheek. Like her companions, she wore dark glasses to conceal her eyes.

She tossed a leg over the bike, slung the rifle from her back, and held it in casual threat.

Fallon scanned the others, tried to keep her heartbeat steady as the throaty sound of the engines shut off.

The leader swung off his bike. "Well, what do we have here?"

"My granddaughter and I are traveling south to look for work."

"Is that so? Hear that? They're looking for work."

The one on the second bike tipped down his sunglasses, sent Fallon a wink that made her skin feel sticky.

If she had to fight, she decided to target the woman first, then the winker.

She wouldn't ride away. She would never leave someone so outnumbered.

"What's in the bags?"

"All we have left in the world." The plea in Mallick's voice put Fallon's back up. "And little more than nothing."

"Then you can make do with nothing. Off the horse, Grandpa. You, too, sweetcheeks."

"Please. She's just a child."

The second woman pulled a sidearm. "She gets off the horse or I shoot her off."

"Don't shoot the fresh meat." The one who'd winked got off his bike, rubbed his crotch. "I got some work for her."

They laughed, all, in a way that didn't make Fallon's skin sticky. It turned her mind, her blood, very, very cool.

She dismounted.

"Six of you," she said with disdain. "Two of us."

The leader drew a knife from his belt. "It's about to be one of you." He lunged at Mallick.

It happened fast, before Fallon could react and she'd thought she was ready.

Mallick's fist flashed out, hard as a hammer strike. He knocked the man back into the woman behind him so they both fell.

With his other hand he hurled a ball of wind that blew the second woman and her sidearm twenty feet back. Even as she landed with a sickening *thud*, Mallick drew a sword.

Two rushed him, and the third left standing ducked aside and charged at Fallon.

She pulled out her knife, and without thinking set it on fire.

"Fucking Uncanny bitch." He snarled at her, drawing his gun. "Bullet beats knife, every time."

"No. It doesn't." She slashed the blade through the air, and the gun in his hand exploded into flames.

When he screamed, dropped it, slapped at the flames over his hand, she did one of the first defensive moves her father had taught her. She kicked him in the balls.

When he went down, she spun, prepared to help Mallick. He stood with his bloodied sword.

Two lay dead on the ground. The other three were wounded, and the one who'd winked at her was curled up moaning, with a hand she doubted he'd ever have full use of again.

"Collect the weapons," Mallick said briskly.

He bent to take the gun and the knife from the leader. Fallon, feeling a little sick now that it was done, fought to keep her hand steady as she took weapons from the dead.

"That one's gun's melted too much to be of use."

Mallick glanced over where the man moaned, cradled his ruined hand. He said, "Hmph," much as he had about her weather forecast.

She slung one of the rifles over her shoulder by the strap while Mallick took two. After they stowed the other weapons, they remounted.

"You didn't tell me to go."

"Would you have?"

"No."

"Then why would I waste my breath?"

"You may not have taken them all."

"May no longer matters. You have courage. You fought your man well."

"We shouldn't leave them like that. The ones still able might come after us, or hurt someone else."

"We don't kill the unarmed and the wounded."

"No, but . . ." She held out her hand, set the tires on fire.

"Injured, unarmed, and on foot, they won't come after us, and it'll be harder for them to hurt anyone else."

Mallick studied the bikes as they crashed to the ground. "Well done. Good tactics."

"Good sense," she corrected, and began to walk her horse down the road again. Her throat was tight and dry, but she pushed the words out. "They would have killed you. They'd have raped me, then killed me. Or taken me to wherever they were going, raped me again, then killed me. The horses they might've kept if they had use for them, or they'd have slaughtered them for the meat."

"Yes. Unquestionably."

"You killed two of them. Maybe three because the one woman's badly hurt. They'll probably leave her there."

"It troubles you I took their lives?"

"No. Yes," she corrected. "I guess it did, until . . . They would have killed us. Not to survive, but because they like it. If we'd just been two people on the road, you'd be dead and I'd be . . . We made the right choice."

"They made the wrong choice. Consider this your first lesson."

With a nod, she glanced toward him. "You didn't have a sword before."

"Didn't I?"

"I think I'd have noticed."

He kicked into a canter. "You have to look to see."

He kept the pace brisk, following the road before veering off when another settlement came into view. At one point she saw another kind of settlement, one of only houses. Large houses stacked close together, many of them very much the same.

Some had boarded windows, another showed damage from a fire. Deer grazed on the knee-high grass and the wind whistled through the empty streets.

But she saw a shadow at one of the windows. Not all the houses stood empty.

"Why wouldn't people till the ground, grow food?"

"Not all know how," Mallick told her. "Some hide and scavenge. Fear locks them in."

She thought of it as they rode on. More than a hundred houses by her count, and close together for good defense. Wasted, she decided, as the ground that could be planted was wasted.

But as she had on several points along the journey, she marked it in her mind like a signpost on a map.

Once again they moved into a wood with rough, rolling ground where rocks shoved through. She heard the bubble of a stream before she saw it and, with Mallick, followed its meandering flow.

It widened, and water fell frothy and quick over ledges of rock. The rocks climbed higher, the water fell faster so its rushing sound filled the woods.

She spotted a few faeries fluttering in the pale rainbows formed by the strike of the sun on the splashing water.

Beyond the waterfall where its rush softened to a quiet music, Mallick stopped in a wide clearing.

Moss grew heavy on downed trees, lichen on an outcropping of rock. On the edges, trees bowed in an arching canopy.

When Mallick dismounted, Fallon assumed he wanted to rest the horses, so did the same.

"We should be nearly there. We could water them in the stream, walk them awhile, and get where we're going."

"We have."

"Here?" While she had no objection to living in the woods, she didn't relish living without shelter for the next couple years. "We're going to make a camp?"

Saying nothing, Mallick handed her his horse's reins, stepped forward.

He lifted his hands, shoulder high, palms out. For a moment there was nothing but the quiet echo of the waterfall, the shiver of the wind through the trees. The sun angled down, its light slipping through the canopy spilling into the clearing, and shadows shifted with the breath of the wind.

Then she heard the hum of power, felt the first pulse of it on the air, felt it raise the hair on her arms, at the back of her neck. The horses felt it as well and shifted restlessly so she shortened her grip on the reins.

Mallick's eyes deepened so his face seemed to pale as the wind rose up, blowing through his hair, and hers.

Light and shadows changed, shapes formed like a sketch blurred behind rippled glass.

Then his voice rang out, his arms snapped wide.

"Open now what I closed. Reveal here what I cloaked. For this is the place of my making. And The One is come."

The blurred sketch sharpened, took on form and color and shape.

Now in the clearing stood a cottage with a thatched roof and walls the color of sand. Smaller than the farmhouse, larger than the cabin, it had windows facing west and a thick wooden door. Beside it a small stable with a pitched roof held double doors, and close by a small greenhouse shimmered in the stream of sun.

Like the cottage doors, protective symbols had been carved around the frame of the stables, the glass door of the greenhouse.

A statue of the goddess, like the one at the cabin, stood beside the cottage door in a pool of polished stones.

She'd seen her mother's magicks, had practiced her own. But she'd never witnessed anything approaching the power needed to conceal and conjure on such a scope.

"See to the horses," he told her. "They've had a long journey."

"You're pale."

"It's more difficult to open than to close. See to the horses," he repeated, "then come inside."

He took his pack, walked into the cottage, and shut the door.

CHAPTER FIVE

She tended the horses, an easy enough task. Though the stable held only two stalls, they had fresh straw already laid and tools for grooming organized. Both mounts seemed content to settle in with some hay in the basket and the water she fetched from the stream.

She left them to it, carried her duffel, the weapons she'd taken, and what was left of the food her mother had packed to the cottage.

There she paused, remembering, and took her canteen, dribbled water for the goddess on the stones before she opened the cottage door.

It seemed larger inside, and the oddness of it gave her a strange, disorienting sensation. The ceiling rose higher than it should have, the walls spread wider.

A fire burned in the hearth with two sturdy chairs facing it. Rather than a sofa, the room held a wide bench covered in dark brown leather. Candles stood in iron holders on a table. A woven rug spread over the rough planks of the floor.

What served as the kitchen ranged across the back. It held a second, smaller hearth, a worktable, a sink with a window over it. Dried herbs hung in clumps. Jars of roots, berries, mushrooms, and seeds stood together on a wide plank.

She hoped he planned to conjure a stove and a refrigerator. And the power to run them.

But for now he sat by the fire with a glass of what she assumed was wine.

"You have the south-facing room. Leave the weapons on the table. We'll have some food when you've put away your belongings."

"There's no stove, no oven."

"There's a kitchen fire."

"No refrigerator."

"There is the box charmed to keep food cool."

She had a sudden and very bad feeling. "Where's the bathroom?"

"You have a water closet for that need, and both a stream and a well with water for washing."

"Are you kidding me?"

"You will, most certainly, find yourself in places without the advantages you've known until now. You'll learn."

"This already sucks."

She dumped the weapons and, more shocked than angry—no *bathroom?*—stomped off to what would be her bedroom.

If she stayed.

At least she didn't have to face lame bunk beds or ugly plaid, she thought with a frowning scan of the tiny bedroom. The bed was a mattress on slats with four short posts, but the blanket on it felt thick and warm.

In lieu of a dresser she had a chest, but she liked the shape of it, liked the painting of three women—goddesses maybe—over it. She had an oil lamp and a rug and a small, square mirror that showed her tired and dissatisfied face.

Still, the window—no curtain—looked out to the woods. She spotted the stone well, which would have saved her the trips to the stream if somebody had bothered to mention it.

She noted a chicken coop, so fresh eggs, and, to her surprise, saw a cow.

So he could do all that, but he couldn't add a damn bathroom?

She didn't bother to unpack, but went back out to complain.

"I want a bathroom. This isn't the seventh century."

"Then you'll have to learn enough to make one. For now, we have what you need to make a stew for dinner, in the cold box and the cupboard."

One shock followed the next. "You want me to cook?"

"I provided your breakfast," he reminded her as he sliced a loaf of bread. "And we have bread and cheese for midday. Your mother taught you to cook. She is an exceptional cook."

"And what do you do when I cook?"

"Eat. We have a cow for milk, chickens for eggs—and meat when needed—a forest for game, and plantings in a greenhouse. You'll eat well enough."

Because she was hungry, she took the bread and cheese. "We need to make a hive. We need to keep bees for honey unless you have a source for sugar. Where do you get the flour and salt and yeast or starter for bread?"

"I barter for it. We'll tend the stock and the plantings together. I have no knowledge of hives, so that will be your task, then you'll teach me how to tend it."

She ate as he did, standing up while they measured each other. "The clearing's too small to hold the house, the stable, the outbuildings. And the house is too small to hold all the rooms in it. You'll teach me how to create that kind of illusion."

"I'm here to teach you."

"If I learn, I want a bathroom. A toilet, a shower, a sink—with hot and cold running water."

He raised his eyebrows. "That seems a great reward for learning."

"What will it take?"

He considered. "I will give you three quests. When you complete all three, you'll have what you want."

"What quests?"

"There is a tree in the wood that bears a single golden apple. A white bird guards it jealously. You'll bring me the apple without harming the bird, bruising the fruit, or climbing the tree."

It sounded amazing—an adventure. But . . . "What's the next?"

"Complete the first task, and I'll tell you the second." He wrapped the cheese in a cloth, replaced it in the cold box.

She could find a golden apple, and she could outwit a dumb bird. "What's upstairs where there shouldn't be an upstairs?"

"A workshop and your classroom." He wrapped the bread. "I'll show you, then the cow needs milking, the eggs must be gathered, and you'll want to start the stew."

She wanted to start the hunt for the apple, but decided she could at least look upstairs.

She followed him up a ladder of steps, then struggled not to look amazed. She didn't want to give him the satisfaction.

Carefully labeled bottles filled shelves along one long wall. Potions, she mused while she—as casually as possible—strolled along to study. Ingredients for spells, some of them glowing with magickal light. Books filled the facing wall, and some looked impossibly old. The west wall held tools: cauldrons, athames, bells, bowls, candles, crystals, wands, staffs.

She wanted to touch everything, so she deliberately slipped her hands into her pockets.

A long table and two chairs stood in the room's center. Another

hearth, cold now, on the east wall had two closed cupboards flank-
ing it. Over it a mantel held more candles and a sword with a carved
hilt.

The only window cut through the roof and let the afternoon sun
stream in.

"Here you'll train and learn and practice. And become."

She gestured at the sword over the hearth. "That's not the sword
you used before."

"It's not mine to use."

"Mine? Is it the one you told my mother about? The sword and
the shield I'm supposed to get?"

"No, but when you're worthy, it will serve you."

"I don't know how to use a sword."

"You'll learn."

She liked the idea of that, and the idea of this room with all its
wonders. She liked the idea of finding a golden apple. But she wasn't
going to unpack, not yet. She'd give it a week. One week—that
was fair. She wanted to find the golden apple and drop it into Mallick's hand. She wanted to learn how to use the sword, and practice
magicks she didn't know in the room with the window in the roof.

One week, she thought. Then she'd decide.

Since Mallick filled the rest of the day and well into the evening,
Fallon didn't have time to think about decisions. He sent her off
to the greenhouse to gather what she needed to add to the venison
for stew. She approved of his work there, though she saw room for
improvement as she pulled onions, garlic, carrots, some tomatoes,
clipped herbs she'd use with the meat and potatoes stored in the
cottage.

She thought her mother would be proud of the way she peeled, chopped, mixed. And though Mallick balked at first about using his wine in the stew, Fallon stood firm.

While she set about making egg noodles—something she'd never done on her own—he told her to write down what she needed to build the hive.

"The bees actually build the hive. We build the bee box." She wiped her hands, took the pencil and paper he offered. "It's going to take some scavenging."

"Just write what's needed. I have a way."

Interested, she looked up. "Magickal?"

"Not precisely. When you're done, come upstairs. We'll begin."

He began by testing her basic knowledge and skills. Lighting candles, levitating small objects, mixing potions, performing what she thought of as kitchen spells.

Baby stuff to her mind.

Then he started testing her on rituals and deities and symbolism and sabbots.

His opinion of her knowledge was a head shake, a sigh. And a stack of books he pushed into her hands with the order to: Read and learn.

Still, she felt smug when the rain came, as she'd predicted, well before nightfall. And the stew she served over egg noodles was better than okay.

She hoped the next day involved sword practice and the hunt for the golden apple, which would be a lot more fun than cooking and making sleep potions and balms for burns.

She read in her room by the light of an oil lamp until mind and body gave way to fatigue.

At first light she took it upon herself to tend to the horses. When she stepped out she found a package wrapped in brown paper and twine at the front door. Scanning the woods for any movement, she picked it up.

She carried it back inside, set it on the table. Considered. It would be for Mallick, but . . . it didn't have his name on it, did it? And she lived here, too. At least for a week.

Justified, she pulled the twine, pulled back the paper.

A round of cheese, she noted, and sniffed it. A sack of flour, another smaller one of salt, and a corked bottle she assumed was wine.

Mallick came out of his room as she studied them.

"Somebody left this at the door."

"Ah." He looked at the supplies. "We're grateful."

"Who left it? Why?"

"Others live in and around these woods. They're also grateful, and pay tribute. They know The One has come."

"Why wouldn't they knock?"

"They have no need, as yet. Have you fed the horses?"

"No, I was just—"

"See to that. The animals need to be fed before we break our fast."

Rather than swords, Fallon spent most of her morning with books. She liked books, but with the woods so bright and clean from the rain, she'd rather have spent the morning outside learning to fight with a sword.

Still, she liked reading about the gods, the heroism, the betrayals, the battles, and the triumphs, even the romances.

He criticized her lack of knowledge and understanding of the spirituality of the Craft, its rituals.

She bristled. "We had to put food on the table, help our neighbors. My mother taught us what she could, what she knew."

"And did well with what she knew. Did well with what she came to know. You must know more. You'll take what your mother taught you, what I teach you, and what you come to know that's already in you waiting."

He paced the workshop in his soft boots as he spoke, then stopped, pointed one of his long fingers.

"Here's a lesson, Fallon. Your spirit is yours as mine is mine. What you feel and know are yours and will never be a mirror exact of another's. But respect for the spirit and the light, understanding of the dark, must be. And that's shown in the tradition of ritual, in its words, its symbols, its tributes.

"Your power doesn't come from a void, girl. There is a source for the light, for all we are, for the air we breathe, the earth we stand on. Life is a gift, even to a blade of grass, and must be honored. We have been given more, and must honor the gift and the giver."

"When we tend the earth and what it grows, the animals, each other, aren't we honoring?"

"Yes, but more is expected of some than to live an honorable life. Even a simple act can be a symbol. If I offer you my hand, and you take it, it's more than a greeting. It's a gesture of trust, perhaps agreement. My right hand to yours. The hands that hold the sword clasped together in that gesture of trust."

She studied his hand—long like his fingers, and narrow of palm. Then looked up at his face. "Some people are left-handed."

He had to smile, had to nod. "So they are. And there are those who would offer the gesture but not honor its symbol, in whichever hand they hold a sword. So you must learn to judge who to trust. And that is another lesson."

He walked to a shelf, selected a crystal. "What is this?" he asked as he set it in front of her.

"It's . . . ah . . . bloodstone." She searched her mind. "It's used in healing spells."

"Even before my time soldiers would carry a bloodstone into battle to stop the bleeding from wounds."

"If that's all it took, there wouldn't be so many dead soldiers."

"Your pragmatism is warranted. It takes more than a stone, even a powerful one, and faith to heal. But a ritualized stone, or one used in ritual, one blessed and used in a spell or potion, may heal. That, too, takes faith as well as knowledge and skill."

"My mother's a healer."

"She has that gift."

"She . . . yeah, powdered bloodstone mixed with honey and, um, egg whites and rosemary oil."

"Good. The stones are gifts and tools. You must learn how to clean them, charge them, use them. Take from what you see here, make a charm for a restful night, another for a clear mind, and a third for calming a jealous heart. Then you can do as you like until dusk."

He turned toward the steps. "Don't leave the wood," he added. "Don't wander far, and be back at dusk. No later."

She poked around the room a bit. The charms he'd assigned were basic, hardly a challenge, but she wanted to do them perfectly— so to invite a challenge the next time. And she preferred making pouches.

She checked in one of the cupboards beside the fire, found cloth, ribbon, cord, chose what she wanted.

She moved to the other cupboard, and found it locked.

And thought that very interesting.

She lifted a hand—opening a lock wasn't a challenge for her, either—then dropped it again. She'd been raised better. Maybe she could regret that at the moment, faced with a fascinating locked door, but it was simple fact.

Mallick was entitled to his privacy, just as she was.

So, some dried herbs from the jars. Anise, chamomile, lavender, cypress. And bits of crystals. Azurite, aquamarine, citrine, tiger's-eye. Some black pepper, oil of bergamot, of rosemary.

She set out everything in three groups, wrote out simple spells for each on a length of white ribbon, and used a needle to carefully sew the cord through the material to form a pouch. She assembled each one, saying the words on the ribbon three times before adding the ribbon to the pouch, tying it three times.

When she took them downstairs, she didn't see Mallick. Leaving them on the worktable, she got her jacket. Thrilled with the idea of freedom, of the hunt for the apple, she ran outside. She followed the stream for a while, but not the way they'd come, as she hadn't seen an apple tree.

Still, it might not *be* an apple tree, she considered. That might be part of the trick.

She searched branches, spotted birds—sparrows, jays, cardinals, finches. A hawk's nest, an owl's roost. But no white bird.

She angled away from the stream into thicker trees. She saw tracks and scat of deer, bear, opossum. She saw signs of wild boar and told herself the next time she'd bring her bow. And Grace, she thought. Her horse would get bored after a few days in the stable.

She saw faeries out of the corners of her eyes, but they darted away when she turned. They would be shy yet, she decided, and needed time to get used to her. But she changed direction, following the bright glint of their light into deeper shadows where thick moss covering trees like coats turned those shadows soft, soft green.

In that green light a little pond spread in the deepest of blues with pale green pads floating on it. On one sat a fat frog, apparently dozing, while a dozen dragonflies darted and swooped on long, luminescent wings.

A faerie glade, she realized, as even the air felt happy and sweet.

She sat cross-legged beside the pool, her chin on her fist, and marveled at the glasslike clarity of the water. She could clearly see the bottom, the soft dirt dashed with tiny colored pebbles, the fish, gold and red swimming in the blue.

"It's so pretty here." Leaning forward, she dipped a finger in the pool. "It's warm! Maybe you'll let me swim here."

She'd bring a gift next time, an offering, she decided.

It was so sheltered, not like the stream where she felt exposed when she took off her clothes to wash. Swimming here would be almost as good as—maybe better than—having a shower.

Content for the first time since she'd ridden away from home, she lay back, breathed in.

And saw the apple glinting gold on a high branch overhead.

"Oh my God! I found it."

And the bird, too, she thought as she scrambled to her feet.

Not the dove she'd imagined, but an owl—the biggest she'd ever seen. It sat on the branch beside the apple, and looked down at her with hard eyes of dark gold.

Like Ethan, she could connect with animals, birds, insects, fish. So she tried charm first, smiled.

"Hello! You're really handsome."

The owl stared unblinkingly.

"I'm Fallon. I'm staying in a cottage only a mile or so from here. With Mallick. Maybe you know him."

She heard the titter of faeries, ignored it for now. It wasn't the words, she knew, but the tone, the intent, the images in her own mind.

When the image of herself holding the apple popped into it, the owl spread its great wings, wrapped them around the apple.

She pushed, just a little. She'd been forbidden to harm the owl, and she'd never cause harm to anything so magnificent, but she tried just a little push. Instead of flying off as she'd hoped, he ruffled his feathers and stared down with active dislike.

"All right, okay. God, I want a shower. I want a toilet. You can't imagine how much. Look, I'm The One, and that makes me important. You should want to do me a favor."

He didn't budge, and the next ten minutes of trying to use her mind to trick him into flying away gave her a mild headache.

She needed a plan, she decided. She knew where he was now. She'd work up a plan, come back.

She shrugged as though the owl and the apple meant nothing, strolled away. She'd return, she thought as she moved from green shadows into dappled light. She'd bring a gift for the faeries so she could swim in the pool, and a plan to distract the owl long enough to get the apple.

She said nothing to Mallick about finding the apple, and though for the second night she went to bed with a stack of books, she spent considerable time plotting her strategy.

And in the morning, for the second time, she found gifts at the door. Stunned, delighted, she crouched down to examine the wood, the screening, the paint, the nails. The benefactor had even found the slats needed to separate the workers from the queen.

She stood again, stared out into the trees.

"Thanks!" she called. "When we have fresh honey, you can share."

She rushed to muck out the stalls, lay fresh bedding. She reminded Grace they'd take a ride later as she fed and watered both horses.

In building the bee box, Fallon was the teacher, and she liked it. It balanced out the morning of lessons, instructions, practice—none of which involved swords—and Mallick's less-than-enthusiastic response to her class work.

But for the hive project she took charge because he knew, in her opinion, zippity zip about hives, bees, and honey production.

"We're doing it from the bottom up," she told him once she had the supplies and tools organized to her standards. "So that's the hive stand to keep the hive off the ground. We're going to do an angled landing for the bees."

She had already measured and cut, so she showed Mallick how to lay a bead of wood glue. And found the scent of it reminded her of her dad.

"We have three hives at home. The first one, my grandmother gave my grandfather the kit and the bees for his birthday the spring before the Doom. The other two I helped Dad build, then the one we built for the ladies at Sisters Farm. They're not really sisters," she said as she worked. "They're witches, really nice, and friends of my mom's especially.

"Now we do the bottom board," she explained. "We're going to use the screen for ventilation, and we need to add the entrance. The bees come and go through the bottom board. So we're making a reducer. It keeps out mice and wasps. Pest and robbers."

She taught well, Mallick thought, working steadily, but explaining each step, guiding him through. She tasked him with constructing a board of slats, for more ventilation, to separate the brood chamber.

"I'm making two medium honey supers. Two's enough just for us, enough to feed the hive, have some for bartering. We're building a queen excluder."

"'Excluder'?" Mallick frowned. "I thought the queen was vital to the hive."

"She is, but we don't want her laying eggs in the honey, right?"

"I confess I hadn't given that a thought."

"You would if she did. She's bigger than the workers and drones, so we just make the excluder. She can't get into the honey supers, but the bees can get to the queen. We're going to build eight frames for the deep super—that's where they start building their wax. The excluder goes between the deep super and the honey supers."

"Your father taught you all this?"

"Yeah. Well, he had to learn. He read his father's beekeeping books because he didn't do much with the hive until his dad died, so he didn't know much about how it worked. Then we built more. My dad likes to build things. He's really good at it. He built the rooms onto the house and the picnic tables and the . . ."

She trailed off, kept her head down, her hands busy.

"It's natural to miss him, miss your family."

"If I think about it too much it's too hard."

He'd told her he'd never loved, but he had. He'd loved his mother. Fifteen hundred years didn't kill the memory of his sorrow at leaving her.

His duty was to teach, not to comfort, he thought. And yet, some comfort, some understanding surely paved a path toward teaching.

"What you do here, the sacrifice you make, the knowledge and skills you earn, you do for them. For the world, but they're in the world. What your mother did to keep you safe, what your birth father did, your life father. And they gave you a life, a foundation. Brothers, family. A reason, Fallon, above mere duty to face what comes. They taught you well and gave you knowledge. Enough that you can teach me how to build a home for bees."

"If . . . If I'd said no, would they die?"

"I can't say. I don't know. But you didn't say no. Yet."

She flicked a glance over at him, went back to her work.

She studied his slatted board, approved it, then had him follow her step-by-step as she built one honey super and he the second.

"Okay, this part's really messy. We've got to coat this plastic with beeswax. It gives the bees a start. We need to melt the wax first. I can take it in, melt it over the fire."

Mallick quirked an eyebrow. "Or you could consider this part of the task practice."

She liked that better.

She'd put the two cakes their benefactor had left them in a small cauldron. And now under Mallick's watchful eye, she held her hands over it, glided them down the sides, up again.

He felt the heat, slow and steady, saw the light shimmering from her palms, her fingertips. Soft, pure white.

Inside the cauldron, the wax began to melt.

"What do you call on?"

"The light," she murmured, her gaze fixed on the melting wax. "The heat. Not fire—not flame. Warmth and light."

"Where does it rise in you?"

"Everywhere. From the belly and . . . below. From the heart and the head. It's through me."

"How do you control it?"

She frowned at that. "I . . . think. Enough to melt, but not to burn or boil. That's enough."

She looked up, smiled. "Now it gets messy."

It took most of the afternoon to build and construct, to paint the exterior a bright white. While Fallon circled around it, crouched down to examine, Mallick stepped back. And found himself foolishly satisfied to have had a part in building something with his own hands.

"It's good," Fallon decreed. "Sound and sturdy."

"You'll give me lessons on the keeping of the bees once we get them. Do they come to the hive, attracted by the box, the wax?"

"You wouldn't get a healthy colony that way, and you'd never draw the queen. You call them, invite them."

"Show me."

"I scouted a colony yesterday. They'll like it here. You've never called bees?"

"No. It's not my gift. Show me," he repeated.

She closed her eyes a moment, a young girl, long-legged, slender, her raven-wing hair in a braid over one shoulder.

"I am in the air, of the air. I am in the light, of the light. I am on the earth, of the earth. I am by the water, of the water. And all these, magicks join. I am of the magicks that join the creatures that walk, that crawl, that fly, that burrow, that swim. We are all of, in, by, on.

The queen nests while others brood, work, hunt, build. Here I offer a home, humbly. Come and see. Come and live. Come and thrive."

She spread her arms. "Come."

He saw nothing, heard nothing but the girl, her arms spread wide, her body statue-still. And her face, he thought, luminous.

A minute passed, then another, then a third. He thought to stop her, to tell her she could try again another time.

Then he heard the swarm.

The air filled with a deep, droning buzz, and Fallon stayed still. The cloud, a swirl, swooped out of the woods. His instinct was to rush to her, to pull her away, inside to safety.

Before he moved, she opened her eyes. And glowed.

A large honeybee—the queen?—hovered over the palm of her right hand. And the swarm covered her outstretched arms, her hair, her shoulders, in a mad buzz.

She laughed as though surrounded by butterflies.

Did she know, could she know, all she had? Mallick wondered. All she might be if he didn't fail her? At that moment, her power was so strong, but still young and painfully innocent.

What would she be, what would she hold when that power matured, and that innocence was lost?

She moved then, tipping her fingertips down in a gesture toward the hive. "Welcome," she said. And as one, the swarm entered the hive.

"How do they—" He broke off to steady his voice. "How do they know where they should go inside the hive?"

Her answer came with a puzzled smile. "Well, I told them."

"Ah. All right then, well done. I'll put the tools and so forth away. You're free until dusk."

"I want to take Grace for a ride."

He nodded. "Don't go too far, and be no later than dusk."

She ran off, young, innocent. Mallick listened to the hum of the bees, and felt very old.

BECOMING

Learning is not child's play;
we cannot learn without pain.

—Aristotle

CHAPTER SIX

Every day for three days, Fallon visited what she thought of as faerie-land. She tried magicks on the owl with no success. She tried bribery, intimidation, and what her mother called *reverse psychology*.

I don't want your stupid apple anyway.

He simply sat, guarding the apple that hung tantalizingly from that high branch.

She swam in the pool so at least she felt clean. The little faeries grew used to her and came out to dance or skim along the water when she bathed.

But she couldn't convince any of them to help her get the apple.

She sat on the grass at the end of her first week, drying her hair, studying the stubborn, hard-eyed owl.

She couldn't climb the tree, but what if she went up *without* climbing it? She'd been practicing—away from Mallick's watchful eye—and though her form proved shaky, she'd managed to levitate about two feet off the ground.

The apple, to her gauge, would require a solid ten-foot lift. And then she had to consider that big, sharp beak, those keen talons. So she'd have to practice until she could go high, and go fast.

She wanted to outwit the owl as much on principle now as for the bathroom.

"One week down, a hundred and three weeks to go," she said out loud as she braided her hair.

She still hadn't unpacked, told herself she could leave in the morning, be home in less than two-days' ride.

She didn't mind the lessons and lectures and practice as much as she'd thought she would. Some of it was interesting, even if it had started to cut into her free time since Mallick had added physical training.

Still no sword.

And while she didn't see how being able to balance herself on one hand or juggling balls of light would help her save the whole damn world, she liked learning. She didn't mind the studying or learning about the people Mallick claimed were her ancestors. She liked the spell casting.

But everything took so long, had to be done over and over again. She couldn't imagine spending another one hundred and three weeks doing the same things over and over. Or having nobody but Mallick to talk to.

Maybe she'd try balancing on one hand over the water. Now that would be really interesting. If she could work with two elements— water and air—balance on the surface of the water.

Even Mallick would be impressed.

She would practice levitating in her room with the apple as the goal, and practice the balancing here in faerie-land. When she had perfected those skills, she'd use them as a lever to start learning how to use a sword.

She wished she'd thought of the water-balancing earlier because now she'd already taken most of her free time for the day.

"Tomorrow," she murmured.

She didn't sense or hear anything until almost too late. She spun quickly toward the *sense* in time to see the boy slip half out of a tree, an arrow already notched in his bow.

Even as she threw up a hand in defense, she saw that he aimed the arrow not at her, but at the owl.

She didn't think, only felt. Outrage, fear for another. And the feeling shot her ten feet in the air, slicing out her hand to deflect the arrow. The keen point grazed her palm before the arrow winged away and thudded into another tree. The shock of pain, the shock of rising, broke that feeling. She tumbled back down, landing with enough force to knock her breath away.

"Are you crazy?" The boy, tumbled bronze hair, furious eyes the color of spring leaves, leaped toward her. "I could've killed you."

"Why would you kill the owl? Nobody eats owl."

"You're bleeding. Let me see how bad."

"It's nothing." It hurt like fire, but she knocked his hand away. "You've got no business shooting an arrow in this place, or at the owl."

"I live in this place." He shook back his mop of hair with its single skinny braid falling over his right ear. "Sort of. And I wasn't shooting at the owl."

"Yes, you were!"

"No, I wasn't. Taibhse is a god of the glade. I would never try to hurt him. I was aiming at the apple. You wanted the apple, didn't you?"

"Why would you care?"

"Why not? You'd have the apple now if you hadn't spoiled the shot, and I'd be the one who tricked Taibhse. That's a deep cut. Mallick will have a healing balm. He's a great sorcerer. You're his student."

"And I can take care of myself."

"Whatever." He pulled out a cloth, shoved it at her. "At least wrap it."

Annoyed, she wrapped the cloth around the slice in her palm, pressed her hands hard together, then yanked off the bloodied cloth, tossed it back to him.

The wound had closed, begun to heal.

"Even if you were aiming for the apple, you could have missed, hit the owl."

His chin jerked up. "I don't miss."

"You *did* miss."

"You got in the way." He shrugged it off. "They're saying you're The One, like some great warrior, witch, Savior. You just look like a girl to me."

He wasn't much older than she was, a year, maybe two at the most. Taller, yes, but hardly older. She bristled at having someone her own age so dismissively term her *a girl*.

"If I was just a girl, your arrow wouldn't be stuck in that tree over there."

Pride every bit as much as power had her flinging out a hand, yanking it out, floating it back until it dropped at the base of the owl's tree.

She'd meant to drop it at the boy's feet, but close enough.

"That's pretty good." He walked over to pick it up while the owl stared down at him with cold disdain.

"Look, I was just trying to do you a favor. You've been trying to get that apple for days." Using the cloth, he wiped her blood from the arrow before slipping it back in his quiver.

"It's none of your . . . How do you know?" Horror, instant and deeply female, flared through her. "You've been spying on me."

He had the grace to look embarrassed, and it pinked up the tips of his ears. "I wouldn't call it spying exactly. I just saw you come in here. Nobody outside knows about this place, and nobody who isn't one of us can come into it. So when you could and did, I wanted to see what you were up to."

"You're a, you're a—" She dug for the word. She'd heard it in a movie. "A Peeping Tom."

"I'm Mick. My father's Thomas, but I don't even know any Tom."

"It's an expression."

"What does it mean?"

"A spyer."

"It's not my fault you took your clothes off, and anyway, you're skinny. And I was just trying to do you a favor. You left out sweet cakes."

Her eyes narrowed. "Are you the one who leaves things at the cottage?"

"One of us does. It's tribute, and no payment's expected or needed. It was kind to leave the cakes—and they were good. My father says you repay kindness with kindness, then there's more of it."

"I bet your father wouldn't like knowing you spied on me." She strode to her horse. "Don't do it again. I'll know." She swung onto Grace. "And don't shoot arrows at the owl or the apple. It's not the right way. It's not fair."

She looked down at him, as regally as she could manage after knowing he'd seen her naked. "We appreciate the tribute, so thank you, your father, and whoever else. Now go sneak around somewhere else."

She nudged Grace into a trot.

"Are you coming back tomorrow?" he called out.

She sighed, thought, *Boys*, and declined to answer.

As she approached the edge of the clearing, she heard the *whoosh* of wings. She reined in Grace, looked up. Her eyes widened in awe as Taibhse swooped overhead, the stem of the apple in his beak.

Some instinct—Mallick would have termed it a call to her blood— had her lifting an arm. And still it stunned her when the owl glided down, landing on it as if on a branch.

She felt his weight—considerable—but not any bite from his talons. His gold eyes stared into hers, and she felt a connection forged.

Mallick stepped out of the cottage, watched her ride toward him, one hand on the reins, the magnificent owl on her other arm.

Hadn't he dreamed that? Hadn't he seen it? The owl, the ghost god, the hunter, would be hers now. As bound to her, Mallick thought, as he was himself.

"I found the apple. I didn't hurt the owl. He's Taibhse."

"Yes, I know."

"I didn't climb the tree. I don't want to take the apple from him. It's like stealing. But you see I found it, and he can take it back. I want the bathroom, Mallick, but I'm not going to steal to get it."

"You've fulfilled the first quest. The apple is another symbol, Fallon. There are many who would be blinded by the gold and not see the true prize. You've won the loyalty of Taibhse, hunter, guardian, wise spirit. He's yours now as you are his."

"I . . . I can keep him?"

"Girl, he's not to be kept or owned. You belong, one to the other. Lift your arm to release him. He won't go far."

When she lifted her arm, Taibhse soared up, settled on a high branch. When he set the apple down, the stem attached as if the golden fruit had grown there.

"He's beautiful, and brave. What's the second quest?"

"We'll discuss it over dinner. Tend to your horse."

"Don't you want to hear how I got the apple?"

"I do, yes. Over dinner."

That night, she unpacked and hung Colin's wind chime in her window. On the sill she placed a little jar and set the stem of Ethan's flower in it along with her birth father's book, and the photo of her with her family.

Looking out through the dark, through the dance of faerie lights, she saw the white flash of the great owl on the hunt.

Tomorrow, she thought, she'd hunt, too. After the chores, after the lessons and the practice and the studies, she and Grace would ride the woods on the second quest Mallick had given her. She would find the gold collar, and the wolf who wore it.

While she dreamed, others hunted. Their fingers probing through the dark scratched at the surface of her dreams. She was the prey, had been since before her birth.

She tossed in sleep, fear urging her to turn away from the images, the voices just beyond reach. Run from them, hide, survive.

What she was pushed to see and hear was blurred and indistinct. To know what to fight.

The circling crows, a gleeful murder heralding death. The flashes of lightning, black for death, red for burning. A circle of stones swimming in fog, and a man wading through it to stand and stare at the scorched and broken earth within the old dance.

The hilt of the sword he carried glinted in a single beam from the moon. Suddenly, his gaze cut away from the stone, and darkly, fiercely green broke through the borders of dreams.

Here the first of seven shields, destroyed by treachery and dark magicks. Here the blood of a son of the gods shed, and here the blood of our blood poisoned. So raged the plague.

Now, Fallon Swift, I wait. We wait. It waits.

He lifted his sword. Lightning struck the lethal point, erupted so he held a blade of white, flashing flame.

Will you take up the sword and the shield of The One? Will you answer the call? Will you come? Will you be?

When he plunged the tip of the sword into the ground, the fog burned. In the stone circle something bubbled and churned.

Choose.

While she dreamed, while others hunted, still others prepared for blood sacrifice.

In what had been, before the Doom, a wealthy suburb in Virginia, a band of Purity Warriors established a base camp. There nearly a hundred men, women, and the children they made, captured, or indoctrinated lived in grand houses and held weekly public executions.

Some, true believers, followed the tenets of Jeremiah White, the cult's founder and self-proclaimed commander. All Uncannys, any who had magickal abilities—or those who sympathized with them— were from hell. Demons and those who trucked with them must be destroyed.

Others joined, bore the symbol of the cult, because they enjoyed the freedom to rape, torture, kill, and a religious fervor baked in blood and bigotry offered the opportunity.

White himself had visited the base. He'd spent two days in one of the grand houses, had given rousing sermons on his twisted god's vengeance, and there presided over the hanging of three prisoners.

An elf, barely twenty, wounded in battle in the outskirts of D.C. A woman, a healer past seventy, who'd tended the wounds of the elf and others—even those who cursed her for a demon. And a man, simply a man, accused of witchcraft for the crime of trying to protect a child of ten from a beating.

Torture preceded the hanging. White called the screams of the damned trumpet calls to the righteous, and those who followed him cheered in a black wave of hate that rolled like a killing sea.

White traveled with an entourage of bodyguards, strategists, sycophants, and soldiers. And some—if reckless enough or drunk enough—whispered some of that entourage were of the Dark Uncanny.

But White rewarded his faithful with food, slaves, those rousing sermons, and a promise of eternal life when the demon threat was eradicated. So most kept silent.

Sundays, the Sabbath, began with worship. Reverend Charles Booker, formerly a grifter who specialized, with mixed success, in bilking the elderly on home repair and security, led the congregation in prayer and verses from the Old Testament to a god thirsty for blood. Announcements followed the service, given by Kurt Rove, appointed chancellor by White as a reward for his part in the New Hope Massacre. While he ran the base with an iron fist and basked in his position, on Sundays Rove reveled.

Rove might announce changes in laws, often arbitrary. He would read dispatches from White, reports from other bases, from battles, listing numbers killed and captured—this to cheers that celebrated spilled blood.

He would end reading the names of prisoners, and those selected— by committee—for that Sunday's execution.

Attendance to worship, announcements, and Sunday executions was mandatory. Only those assigned guard details were granted dispensation. Illness only served as an excuse for absence if the base doctor, who'd had his medical license revoked before the world ended, issued a waiver.

Those who failed to attend risked, if reported, twenty-four hours in the stocks erected outside the three-car detached garage that served as the prison.

Since Rove's appointment, executions took place at precisely midnight. Not a minute before, not a minute after. "Escorts" selected by lottery led the prisoners from the garage to the public green and the scaffold. Each prisoner bore the brand of a pentagram on their forehead—a Rove flourish White had decreed into Purity Warrior policy. Their hair, roughly shorn, often showed bloody scalps. They were allowed no shoes, only a rough garment of burlap fashioned by slaves.

If the prisoner had wings, they were sliced off. Witches remained as they were since capture, gagged and blindfolded, lest they try to cast their evil eye or speak an incantation.

On this Sunday night, when images of shadows and shapes pushed into Fallon's dreams, as crows circled over the scaffold and those already gathered, two of the six prisoners being held took the forced march.

The witch, raped, beaten, all of her fingers broken, struggled not to limp, not to trip. If she fell, they'd kick her, and they'd already broken her spirit with pain. She was ready to die.

Beside her, fighting to be brave, the shapeshifter, barely twelve, kept his head up. He'd run to draw the hunt away from his little pack. He'd saved his brother and the rest, so he kept reminding himself he wouldn't die a coward.

He could ignore the jeers and taunts of the escort, of the people who ran along the street. He had to ignore the sad, hopeless eyes of the slaves or he might give in to the screaming inside his head.

He wasn't ready to die. But he wouldn't beg.

A stone grazed his cheek. The quick pain, the scent of blood had the animal inside him straining for freedom. He reined the cougar in. These filth would never see his spirit.

One of the escorts shouted, "Stoning's forbidden! Knock that off unless you want an hour in the stocks." Then he gave the boy a shove. "Keep moving, you demon bastard."

Inside the boy, the cougar growled low. Its powerful forelegs pulled against the rope binding the boy's hands behind his back.

Then he saw the scaffold, the pair of nooses, the crowd of people lit bright on the green. They'd kill him, he thought with a cold assessment his youth had helped him deny. At midnight, they'd hang him so he'd choke and kick while they cheered.

They'd kill him, so why shouldn't he die fighting? Why shouldn't he fight with all he was? And maybe take a couple of them with him.

He breathed in deep of the night air, let the cat stretch inside his bones, his muscles, his skin. They could kill him, he thought, but they wouldn't break him.

As he opened himself to the change, welcomed it for what he believed was the last time, an arrow winged out of the dark.

The escort who'd shoved him let out a kind of grunt, then fell to the ground. Jeers turned into screams as more arrows flew and people scattered.

With arrows whistling, the cougar slipped its bounds, dropped to all fours. Its eyes glinted as it leaped into the panicked crowd. He saw a man—a boy?—pull the gag and blindfold from Jan—the witch—then pick her up when she swayed.

He ran with one purpose, one destination in mind. What had been his prison. He heard gunfire, more screaming, rushing feet. He scented blood, scented fear.

He wanted blood. He wanted fear.

But when he reached the prison, his prey lay on the ground bleeding, senseless. A girl stood over him, and then she turned, stared into his eyes. Shifted to stand between him and what he wanted most. The taste of that blood in his throat.

"He's down, and he's unarmed now. You might be able to get by me long enough to rip out his throat. But you'll never be the same if you do. We have your brother safe, Garrett. We have Marshall and the others safe."

He shuddered, dissolved into the boy. "Marshall? Everyone?"

"Marshall and everyone. All eight. Nine now, with you. You're safe, too. And we need to get everyone we can away from here. Jonah!" she called toward the garage. "I've got the kid. The shifter."

"Get him to the rendezvous. We've got four in here, and we need to transport them out."

"Roger that. You need to—" She broke off when Garrett swiped out—cougar claws on a boy's hand—and scored the guard's right arm.

"They beat us and burned us and broke pieces of us. They marked us. And things . . . He raped me." Garrett drew a shuddering breath. "Now I've marked him."

"Okay." She put a hand on his shoulder, drew him away. "We have to move fast, get as many people who're being held out as we can. Can you run? It's less than a quarter mile."

"I can run."

She broke into a sprint, making him prove it.

She had dark hair in a lot of curls that sort of burst out of a band. She ran fast, scanned everything as she moved. He thought her eyes were blue, but it was hard to be sure when the moon kept going in and out.

She wore a short sword and a quiver, a bow.

"Did you shoot the arrow?"

"Which one?"

"The one. The first one."

"No. My brother did. He won the toss. I'm Tonia." Grinning, she shot a hand in the air, circled a finger, forming three circles of light. Just ahead, Garrett saw the answering light. Then two men with rifles beside a truck.

"I've got Marshall's brother. I've got Garrett."

"Marshall's going to be a happy boy tonight. You hurt, son?"

The man looked really, really old, but he held the rifle like he knew how to use it. "I'm okay."

"I'm Bill, and this is Eddie."

"How's it hanging, my man? Hey, why don't you get on up in the truck there, keep Joe company."

"Who?"

"My dog, Joe." Eddie pulled down the tailgate. A big dog stood up, a little slow, a little stiff, wagged his tail.

"I've got to get back."

Eddie nodded at the girl. "Go on. We've got him. Come back in one piece or your mom'll kick my ass."

"Can't have that." She dashed off, swallowed by the dark.

"Let's get you on up there, dude."

"I can do it." Garrett climbed into the back, dropped down, and when the dog leaned against him, he gave in to the little boy, wrapped his arms around the dog, pressed his face to the fur so nobody saw the tears.

He jolted at the sound of explosions, shivered as he saw fire shoot to the sky.

"What's that? What is it?"

"Just taking care of business," Eddie said while Bill leaned in, wrapped a blanket around Garret's shoulders. "You don't want the assholes following you? You steal some of their vehicles, and go boom to the rest. Much as you can anyway. How about you and Joe make some room back there? We're expecting more riders."

Some ran, as he had. Others were carried. Another truck pulled up, and the man behind the wheel gestured ahead.

Others piled into the bed, boosted in by Eddie or Bill. Kids mostly, some women. He recognized one or two. Whenever they'd bothered to feed prisoners, the slaves had brought in the slop they called food.

The boy beside him, younger than the youngest in his own pack, shivered with the cold.

"Here, you can share my blanket. This is Joe."

He heard the roar of an engine, saw the girl he'd run with on the back of a motorcycle, behind a boy. Dark hair like the girl's, not as curly.

The one, Garrett realized, who'd helped Jan.

He swung the bike in a half circle, stopped. "We got all we could get—some just ran so we couldn't pull them in. They're going to be busy putting out fires, so the ones who ran might make it."

"Jonah said move out," Eddie called and hopped behind the wheel.

"We'll take point. Flynn and Starr have flank."

He roared off, dark hair flying.

Eddie opened the window to the bed, raising his voice as he pulled into the convoy. "Hi there. I'm Eddie, and I'll be your driver tonight. Just settle back, 'cause we've got a ways to go. There's water back there and blankets. Be sweet, everybody, and share."

Garrett shifted closer to the window. "Who was that on the motorcycle?"

"Duncan. Tonia's twin brother. Our resident hell-raiser. Get yourself some water, dude, catch a nap if you want. We've got a good hour's drive—and food and medical attention once we get you there."

"Marshall's there? And everybody?"

"That's a fact, Jack." Eddie took a hand off the wheel, angled himself to reach a hand back through the little window, give Garrett's a squeeze. "They're all waiting for you, so you can chill now."

Because more tears wanted to come, Garrett blinked hard. "Where are we going? Where is 'there'?"

"My man, we're heading to New Hope."

CHAPTER SEVEN

Fallon mangled a basic incantation—twice—and very nearly added belladonna rather than bergamot to a simple potion before Mallick stopped her.

"Do you wish to poison an enemy?"

"What?" Her brow furrowed as she looked up. "No." Then she looked down at the clearly marked bottle in her hand. "Oh." She put the bottle back and, after a moment—too long a moment to Mallick's mind—chose the bergamot. "So I made a mistake."

He objected nearly as much to the dismissal of her carelessness as to the carelessness itself.

Both were unacceptable, but the dismissal showed weakness.

"A mistake with belladonna can kill. As a mistake with an incantation can have far-reaching and disastrous consequences. Your words and actions, the precision of them, matter."

"Maybe if you didn't expect me to remember *everything*, and stand around watching me all the time, I wouldn't make a mistake."

"Perhaps my mistake is believing you'd progressed enough to know the properties and uses of extracts, oils, and powders. Sit then, and we'll start at the beginning."

"I know the stupid properties, okay?" Because it shook, the snap in her voice lost most of its sting. "I just picked up the wrong bottle. And ingredients like belladonna and foxglove and other deadlies should be separated out into their section instead of everything to-gether in alphabetical order."

He inclined his head. "That is a fair point. You may begin that task now."

"There are hundreds! It'll take half the day."

"Then you should begin. The task should help calm and focus your mind."

"I don't want to spend all day cooped up in here doing something you should've done in the first place. I want to go outside. I want some air. I don't feel good."

Clearly, he thought, she didn't. The misery in her eyes, the sheen of tears in them unnerved him more than a little.

Why had he, a man who knew so little of children, and less about female children, been tasked with the care and training of a girl child?

For despite her power, she was still a child.

A female child, he remembered, and cleared his throat.

"Ah. Have you begun your monthly courses?"

"My . . ." It took her a minute, then misery flashed into disgust. Disgust edged right over into contempt.

"God!" Pulling at her hair, turning in a circle, she inadvertently had the candles flaming. "My mother was right. She was right! The minute a woman's out of sorts or upset, men think or are even stu-pid enough to say something about her period."

"I . . . am at a loss."

"And until men start cramping and bleeding every month, they should just shut up about it."

"Done."

Fallon dropped her hands, then lifted them again to press her fingers to her eyes. "I'm just tired. I'm just tired. I didn't sleep very well."

"You made a fine charm for quiet sleep. Take it, use it. I'll help you reorganize our ingredients, as you're right about the separation. Then we'll make a sleep potion, a fresh one, for you. And you'll take a ride later, in the air."

He stopped because while the fire had gone out of her eyes, those potent gray eyes, the misery only increased.

More than a sleepless night, he thought. And he was a fool, bungling her care as surely as she had the incantation.

"You long for your family, and I am not your family. You wish for your mother's comfort, your father's shoulder. I can't be that for you. But will you not trust me enough to tell me what troubles you?"

"I had dreams."

"Dreams or visions?" He put up a hand when those eyes filled. Yes, he was a fool and a bungler. "No matter just yet. Come, sit. Sit," he repeated. "I'll make you tea."

"I don't want—"

"Only to soothe," he assured her as he moved to choose herbs to steep. "I'll have some as well. I can teach you and train you, I can guide and defend you. But I know little of young girls and their needs beyond the training. You must give me time to learn, to practice. Your dreams disturbed you."

"I—I unpacked. I hung up Colin's wind chime and put out Ethan's flower. I put out the picture my parents had made for me, of the whole family. So the room is more like mine."

She knuckled at her eyes, not at tears, Mallick noted, but at fatigue.

"I found Taibhse, and that was—it was the best. And, like I told you, I met Mick. He's kind of a jerk, but . . ." She shrugged. "And I thought about tracking the wolf with the golden collar, and that would be fun. So if I have to do this, at least after I study and train and practice, I have Grace and now Taibhse, and jerky Mick. So maybe I can learn enough. Like building the beehive. It's one step, one piece at a time. Like Dad says, you do this, then you do that, then the next thing.

"I felt happy."

He brought the tea to the table, sat across from her. "Then you dreamed. Will you tell me?"

"The first was a place. It's stupid."

"The place is stupid?"

"No, no. I've never been there. This is the farthest I've ever been from the farm, so I've never been there, but I felt I knew the place. With the stones in a circle, coming up out of the fog, and the empty fields, the woods dark and close. Then a man walked through the fog to the stones. I know I've never seen him before, but there was something, and I felt . . . I felt something. He had dark hair, and a sword. And green eyes. Dark green like the shadows in faerie-land."

" 'Faerie-land.' "

She flushed just a little, lifted her tea. "It's what I call the glade where I found Taibhse. I know the color of his eyes because even though I wasn't in the dream like you sometimes are, I wasn't in it, he turned his head and he looked right at me. Like through a window or a mirror. And he spoke to me."

"What did he say?"

"He said my name, and he said how the circle was the first of seven shields, and how the blood of the gods—the blood of our ancestors, his and mine—was shed there, and how it was poisoned and destroyed the shield and started the plague. And he took out his sword and lifted it. Lightning hit it and it went to fire. White fire. He asked me if I'd answer the call, if I'd take up the sword and the shield, if I'd fight and be strong, if I'd, like . . . come to be. He told me to choose.

"I don't know if it was a dream or a vision."

"It can be both."

"Mom has visions, and sometimes . . . Sometimes I know where the boys are hiding or if they're going to play a trick on me. I see it in my head. Not every time, but sometimes. Once a man stopped at the farm. He had scars on his arms, and on his face. I saw him in a fire, screaming, and running, and falling in the dark outside where they left him for dead. Raiders. I saw it."

"It frightened you."

She nodded, sipped her tea.

"You said 'the first.' You had other dreams."

"One other. Longer, and it wasn't clear like the first. It was blurry. Mostly. Like the glass was dirty, and the voices were far away. I could hear some, but not all. It was a different place. Like that place we rode through with all the big houses, all together?"

"Yes. They called them developments. A kind of community."

"Okay, it was a place like that. Really big houses. Purity Warriors lived there. I know who they are."

Some of the misery burned off in anger.

"They hunt us, kill us, just because we're not like them."

"They fear us, and any who are different."

"They have slaves," Fallon told him. "They make slaves out of people who don't believe like they do. Even kids. And they keep magickal people locked away. They do terrible things to them. There was a boy, and I could see into his head. A little. Pieces of his thoughts, so I know the terrible things. They were going to hang him, and the woman with him, a witch. Her name . . . I lost it."

"It's all right."

"He's Garrett. Was Garrett. I don't know when. Was it now or before or not yet? I don't know. But he was Garrett, a shapeshifter. Younger than me. They'd beaten him and burned him and cut him and . . . and raped him. They'd cut off his hair, and the woman's. They had her blindfolded and gagged, and both of them had their hands bound behind their backs. They had to walk barefoot down the street while people shouted at them, and one threw a rock that hit the boy's head. They had—the boy and the woman—a mark here." She touched her forehead. "Burned into them. A pentagram."

"The Purity Warriors brand those like us they capture."

"The slaves, too. But here." She tapped the back of her left wrist. "They burn a symbol there. A circle with a cross in it. The boy, Garrett, could see, so I could sort of see, they walked toward this platform, with two nooses."

"Scaffold."

"Okay, a scaffold. And this I heard from his mind, clear. He would change, become the cougar that lived in him. He would fight before they killed him. Then, an arrow came out of the dark and killed the man who forced him to walk. Then another, and another, as the boy changed, and the cougar ran through the people who were screaming and running. But I saw a boy, another boy. Older though, older than Garrett, than me, go to the woman and take off her gag and blindfold, and pick her up when she fainted. I saw that, too. And I think he was maybe the younger brother or the son of the man from the first dream because I don't know when that happened, either. And I only saw him then for a minute, with the woman who fainted, because I was with the boy, the cougar, and he was racing toward this place where they kept the others locked up."

She took a breath, she took some tea, and found some of the twisting in her belly eased away.

"He'd never killed before, Mallick, not as boy or cougar, I knew that, felt that. But he wanted to now. But the man guarding the jail was on the ground. Bleeding and dazed, but not dead. I felt life still. There was a girl, really pretty, and she wasn't afraid of the cougar. It gets all mixed up. I think there were others helping inside the jail, and the boy changed back so the girl helped him get away to where other people were waiting. A man and an old man, and a dog. An old dog. I heard the man say his name was Eddie and the dog was Joe. I know those names, Mallick. I know them."

"Yes."

She shivered a little at having Mallick acknowledge what she knew.

"The girl went back, and others came. The slaves and the captured. Another truck with more. Explosions back in the—the development? It was like a raid, but to save people, to free people and help them. Then the girl came back, riding on a motorcycle with the boy who'd helped the woman. Duncan and Tonia. I know those names, too."

"Yes."

"They all drove away, and when the boy, when Garrett asked Eddie where they were going—because I heard that clear, too—he said New Hope. I know that place. My father died there. My birth father, when the Purity Warriors came to kill. To kill me especially."

The words tumbled out now, fast, fast, to lift the weight inside her.

"My mother ran from there to save me, to save the people who lived there. Her friends. Eddie was her friend. He had a dog named Joe. Duncan and Tonia—Antonia—were twins, just babies when she lived there. Their mother was my mother's friend. They—Eddie and Duncan and Tonia and the old man, all the others, they risked their lives to save Garrett, the woman, the other people. It was too . . . tactical," she decided, "to be the first time, the first rescue. I don't like *raid*. *Rescue*'s better. Duncan and Antonia aren't much older than me, and they're already fighting. Garrett's younger than me, but he was ready to fight."

"Do you question why you've been shielded?"

She hadn't realized, not fully, that this was the weight, so much heavier than the rest.

"If I'm The One, why aren't I fighting? Why aren't I helping people?"

"You will. Your mother and your life father provided your foundation not only with what they both taught you, but by giving you vision. A family, community, loyalty, and love. A war such as this can't be only blade and lightning. You must believe, into your bone, the cause you hold is worth dying for. Killing for. And what you have yet to acquire, to know, to hold, even to believe is vast, girl. Vast. Some are warriors, some are leaders, some are symbols. You will be all. But your time is not yet come."

"Is that why the sword stays up there, and that cabinet is locked?"

"You'll hold the sword soon enough. Why haven't you tried to open the cabinet?"

"How do you know I haven't?"

He smiled. "I'm not without vision, girl."

"Fine. Because that would be rude and disrespectful."

"And you wouldn't have that understanding and sensibility if you'd been denied the years with your family. They serve you, and will serve you."

Maybe that was true, she thought. But . . . "Do you know the place in the first dream?" she asked.

"Yes," he replied.

"There are six more. If destroying the first killed almost everybody, what happens if the others are destroyed?" She had so many questions.

"The first wasn't broken quickly or easily. It took a great concentration of dark power, and a lack of the light. Beliefs can fade, and when faith pales, so does power. Fears of the dark? They're intrinsic, and so dark can build. And as it became easier to dismiss the light, it dimmed and the protection around the shield weakened. Just enough. It may have taken this horror to wake the light, to bring it beaming, but it is woken."

"That doesn't answer the question," she complained.

"The shields are now more carefully guarded."

"But?"

He sighed. A relentless mind, he thought, and had to respect it.

"One by one, shield by shield? More would die, infected by a madness, crops would fail until they burned in the field, withered on the vine, rotted in the earth. So famine follows. And a plague runs through the animals. Fish and fowl, mammal. Only what slithers and crawls remains. And the rivers and streams, the lakes and oceans bloated with blood and death and rot become tainted even as they rise up in a flood to spread their poison."

Already pale, she lost more color as he spoke. But the question deserved a full and true answer.

"And a great heat bakes the earth, burns the trees with lightning striking down forests. The world is fire and smoke. Then the dark descends, and the slaughter of all who remain begins. The ground will shake and split, and what rules the dark rules all."

"Why? Why?" she demanded. "There'd be nothing left to rule."

"That is the purpose. All that is light extinguished, all that is good silenced, and all that is hope murdered."

"That's just stupid."

"Then those of us who fight that purpose must be smart."

She fought to steady herself, to understand. To . . . *not* be ignorant.

"So when the shield broke and the Doom killed billions, some people who thought they were just regular people found their magicks. So people would believe again?"

"Faith is a sword and a shield, as long as one bolsters it with courage and brains and muscle. Some who found their magicks turned to the dark, some went mad from it. And some, like your birth father, learned to lead. Like your mother, learned to embrace and build and protect. Some, like those in your vision, learned—magickal and not—how to come together, how to fight, how to work together to help others. A foundation again, for you, The One, to build on."

She could only sigh. "I can't even get my stupid brothers to do what I tell them half the time. More than half. How am I supposed to lead everybody?"

"How did you build the hive? With knowledge and skill learned. How did you call the bees? With faith and light and power innate."

Fallon pushed the tea away. Maybe she felt calmer, but she didn't feel any smarter, or any more certain.

"I shouldn't have made the mistake with the incantation or the belladonna just because I was upset. I'll be more careful."

"Yes. I should have stocked the supplies in wiser order rather than by old habits. I'll be more careful."

"Mom always put the deadlies on the highest shelf, and away from . . ." It all welled up in her again, and spilled out of her eyes before she could stop it. "I'm okay." She pressed the heels of her hands against her eyes. "I'm okay."

A child, he thought again, and often the gods asked too much.

"Look into the fire. A minute only. Look," he repeated when she dropped her hands. "And see."

When she turned, looked, he opened the window for her. Just a little, only for a moment.

And in the flames she saw the farm, leaves falling fast in a quick wind. Her brothers, all three, stacked firewood while her father repaired a section of fence in the near pasture. Her mother worked in the garden.

As Fallon looked, as she saw, as she soaked it in, her mother straightened. She laid a hand to her heart, smiled even as tears shimmered. And tapping a finger to her lips blew a kiss before the image faded.

"Did she see me? Did she?"

"Felt you. I could do only that."

"She felt me. Thank you."

"Take your horse. Take the air."

"I will, but I'll finish the potion first, and we'll organize the supplies. I'm all right now."

———

For a week Fallon did her best to study, work, and improve her physical training. She could now juggle five balls of light, but had yet to
learn how a sword felt in her hand. She'd yet to master balancing on
her hand on the pool—something she did within a curtain she conjured in case Mick tried to spy again. But she only practiced that for
twenty minutes a day.

The rest of her free time she spent in search of the wolf with the
golden collar. She combed the woods but not only couldn't find the
wolf, she found not a single track, no scat, no sign.

She did spot Mick a few times, and deliberately changed directions just to make a point. But as the leaves fell, swirled, left branches
empty, she decided to let him catch up with her.

When he popped out of a tree in front of her, she stopped Grace.
"Don't you have anything better to do?"

"You don't own the woods." He watched the owl swoop down onto
a branch. "He goes where you go now."

"When he wants to. The apples this morning are nice. If I had
some more, and some sugar—brown sugar's best—I could make
apple butter."

"How do you make butter from apples?"

"My mother taught me. It's good. If I made some, I could leave
some out for you. You can spread it on bread or biscuits."

He walked along beside her horse, occasionally running up a
tree and flipping down again. A trick she decided she needed to
learn.

"What are you looking for?" he asked her.

"Who said I'm looking for anything?"

He gave her a smirk. "I know when somebody's trying to track.
But you haven't been hunting."

"We have enough venison. Plus, Mallick likes to fish. I might hunt for a boar, but not yet."

"So what are you looking for?"

"Well, if you must know, I'm on my second quest."

"What was the first?"

"Taibhse and the golden apple, dummy."

"Oh, yeah. Right." He slid into a tree and out again. "What's the second?"

"A wolf with a golden collar. I have to get him to give me the collar."

At that, Mick laughed until he fell down. "That's never going to happen."

"What do *you* know?"

"I know Faol Ban would eat your liver before he turned over his collar."

"Is that his name? You know about the wolf?"

"Everybody knows about Faol Ban. Boy, were you born last week? He lives in a secret den and roams the woods at night. The goddess of the moon gifted him the collar for his loyalty and bravery. He's sure never going to give it to some girl."

"Which moon goddess?"

"I don't know. One of them."

It probably mattered, Fallon thought. Now that she knew the name, more of the story, she might find more in one of Mallick's books.

"Anyway," Mick continued, "we're having a bonfire for Samhain. It's fun. You could come if you want."

"I have to do a ritual with Mallick, and honor those who've traveled behind the veil. We always did a bonfire at home—a ritual, too, but then we got to wear costumes we made and play games and carve faces in pumpkins."

"Where is that? Home?"

"A full day's ride north of here. A farm. My mother was a chef and my father was a soldier, before. I have three brothers. Do you have any sisters?"

"No, just me and Dad, but we're part of the clan. There are thirty-three of us. Thirty-four now," he corrected, "because Mirium just had a baby.

"There's the shifters," he continued, flipping over to walk on his hands for a few feet. "I guess there's, oh, about a couple dozen. There's a faerie clan, too."

He flipped back over. "There are a lot more of them if you count the little ones, the pixies and the nymphs. They left the apples, and the flowers the other day. They're really good at getting things to grow. One of them only has one good wing because he got hurt in a Purity Warrior raid, and nobody can fix it. But he gets around okay."

"Maybe Mallick could fix it."

"He couldn't. He tried. He's good at healing, too, but he couldn't fix it."

"I'm sorry. They killed my father. My sire."

"I know. Everybody knows the story of Max Fallon and the New Hope Massacre."

"They do?"

"Sure." His head tilted as if he heard something from far off. "I gotta go. The bonfire's fun. Maybe Mallick will let you come after the ritual and all."

He raced off, a blur, and was gone.

A bonfire would be fun, she mused. But even if Mallick loosened the reins enough to let her go, she didn't think she'd have time.

She'd be waiting until Mallick slept at night now so she could hunt the woods for Faol Ban.

The night the veil thinned between the living and the dead held crisp and clear. The wind, light and free, sent leaves dancing. As dusk fell, little faeries, glimmers of light, watched from a distance as Mallick fashioned an altar out of stones. At his bidding, Fallon brought out the athame, the candles, the apple, the herbs. She made more trips to fetch the pumpkins and gourds left at the door that morning, and the cauldron.

Following her mother's teaching, she decorated the base of the altar with the pumpkins and gourds, some wildflowers that had survived the first thin frost.

She went back in one last time for a small plate of bread, a bolline, and her father's book.

When she set the book on the altar, Mallick nodded approval. "This is the night of ancestors. You show respect."

"Do you have anything from yours?"

"The athame you chose was my mother's. Perhaps her hand guided you to place it on the altar tonight. Cast the circle."

Her eyes went wide. "Me? I've never cast a circle for a sabbat."

"Do so now."

Nervous, afraid she'd make a mistake and earn his wrath, she started slowly. She placed candles at the four points. Lighting another with breath, she moved clockwise around the altar. With her will, she flamed the East candle.

She had to take a couple of calming breaths, work to clear her mind of nerves and doubt.

"Guardian of the East, goddess of the Air, we call you, we beseech your powers of knowledge and wisdom, keep watch over us within this circle, cast in love and trust."

She glanced toward Mallick for approval or criticism, but he said nothing. She moved to the South point, called upon the guardian, the energy and will of Fire. Then, as her confidence built, she moved West, to water, to passion. And finally North and Earth and strength.

Despite the wind, the flames rose true when she turned to Mallick. "And so the circle is cast. Will you enter in the light and the love of the goddess?"

"I will." He stepped in. "You are priestess tonight. Call."

Fallon's throat went dry as she lit a black candle. "Dark Mother, goddess of death and rebirth, hear your servant who honors you. I ask your blessing. At this place, in this hour, I call you to use your power. Lift the veil between the worlds so those who came before hear our words."

She lit the next. "Dark Father, Lord of the Underworld, hear your servant who honors you. I ask your blessing. At this place, in this hour, I call you to use your power. Guard and protect as the veil thins, keep safe all without and within."

"And the flames rise," Mallick said, "as the goddess and her consort hear you."

She felt power, flickers of it like the candle flames—tiny burns that brought both pleasure and pain. Without Mallick's bidding, she continued, speaking words that simply came to her mind, her heart, her tongue.

"On this night, with this light, embracing dark its counterpart, we welcome spirits with full heart. All from world to world did pass, we offer our hand to grasp until with daybreak you depart."

She stepped forward, took the apple and bolline, cutting the fruit crossways, exposing the symbolic pentagram within. After taking a small bite from one half, she placed them in the cauldron, added herbs, bits of bread, wine from the chalice, and struck the flame beneath with her hand.

Taking the wand, she lifted it, thrust her power into it so it shot stars through the smoke.

"Here an offering to all who come, with love to all and hate toward none. And this light, burn bright through the night your steps to guide while you abide."

Did she feel the wind stir? Mallick wondered. Did she feel the breath of the gods on her?

"Here, Dark Mother, cauldron of death and rebirth, one of Air, one of Earth. Dark Father, blade of protection, blade of blood both strong and keen, if I am what you have foreseen, take mine."

She took the athame, scored her palm, let her blood drip into the cauldron.

To Mallick's dazzled eyes, light burst from it, showered over the altar, turned the circle into sunlight.

"Blood of your blood, blood of mine here in tribute they entwine. As slowly dies the year, living and dead have much to fear. Your light, my light, light of those spirits passed and yet to be, I call you now to join with me to fight the dark, to make our mark. If I am your child, inhabit me. As you will, so mote it be."

She set down the wand as it went quiet. Taking her braid in one hand, she sliced it off with the athame. "And here I make my pledge. And here, a symbol of the child rising to warrior."

She let out a long, long sigh. The light of the cauldron ebbed to a quiet glow. The candles that had speared up like torches slipped into gentle flickers in the dark.

With his skin still tingling, his heart still drumming, Mallick stepped toward her. When he laid a hand on her shoulder, she jolted as if she'd awakened from sleep, or a trance.

And so, he thought, she had.

She stared at him, her eyes dark and dazed.

"It was . . . all through me, all over me."

"Yes, I know."

"At first it was what I knew from Mom, or mostly. But then . . . it was just what I knew, and it got stronger and stronger. I feel a little sick."

"It was a great deal all at once." Without thinking, he picked up the chalice, offered it.

She sipped, and the child of thirteen made a face of pure disgust. "What is that?"

Amused, he shook his head. "It's just wine. A sip won't hurt you. We'll close the circle, and you can have a little food, some water, rest."

"I feel all . . ." She stopped, staring with dismay and horror at the braid still in her hand. "I cut my hair."

"Yes."

"I cut my *hair* off. Why didn't you stop me?"

"Girl, I'm not certain the power of the gods could have stopped you."

"But my hair."

"Will grow again. Can you close the circle?"

"Yeah, I can do it."

When it was done, he heated a little of the soup they'd had for supper. Though she only ate a few spoonsful, she drank water like a camel.

"You offered your blood."

She frowned down at her palm, unmarked. "Did you heal it?"

"No. I might have stopped you from the sacrifice, the symbol and power of it, if I'd known your intent. I would have been wrong. Your offering was well received."

She reached back to the ends of her shorn hair. "I guess."

"You honored the gods, honored the ancestors, and you made a pledge."

"It was like I was somebody else, but not. Like I knew what I was doing, but didn't."

"I can help you know, and will. You made a pledge. You've made your choice, for good and all?"

She poked at the soup. "I guess I made it when I unpacked. I'm afraid."

"You'd be foolish not to be. But know you did well tonight. And tomorrow you'll take up the sword."

Her eyes lit. "Really?"

"Tomorrow. For now, go to bed."

CHAPTER EIGHT

She didn't sleep. Fallon waited until she was certain Mallick had gone to his own bed, then slipped out the window. Though she didn't feel compelled to hunt for the wolf—as she'd done the night before with no success—she needed the night, the air, the woods.

However weary her body, her spirit remained awake, engaged, alight as if on a quest of its own. So she slipped through the shifting shadows, through the looming, denuded trees, through the sighs and murmurs of night. In the distance the glow from the elfin clan's bonfire shimmered against the dark. There would be feasting and games and dancing in the glow. There might be girls her age to talk to.

Yet she turned away from the shimmer, kept to the shadows. Too much beat inside her tonight for games and girl talk, and the beat struck, struck, struck as insistently as the tribal drums from the camp.

Heart music, from the trees, the earth, the drums, the spirits who slid in and out of the thinned veil, all quickened inside her. Night creatures, hunter and prey, crept and stalked through those shadows with her, and the skeletal branches overhead creaked like an old man's bones.

She had no fear, only a deep, thirsty need to be out, to look for something she couldn't yet see.

She lifted her hand, ran it over the hair that stopped at the nape of her neck. Shorter than her brothers', she thought, still shocked by it.

Maybe the same knowing that had driven her to shear it off drove her now, to seek the night. She wandered toward the faerie glade but found she didn't want that, either. Restless, as if something tickled up and down her spine, she wandered without aim or purpose.

And perhaps because she didn't hunt the wolf, she found him.

He stood, pure white, between two trees. Eyes of bold, sharp blue watched her. Around his neck the thick collar of gold glinted.

She couldn't claim he looked friendly, but Fallon reasoned Mallick wouldn't have sent her on a quest to find a wolf who'd eat her.

And something, something about the night, the way the air tasted on her tongue, the steady pulse beat of the power that had flooded her during the ritual, made her fearless.

"Greetings, *Faol Ban*. Ah, blessed be. I'm Fallon Swift, child of the Tuatha de Danann, student of Mallick the Sorcerer. I've been looking for you."

She took a cautious step forward. The wolf bared his teeth.

"Okay. I'll just stay over here." She slid her hands into her pockets, and found the bit of pumpkin bread she'd forgotten she slipped there that afternoon.

She took it out, held it up to show the wolf. "It's pretty good. I made it this morning. It's not as good as my mom's, but I never made it by myself before. You want it?"

She saw the wolf's eyes shift to the bread in her hand, then cut right back to hers.

Considering they'd trained Jem and Scout with hard biscuits her mom made for that purpose, she tossed the bread.

Maybe she could make the dog biscuits and bring some next time.

Faol Ban studied the bread, sniffed at it. He gave Fallon another cool stare, then snatched up the bread.

"It's okay, right? I think I should've used a little more honey, but it's okay. Anyway, Mallick's cooking really sucks, so I'm trying."

She sensed rather than heard movement behind her. Drawing her knife, she whirled to defend the wolf. She saw the shadow of a man.

With the knife in one hand, power rising in the other, she prepared to protect. "If you try to hurt him, I'll hurt you first."

"I'd never hurt the wolf god, or you."

The shadow stepped out of the shadows, and her hand trembled on the hilt of her knife. Inside her chest, her heart stumbled.

"I know you," she whispered.

"And I know you. You have my eyes, and your mother's mouth. Look how tall you are, how strong and brave and beautiful."

Her father, her sire, walked toward her. He seemed taller than she'd imagined him, and leaner than the picture on the book. His hair, dark as hers, waved around a face she'd studied so many times.

"I'm not dreaming. I didn't go to sleep."

"You're not dreaming," Max told her. "You called for me."

"I—"

"In your heart. The veil's thin tonight. Thinner still with your power. And you brought me through."

Cautious, curious, she reached out and discovered the arm under her hand was solid. "You're real."

"Corporeal for a brief time. Will you let me . . ." He touched a hand to her cheek. His smile bloomed, moved his lips, his face, moved into his eyes. "There you are."

"You died for me."

"Protecting you was my right, my purpose, my joy. Walk with me while we have this time. You've been happy, and well?"

"I . . . She loved you. My mother."

"My sweet girl, I know. And I loved her. We had such a short time together to love, to learn. So much of it, too much of it, riddled with fear and violence. But we had more than that, we had pleasure and laughter, too. And wonder and joy. I fell in love with a pretty witch who'd rather shop for new shoes than practice the Craft, and I watched her grow into a strong, fearless, powerful woman. You were part of that, the change that made us better than we had been.

"But I want to hear about your life. Some I can see, some I can't. Tell me your happiest memory."

Tears burned at her throat, guilt twisted her heart. "Learning to ride, I guess. Being allowed to ride by myself the first time."

"What's this?" Because he heard the tears, Max turned her face to his. "No, no. Do you think I'd begrudge you a father who'd teach you to ride? Or Lana a man who'd build a life with her?"

"I don't know." Had never known.

"How could I love you and begrudge you all he is to you, and you to him? I'm grateful to him."

"You—you are?"

"I am, and he sure as hell should be grateful to me. I made you with your mother, and with your mother he brought you into the world. Love isn't finite, Fallon. If you take nothing else from me, take that."

As he spoke, he stroked a hand over her hair. "Love has no end, no borders, no limits. The more you give, the more there is. Your mother gave you my name, Simon Swift gave you his. He's your father, and so am I. I'd say that makes you blessed."

"That's what Mom says."

"There you have it," he said simply. "Is it any wonder I loved her?"

"Dad—Simon—he is grateful. He says you're a hero, and he owes you for everything that matters most to him. Mom and me, and I have three brothers. I wish you could meet him. That's weird."

He laughed, put an arm around her shoulders as they walked. "The world's full of the strange."

"You wrote about strange things. I read your books. Mom said you were writing another when you died, and she had to run to protect me and the people of New Hope. What was it about?"

"About love and magicks, the dark and the light of both. About battle and bravery, and the rise of a Savior."

"I don't know how to lead people."

"Neither did I. I'd rather have built a simple life with your mother. Simple seemed precious after the Doom. But I was needed, and so are you. I might wish a simple life for you, Fallon, but the world needs more. You'll lead, and well. I believe it absolutely."

"The man in my dream said I had to choose. I did."

"What man?"

"I'm not sure. I think, maybe, it was the boy grown up. Maybe."

"And what boy is that?"

"Duncan, I think. From New Hope. I saw him in a different dream."

"Katie's Duncan? Hmm." Dead or not, Max felt a little twinge at the idea of his daughter dreaming about a boy.

"He saved people from the Purity Warriors. They're the ones who killed you."

"My brother killed me. The dark he chose killed me. His blood, my blood, yours." Pausing, he gripped her hand, firmly, looked directly into her eyes.

She felt the link and the power in their joined hands.

"The same blood," he continued, "yet Eric turned away from light and love and loyalty. He's never to be trusted, Fallon, or underestimated."

"Mom thinks he's dead. She thinks she killed him and that woman."

"Allegra. I don't know the answer. Even the dead have questions. But if he lives, what's in him will do all evil can do to end you. He tainted his blood and all that comes from it. Watch for him. Watch for the crows."

"I will." And if he's still alive, she vowed at that moment, she would end him. "Mallick's going to teach me to use a sword."

"Good God."

"You can't only fight with magicks. *The Wizard King* had a sword."

Max laughed a little. "So he did. Tell me more about your life, your brothers."

It was amazing. It was magickal to walk and talk with the man she only knew from stories, from a picture on a book. Now she knew the sound of his voice, the way he moved, the things he thought.

Now she knew why the night had called her, had struck that beat inside her. She'd reached for him through the veil; he'd come through for her.

She took him to the faerie glade, where they sat and talked while Taibhse swept in to sit on a branch like a guard, and the wolf who'd tracked them as they walked stayed in the shadows.

When she asked him to tell her of the escape from the great city and all that came after, he didn't censor his words as she'd always suspected her mother did.

He spoke frankly of the horrors and hardships, of the wonder and weight of feeling his power expand. And when he spoke of his brother, of trying to take Eric's life, trying to take a life of his own family, she heard both the lingering grief and the cold determination.

"You had to choose." As she spoke, Fallon leaned against him. "My mother, me, the others you protected."

"Yes, I had to choose, and there was no question of what was right. But using the gift to cause harm is a hard choice, Fallon. Causing harm to family, to someone who shares your blood, harder still."

She understood. Wanted to. Tried to. But . . .

"I'm here because you made that choice in the mountains, and again in New Hope. You died because your brother made his choice."

"As a leader you'll face hard choices."

"Did you wish you didn't have to be one?"

"All the time." He turned his head, brushed his lips over her temple. "In the end, we are who we are."

"You believe that?"

"I do, yeah."

"Then you should stop feeling even a little bit guilty for trying to kill Eric. In the end, he was what he was."

Max let out a half laugh. "You got me on that. You're right."

"Tell me more about New Hope. Mom's told us a lot, and sometimes when we use the ham radio Dad got, we hear the reporter."

"Arlys? Arlys Reid?"

"Yeah, she gives reports on Raiders and the Purity Warriors and rescues and things like that. And other stuff. She changes frequencies a lot, for safety. Dad said he could probably fix it so Mom could talk to her over the radio, but Mom wouldn't."

"She worries."

"Yeah, that they'd figure out about the farm, or use her somehow to attack New Hope again. But I know she was really good friends with some of the people there."

"We had good friends," he agreed. "We traveled there with Poe and Kim and Eddie and Joe, from the mountains, and Flynn and his group from the little village below."

"The boy with the wolf." She glanced back, saw the white wolf in the shadows still.

"Lupa. And along the way, there were others."

He painted a picture for her, more detailed than her mother had. And she began to see her mother, too, through his eyes. Young, brave, beautiful, learning to drive, nervous about becoming a mother, standing up to a bully at the town meeting.

She dozed off with her head on his shoulder, his voice in her head.

And his voice woke her.

"Fallon. Wake up, baby, it's nearly dawn."

"What? But . . . I fell asleep. I didn't mean to."

"You gave me the chance to hold my daughter while she slept. One more gift. Come on now. I'll walk you back as far as I can."

"I don't want you to go."

"You know, it's true when people who love you say they'll always be with you."

"It's not the same," she told him as she dragged her feet.

"I know, but that doesn't make it less true. What will you do today?"

"Feed the chickens, gather the eggs. Mallick usually milks the cow. After breakfast we have lessons in the workroom. Sometimes it's boring, sometimes it's not. We have to tend the greenhouse plants, too. And today he said I can start learning how to use a sword."

"And you look forward to that."

"I learn with a sword chosen for the girl I am. But on a night, like my birth, wild with storm, burned in lightning, on a night after I hold the Book of Spells, after I travel in the Well of Light, I take up the sword and shield of The One. Of the daughter of the Tuatha de Danann, the Warrior of Light. With these I challenge the dark and give no quarter. In these my power and my blood run in ice and flame."

Her eyes that had gone dark and fierce blinked. And the child came back.

"You looked like your mother just then when a vision came on her."

"I felt different. I felt strong."

"You are strong." He kissed her forehead. "I have to go."

"Dad." She threw her arms around him, held tight. "Will I ever see you again?"

"I know you will." He kissed her again, drew her back. "We are who we are, Fallon. I see who you are, and I'm so proud. I love you," he said, stepping back into the shadows as the first hint of the sun shimmered over the eastern hills.

"I love you, Dad."

Furious, and more than a little frightened, Mallick stormed out of the cottage. The girl hadn't slept in her bed, and was nowhere to be seen. When he found her, by the gods, she'd know the punishment for a night's foolishness.

As he turned toward the stables intending to saddle his horse, he saw the white owl fly out of the woods. Then the girl walked out. And the wolf, the damnable wolf she'd surely spent the night tracking, stopped at the edge before slinking back and away.

The hand on the hilt of his sword, one belted on in haste, went lax with relief. And his temper rose in one hot flood.

"Are you mad or simply stupid? To wander off through the night, without leave. I was about to do a searching spell with hope I wouldn't find your mangled body. There are predators, girl, on four legs and two, that would find you a tasty meal. You would climb out your window and wander alone through the night?"

"I wasn't alone. I was with my father."

"You risk yourself for . . ." His hearing caught up with temper, as did his vision. Her eyes were heavy, yes, but also dazed and damp. "Your father? Your sire?"

"He said I called him, with my heart, and he came. He came through the thinning veil. We walked in the woods, and talked and talked. I took him to faerie-land, and we talked. I fell asleep for a little while. I wish I hadn't. Then he had to go."

"You've been given a gift."

"I know. I'm not really sad." But tears spilled. "He's like Dad. Simon. I mean, strong and brave and kind. He said he was glad we had Simon, my mom and me, and my brothers, just like Dad said he was glad Mom and me had Max."

"You're a fortunate girl."

"Are you still really mad?"

While the sorcerer felt considerable awe she'd had the power and will to bring her sire into the living world, the teacher had to be firm.

"You broke my trust, or the trust I believed we had between us."

"I'm sorry. The wolf hunts at night, and I wanted to track him. I should've asked if I could, but I was afraid you'd say no."

"You've slipped out before?"

"Yes. But this time I found Faol Ban. I still need to get him to come to me, but I found him last night before my father came. If I'm to be a warrior, I should be able to go into the woods at night."

"You're not a warrior yet, and it's within my power to bar you from the woods altogether."

"Oh, but—"

"Did your parents permit you to wander at night, alone?"

Her head drooped. "No. But I'm thirteen now, so—"

Head inclined, Mallick folded his arms. "A great age when you wish it to be, a small one when you don't."

With her eyes cast down, he didn't see calculation come into them. "You gave me the quest. I should've told you I needed to track at night, and I'm sorry I didn't. But I can't fulfill the quest if I can't track the wolf."

"You're a clever girl," he muttered.

She kept her head down, but shifted her eyes up. "It's all true. I am sorry, and you gave me the quest. He took the bread I had in my pocket—not from my hand yet. I know how to make the biscuits our dogs like. I can get him to come to me, let me borrow the collar if I have time."

Now Mallick calculated. "Mick will go with you."

"Mick? Why—"

He cut her off with a steely stare. "Mick knows the woods—and better than you. He's a dead shot with a bow."

"I don't need a boy to—"

"His sex is of no consequence. His skill is. And I would be more inclined to let you track at night—two hours only—if you take a companion. Those are my terms."

"Fine."

"Your word, here and now, you'll abide by them."

"I'll abide by them. You have my word."

"Very well. You may sleep for an hour before lessons."

"I'm not tired, honest. I feel . . . really good."

"In that case, take your energy, deal with the chickens and the cow before you make breakfast and bring in more firewood. Later you'll harvest from the greenhouse what you need to make soup."

"Why am I doing all the chores?"

"A small punishment for the scope of the crime. We'll see if you can earn Faol Ban's trust, and regain mine."

"Are you still going to teach me to use a sword? I had a vision about the sword—the one on the mantel, and the sword and shield I use to fight."

"Damnable girl! You wait so long to tell me."

"You were mad." And still was, she realized.

"Tell me now."

"Okay." She closed her eyes to bring back the words if not the feeling that had coursed through her, and told him.

"I almost felt them in my hands. It's hard to explain, but I almost felt them. The sword in my right, the shield in my left. I can't take up that sword until I take up the one on the mantel and learn how to use it."

"Yes, a clever girl—and yes, no less true for the slyness. Do your chores, and do them well. If I'm satisfied, you'll take up the sword chosen to teach you."

When she gave a quick cheer and raced off, Mallick looked toward the heavens. He prayed to all the gods he had the strength to deal with the child and prepare the warrior.

Despite Mallick's charm on the blades to prevent them from breaking flesh and drawing blood, Fallon ended her first lesson bruised, aching, and exhilarated.

At dusk she walked out, hard biscuits in her pocket, to meet Mick, who waited at the edge of the woods.

She took her bow and quiver as well. They'd see who was such a dead shot.

"Hey. So did you really find Faol Ban or did you just make it up because Mallick was pissed at you?"

"I don't make things up. I found him, and I'll find him again."

"Maybe. You have to be crazy to go into the woods on Samhain night. You could have spirits walking around, and not all of them friendly. Plus, the faeries like to play tricks."

"I can take care of myself. You're only here because Mallick made me. Besides, I met my father last night."

"The dead one? Are you making that . . ." He shrugged, ran up a tree and down again. The hawk feather he'd added to his braid fluttered. "You don't make stuff up, so that's cool. I've never talked to a real spirit. What was it like?"

"It was my father, my sire. It was a gift."

"My mom died right after I was born. I guess I'd like to talk to her."

Because she knew the pain and the wondering, she softened a little. "Maybe you will one day."

"Maybe. Hey, you cut your hair. Why'd you do that?"

"I wanted to." Or some part of her must have. "It'll be easier to deal with short. If you keep talking, we're never going to get anywhere near the wolf."

Mick snorted. "He can hear us breathe. You won't find him unless he wants you to. And why would he, since you want to steal his collar?"

"I'm not going to steal it. I'm going to borrow it—with permission." She felt the shadow of the owl pass over her, and smirked. "I'm not the one who shoots arrows at owl gods to steal their apple."

Mick shrugged it off, leaped up ten feet to a branch, dived off, flipped, and landed lightly on his feet.

If she had to be stuck with him, Fallon thought, maybe he could teach her to do tricks like that. After she found the wolf.

When the wolf stepped onto the path in front of them, Mick fell into a rare and reverent silence.

Fallon took one of the hard, round biscuits she'd made, crouched down and held it out.

"Wow. He's really big."

"Quiet," Fallon hissed.

"I never thought I'd actually get to see him."

"Be quiet! Be still."

"Like he's going to take that cookie out of your hand. He's a freaking god."

"He's just a boy," Fallon told Faol Ban. "And he talks too much. I made this for you. A tribute. Can you read me, Faol Ban, as I read you? Can you see my heart, my head? What I am respects and honors what you are."

She tossed the biscuit. The wolf sniffed it, picked it up in his jaws, and melted away.

"Told you."

"He took the tribute," Fallon pointed out. "I don't expect him to eat from my hand yet. It takes time."

"Could you read him?"

"A little. Dogs and horses and cats are easier. He's powerful, and he's not ready to let me in. It'll take time," she repeated.

"You want to track him?"

"No," she decided. "I think it's better if I let him find me when he wants to."

"We've got nearly the whole two hours left."

"That's all right. You can start teaching me how to flip in the air and run up a tree."

"You're not an elf."

"That doesn't mean I can't do it."

For two weeks the nightly routine remained essentially the same. Mick would wait for her to join him, then talk too much. Faol Ban would step onto the path, take a biscuit, and slip away.

But to Fallon's mind, he stayed a little longer each time. And he began to watch her practice her flips and tumbles from the shadows where she felt him linger.

In deep November, after a hard frost that made the ground ring and the waters of the pool mist, she met Mick on a night of a white moon and cold stars.

"You're going to be a million years old before he lets you get within a foot of him. Probably older than a million. Why don't you . . ." Mick flicked his fingers. "You're supposed to be a witch, you're supposed to have powers."

"I am a witch, and I do have powers. It's just going to take time."

"You always say that. We could trick him."

"Didn't you learn anything from Taibhse? He won't be tricked, and it's disrespectful to try. Taibhse offered me the apple because I *didn't* trick him, and I bled rather than see him hurt."

"I can shoot an arrow at him, and you can get in the way again."

Fallon only let out a sigh. "Ignore him," she said to Faol Ban when he stepped onto the path. "He's an idiot."

"You're the one bringing cookies to a wolf god every night, and I'm the idiot?"

Insulted, determined to prove himself, Mick lunged forward. Fallon sent him tumbling back with a wave of her hand.

"He doesn't mean any harm." This time instead of crouching, she knelt. "I am Fallon Swift, daughter of the Tuatha de Danann. I am of the light and the sword. I am of the woods and the glade, the valley and the hill, the great city and the humble cottage. I am all who came before me, all who come after. As I am bound to Taibhse, the owl god . . ." She lifted her arm, elbow cocked. Taibhse glided down to her. "So will I bind myself to you."

She took out a biscuit. "It's a small thing, a small tribute, but made with my hands to please you. Will you honor me and take it?"

He stared into her eyes, and she felt him slip into her. A test, she thought, of her courage and her spirit.

Then he stepped forward, came toward her until they were face-to-face. And he took the offering from her hand. Watching his eyes, she laid her hand on his head, stroked his silky fur.

"I can't take the collar. I won't. It's yours. Will you come, show yourself to Mallick so he knows I've completed the second quest?"

As she rose, Mick poked at her back. "Can I touch him?"

"I wouldn't," Fallon said shortly. "Not after you talked about shooting an arrow at him."

"Not *at* him. I'd never . . . He took food from your hand. He let you touch him."

She glanced back, saw awe and a little fear on Mick's face. "I'm the same person I was before. I have to skip the practice tonight. I need to tell Mallick."

"Do you think Faol Ban will go with you?"

"It's his choice, but I need to tell Mallick either way."

Now with little to say, Mick walked with her to the edge of the woods.

"You could meet me in the afternoon tomorrow for more practice." She sent him a glittering look. "Unless you're afraid of me now."

"I'm not afraid of you. Next time you swipe at me, I'll swipe back."

She shrugged that off, stepped into the clearing.

As if he knew, Mallick came out of the cottage and watched her walk with the owl on her arm, the wolf at her side under the light of the white moon.

CHAPTER NINE

Fallon's initiation to swordplay left her considerably bruised and battered, and a lot determined. Her third and final quest left her baffled.

She argued about it as she worked to block and parry Mallick's strikes and thrusts.

"But I have a horse. I have a great horse. Why do I need to find another one?"

She ended up on her butt again, and that abused area burned, yet again, at the rude contact with hard, frosty ground.

"Balance, girl. The sword is about more than strength and strike. Balance."

"Yeah, yeah, yeah." She got up, butt and sword arm aching, tried again. "And a golden saddle? That's stupid. It would be too heavy, too hard."

"If you think so, there's no need for you to look."

"I want a bathroom, so—" And once again, on her ass, this time with Mallick laying the charmed tip of his sword on her belly.

"Gutted."

"Your sword's longer than mine. So are your arms."

"And do you expect to fight only those who are of your size?" Stepping back, he gestured her up.

"I'm just pointing it out."

She managed to block, stay on her feet. "Anyway, I'm going to look for the horse and the saddle, but I don't need a horse and a saddle." She blocked, and well, a second time. "What do I do with them if the horse comes with me like Taibhse and Faol Ban?"

"It might be a question to ask when and if you find them."

"Oh, I'll find them."

Newly confident with a third successful block, she tried a thrust under Mallick's guard.

He blocked, pivoted, and slapped the flat side of his sword hard enough on her aching butt to send her sprawling on her face.

"Damn it!"

"There will be times when you fight amid countless distractions, and still, without focusing on your opponent, you'll fail. Put the quest out of your mind, put everything out of your mind but the sword, my sword, my body, your body. My eyes. And learn."

She did her best to concentrate, and still ended up on her ass, on her knees, or with her face in the dirt. Often with a limb cut off, her throat slit, or some other part of her impaled.

At the end of the lesson, her sword arm wept, and her ass burned like the fires of hell.

As fall blew toward winter, she practiced, and though Mallick tended to be stingy with compliments, she knew she improved. To build her upper body strength, she started each morning with push-ups, like her father had shown her, and ended each session with some of the yoga her mother enjoyed to try to increase her flexibility and balance.

For more challenge, she scaled trees—she was getting better at it—and practiced yoga poses on a branch to increase balance and focus. Plus, that was just fun, and she imagined making her brothers laugh when she held a tree pose.

She'd be a tree in a tree.

She lifted buckets of water in curls and shoulder presses until her muscles trembled and burned.

When she was absolutely, positively sure no one could see her, she danced in hopes of improving her footwork.

She studied, the gods, the histories, the traditions, the magicks, practiced with Mick, and searched the woods for a white horse known as Laoch and his golden saddle.

With Mallick, she performed the ritual for Yule, lit the fires, the candles to represent the return of light after the darkest night of the winter solstice. She made and hung the wreath, the symbol of the Wheel of the Year.

Though she wished for a vision, for a night with her mother as she had had with Max, she felt only ripples of power, heard only the voices of the gods.

When the ritual was done, they left some of the cake for the birds, poured some of the wine on the ground for the goddess.

Her first Christmas away from home made her heart ache as keenly as it had when she'd ridden away from the farm. Even the Yule tree Mallick had allowed her to choose and light and decorate didn't cheer her.

But the Wheel of the Year continued to turn, and turned into the next.

January brought snow, and chunks of ice in the stream that glinted in sunlight. It brought cold hunts for game, and for the elusive white horse Mick claimed was a great stallion fully twenty hands high, who would take no rider on his back.

It brought nights that lasted too long, and had too much room for dreams of circling crows, of gathering storms. Of a stone circle rising out of the fog, and things that slithered in the dark.

As winter took Fallon's world in its frigid grip, the community of New Hope shoveled snow. They hunted game, harvested from their greenhouses. The community kitchen Lana had established years before produced vats of soups, pounds of bread, baked pies, made butter and cheeses.

Children went to school to learn academics and practical skills. The Max Fallon Magick Academy helped children with abilities learn control, respect, and inclusivity.

With the community now numbering more than five hundred, security—within and without—remained essential. They had a duly elected mayor and town council as well as a small police force and fire department.

More than fourteen years since the first group of survivors stopped there, New Hope lived in the founders' vision of community.

None who'd lived through the Doom, who'd survived the journey, who'd survived the Fourth of July massacre forgot how vital protecting the community was, and how tenuous the line was between the light and the dark.

Katie Parsoni had survived all of it, and knew more than most how tenuous the line was. She'd not only lost her parents, but knew her father, through no fault of his own, had unleased the virus that would kill him, her mother, her husband, her entire family save for the twins still in her womb, and spread to take the lives of billions.

A plague that had toppled cities, governments, had unleashed magicks that inhabited both sides of that tenuous line.

She'd survived, and with the kindness, compassion, and heroics of two people had brought two children into the troubled world, and taken another orphaned infant as her own.

She'd wondered why her precious twins held magicks when she didn't, their father hadn't. But over time she'd seen children with no magickal parent bloom in gifts, and others born of magicks show no abilities.

It came through the blood and the bone, of that she was certain, but not always from the parent. She believed Duncan's and Antonia's great gifts came, like Tonia's eyes, from her father, their grandfather. A good man who hadn't known what ran in his blood, or that the dark across the line would somehow use him to destroy.

She worried as the powers her twins held made them targets outside the borders of New Hope. Targets of the murderous Purity Warriors—targets, rumors abounded, of secret forces inside the beleaguered and fractured government that wanted to enlist and train, or harvest those with powers.

And with their gifts, their skills, their fearlessness, even their mother couldn't keep them inside those borders.

In the old world, her three children would have given her grief about so many other things. Schoolwork, teenage sulks and rebellions. Not that she didn't deal with some of that, but in the old world, she wouldn't have to deal with her babies going out on scouting parties, hunting parties, rescue raids.

Her fourteen-year-old son sure as holy hell wouldn't be driving a motorcycle—and she still kicked herself for allowing that one. In the old world, her twins would never have taken combat training, much less be advanced enough to train others.

Her sweet Hannah should be mooning about boys or playing

music too loud instead of stitching up wounds and setting broken bones at the community clinic.

The dark had robbed them, all three, of childhood. It had robbed them all.

Still, there were bright spots, she reminded herself as she dressed for the day. Friendships as solid, as strong and precious as diamonds. Being part of building something good and united.

And love—unexpected, sweet, and fleeting—had come to her through a man, a good man, who had taught history, had embraced her children and lightened her load.

When Austin died on a scavenging mission, she'd grieved again. But time softened grief, and she had the bright spots of memories.

Most of all, she held on to the joys of watching her children grow into the bright and bold and ferociously true.

She needed to believe what she'd helped build here, for them, would hold, would sustain them all. So she had work to do.

She went down the stairs of the house where she'd raised her kids, noted the fire already simmered in the living room.

And found Duncan in the kitchen, not only dressed, but putting on his outdoor gear.

"Hey." He gave her his megawatt smile, but a mother's eyes caught the little twinge of guilt in his. "Morning. I was just going to leave you a note."

"Were you?"

"Yeah. Scouting party's heading out this morning. I said I'd go with Flynn and Eddie."

"It's a school day."

He rolled eyes as green as her own. "Mom." And, God help her, she heard her own voice to her own mother at fourteen. "I'm caught up, you know that. I'm helping teach half the classes at this stage, and they don't need me today. Anyway, Tonia's going with Will and Micha and Suzanne on a hunting party."

"I was going to *ask* first." Tonia walked in, sparing her brother one hot glance.

"Yeah, right."

"I was."

Katie shoved at her curly brown hair, then lifted both hands in warning. "Nobody's going anywhere until they've had breakfast. Is Hannah up?"

"Yeah." Tonia, tall and slim, her dark hair already in what Katie thought of as her hunter's braid, opened the fridge for the jar of mixed vegetable juice her mother made in an ancient blender. "She'll be right down."

"Hannah's doing a half day," Duncan said, always willing to toss either of his sisters under the mom bus. "Then going to the clinic."

"Which is called community service," Katie reminded him, "and part of education."

"So's scouting and hunting." He smiled again when she sighed. "Just saying. If we're eating breakfast first, can it be French toast?"

He edged over to Katie, wrapped an arm around her. "You make the best."

A charmer, she thought, when he wanted to be. And she still had trouble accepting she had to look up at him. Tonia, too, she thought, though not quite as far up. Only with Hannah did she see eye to eye—often philosophically as well as literally.

"Take your coat off."

"Yes, ma'am, Ms. Mayor."

Katie shook her head. The job of mayor was something else she'd been talked into. Still, she thought she was pretty good at it. She got out eggs, a jug of milk, and her precious store of sugar and cinnamon.

No syrup—those were the days—but the kids just heaped on applesauce and ate like horses.

"French toast? Yum!" Hannah strolled in, glossy, bouncy golden-brown hair, doe-brown eyes, and a curvy figure Katie knew already had teenage boys giving her baby girl long—too long—looks.

Not that Hannah showed much interest—yet. Her interest centered around the clinic and learning all she could learn from Rachel, the town doctor, and Jonah, the paramedic, Rachel's husband, and the hero who'd delivered the twins in the horrible days of the Doom.

As she cooked, Katie listened to the sibling noises behind her. Poking at each other, and she had no problem with that. Let them poke, work off steam. When the chips fell, they'd stand up for each other. Always had, she thought, and always would.

Before Katie could stop him, Duncan snatched the first slice off the plate, rolled it up, and ate it where he stood.

"Sit down like a human being. Hannah, you're working at the clinic later?"

"If that's okay. Rachel said they could use me. Ray's doing visiting rounds, and Carly could have the baby any day, so she's on desk work. Vickie and Wayne have the dental clinic open today, so the medical clinic's going to be shorthanded."

"Storm's coming in," Tonia said easily. "By tonight. We're going to get dumped on."

As he dropped slices on his plate and added applesauce, Duncan nodded. "Could get a foot, and wind's coming with it."

They'd know, Katie thought. Part of their gifts.

"It'll take time to dig out from this one," Tonia continued. "So hunting and scouting parties are as important today as the clinics."

Katie caught the wink Duncan sent his sister as he shoveled in food. And she gave up.

"You don't drive." She jabbed a finger at Duncan.

"Mom. Come on. I—"

"Deal breaker. Eddie or Flynn does the driving. We've been dumped on already, and the roads outside of New Hope are bound to be treacherous. You don't have any experience driving in those conditions."

"How do I get it?"

"You don't get it today. Did Eddie or Flynn put in for the gas ration?"

"Sure they did. We'll maybe bring some back. Still plenty of cars out there. We'll siphon what we can."

"You should take some food in case—"

"Eddie's getting supplies from the community kitchen. We shouldn't need it, but we'll have it. This was great, thanks, Mom. But I gotta go."

He rose, grabbed his coat.

"You need gloves, and—"

"Got it all, in the pockets." Leaning over, he hugged her. Then added an additional squeeze. "Don't worry so much."

"It's my job. My first job. My best job."

She knew he'd take the sword and the bow from the utility room, and comforted herself that he knew how to use those weapons, and all the ones inside him.

"That's one way to get out of the dishes. I've got to get out of them, too," Tonia added. "Or I'll be late."

"Go ahead. Stay with the others, Tonia."

"I will." She kissed Katie's cheek. "We'll both be back before dinner. Have a good one, Hannah."

"You, too. I got the dishes, Mom. I've got nearly an hour before school. And they'll be back before dinner. It's spaghetti night, right?"

It made Katie laugh. "Yeah, it is. You're right. They won't miss that. I love you, Hannah."

"Love you right back."

They had to grow up too fast, Katie thought as she pulled on her boots—a treasured pair of UGGs Duncan had scavenged three years before. Eleven years old, and he'd already been scavenging abandoned houses, cars, pillaged malls.

Much too fast.

She put on the parka she'd bartered for fiercely, and had worn every winter for more than a decade, then the hat and scarf Hannah—the only one in the family who could knit worth a damn—had made her for Christmas.

She picked up her briefcase—old and battered and passed to her by New Hope's first mayor—and left the home she'd come to love for a job she hoped she proved worthy of.

In another life she'd been the youngest child and only daughter of a solid family, born and raised in Brooklyn, happily married to her college sweetheart. She'd worked in her family's marketing firm, and when she and her Tony learned she carried twins, she'd planned to become a stay-at-home mom and devote herself to motherhood.

Maybe—maybe—she'd help out at MacLeod and MacLeod now and then, but she'd imagined herself taking her babies to the park, hosting playdates, documenting their firsts in pretty baby books, photo albums, videos.

She, along with her mother and mother-in-law, had outfitted and decorated the nursery. And she'd considered herself the luckiest woman in the world.

Then that world crashed down. She'd lost her father and her mother within hours of each other, her brother, her husband, and all of his family, too. In the weeks that followed, alone, grieving, terrified, she'd fought to survive for the lives inside her.

She'd come to believe she'd survived because of the lives inside her.

Now she walked along the sidewalk of a community built by survivors and based on hope. Smoke curled from chimneys into a sky of hard, clear winter blue. She saw no sign of a coming storm, but didn't doubt the twins' forecast.

If Tonia handed her an umbrella on a sunny day, Katie took it.

She walked toward the town center, past the house where her former roommate, the town doctor and Hannah's mentor, lived with her husband—Katie's hero—and their kids.

And there was the house where Arlys and Will lived with their family.

Lana and Max had lived there once, she remembered, with Poe and Kim and Eddie in the attached apartments.

Now Poe and Kim had a house a block off Main, two kids of their own. And the odd, sweet couple of Eddie and Fred had their little farm on the very edge of New Hope's boundaries.

And Fred, the cheerful, indefatigable faerie, was expecting her fourth child.

Did Fred worry when Eddie went off as he did today, to scout? Raiders still cruised, Purity Warriors hunted, hard-line factions still cast nets. So much to worry about outside New Hope. And not little to cause concern within.

It looked calm, peaceful, like a small town might in any history book. She saw the OPEN sign on Bygones, the supply shop Bill Anderson ran; the CLOSED sign was still posted on Cut, Color, and Curl, the tiny barber and beauty shop created and operated by a beautician, a barber, and a witch.

The sandwich shop, converted to the community's police station. The chief of police, Bill Anderson's son, Will, would be leading the morning's hunting party. Deputies included a former cop, a shapeshifter, and an elf.

Part-time work for the elf, as Aaron also worked as an instructor at the academy.

A balance, she thought. That was part of the plan, an essential element of the blueprint drafted years before in the living room of her home. A mix of the magickal and non in all aspects, creating a sense of unity.

Most often it worked.

In fourteen years only five people had ever been sentenced to the community's ultimate punishment. Banishment.

She'd served on the panel for two of the five, and prayed with all she had she'd never be called to do so again.

She paused to watch the dash of a fox, a slinky streak of red through the snow. Then she crossed the quiet street to the old building—once a house, once a real-estate company, and now town hall.

She let herself in, switched on a single light. Power conservation remained a town ordinance.

The mayor went to her office, one she'd chosen for its window over-looking Main Street, sat at her desk, opened her briefcase. And got to work.

Within the hour the town planner arrived with her agenda, and the town clerk with his.

She had reports to read on the converted laptop their head of IT and communications had built for her. Without Chuck, they'd likely need town criers. Or smoke signals.

Supply requests, submitted by various community entities. The schools, the kitchen, the gardens, the clinics.

Refuse reports, power reports—and requests to expand power to areas outside the current grid.

The school and former furniture store—kindergarten through high school—needed more updating and, as always, more supplies. Fifty-eight kids currently attended, she mused, but there would be more.

The town council would meet, discuss, debate, and, she deter-mined, find a way.

The town planner, an energetic woman of seventy, rapped knuck-les on Katie's open door. "Got a minute?"

"Sure. What do you need, Marlene?"

"It's what we all need. A good cup of coffee and chocolate."

"Marlene, why do you torture me?"

With a quick, cackling laugh, Marlene walked in on her scarred Timberland boots and sat in one of the wingback chairs Will and Jonah had hauled in for her when she'd taken the office.

"Here's the deal. Fred, Selina, Kevin, and some of the others think they can do it this time. They think they know what went wrong before."

Katie had heard this song before. "Attempting to create a tropical climate within a designated space inside a mid-Atlantic climate— what could go wrong? Oh, yeah." Katie tapped a finger to her temple as if just remembering. "Several tornadoes."

"Really small ones," Marlene said with a smile. "And minimal damage."

"We lost six trees."

"More firewood."

"One of them fell on Holden Masterson's garage and started a fire."

"A really tiny fire, which Kevin put out right away. And Holden didn't need that garage. They've worked out the kinks in the spell."

Katie stared up at the ceiling. "Kinks."

"Honey, I don't know any more about spells and all that than you do, but Fred's pretty high on the idea."

"Fred's pregnant and hormonal and wants chocolate."

"That may be. I'm not pregnant and hormones haven't been my problem for a long time. I want some damn chocolate. More than that. Lemons, oranges, bananas—and not the little guys they're growing in the greenhouse. Sugarcane. Pepper—more than we've managed from what the group brought in from down south. Medication," Marlene continued, ticking off items on her fingers. "Our herbalists and holistic groups are all for it."

Kim chaired the holistic group, and no one was more sensible to Katie's mind. But still. Tornadoes.

"And, Katie, Fred says if they can do this, they can do other climates. We could find a way to mine salt so instead of having to send people farther and farther out to scavenge for those basic needs, we'd generate our own."

The salt stung. Salt had been a top priority on the scavenge list when Austin had died.

But as mayor she had to put that aside, handle the right now.

"I'll take it up with the town council. I will, but I can tell you that Fred and her group are going to have to come in and make the case. Make a strong case."

"I'll let them know. And I should let you know they think they have a secret weapon. The twins."

"My kids?"

" 'Power boosters,' Fred said. She thinks they have enough, but she claims with Duncan and Tonia, they'll have a better shot at making it work."

"Has she said anything to them?"

"Katie, you know she wouldn't without talking to you. She's a mom, too."

"Okay, all right." Katie pressed her fingers to her eyes. "I need to process, and I need to talk to the council. Then we'll talk to Fred and her group of climate wizards. God."

"You wanted the job, Mayor."

"Did I?" Katie gave the ceiling another wistful look. "I can't imagine why."

"How about I have LeRoy zap you up some of his energy tea? It ain't a good cup of joe, but— Hey there, Arlys."

"Hi, Marlene. Would LeRoy have enough for two cups of that tea?"

"Don't see why not." She pushed to her feet. "Have a chair."

"I will, thanks. Got time for me?" Arlys asked Katie.

"Which hat are you wearing?"

Arlys smiled. "All of them."

"It's a shame because your hair looks fabulous."

"Carlotta's a genius." Arlys gave her short, sleek brown bob—with subtle highlights of bronze—a fluff. "Plus, Fred popped in while I was in there."

Now Katie sighed. "So you know about Project Tropics."

"I do, and I won't report anything on it. Yet."

"Appreciated." She paused as Marlene came back with two steaming mugs. "And ditto, Marlene."

"Happy to serve. Want the door closed?"

"Do we?" Katie asked Arlys.

"If you wouldn't mind."

"No problem." Marlene went out, shut the door.

Arlys didn't waste time. "Chuck hacked into some communications. Purity Warriors. They're planning a major raid."

"Where?"

"An Uncanny settlement in Shenandoah National Park. From what he could tell, they've created a kind of commune there. Peaceful. The PWs' intel says there are between thirty and forty of them, and they don't have any weapons."

"What? *No* weapons?"

Shifting, Arlys leaned forward. "They've taken some sort of vow, something—it's not clear from the communiqué—that forbids the use of weapons, the use of magicks."

"To harm, you mean? That's the basic tenet—the do no harm, not even against an attack, not to protect, defend."

"No use of magicks, period. I'm assuming religious sect, and I'm working to verify that. In any case, they'll be defenseless. The PWs are mobilizing, and plan to move into that area by day after tomorrow. They're going to surround the commune, and wipe it out."

"Can our people get word to them, warn them?"

"We can try, but Chuck doesn't think it'll make any difference.

They won't fight back. Among the thirty to forty are approximately twelve children, including infants."

"Okay." After blowing out a breath, Katie pressed her fingers to her temples. "Take it to Jonah. We'll need Will and Eddie as soon as they get back. We need Chuck to try to pinpoint the location of the commune from his intel, then we need one of the Uncannys who's good at astral projection. Not my kids," she said before Arlys could speak.

She shoved up from the desk, paced. "And not because I want to shield them, but because they are kids. To relay something this important, to convince those people to move or hide or fight, we need an adult."

"I agree with you. On everything. Chuck's already talking to Jonah, and he thinks he has the location pretty well nailed."

Katie stared out the window, watched one of her neighbors with a toddler, and a young dog on a leash. "Will it ever stop, I wonder? Will it ever just stop? We're going to send people to fight for people who won't fight for themselves."

"I'd have to say, that's what Will and Jonah and Maggie as the heads of our mobilization forces are going to decide."

"Duncan and Tonia will go." It already twisted in her belly. "I won't be able to stop them. I could try. I could lay down the law, but I'd just be postponing the inevitable. This is the world they live in. The world I brought them into. You brought your babies into. Yours are too young yet, but—"

"They won't be for long. Theo's eleven, Cybil's nine. And she's showing stronger abilities every day. Where does it come from? I say her father's side."

Smiling a little, Katie turned. "She looks just like him."

"Doesn't she? Well, except for the wings." Rising, Arlys walked over so she and Katie looked out at the town together. "We built something good here. We made something that matters. We can't stop now. As long as we build, as long as we fight back, we're winning. And you've got to believe, you've got to believe that one day the world . . . will only be as screwed up as it used to be."

Rather than laugh, Katie tipped her head toward Arlys. "Duncan dreams about a girl. A woman."

"What fourteen-year-old boy doesn't?"

Now she laughed. "He doesn't tell me, but he tells Tonia, and she tells Hannah, and Hannah tells me. A tall, slender woman, dark hair, gray eyes. Beautiful. Sometimes she's bathed in light. Sometimes she's fighting side by side with him in the dark, in the storm. Arlys, do you think it's Lana's daughter? Lana and Max's? This Savior some of the Uncannys talk about—The One?"

"I think about Lana all the time." Miss her, every day. "I think about that horrible day when Max died. When so many died. When she ran to protect her baby, to try to protect us. And I have to believe she got somewhere safe, somewhere safe and had her baby. Fred believes it absolutely, believes Lana's daughter is the answer."

"She'd be younger than my kids," Katie added.

She stepped away from the window. "First things first. As soon as everybody's back, we'll have a meeting, and figure out the best way to save a group of pacifist Uncannys. Let's say eight o'clock to be sure."

Arlys nodded. "I'll get a sitter."

CHAPTER TEN

A dedicated and somewhat fanatical witch founded the commune simply called: Peace. He believed, with his entire being, peace answered all.

Javier Martinez, once an undocumented immigrant who'd worked the cotton fields in Texas, hauled cement in New Mexico, picked and packed cauliflower in Arizona, dedicated the life he believed God had spared to peace.

He'd woken to his abilities the day the woman he loved died of the terrible sickness the devil had cast over the world. He'd been twenty-six. Fear and grief had spewed lightning from his fingertips, and that lightning had set the little house where he'd lived with Rosa and three others—all dying—to blaze.

Only he had escaped with his fingers burning, his soul screaming. In his madness, he'd sent the lightning over the fields, into other buildings, even people.

Everything burned and burned.

But he survived.

He wandered through the desert, skin burning and blistering under the unrelenting sun. And followed, gibbering to the demons only he could see, the rise of smoke, the circling crows. For a time he starved, ribs poking through his scorched skin. For a time he glutted his hunger on the burned bodies of the rats and rabbits he struck down.

For months he stole whatever he could steal, he quenched his grief and rage in bottles. And burned more in drunken glee.

He raged at the dead when he found them.

He survived. Later he would believe with all he was that the divine had shielded him, taken pity on him, tested him. How else had he known when to hide when parties of Raiders roared by? Or when to conceal himself, to watch military convoys herd people into trucks? How many times had he heard the screams of the damned like him captured by Purity Warriors?

But they never found him. Not in a year, then two, then three. Not in all the miles he walked, through desert and forest, over highways littered with cars and bodies.

So he had a vision.

While he shivered and wet coughs racked his body on a brutal winter night in what was left of a mini-mart off I-70 outside of Topeka, Rosa came to him.

Pretty Rosa, with her soft hair and soft eyes, laid her hands on him in the dark, in the cold, and warmed him.

The relief, the sweet relief from the biting, gnawing cold brought tears to his eyes.

Through those tears, he saw her for what she was, what she had always been. An angel, a messenger of the divine with wings white and luminous.

Rise up, rise up! she told him. *Cleanse yourself, body and soul. Rid yourself of the demon inside you, for only then will you serve your great purpose. Rise up, for you are the Chosen.*

He reached for her, and she took his hands in hers. In his delirium, Martinez struggled to his feet.

The demon is wily, Rosa warned him. *You must close your eyes and ears to him. Purge yourself. Reject him and his power, for if you let him free, he will consume you, and all is lost. Go forth, go forth and teach the word. Go forth and gather the flock of the damned. Cleanse them, anoint them, bring them into the peace. Lead them into the valley, show them the mountaintop, cloister yourselves from the evil of man and demon so on the day of final reckoning, you are pure.*

Tears burned out of his reddened eyes. "Stay with me, Rosa." His voice croaked out, the words like razors in his throat. "Show me the way."

You will find the way when you are cleansed, when you are pure. I will protect you as I have through your terrible trials. Repent and be saved. Be saved and save all.

Sick in body, sick in mind, Javier Martinez stumbled out to cleanse himself with snow under the cold, slitted white eye of the moon.

And so began his new journey.

He fasted, he found gloves to cover the fingers cursed by the demon. He raged and prayed as he limped on frozen feet. Feverish, delirious, he stumbled into a small settlement. Lights blinded him, shadows moved around him. As he fell unconscious, he heard Rosa say again, *Repent and be saved. Be saved and save all.*

For days he hovered between life and death, even with the care of a healer. His hair, gone gray, fell around a face honed by sickness and starvation to prophet's point.

But he survived.

In the weeks that followed, he regained his strength and his mind cleared. He explained kindly, gently, to the healer who'd saved him with her gifts that her powers were ungodly, urged her to repent, felt sorrow when she refused to reject her demon.

He preached in that same gentle way to all who would listen, and to many who wouldn't. When he was strong enough, he walked among them, a thin man with kind, compelling eyes who spoke of a world without weapons, without death, a world of peace and prayer.

Of a valley blessed and a holy mountaintop where those who followed him would live forever.

When he walked away from the settlement, two went with him.

By the time he reached Tennessee, he had twelve apostles, and created the commandments told to him by angels in his dreams.

Only those infected by demons who repented would be allowed to enter onto the blessed land.

No member of the faithful would own or use a weapon of any kind. A knife used for harvesting roots or in preparation of food would be sanctified.

No animal flesh would be consumed, nor any part of a living creature used by the faithful.

What belonged to one, belonged to all.

Women, from the age of twelve, would fulfill their divine duty and seek to conceive and so propagate the earth with the faithful.

None would lift a hand in anger or strike a blow.

Any who used the power of the demon would be banished from the holy land.

As he walked east (his angels forbade the use of any motorized vehicle) his flock ebbed and flowed. Of the thirty faithful who rested for two weeks near Shelbyville for a birthing, only eighteen escaped an attack by a scouting party of Raiders.

Those left behind, living or dead, had gone to glory, Javier explained. The sacrifice demanded by the divine was for the others to walk on.

Some died of illness or in birthing. Some fled in the night. Others joined simply for the safety in numbers, and most of them fell away.

On a day green with spring, three years after his redemption, he led his flock of twenty-three—to the mountaintop.

And there, his gray-streaked hair flowing, his sunbaked face luminous, his eyes kind and crazed, he opened his arms to the valley below.

In this sacred valley, we will live, he told them. In this cup of holy ground we will worship. And with our prayers and with our faith, the world will be cleansed as we are cleansed, and made worthy for the coming of the divine.

It took days to reach the valley, and there the river flowing through it swelled with the beat of spring rain. They built their fires, pitched their tents.

Women, as their hands and hearts were more pure, prepared the meal of berries and oats. Men, as their backs were stronger, their minds keener, gathered stones and twigs and mud to build stronger shelters.

There in that quiet valley, a devout madman created his image of peace.

Eight years later, Duncan crouched on the snow-covered ground. Dusk sighed down, thin and gray. Through it he studied the commune.

"No defenses. Nada," he said in amazement to Will. "No guards, no checkpoints. Jeez, Suzanne tried to warn them, and they ignored her, preached at her. They didn't listen, so now the enemy could settle down on one of those ridges, pick them off like flies."

Will nodded, shifted slightly while his eyes, dark blue, scanned the ridge. "I figure they'll put some up there, pick off runners. They're going to want to capture plenty. Executions are their big show."

Beside them, Eddie grunted. His straw-colored hair straggled out from under the black ski cap Fred had knitted for him.

"They got themselves a freaking carnival ride here, man. Not only no defenses, but who the hell camps where you've got no way out? You make it to the river, then what the fuck? Can't swim across this time of year for sure. Cold'll kill you sure as a bullet. You got the mountain blocking that way. Head for the woods, okay, how far you gonna get? Not a one of them wearing decent boots. And, dude, what's up with those weird-ass robes?"

Flynn, half in, half out of a tree, laid a hand on the head of his wolf. "We can ask them about their wardrobe after we save their pious asses. Starr and I can get closer from this point."

Starr, quiet as smoke, eased out of a tree, simply nodded. If she could say something in two words, she wouldn't use three.

"Steve and Connor move in from that point." Flynn gestured toward a band of trees where others waited, including the two elves.

"Okay then." Will shifted. "Let them know."

Easily done, as elves could communicate mind to mind.

"And let's have Maggie take her group up to that ridge. Any PWs who move up there need to be taken out, quietly. Eddie?"

"My man."

"Take your team to the south end with Jonah's. The PWs will be coming soon."

"They're coming now." Flynn, tall, lean as a whippet, angled his head. His eyes, sharp green, narrowed. "I hear engines."

"Elf ears," Eddie noted.

"Direction?"

"Southeast. Maybe a quarter of a mile." Flynn glanced toward Starr for confirmation, then held up a hand. "They stopped."

"Coming on foot, bigger surprise. Take positions," Will ordered.
"Let's ambush the ambushers."

As they moved into positions, Duncan watched the targets gather
together. They came—in those weird-ass robes and strange shoes—
out of tents and what looked like huts of mud and freaking twigs to
stand in a circle around a central fire.

Kids, too, he noted. Babies carried in slings.

No one spoke. When one of the babies squalled, the woman carrying it bared her breast, offered it.

Then there was silence, just the wind sloughing through the trees,
as the circle, even the children, drew hoods over their heads, and
bowed them.

Sitting ducks, he thought. Every last one of them. The wind kicked
up the robes some, exposing bare legs that had to be freezing.

A man came out of one of the huts, long, unbound gray-streaked
hair blowing. He moved into the middle of the circle. He lifted his
arms high.

"We are the Chosen."

"Let us be worthy," the circle responded.

"We have been sinners, all."

"We do repent."

"Do you reject the demon inside you?"

"We do reject him and all his evils."

"Do you embrace the divine?"

"We do embrace him. And we pray for his embrace."

During the call and response, Duncan edged over until he was
shoulder to shoulder with Tonia. "If the faeries can't manage to pluck
up all the kids," he whispered, "we need to block them or herd them
toward the woods, where we can pick them up after."

"There are three women with babies. If we can't get the women
clear, we get the babies clear."

Two infants, he counted, and one maybe a year or so. "Agreed."

"Dunc? They're a bunch of lunatics."

"Oh, yeah, but that doesn't mean they deserve to be slaughtered."

"No, but we save their butts tonight, even get them out of here to safety? They're just going to come back. Because they're lunatics."

Though he didn't disagree, he shrugged. Tonight was tonight. Tomorrow was whatever it was. Plus, the chance to take on and defeat a squad of PWs couldn't be overstated.

He wanted the battle.

Will held up a hand, then seven fingers before pointing to the ridge.

Comm from the elves, Duncan thought. Seven PWs moving up to the ridge. Then he pointed toward Eddie's position, flashed ten fingers twice. Twenty moving toward the south of the camp. Fifteen, Duncan confirmed, reading the next signal, heading west—their position. And another eight moving east.

With a team of six spreading out through the woods—a cleanup crew, Duncan concluded.

Elves were damn handy, and a lot quieter than walkies.

He heard the movement, the snap of a twig, while the group around the fire continued to call and respond about angels and demons. He touched a hand to his sister's knee.

"Ready?"

"Oh, yeah." She moved, quick and quiet as a snake, rising, pivoting behind a tree. Notched an arrow in her bow. Duncan grabbed the hilt of his sword, rolled onto the balls of his feet.

"Ridge secure," Will murmured. "Hit the lights."

Duncan pumped his free hand in the air and turned the night to midday. It effectively blinded any enemy wearing night-vision goggles. And the screaming began.

Some in the circle simply fell to their knees, maybe, Duncan thought fleetingly, thinking the light was a sign from their divine. Others scattered.

Gunfire erupted, and Purity Warriors flooded in.

He'd heard the saying about bringing a knife to a gunfight, but Duncan considered a sword a different matter. Plus, a gun didn't do much good when the hand holding it was cleaved off.

The man he'd wounded let out a shrill scream as his blood spurted. The keen aim of Tonia's arrow took out another, and Will's return fire still more.

With his sword slashing, Duncan threw out a wave of power, sent two men and a woman flying back. He sensed a movement to his left, spun to block an attack. A good thing, he'd think later, as he heard a bullet whine past his head.

They had shotguns, the shells loaded with bits of metal. The shrapnel peppered trees, huts, the ground. He felt a sting at his hip, ignored it, and punched power toward the gun. As it turned molten, the shooter cried out, dropped it.

One of the elves rose out of a rock, dropped the shooter.

Chaos swirled. Within it one of the healers rushed, pulling the wounded to safety. Faeries risked their lives to swoop down, lift children away from flying metal. Duncan fought with the single-mindedness that had been trained into him. Beat the enemy back. Protect the innocent and your own people.

Then, to his horror, he saw that three of the Purity Warriors had broken through the northern flank. And one had a flamethrower. He fought off another attacker, drew blood and shed it before he could turn and run toward the cleared land.

Not soon enough, not soon enough to stop the woman who screamed in triumph from engulfing one of the kneeling men in flame.

The terrible high-pitched scream, the horrible sound of crackling flesh blocked out the gunfire, the shouts, the whizzing arrows.

Duncan didn't think, and years of training fell away, crushed under his charging feet. On a wild cry, he rushed them, all three, barely threw out power—enough and soon enough—to block the flame that washed over him.

His sword seemed alive in his hand as he struck her down; and with that horror, that rage consuming him, he sliced and hacked at her companions. He didn't see the knife, wouldn't have seen it through his blind fury before it gutted him.

But he saw it slip from the hand of a fourth man who rushed at his back as that man pitched forward with an arrow in his heart.

Then it all seemed to stop. A few dim shouts from the distance, calls for healers. He stood with the fire flickering over his face, with the nightmare scent of burning flesh fouling the air. And four people dead at his feet.

He heard Will shouting orders for a search—for the enemy and for the targets—and only stood there with his bloodied sword heavy in his hand.

Tonia stepped beside him. "Let's go."

"I kind of lost it." Still felt a little lost.

"Yeah, I noticed."

He looked at the dead man, the arrow piercing him. "Thanks for having my back."

"Mom'd be pissed if I came home without you."

With a forearm he wiped sweat, blood, and God-knew-what off his face, turned to her. "Hey, you're bleeding."

Tonia winced as she looked at her biceps. "Yeah, I caught some shrapnel. It really hurts."

"Tell me. Me, too." He gestured to his hip. "I'll do you. You do me. And we'll never tell Mom."

Tonia lifted her eyebrows, rolled her eyes under them. "She'll see the hole in your pants, my jacket and shirt."

"Right. We'll worry about that later." He laid his hand on her arm; she pressed hers to his hip. Eyes locked, they wound together the cool and the warm to heal.

When Will strode up, Duncan knew from the look on his face that he was in for it.

"You're on your own now," Tonia muttered.

"What the goddamn hell, Duncan? We don't need any damn dead heroes. You run out, no cover, three against one?"

"I just—"

"You just nothing." Will snapped it out.

"They set him on fire, Will. He was just kneeling there, and they set him on fire."

"So you risked your life for a dead man. We fulfilled our mission here without a single casualty on our side. We'd have had one if your sister hadn't been quick enough to take out the one about to cut out your liver because you were too busy playing fucking samurai to notice."

"Okay, I get it." But part of him didn't believe he'd been wrong. "I'm sorry."

" 'Sorry' doesn't cut it. Jesus, I have to trust you, everybody, to think, to follow the training—and, worse, what would I tell your mom?" Pausing, Will rubbed his hands over his face.

Duncan figured he'd be in for more, but Eddie limped over and drew Will's attention.

"You're hurt?"

"Ah, just banged my knee up some. Rachel can fix me up. But, Will, I saw Kurt Rove. Rove was with them."

"Rove? You're sure?"

Something came into Eddie's eyes that merged cold rage and hot grief. "I know the bastard, Will. He's older, some fatter, but I know the bastard. He was running, fucking coward. I'm going to tell you I broke ranks to go after him. That's when I banged up my damn knee. I couldn't get him, Will. I couldn't get him."

"Okay, it's okay. Now we know for certain he's still alive. We'll get him, Eddie. One day we'll get him."

Duncan wanted to ask why Eddie got an "okay" when he'd broken ranks, and he got a lecture. But he knew about Kurt Rove. Knew he'd been part of the Fourth of July massacre.

"Come on," Will said, with a hand on Eddie's shoulder. "Let's get these people to New Hope. And the ones who won't come, well, we'll give them some supplies. Let's go home."

"I hear that."

Duncan waited until they'd walked away—to avoid having Will remember to finish the lecture.

"He's not going to tell Mom," Tonia said. "He may threaten to, to scare you, but he won't because it would scare her." She waited a moment. "You scared me, too, but I know why you did it. It's in us. Will can't understand. Mom can't, either, because it's in us. It comes with the gift—I don't know. It just is."

She let out a breath that whisked away in a little cloud. "Let's help clean up and get home. This one, I don't know, Duncan, this one didn't give me the lift I usually get from a rescue."

"That makes two of us. Yeah, let's clean up, get home."

As he turned to walk with her, he caught a movement out of the corner of his eye. His sword all but flew back into his hand. The girl hiding behind the hut cringed, whimpered. Eyes blue as cornflowers gleamed with tears over fear.

On an expelled breath, Duncan sheathed his sword. "We won't hurt you. You're safe now."

But she shook her head, curled into a tighter ball. "You need to come with us." Tonia tried to mimic her mother's no-bullshit tone. "We'll take you somewhere safe and warm."

"The women aren't ever to leave the sacred valley."

Duncan figured she was maybe his age, maybe a little younger. He didn't think that qualified as woman, but let it pass. "It's not safe here anymore. The PWs know about it, and they may come back. What's your name?"

"I—Petra."

"Listen, Petra. Is your mom, or maybe your dad here? We'll help you find them."

"My mother died giving me life because I'm cursed. My—my father . . ."

She pointed toward the blackened husk on the ground.

"I'm sorry." Tonia crouched down. "I'm really sorry. You need to come with us. There's nothing left for you here."

"Javier the Blessed says—"

"He's not here." Out of patience, Duncan threw out a hand to show the dead, the blood, the destruction. "You see him?"

"They took him away."

"Who?" Tonia demanded.

"The people who came to defile the sacred valley. I saw them drag him away."

"So he's not here," Duncan concluded. "Neither is anybody else right now. So you need to come with us."

"It's a good place," Tonia added. "We're going to a good place."

"Holy ground?"

"It's a good place," she repeated and offered her hand. "We'll be taking some of your . . . people there, too. Anyone who wants to come. You'll have food and shelter." And a shower, Tonia thought, because, boy, she needed one. "No one will hurt you."

When she took Tonia's hand and rose, Duncan noted she was about his sister's height. Her hair, in a long, matted braid, read dirty blond. Really dirty.

The robe—more of a sack, he thought—looked like some sort of woven material. The same as the useless shoes that came up to her ankles.

But she went quietly enough with Tonia now, so he considered that problem solved. He decided to stay back—his own disciplinary action for breaking ranks—and help burn the dead, as the ground was too hard for burial.

Once they'd settled those of Javier's cult who came with them—eleven minors, including the infants, and three adults—Eddie made his way home.

They didn't need him at the clinic, where Rachel and Jonah and the other medicals and healers would deal with the wounded. He'd have her look at his knee in the morning. He just wanted to go home.

They didn't need him at the kitchen, where volunteers put food together for the people they'd brought in. They didn't need him to pass out clothes and supplies or to move them into the house more volunteers had readied for just that purpose.

He wanted Fred. He wanted Joe. He wanted to look at his kids, who'd be sleeping. Just look at them.

He walked into the house Fred had turned into a happy, colorful home. Climbed the stairs. He looked into the girls' room first. Rainbow, their oldest, cuddled under the multicolored blanket with a cat, a puppy, and a smile on her face.

Angel, their youngest, sprawled over her bed, all but buried in her collection of stuffed toys.

He moved on to his son's room. Max. His middle child, named for a dead friend, slept with another puppy, his favorite truck, and even in sleep looked ready to cause trouble.

His eyes burned.

In all of his life, Eddie had never imagined loving anything, anyone, the way he loved his kids. Would he have them, would he have Fred, who just lit up his freaking world, would he have this life if not for Max and Lana?

He walked toward the room where he knew Fred would be waiting up for him. She sat up in bed, her red hair a glorious halo of curls, her belly rounded with their fourth child as she worked on crocheting a blanket for their new baby.

On the floor, curled on the rug with yet another puppy, Joe thumped his tail in greeting.

"I heard you come in." Fred set the blanket aside. "Bryar sent word a couple hours ago that everybody was okay." Her smile faded. "You don't look okay. I'm going to fix you something to eat."

"No. No, don't get up." He waved her back, walked in, and sat heavily on the side of the bed, one he'd brought back from an abandoned house sixty miles away because he knew she'd like the canopy. "I'm not hungry."

"You're limping."

"Just banged up my knee."

"Rachel or—"

"Tomorrow, okay? I needed to be home. Somebody'll look at it tomorrow."

"I'll make some ice so—"

"It's okay, Fred."

She shifted, pressed herself and the baby against him. "What happened? What's wrong?"

"It was bad. Those people, just standing around in a circle praying or some shit. Kids, too, and they don't have decent clothes, decent shoes. Skinny and dirty and . . . I think they must be all fucking crazy, Fred."

"People have different ways of coping, I guess. Even crazy ones."

"We had a good plan, good positioning, and it worked. Mostly it worked. The bastards got about ten of them, and more just took off, but we got all the kids. Babies, some of them, Fred. Just babies."

In comfort, he laid his hand on her belly.

"We had some injuries, but nothing too bad. Everybody got fixed up, or Rachel'll finish that job. Nothing too bad. We brought fourteen back—eleven of them kids. Some of the crazies scattered, and the scouts didn't find them, or bodies, so . . . Some just wouldn't come, and we're not going to make them. But we brought fourteen back and that's something."

"What is it, Eddie? You need to tell me."

"I'm working on it." He gripped her hand, hard. "I saw Rove. Kurt fucking Rove. I saw him shoot one of the crazies, a woman. Shoot her in the back. Then he started running because we were taking them down, Fred. We were whipping their asses, and they were running like the cowards they are. I went after him. I broke ranks, and I took off after him. But I didn't see the goddamn stupid root. Didn't see it because all I could think was Rove, that son of a bitch. And I banged up my knee, and he got away from me.

"I couldn't get him, Fred. I couldn't get him for Max. I couldn't get him for Max and Lana. I couldn't get him."

Fred wrapped her arms around him and held him while he wept.

VISIONS

Who looks outside, dreams;
who looks inside, awakes.

—Carl Jung

CHAPTER ELEVEN

Within three days one of the women they'd saved slipped out of town with her baby and two of the children. The single male who'd come with the rescuers ran off with a bag of supplies, leaving behind a five-year-old girl he'd claimed as his daughter.

Rachel sat in her office reading over the charts of those who remained.

Malnutrition, exposure, ringworm, impetigo, bad teeth—dentistry would be busy—kidney infection. Two girls no more than fourteen pregnant. A case of double pneumonia, several old breaks, poorly set. Several wounds—animal bites or gouges—poorly stitched.

And that didn't begin to address mental and emotional issues.

She sat back, took off the cheaters she'd started using a couple years earlier, rubbed her eyes. She had dense, curly hair clipped back and, because it made her feel better after several long days running, had used some of the organic makeup Fred gave her.

Jonah came in, sat on her desk. He handed her a mug. "Pretend it's strong black coffee."

"I wish I could forget what that tasted like. A good, dark French roast, beans freshly ground."

She drank some of the echinacea tea instead.

"Fred's bound and determined we're going to have coffee beans."

She sighed. "Right now I'm ready to say it's worth the risk of them trying—again. But I'm weak."

"Never." He leaned down and kissed her.

He needed a trim, she thought, though she liked his hair when he didn't take time to go to the barber. "You got the kids breakfast and off to school?"

"Hey, I do my duty. Henry made you the tea. He said you needed it. Luke did the dishes. Under protest, but he did them."

"They're good boys, our boys."

"Speaking of boys, there's one from the cult. And I'm calling it like it is, Rachel, believe me."

"I'm not arguing."

"So this boy? He's only three. He says his name's Gabriel. He talked to me. I didn't bring it up last night because you were tired. We were both tired."

"We've got a group of people resisting basic treatment—or enough of them intimidating the rest to resist. And those who'll agree to it are going to take a lot of time and care to get healthy. We've got an infant severely malnourished and dehydrated because his mother's the same, and her milk isn't enough, and another a year, maybe fourteen months, not yet weaned, whose mother died in the raid, with a raging ear infection."

As she took another sip of tea, Rachel rubbed her fingers at her temple.

"They won't accept blankets if they're wool, won't wear the boots because they're leather."

"Cult. Indoctrinated." Jonah stepped behind her a moment, massaged some of the tension out of her shoulders. "But the kids can and will learn better. Sooner. This one."

"Gabriel, age three, male, malnutrition, ringworm, another raging ear infection."

"Yeah, that one. There's something about him, Rachel. I can see he's going to make it. Just like . . . the double pneumonia, the—"

"Goes by Isaiah, age about sixty."

"He's not going to make it."

"If he'd accept treatment—"

"Maybe, maybe not. But he's not going to make it."

As Jonah's gift caused him to see death, and often the life of the dead, Rachel didn't argue.

"All right."

Jonah came back around, sat on the corner of the desk. "The kids are going to need family."

"The cult—and you're right—considers themselves family."

"They're not. Family wouldn't allow children to half starve when there's game. Wouldn't let them freeze when there are places that offer shelter. Maybe the adults couldn't be debriefed or detoxed or whatever the hell, but the kids can. Certainly the young ones. He's three, Rachel. His father, or the man he thought was his father, died in the attack. His mother died when he was born, or soon after. He isn't sure."

She'd been nodding along, then something in his tone got through. "Jonah, are you asking what I think you're asking?"

He took one of her hands, rubbed it between both of his. "He needs a home. We have a home. He needs family. We're a family. There's something about him, Rachel. I can't really explain, but there's something about him. He needs us."

She flopped back in her chair. "Jonah. A three-year-old. Our boys are eleven and eight. A three-year-old. One who's never seen a toilet or bathtub—or hadn't until a couple of days ago. And our boys—"

"We'd need to talk to them. They'd need to be okay with it."

"Henry would be. Soft heart. But Luke . . . harder sell." More like her, Rachel thought, in looks and temperament. "And I'm not sold. You are."

Still a little baffled himself, Jonah spread his hands. "The minute I looked at him, him at me. It was immediate. Not like the first time I looked at Henry and Luke, held them. That overwhelming, stupefying love. But more . . . Oh, there you are. Yeah, I see you."

"Is it your gift or your soft heart?"

"Truth? I think both."

"We'll talk to the boys."

He gripped both her hands, brought them to his lips to kiss. "I love you. Thanks."

"I love you, too, but there's a way to go before thanks."

Duncan walked toward home after a stint at the academy with his best friend, Denzel, a shifter. As Denzel had yet to pass combat-and-weapons training, he'd never fought in an actual battle, worked an actual rescue. Simulations only. So, as usual, he wanted every detail of the fight in the Shenandoah.

Antonia walked several paces back with April. Duncan could hear the girls giggling—mostly April—as April fluttered in circles. Talking boys, Duncan decided. The faerie girl was obsessed with romance.

"Gimme your score, man. How many'd you take out?"

"It's not like that. I told you. It's not like one of Chuck's games or sims."

"Cut me some breaks." Denzel, a big guy who shifted into a

panther—that was cool—gave Duncan a shoulder bump. "Word is you took on three, at the same time, and nearly got your ass crisped by a freaking flamethrower. Is that the straight shit or not?"

Duncan had a flash of the kneeling man, dirty robe, dirty beard, eyes blank with fear and . . . something like rapture. And the way the flames caught him. The way they ate him alive.

That wasn't something he would share with Denzel, best friend or not. Denzel was a lot softer than he thought he was.

"What I did was break ranks, which is why I'm stuck writing a stinking essay on chain of command."

"Unfair, man. I gotta get me some action."

"You flunked archery, hand-to-hand, and still can't hit the target with the rubber bullets. You keep tanking chem, and you need it, man, you need it because you might not have a witch around to make fire or throw a blast, whatever. You barely passed basic tactics."

Denzel rolled his huge dark eyes, then flashed a wide, white grin. "I just bring out Kato and tear 'em up."

"Yeah, yeah." Personally Duncan thought Denzel should stick with sports, where he shined, whether it was catching a football, dunking a basket, or swinging a bat.

Not everybody belonged in battle.

"Hey, wanna hang tonight? Magna got a horror flick in the DVD rotation."

Magna, eighteen, and the only lazy elf Duncan knew, lived in an apartment in what everybody thought of as Elf Central because so many of them lived there.

Magna's place often reeked of dirty laundry, unwashed dishes, and garbage he'd neglected to haul to the community waste and recycling center.

Not that Duncan considered himself overly fussy—his own room could and did resemble a trash heap until his mom laid down the law.

Though Magna refused to fight—claimed it was against his moral code—and often slipped and slid around any community work, he was harmless and good-natured. Duncan liked him fine.

But.

"Essay, remember?"

"Bummer. You ought to ditch it, man. Trot's going, and he'll bring Shelly. Where Shelly goes, Cass goes. You've had half an eye on Cass."

He'd had both eyes on Cass right at the moment, the pretty brunette who went to what he thought of as the civilian school. She'd grown really interesting breasts the previous summer.

But if he ditched the essay, he'd pay for it. Not only with Mom Wrath, but an automatic cut from the next operation.

"Can't do it."

"Sucks for you. Want me to help you on it?"

He would, too, Duncan thought. He'd blow off the fun to huddle over a damn essay if Duncan asked.

"Nah, I got it."

"If you get it done early, come hang out. I gotta book it. Later, gator."

"Yeah."

He watched Denzel, broad shoulders, beefy arms, lope across the street with his tightly curled tail of hair bouncing. He saw the kid from the rescue late last year—Garrett, he remembered—with his pack, racing along the opposite sidewalk. One of them rolled into a wolf and back out again, making the others laugh.

Garrett paused, shot Duncan a huge grin, waved. Then shouted out to Tonia.

Crushing, Duncan realized. The kid was crushing on Tonia—which could afford significant ammo for teasing his sister relentlessly.

Good intel.

Pleased, he slipped his hands into his pockets while Tonia caught up with him. April, with her flutters and giggles, had peeled off for home.

"Who's she in love with now?"

"Greg."

"Greg, the elf with the red hair and face full of freckles, or Denzel's brother, Greg, or—"

"Freckles. She thinks he's adorbs."

"A what?"

"Short for *adorable*. She heard that on some DVD. It's her favorite new word."

Adorbs. Seriously? "Why do you hang with her?"

"She's fun. She's silly, but she's fun. And she's smarter than you think. She was smart enough to get over being in love with you."

He hunched his shoulders, as the memory of having April giggle and flutter around him still mortified. "She's not my type."

Tonia snorted. "You're fourteen. I know this because, hey, so am I. So you don't have a type yet. Guys our age, the ones who like girls, have just one type requirement. Breasts."

He thought of Cass's—and the stupid essay. "What do you know about it?"

"I *have* breasts."

He nearly gave a snort of his own, then it struck like lightning, pulled him up short. "If some jerk tries to touch you, I hear about it."

"If some jerk tries to touch me, I can take care of myself."

"Bullshit. If anybody tries to . . . with you, I break his hand, then his face."

Tonia flipped back her hair, long and loose under her knit cap. "I don't need you to fight my battles. And maybe I'd like somebody enough to let him try."

"Screw that!"

The thought of some guy doing to Tonia what he imagined himself doing to Cass had his temper flashing like a grenade.

"I break his hand, then his face, then I deal with you."

"You don't *deal* with me, stupid." She shoved him.

"Watch me." He shoved her back.

"You just mind your own business." She elbowed him aside.

"I am." He grabbed her arm, yanked her back.

Right before she kicked him—hard enough to make him see stars—he spotted the blond girl, blue eyes wide with shock, as she tried to hide behind a snow-covered shrub.

He turned his grip on Tonia's arm to a warning squeeze, shifted so they both faced the girl.

"Hey, ah . . . Petra, right?"

He nearly hadn't recognized her, since she'd hidden a lot of pretty under the dirt. Her hair turned out to be a sunny, golden blond and her skin was sort of soft-looking. But she cringed back just as she had in the camp.

"We're just messing around," he said, with another warning squeeze for Tonia.

"Boys." Tonia gave an exaggerated shrug. "Come on out."

"I—I shouldn't be outside."

"Why not?" Tonia solved things by walking to her.

"Because . . . We're supposed to stay separate. Mina said."

"Not anymore. We live right there." Tonia pointed toward the house. "Come on in for a while."

"I don't know if it's permitted."

"Sure it is." In her take-charge way, Tonia took Petra's hand, pulled her up, and kept it gripped as she walked. "How's it going?"

"I don't know."

"I like your shoes."

Petra looked down at the black, gently used Chucks. "They're not really mine, but they took mine away. They brought others, but they were made from animal flesh."

Tonia just led her up to the house, through the unlocked door. Then flicked a hand to start the fire.

On a gasp, Petra reeled back. "The demon—"

"Why demon?" Duncan demanded, peeling off his coat to toss it over the back of the couch. "We don't believe that. You can if you want, but we don't. We have a gift, and for us it comes from the light. Anyway, I'm starved."

"He's always hungry," Tonia commented as Duncan wandered back toward the kitchen. "So, take off your coat."

"It's not really—"

"It is now." Tonia took off her own, tossed it with Duncan's, waited while Petra carefully took off a blue parka just a little too big for her thin frame. "Our sister Hannah's probably over at the clinic. Maybe you met her."

"I don't know."

"You got checked out, right?" Once again, Tonia led Petra, steering her back to the kitchen. "The doctors and all that."

"They said I had bad nu . . ."

"Nutrition. So let's eat."

"Mom scored!" Duncan let out a whoop. "We got pizza."

"They make it at the community kitchen," Tonia explained as she hunted up a sealed bottle of ginger ale. "And we can freeze it, then cook it up. And we've got this."

"What is it?"

"Ginger ale. Ginger root and sugar and lemon and yeast—for the bubbles—and water. Hannah made this batch, but we all have to take cooking lessons, and chem. Making stuff like ginger ale, it's chemistry. Plus, it's good."

Tonia poured out three short glasses while Duncan held his hands over the pizza until the crust browned and the cheese bubbled.

"What's your gift?" he asked Petra, casually. Then shrugged it off when her shoulders hunched. "Okay. So, how's it going over at the group house?"

"The doctor—the doctor said some of us are contagious, and need medication, and the nursing babies need better milk. And Clarence and Miranda both took the boots of animal flesh, and now we have to shun them."

"Harsh." Duncan cut the pizza into slices.

"It's hard, I guess, because you lived somewhere and some way, and now you're living here, and a different way." Tonia got plates. "But you couldn't stay there."

"If the divine brings violence to take our lives . . ."

"You just lay down and die?" Duncan slid pizza onto the plates. "Doesn't sound very divine."

"How old are you?" Tonia asked, then sat at the counter and pointed to the stool beside her.

"I'm not sure. I've come into womanhood, but I haven't conceived."

"What?" A slice halfway to his mouth, Duncan froze.

"I've come into womanhood," Petra repeated. "And though I have given myself, even to Javier, I haven't been blessed with child."

"You're saying you have to do it, and with that old guy?"

"Javier has no age," Petra said, beaming. "It's a great honor to conceive a child with him."

"Bullshit. It's sick and twisted."

"Duncan—"

But he ignored his sister's warning. "Did you want to do it with him? Or did you have to because he made it his law or something?"

"It's a great . . . I was afraid," she whispered. "But that was my weakness. And it hurt me, but that's the sacrifice of all women for the sin of Eve."

"And that's more bullshit."

Tonia waved Duncan off as Petra's head drooped. "I'll take this. That's not how things work here. And if you read books and listen to the older people, it's not how it worked before. People who did stuff like that got punished if they got caught. You have rights. Everybody does. And just because we're women doesn't give anybody else the right to hurt us or make us have sex. No one's going to do that to you here."

"But there must be children to increase the flock, to care for the elders, to spread the word. So many of them die, inside the womb or soon after birth. We all do our duty."

Tonia, a born feminist, but more diplomatic than her twin, kept her voice easy. "Around here and in a civilized society, people have kids because they want them, and because they want to take care of them, love them. How long were you in that camp?"

"I'm not sure. I wasn't born there. Two winters, I think. Before, we just moved and walked and hid. And my father hit me and cursed me because of my curse, even though he was cursed, too. Javier and our people didn't hit me or curse me. And my father stopped, too, when he embraced redemption."

"He stopped hitting you, but the rest is just a different kind of abuse." The thought of it, all of it, burned Duncan's craw. "We have laws here, too. If somebody deliberately hurts somebody else, he's punished for it. Everybody pulls weight in whatever way they can. We take care of each other."

"One question," Tonia put in. "Were you happy there?"

"It was . . . I don't know." Obviously distressed, Petra twisted her fingers together. "I don't know."

"Maybe you'll figure out if you're happy here. Pizza's getting cold."

Petra looked down at her plate. "I'm thankful for the food, but . . . is this animal flesh?"

"Pepperoni." Duncan bit into his slice. "Pick it off if you don't want it."

"They mostly make it at the big farm," Tonia told her. "And distribute it to the community kitchen."

Petra carefully peeled off the disks of meat, then took a tiny bite of pizza. Her eyes widened. She took another, bigger bite. "It's so good!"

"They can make it without the pepperoni," Tonia said, then handed Petra one of the napkins stacked on the counter.

"You can just have it?"

"Everyone pulls weight," Duncan repeated. "Everybody eats."

"You have this big house and all the things." With wondering eyes, Petra looked around the kitchen. "Just you?"

"And our sister, Hannah, and our mom. Kids don't live on their own until they're at least sixteen. Some kids come in without parents or adults. But somebody takes them in, takes care of them."

Petra bit her lip. "Clarence can go, and he wants to, with others. To live. He tried to run away from the divine, but they brought him back. His curse is wings, and balls of light and—"

"Faerie," Duncan finished.

"He had to be shunned many times, and closed into the redemption hut before he stopped giving in to his demon. Because he was a child, he wasn't cast out, but we were afraid he'd give in to his demon again when he reached the age of judgment."

"Not his demon, his nature," Duncan corrected. "His gift. Did he ever hurt anyone?"

"Once—twice," she corrected, "he fought with other boys who said hard things to him."

"That's different. That's called standing up for yourself."

"He's going tonight with people called Anne and Marla."

"They're nice," Tonia said with her mouth full. "They live near the academy. They raise sheep and llamas, and weave blankets and sweaters. And make art, too. It's pretty. Anne's an elf, but Marla's a civilian—no abilities. I heard before the Doom, when they lived in Baltimore, they were going to have a baby together."

"They're both women. It's not possible. And it's sinful."

"It's not sinful to love someone. And before the Doom there was science and medical technology to help people have babies when they wanted them. They're really good people. Clarence is lucky to have them."

"He said . . . He told me Miranda can go with him. And that these women would take one more. I could go."

"You should give it a shot—try it," Duncan explained. "If you don't like it there, you don't have to stay."

"I could go, then not stay?"

"Anne and Marla wouldn't make you stay if you weren't happy."

"It's so different. Everything's so different."

"Don't cry," Tonia comforted. "It's going to be okay. Have some ginger ale."

Obediently, Petra lifted the glass, sipped. And laughed as she wiped at tears. "It tickles."

"It's the bubbles."

"I never drank bubbles before. Or don't remember. So much from before is blurry or mixed up. Esme said we had to go back."

"Esme?"

"She left, with her baby, and took two of the young ones. She said we had to go back or be damned. But no one wanted to go with her. She left and said she was going back to the holy ground, to the sacred valley. And Jerome left, too. He took things from the place we're living, and went away. He said I could go with him, but I didn't want to go with him. It's good to be warm and to have shoes, and the clothes that don't scratch, and to eat the pizza and drink the ale. Before is blurred and hard and I was afraid and hungry and cold."

"Well." Duncan put another slice of pizza on her plate. "Now starts now."

"Now starts now," she echoed, and smiled at him.

She ate the second slice, and since ginger ale had to be rationed, Tonia gave her juice for the next round.

"I'm very thankful for the food and drink. I need to go back. They'll worry and wonder." She stood, hesitated. "If I don't go with Clarence and Miranda to the women, and stay with Mina and her baby, will you still talk to me?"

"Sure we will. We'll see you in school, and you can hang out with us."

"I don't know how to go to school."

"Don't worry, you'll catch on. I'll walk you out."

Petra started out with Tonia, then stopped, turned back to Duncan. "It's hard to talk to those I don't know. It's good, but it's hard. You killed the men with your sword and your curse—your gift," she corrected quickly as color rose up to her cheeks. "I know they would have taken my life. We're taught the divine demands we never lift a hand to another, never take up a weapon, even when our life will be taken, or the life of another. It's the greatest sin. But I was afraid to die. I was afraid."

"To stand by and do nothing to help someone else? I've been taught that is cowardice, and if it's not a sin, it's the greatest weakness."

"Then you're not weak."

He sat, brooding, while Tonia took her out. Brooded a little more when his sister came back. He knew Tonia dealt with the dishes right off, without pushing him to help, because she wanted her hands busy. Her way of brooding, he supposed.

"I could've been her," Tonia said.

"Not in a million years."

But Tonia shook her head. "She's about our age, maybe a little younger. It's hard to tell, but we're about the same age. If we didn't have Mom, and if she hadn't had Jonah and Rachel to help her get all of us out of New York. If they hadn't met up with Arlys and Chuck and Fred, and . . ."

"A lot of ifs that didn't happen."

"Ifs are about what hasn't or didn't. I'm saying I could've been taken to a place like that, forced to live like that, had my brain washed—because that's it, right? Had my brain washed into thinking I was nothing. Just some nothing to be used to make babies and worship some *asshole* who claimed to talk for some divine bullshit. And I'd have just laid there while some . . ."

"*Fuck*'s the word you're after. Mom's not here so you can say it. Sick, twisted fuck."

"Yeah, sick, twisted fuck raped me. Because that's what it was. And I'd believe that what's in me is evil, like she does."

"Here's where you're wrong." He rose then, put the plates she'd washed and dried away. "You'd never be like her because you're strong and smart and you'd kick that sick, twisted fuck in the nuts before he raped you."

Because he made her feel better, she offered him a smirk. "I thought I needed you to break hands and faces for me."

"I didn't say you needed me to, I said that's what I'd do. You'd never be like her. Nothing and no one could make you like her. Maybe, and who knows, but maybe if she sticks here, if she lets herself, she'll be who she's supposed to be."

"I'm glad we didn't save him. That Javier," Tonia said. "I know I shouldn't be, and it goes against everything, but I'm glad the PWs dragged him off before we saved him. If we had, if he was here, she wouldn't have a chance to be anything. None of them would."

Duncan realized—and realized he should have realized before—the entire conversation with Petra had upset his sister even more than it had him.

"I know there's this—what's it called—school of thought? That. And some who go with that believe how things are meant, and fate and destiny and all that crap. I don't buy it."

He flicked the theory away. "People make things happen, one way or the other. But if I did buy it, I'd say we weren't meant to save him. We were meant to save kids like Clarence and Miranda and her."

Tonia wasn't quite as sure either way. "Meant or not, that's what we did."

"We should tell Rachel—Mom, too, but Rachel because of the doctor deal—about the sex shit."

"I'm pretty sure somebody as good a doctor as Rachel knows. Especially since one of the kids I loaded, again about our age, was pregnant. Pretty far along, it looked to me."

"Jesus."

"But you're right. We'll make sure Rachel knows. We could walk over, talk to her now."

"It's a girl thing." And he'd had more than enough girl-thing talk for the day. For the freaking year.

"*Girl* thing?" said the born feminist, with dripping derision.

"You're a girl, and since you're on it," he added, "it can be a girl thing. Anyway, I've got that stupid essay."

But when he went up to his room, Duncan flopped down on his bed to stare up at the ceiling. He thought of Cass's breasts. He thought of Petra's golden hair.

And he thought, as he often did, of the tall, slim girl with the short dark hair and storm cloud eyes.

He didn't wonder if she was real. He'd seen her in his head, in his dreams too often to believe otherwise.

But he wondered where the hell she was.

CHAPTER TWELVE

By spring Fallon could hold her own with a sword. Mallick knocked her down, disarmed her, and metaphorically beheaded her more often than she liked, but she reminded herself he'd had centuries of practice to her handful of months.

Spring meant planting, and the farm girl found comfort in the familiar. She knew as she worked the earth her family did the same. She didn't need the math lessons Mallick swamped her with to calculate she'd passed a quarter of her training time.

Mallick schooled her in the basics—math, history, literature, and the practicalities of tactics and strategies and mapping. When he expanded her lessons into engineering and mechanics, she took some pride at his surprise over what she already knew.

She had, after all, helped her father build, had learned how engines worked, how to repair them, even build them from scavenged parts.

He pushed her further and harder on magicks than her mother

had done, and this she welcomed. The more she knew, the more she opened, the brighter the beat inside her.

And still the crystal he'd given her when she was a baby remained clouded.

Her archery improved—partly from her innate desire to match Mick's skill, or even outpace it.

As the air warmed and the leaves greened, Mallick allowed her to visit the elf camp, the faerie bowers, the shifter den. She took gifts of food and charms and healing balms, considered the visits a kind of reward for her progress, a break from tasks and studies.

But she also learned, as Mallick intended, of other cultures, rites, beliefs, histories. Though she liked talking to the girls now and then, she found herself more drawn to the boys, with their contests and races, or to the elders who spoke of hunts and battles.

Once when she ran the woods with the young elves, practicing her tree scaling, a young elf, no older than Ethan, fell when a branch cracked beneath her.

She landed hard, her right arm cocked beneath her. Dazed, she whimpered, but when the others ran to her and turned her, she screamed in pain.

"Bagger, get her mom," Mick ordered. "Fast! I think her arm's broken. It's okay, Twila. It's going to be okay." He smoothed back her dense black hair from a face gone pasty under brown skin. Blood trickled from scrapes on her forehead and cheekbone.

She just screamed again. "Mama!"

"I'm going to take you to your mom, okay? I'm just going to pick you up and—"

"No." Though she understood the elves had their ways of healing, and that a child so young needed her mother, Fallon stepped forward. "Don't move her. She may have hurt something else."

Fallon knelt down, laid a hand on the sobbing girl's shoulder.

Tears rolled like liquid glass down the girl's cheeks. "I want my mama."

"I know. She's coming. Do you see me, Twila?"

She murmured it as she glided her hands just above the girl. Head, throat, heart, torso, limbs. "Do you see me?" she said again with her eyes on Twila's. Those dark, pain-filled eyes that pulled at Fallon.

Slowly, she let what rose in her ease out. "Do you see me?" she repeated, and watched those dark eyes glaze with the trance.

"I see you."

"Do you hear me, Twila? Do you hear my voice? Do you hear my heartbeat? Do you hear what lives in me stir and rise?"

"I hear you."

Fallon ignored the sound of running feet, a cry of alarm, and kept what she was, all she was, focused on the girl.

Behind her, Mick's father gripped Twila's mother's arm. "Wait. Wait. The One has her."

"I will be in you, you will be in me. Your bones are soft still, and the break is clean. I'm in you, you're in me. We share the pain, and it lessens. Here. See me, only me."

Fallon laid her hand on the break, gave herself to the knowing. "With me, Twila. Quick."

And gripping the snapped bone, squeezed. Her breath caught as the girl's did in that shared moment of heat and pain. Twila's eyes widened in shock, pupils going from saucers to pinpoints, then back again until her eyes closed on a whimpering sigh.

A new tear slipped out.

"You're all right now. She's all right." With the power still bubbling in her, Fallon eased back. How could she feel so strong, she wondered, with that ghost ache in her arm, with her stomach shaking?

"It was her arm," she managed as she rose. "The rest is just bumps and scrapes. She's all right."

On a cry, the mother leaped forward, gathered Twila up, rained kisses over her hair and face. Cuddling her daughter, she reached up for Fallon's hand. "Thank you."

"Sure." She turned to Mick's father. She thought of Thomas as a kind of scarecrow man because of his tall, thin build and the mass of corn-silk hair he wore in a bushy braid.

Just then he seemed a little blurry.

"The branch broke. It was the way her arm was bent when she fell on it."

"Yes. Here." He pushed a canteen on her. "Drink some water."

Realizing her throat burned with thirst, she started to gulp, but he laid a hand on the canteen. "Slowly now. Slowly."

She did as he said, found the world clearing, settling.

"We won't forget your care for one of our children." He touched her hand when she started to shrug off his gratitude. "Caring for another matters most of all. We'll get Twila back to camp, and Mick will walk you home. Mick?"

"Yes, sir."

Thomas turned, picked up Twila. "We won't forget," he vowed, and carried the girl away while her mother stroked her hair.

The others scurried after them.

"I didn't know you could do that."

Neither did I, Fallon thought.

When Fallon got back to the cottage, she found Mallick harvesting honey, a chore he'd come to enjoy—despite the occasional sting.

He wore the big hat with the net, and gloves. She could see the last wisps of smoke he'd conjured to chase whatever bees weren't out hunting from the combs as he slid out the rack, slipped in the spare they'd made.

With the rack in the bucket, he turned, saw her.

"Our bees have been productive."

As she'd instructed him, he began to walk with the bucket toward the greenhouse—to get out of the open air because the scent of the honey would attract bees.

She walked with him and into the scents of the earth and growing things.

"Something happened."

He gave her a quick, sharp look, but whatever he saw on her face had him relaxing again. He reached for a knife, warmed it, and began to uncap the comb.

"What happened?"

"One of the girls—her name's Twila. She's about five or six, I guess. She fell. She was tree-climbing and a branch broke. She hit really hard, and her arm . . . Anyway, she broke her arm."

He paused, concern renewed. "Do they need our help?"

"No. I . . . I healed it. Her. The arm."

He nodded, continued to work, separating the honey, the propolis, and the beeswax. All could be used. "How?"

Automatically, Fallon got a fresh jar for the propolis.

"I just knew. It was more than I'd done before. I've never healed a broken bone. And she was really scared and it hurt her. She was crying for her mother, so I had to calm her down first. I put her in a trance, a light one. I've never done that, Mallick, but I just knew. I didn't have to think or wonder how."

"That was wise. A child so young wouldn't calm on her own."

"I did what I knew, and what my mother taught me. How you look for injuries with your mind, your light. It was just the arm, or mostly. And it was like a snap—not jagged, but clean. I did a merge. With small injuries, you don't have to. It's just . . ."

"Surface," he said and kept working.

"Yeah, surface. But to heal a bone, it takes more. But I think it went quick because I was right there, because it was fresh, and she was so little. I think. I had to hurt her a little."

"You shared her pain?"

"It was just for a second." A second she'd never forget. "The bone knit so fast, just that second of fire and pain, and then, she was okay."

"And you?"

"I felt strange. Strong, but strange, and everything was a little blurry. And I was really thirsty. Thomas gave me water, and they took Twila home."

"You did well. You learned."

"Learned what?"

"Sometimes you think and plan and weigh. And sometimes you feel and act. And always, always, you trust what's in you. Trust what you are. You did well."

The next morning Fallon found a bounty on the doorstep. A small bag of salt, another of sugar—both precious—and a little jar of peppercorns, more precious still.

All had been arranged in a pretty woven basket and scattered with flower petals.

As she lifted it, she saw Twila and her mother. The woman gave the girl a little pat on the butt, sending her forward.

"I came to thank you."

"You're welcome."

"I made you this."

She held out a crown of flowers twined with white rosebuds and starry white daisies.

"It's really pretty." Accepting it, Fallon made the girl smile by putting it on her head.

"You look beautiful. Like a princess, but Mama says you're a queen."

"I'm not—"

"I was in your light." Twila smiled up at her, a face filled with trust. "It was so bright and warm, and nothing hurt so I wasn't scared."

Fallon crouched down. "I was in your light. It was soft and pretty, like the flowers."

Twila giggled, then wrapped her arms around Fallon in a hug before she raced back to her mother.

Because Mallick was pleased with her, he allowed her an extra hour to devote to her quest. She went alone, convinced having Mick or even Faol Ban and Taibhse with her kept the horse elusive.

Though, she had to admit, she'd gone alone before, with the same results.

She'd made progress on so much—her spell casting, her class work, her archery, and her swordplay. She mastered balancing with one hand on the pool as well as the ground.

But she'd made no progress, at all, in her hunt for Laoch.

She'd told herself, during the winter, it was just a matter of waiting until the snow melted. Then she'd find him.

In the early days of spring she told herself she'd find him as the leaves grew thick again.

But winter or spring, alone or with companions, she found no trace of him.

That day, like so many others, she set off, choosing a direction at random. She comforted herself that even if she didn't find the horse, the days grew longer, the air warmer. And the woods birthed flowers. She cut some, dug up others—not just for their magickal and medicinal uses but because having them in the house reminded her of home.

Because she could, she danced her light over some lily of the valley, thickened its spread, then had the little bells tolling. The light, pretty music lured blue and yellow butterflies.

Magick, her mother had taught her, should bring joy where it could.

And the tinkle of the flower bells, the fluttering, colorful wings brought her joy.

She heard a rustling as she smiled down. And a kind of clomp, then the blowing breath a horse would make.

For a moment, she was fooled, and her heart did a fast jump.

Then her senses tuned in, spread out. And she rolled her eyes.

"Don't be such an ass, Mick. Like I don't know the difference between a horse and some goof-off elf trying to trick me."

"Come on, that was a good one!" He somersaulted from a thicket, bounded to his feet, and grinned at her. "We were out on a hunting party—and we'll be eating like kings tonight—then I saw your tracks."

"I wasn't trying to hide them."

"Wouldn't matter. I can track anything, anyone."

"Really? You've been out with me for weeks but you haven't tracked the horse."

"That's different. Laoch doesn't leave tracks, and he's invisible most of the time."

"You're just making stuff up now."

"He's probably not even around here." Mick jumped on an outcropping of rock, sank into it to his waist. "I've heard he lives in a mountaintop meadow where it's summer all the time."

"You're not even good at making things up."

He popped out of the rock and straight up to swing on a tree branch. "It makes as much sense as a horse living in the woods like a deer or a bear."

"Mallick says he's here. Mallick doesn't lie."

"So he's here one day a year. That could be it," Mick said as he dropped back down, and they began to walk again. "Maybe only on the summer solstice. That's not too far off. Why don't you just do a spell or something?"

"Oh, why didn't I think of that?" Sarcasm dripped. "Which I did, but it's not the way. I didn't find Taibhse or Faol Ban with spells."

"You're the one who wants a bathroom so bad."

She started to snap back when realization struck. "It's not about that anymore. I guess it was never about that for Mallick. He just used it to give me the quests. And now it's not about that for me, either."

"What then? You've already got a horse. She's a nice horse."

"Grace is a great horse. This is different, this is . . ."

A slant of sunlight struck her. She stopped, turned.

"There are three spirits. And they are pure and powerful. They are one, and they are separate. They choose to give their loyalty and allegiance or withhold it. Is there faith, is there courage, is there compassion? These, too, are one and separate.

"When the three spirits join together, when the three spirits join with The One, they are a hot, flaming sword to strike the dark, a bright, shining mirror to bring the light."

Mick said nothing for a moment. "Okay. You get really weird when you talk like that."

The vision faded off but left her skin tingling. "I *feel* really weird when I talk like that, but it's true. And there's more. They're three, and it's like Mallick and his symbols. The owl's wisdom, the wolf's cunning, and the horse is heroism."

"What's that make you?"

"Someone who needs them." As she spoke, she felt. And put a hand on Mick's arm. "Slow," she warned.

She wound through the trees, and knew when Mick caught the scent as she had. The scent of horse, the scent of flowers and horse and leather.

He stood, not in a meadow on a mountaintop in perpetual summer, but in a small clearing. Flowers grew wild to cover the ground.

She'd walked over that ground countless times, and there had been no carpet of flowers. There had been no magnificent white stallion with deep green eyes, with its mane fluttering in the spring breeze.

The saddle was gold, as Mallick had told her, but not the hard, heavy metal she'd imagined. She could see—and smell—the soft, supple leather as well as the glint of the bright stirrups.

"Holy shit." Mick breathed it out. "He's really real. And he's really, really big. I never really believed he'd be that big. Like twenty hands."

The farm girl took her own measure. "Twenty-two." And likely, she thought, over three thousand pounds. "Laoch." She tried a bow. "I'm Fallon Swift. Mallick the Sorcerer gave me three quests. The first to find Taibhse, the white owl, and his golden apple. The second to find Faol Ban, the white wolf with his golden collar. And the last to find you, the magnificent Laoch and his golden saddle."

She started to step forward, and Mick grabbed her arm. "Just wait. If he charges—"

"Why would he? I'm not his enemy."

When she stepped into the meadow, Laoch swished his long tail, shifted on his great legs. And reared back, lifting his forelegs to paw the air.

Mick moved in a blur, snatching Fallon back, putting himself between her and those powerful, slashing hooves.

"Try to hurt her, just try it! And you deal with me."

The ground shook when Laoch brought his hooves down. Fallon swore the trees trembled on their roots.

And he lifted his right foreleg, favored it by leaning left.

"He's the one who's hurt. It's all right, Mick, it's all right." She shoved past him. "I can help you. Let me see what's wrong. Let me help."

"Damn it, Fallon, he'll crush you like a bug."

"No, he won't. Because he sees me, and he hears me." She looked into Laoch's eyes as she laid a hand on his leg. "And he knows me. Let me look. Let me help. You showed yourself to me so I could."

She lifted his foreleg, running her hands gently over it. "I don't feel a sprain. Ah, here we go," she murmured when she examined the hoof. "He's picked up a stone. A big one. It has to be painful every time he takes a step."

She looked up into those deep green eyes. "I can fix it. You see me," she said as she slowly took out her knife. "You know I'd never harm you."

"Fallon."

"I've got this. I need you to trust me—you, too, Mick. I need you to be very still. I can get the stone out. I want to get it out without hurting you, so you have to be still. It's bruised, so it may hurt a little. Just a little."

She took a breath, then another, then with great care worked the tip of the knife around the stone. "You've worked it in deep. I'm sorry it hurts. I've nearly got it. Stay still, stay still, just another minute."

She had to dig more than she liked, but she loosened the stone, carefully drew it out. And tossed it to Mick. "Another minute," she all but crooned as she stroked the leg, slid her knife back into its sheath to free her other hand.

She held it over the bruised hoof, that tender area, soothed it. "If you come with me, I have balm that will make it feel even better. You don't have to stay. Or I can ask Mick to run back and—"

"Fallon."

"I'll be fine. You can get there and back in no time. Mallick will know what to give you."

"Fallon," he said again, and with some impatience she looked around.

Saw Taibhse cast his shadow over the ground before he chose his branch. Watched Faol Ban step out of the shadows.

"They're together. We're together." Filled with joy, she stroked a hand up Laoch's leg. She felt the quiver, felt that strong bunching of muscle, and instinctively stepped back.

In wonder, she watched with Mick as the silver horn speared out of the great head. And when he once again reared, bugled, the silver wings that flowed out.

"Man. Jeez. Shit! He's not a horse."

"An alicorn." Fallon let out a reverent breath. "His breed is called alicorn. And he's mine. He's mine, and I'm his. As he's Taibhse's and Faol Ban's, and they are his. As we are ours."

She pointed skyward, and color flashed, spread. Joy, she thought again. And laughed as she let hers fly into dozens of rainbows.

She gripped the white mane to launch herself into the golden saddle.

"He—he doesn't have any reins," Mick stuttered.

"We don't need them. Want a ride back?"

"I think I'll walk. I'm fine down here. Nobody's going to believe me."

"Tell them to look up."

Laughing, she threw her arms up. In one smooth leap, Laoch rose, and with the owl gliding after, the wolf racing below, she rode the alicorn into her own joy.

Mallick watched her streak across the blooming sky on the white horse. A shooting star, he thought, bright and glorious.

The man responsible for the girl felt his heart drop as she dipped and rose, circled and spun. The sorcerer responsible for The One felt his soul lift.

"At least she could hold on," the man grumbled.

Instead, she flung out an arm for the owl, dived down, and landed a foot away from the charging wolf.

So they came to him. She came to him glowing like the sun.

And the beauty of it, the power of it, all but closed Mallick's throat.

"I found him! You didn't say alicorn."

"It wasn't for me. Laoch chooses whether to reveal his full nature."

"Well, he sure did. Mick might've wet his pants." Laughing still, she rubbed a hand over Laoch's neck. "He's so beautiful. But he needs some balm. He had a stone in his right front hoof. I got it out, and eased most of the bruising, but it was deep, and he needs more care."

"We'll see to him."

"I know what they are to me, what we are to each other."

"He would never have allowed you to find him otherwise."

"We need to add on to the stable, for when he wants to stay."

She tossed a leg over the horse, dropped down to the ground—a considerable drop—with a kind of careless fluidity.

"Yes."

"But not a stall. Just a shelter. He wouldn't like to be shut in. Just a lean-to and bedding and water. He needs to come and go as he pleases."

As Taibhse flew off to a nearby tree, Fallon gave the wolf a rub before she walked to Laoch's head. "I understand now. Grace is mine, but she's not built for war. But he is, and he's mine, too. I wish he could just fly or run or just be." She laid her cheek on the horse's. "That all of us could. But we can't, can we?"

"There are battles ahead. But not this day."

"Not today." She stepped back. "I'll go get the balm."

"You've said nothing about your great wish."

"I just said I wished we could just be."

"The bathroom."

She stared a moment, then laughed. "I nearly forgot all about it. That doesn't mean I don't want it. A deal's a deal. We're going to need supplies. But Laoch needs the balm. And an apple."

Mallick stood with the horse, the owl, the wolf under a sky still rioting with color. He watched the girl he would send to war run into the house.

And felt a wild pride and a sick dread.

CHAPTER THIRTEEN

On a sunny day in June, Fallon knocked Mallick on his ass.

Though her skill with a sword had improved steadily through the spring, the moment stunned them both. Mallick sat on the ground, his breath gone, his sword beside him where it slipped from his hand at the force of her blow. Fallon stood, feet planted, both hands gripping the hilt, as she'd swung back for another strike.

Her own breathing ragged, her face dewed with sweat, she slowly lowered the sword. Then lifted it again, along with her other hand, pumping them toward the pure blue of the sky while she let out hoots. And danced.

"Yes, yes, yes! *Finally!*" She jiggled her shoulders, shook her butt and, sword in hand, executed a kind of boot-stomping pirouette.

"And with your back turned toward me, your foolish dancing, I could kill you half a dozen times."

"Oh, let me have it, will you? Let me have my *victory!*" Then she stopped, swiped at the sweat on her forehead with the back of her wrist. "You didn't let me take you down? You didn't, did you?"

It shamed him to realize he wanted to claim he had. The girl, who'd come at him both fierce and wily, had wounded his pride and his arse in equal measure. But that was more foolish than her dance. True enough a girl of thirteen had bested him (this once), but he reminded himself he'd trained her.

So the victory was his as well.

"No. What would be the point of that?"

She hooted again, danced a little more, then rolled her shoulders. Set. Smirked. "Let's go again."

"When one acts cocky in battle, one loses."

"I feel cocky, and I'm going to take you down again."

He shoved to his feet, muttered, *"Nid wyf yn credu hynny."*

Grinning, she took a two-handed grip again. *"I yn gwybod."*

Mallick shoved his hair back, started to set. Then simply stopped and stared. "What did you say?"

"I said I'm taking you down, again."

"No, after that."

"You said you didn't think so—all grumpy. And I just said I know. Like, I know I will. I'm ready."

"I spoke in Welsh."

"What?"

With his sword at his side he stepped toward her. *"Ydych chi'n deall?"*

She stared a moment, let out a breath. *"Dwi'n gwneu."* I do. "How?" she demanded. "I understand the words, but I don't understand how I understand."

"An dtuigeann tú?"

"Tá." Same question, same answer, but that was Irish. How do I know that's Irish?"

"Come ti chiami?"

"I don't understand that, or what it is."

"I asked your name in Italian. That will come."

"What will come? This is crazy." Panic punched through her. How could she know what she didn't know? "I haven't studied those languages, the Welsh or the Irish. How's Irish a language anyway? How do I know it is? And now I know when you mumble *damnar air*, you're saying 'shit' in Irish. I figured you were swearing in Welsh because you said you were born in Wales."

"And I will now have to be more guarded with my cursing."

"That's not the stupid point. I don't understand how I know. Wait, wait." She squeezed her eyes shut, pressed a hand to the side of her head. "Scots Gaelic, that's in there, too."

"They have a root," Mallick told her. "The root has sprouted in you."

"How? How do I know what I don't—didn't know?"

He planted his sword, leaned on it, a man who'd waited a millennium for moments such as this.

"You are The One, Fallon Swift. It is inside you. The knowledge, the answers, even your ability to knock down your teacher. Do you think all you'll meet, all friends, all foes, will speak only English? Those you lead, those you fight, those you protect? You must understand them, and they you. Language is only thoughts put into words, after all."

He rarely touched her, but now put a hand on her shoulder. "This is another victory for you. I hadn't expected it to come this quickly. That's to your credit, not mine."

They swarmed in her head, so many words, like bees building a hive. "I can't think. It's all banging in my head."

"Quiet your mind. Knowledge is a blessing, and a power, and a weapon. For now, while the roots sprout, take the blessing. You can now curse me in several languages."

That made her smile a little, and the smile pushed back the leading edge of panic.

"Sometimes I feel I'll be ready. I'll know what to do, how to do it. And other times . . . I just want to go home."

So much, Mallick thought, for one young girl on a bright afternoon. He'd sworn to train and protect, but what were those without some tending?

"Do you hear the bees buzzing? Do you see the garden we planted flourishing? You can smell the earth, the growing things. Do you feel the air around you, warm from the sun? Listen, feel, look. Deeper."

With his hand still on her shoulder, he waved the other in the air. And they stood on the rise where her mother had stood so many years before, looking down at the farm.

Her mother, taking in the wash. Sheets that rippled in the breeze. Ethan throwing a red ball for all the dogs to chase at once. His laugh bright on the air. Travis trying to walk on his hands while Colin taunted him. The exchange of jeers so normal, so real.

And her father striding up behind her mother to grab her, spin her, kiss her. The love, as true as anything she knew, struck her heart.

The bees buzzed, the garden flourished with the scent of earth and growing things. The sun warmed the air.

"The time will pass," Mallick told her. "You won't come back as you left, but you will come back."

Her father's shirtsleeves rolled to his elbows. Ethan's big, happy laugh as the dogs leaped for the red ball. Sheets billowing at her mother's back. Travis's face pink with effort as he walked on his hands while Colin danced in circles around him.

God, God, a part of her, the deepest chamber of her heart, wanted to run, just run toward them. But the rest, what she knew in the blood, stopped her.

"How will I come back?"

"Stronger."

"Can I come like this again? Just to see them for a minute?"

"When you learn how."

"Then I'll learn how."

Now her brothers wrestled, and so did the dogs. Her mother carried the wash inside, and her father picked up the red ball, threw it so boys and dogs gave chase.

And Fallon stood back in the clearing, hearing the bees, smelling the garden, feeling the sun.

"Thank you."

"Victories should be rewarded." He stepped back from her.

"Okay. Pick up your sword, because I want another."

On the longest day, when the sun stood at its peak, Fallon cast the circle. With her sword, within the circle, she drew a pentagram, and at each of its points placed a candle. Brought them to flame.

She'd placed sunflowers and bounty from the garden, herbs fresh cut, water drawn cool and clear from the stream.

She called to the god of fire, gave thanks for his light. She thanked the goddess for the fertility she granted the earth.

Mallick watched her perform the ritual and thought of Samhain, when he'd seen her power rise.

He saw it now as she lifted her sword, as her hair, shorn short, fluttered in the air she stirred.

"His sword will flame. He is blood of my blood. My sword takes fire from the gods. I am bone of their bone. My light, his light, their light, our light will strike the dark. My life, his life, their lives, our lives join for this purpose. The sun will rise and set, rise and set. The earth will bloom and rest, bloom and rest. Magicks awakened will not sleep again. The time for sleep is past, and here I make my pledge.

"On this day, at this hour, beneath the sun, among the flowers, I am your servant, I am your child. I will face what comes to me be it tame or be it wild. You who forged my destiny light the flame inside of me, and against the dark I vow to blaze though it takes ten thousand days. I give what you ask of me. As you will, so mote it be."

She lowered the sword, stood quiet. She didn't pale as she had before. Already, Mallick thought, showing the soldier she would become.

"I can't go back now." She spoke quietly, and not at all like a child. "I've come too far, I have too much in me to go back now."

"So you made your pledge."

"I'd planned to do the ritual my mother does for Midsummer. It's really pretty. Spiritual, I guess, but it's just pretty. But then . . . I made a choice. *J'ai fait un choix.*"

His brows lifted. "French."

"*Parlo italiano anche.* I didn't before I started the ritual. I don't think. It's not banging this time, but it's a lot."

"Yes, it is. You need to close the circle. And you'll have the rest of the day free."

She wanted that, but . . . "It's a lot, but there's more than a lot left to learn. I need more practice. I need more."

"Then we'll work. Tonight you'll go to the balefire. Celebration gives balance to work and study."

"I want to go. You should come, too. You should," she pressed, sensing his excuses. "Celebration provides balance."

"Very wise."

She smiled. "I heard it somewhere."

That night after the sun set on the longest day, she danced around the balefire with elves and faeries and a pack of shifters. And the weight of work and learning and tomorrows fell away. For a night, one night, she could be just a girl at a party.

She wore the flower crown Twila had made her; she'd spell casted to preserve it. She brought honey and apple butter and bread sweetened with currants as gifts for her hosts. Because during her months with Mallick she'd gained a full inch of height, she sought out the sly young elf Jojo, who had a reputation for her skill in finding anything, and requested new pants. In trade, she offered a bracelet she'd made of braided leather.

As the smoke curled, the fire crackled, and drums beat, she sat with an elf nursing her baby. She'd been an exchange student before the Doom. Testing herself, Fallon held the conversation with Orelana in French.

"The family I stayed with was very kind. I had gone home for Christmas, and came back to America on the second of January. No one knew, not then, what had already happened. No one knew, so I left my family and came back to America. I went back to school, and you began to see, began to hear. But still, no one seemed to know. The father of the American family took ill first. While he was in the hospital, the mother became ill, and then Maggie—this is the girl of my age, the daughter. So fast, all so fast and horrible. At the hospital, so many ill, so many dying. I called my family, and my papa was already ill. I tried to get home, but I couldn't get a ticket. I went to the airport to try to get one there, and it was madness."

Smoothly, she shifted the baby to her other breast. "People sick, people desperate, people angry. Shoving, striking, shouting. Police. Soldiers with guns. I ran from there. It took hours to get back to the house, empty now, where I stayed. So many cars, coming and going, so many people in them sick. I tried to call my family again, but I could not get through. I never spoke with my mother again, or my papa, or my brother."

Fallon stared into the fire, watched the crackle of red and gold into the hot blue heart. "It was a terrible time, but it had to be more terrible for people like you, people who couldn't get to their family."

"I know my papa is gone. He was already ill. But I have hope my mother, my brother survived. Afraid, so afraid, I stayed in the empty house. Afraid, too, because I felt the change in me."

"Your elfin blood."

"Yes, it frightened me. What was I? Why was I? The family lived in what is the suburbs. Do you know this?"

"Yes. On the way here, Mallick showed me. Communities outside the towns."

Orelana nodded. "This was such. Quiet, wealthy, a lovely big house, but inside it, I was alone and afraid. Outside it, I would hear gunfire and screams, horrible laughter. And I would also see beautiful lights."

"Faeries."

"Yes." She lifted the baby to her shoulder, rubbed his back. "What was in me knew the lights were good. I took what I thought I would need. I was only nineteen, you see. A child of privilege. A young girl on her first trip to America, away from home. A good student with dreams of becoming a designer of fashion. A designer of fashion," Orelana repeated with a laugh. "I took what I could carry in the backpack, and I followed the lights."

"How did you get here?"

"Inside me was a need, not only to follow the lights, but to take this road instead of that, make this turn instead of another. For days I let the need guide me, just as it guided me to become one with a tree or the slope of a hill when something bad came near."

She looked toward Fallon with a smile as the dozing baby burped. "I learned not to fear what was in me, but to use it. Whenever I saw crows circling, I would hide. When I heard fighting, I would hide. Or run, fast as elves can, so I wouldn't be caught. But men did catch me. Soldiers."

"You were swept? I didn't know."

"They said they'd help me, take me somewhere safe." Remembering,

Orelana cuddled her baby, swayed a little to keep him lulled. "They gave me food and water. I was so tired, so afraid, so hungry. But elves hear very well, as you know, and can hear thoughts as well if they're loud enough. So I heard them talk and think about the containment centers and about laboratories and tests. Isolation camps, all these frightening words and thoughts. I was with three others in the back of a truck with heavy material on the sides so we couldn't see where we were, where we were going."

"I didn't know you'd been in a containment center."

"I never got there. One of the soldiers thought very loud, very loud to speak to me. Minh."

Fallon glanced over at the elf talking to some of the men and bouncing a sleepy toddler on his knee. She knew he was Orelana's man, and his parents had come to America from Vietnam. She hadn't known he'd been a soldier.

To lead, she thought, would take more than understanding words in any language. It would take knowing the stories of those who said the words.

"What did he say to you?"

"He thought: *This isn't help. It's prison. Be ready.*"

"What did he do?"

"First, I should tell you he was a good soldier, wanted to serve his country. But he'd hidden his true nature from the others he served with. He knew, because he'd seen the camps and centers, what would happen to him. What was happening to others. There were others who served who did the same, and they had found each other. Some of them."

She paused to shift the baby, free a hand so she could pick up a cup and drink.

"*Be ready*, he thought to me, and not long after, the truck stopped. It stopped because one of the resistance, a witch, made it stop. They made an explosion, not on the truck, but close. And another.

"In the confusion, Minh came around, elf quick, he took the little boy—a shifter, no more than three—and told the woman who cared for him, who had become his mother to go, go. I took the hand of a girl, an immune, pulled her out. We ran into the trees where more were waiting to help us. And we escaped.

"Minh led strikes against one of the camps, one of the centers. With Thomas and others. They freed some, and some were lost on all sides. We came here to make our lives. You know the boy there, Gregory?"

Fallon looked toward a group of teenage boys pretending to be bored. "Sure. Wolf shifter."

"He was the little boy with me in the truck. Darla, though she is not Uncanny, lives with the pack. She is his mother, after all. The little girl, the immune? She's a soldier with the resistance. She sends word to me, to Minh, now and then."

"It's a good story. A strong story."

"It's important never to forget who and why we are." She set aside her cup, let out a contented sigh. "I haven't spoken in the language of my birth for so long a time in years. You've given me a gift."

"It's my first conversation in French, so a gift for me, too. I'm glad Minh was there for you. Glad he was a soldier and wanted to serve. And glad he understood how to serve, was brave enough to do what's right."

"I felt grateful to him that day. I admired his courage over the weeks and weeks that followed, his ability to help lead, to provide. But I fell in love with him on a spring night just here, just here where we sit now when I came upon him singing to a little girl who'd had a bad dream."

Fallon knew the light in Orelana's eyes when she looked at Minh. She'd seen it in her own mother's toward her father.

"Here is a man who would fight, I thought, who would choose what's right and risk himself for it. A man who would provide. And one who would soothe a child with a song.

"I thought too loud," she said with a laugh. "I hadn't learned how to quiet my thoughts, to protect them. So he heard me. So he heard me, and he looked at me, and because he was brave, let me hear his." She sighed. "Litha is a time for love and lovers. One day you'll look, and you'll know."

She gave Fallon a pat on the knee. "But now, I need to put the baby to bed."

Fallon sat studying the fire. She wasn't sure there would ever be a time for her for love or lovers. Wasn't sure she had inside her what would put that light in her eyes.

She'd made a vow. Balance, she mused, yes. A dance around the balefire on the solstice, good food, and friendships. Her first conversation in French. But to balance *that*, she'd learned Minh was a soldier, part of the resistance. Someone who knew, if she needed to know, where camps and centers had been.

Might still be.

Even now she could see Mallick enjoying wine. But while he did, he huddled with Minh, who'd passed the little girl to her older brother, and Thomas, some of the elders.

She doubted they spoke of love and lovers.

Battles, raids, supplies, strategies, security.

She didn't need elf ears to know what those charged with leadership spoke of.

She'd made a vow, accepted her duties. One day they would look to her for those plans, those answers. She needed to be ready. Propping her chin on her fist, she looked into the fire, the blue hearts of flame, the snap of red heat, and wondered if she'd see her future.

When she did, she pushed to her feet and walked away from the music, the voices, the dancing.

"Hey!" Mick caught up with her. He had a goofiness in his eyes that made her sure he'd managed to sneak at least a couple sips of the faerie wine. "Where're you going?"

"Home. It's late."

"It's Midsummer." He raced up a tree trunk, flipped. When he nearly fell on the landing, she thought he'd sneaked more than a couple sips. "Some of us are going to the glade, going for a swim. Come on." He snatched her hand.

"No, I can't. I have to get started early tomorrow."

"That's tomorrow. Tonight's tonight." He gave her a tug, trying to draw her back to the party.

"Mick, I'm tired." In the mind, in the heart. To the bone. "I'm going home."

"You'll feel better after a swim." He turned to her in the leaf-filtered moonlight. "It's Midsummer night. It's magick. Everything's magick tonight."

She heard his thoughts. They gave her a jolt, a warning, but she didn't evade in time. Maybe, just maybe, part of her wondered. Even wanted.

So on the warm Midsummer night, under the leaf-filtered moonlight, she let him kiss her. It had a sweetness, maybe the faerie wine, maybe the moment. How could she know? It was her first kiss. It felt . . . comforting, even as it lightly stirred something she didn't recognize.

Sweet, she thought, analyzing even as she experienced. And soft. For another moment, she let it linger, wishing for the sweet and the soft.

But then she drew away. Not so much a goofiness in his eyes now, she noted. She saw wishes there, too.

"You're so pretty," he murmured, reaching for her again.

"I can't." Something else stirred in her, and this time she recognized it as regret. "I'm sorry."

"I like being with you. I like you."

"I like you, too. But I'm not . . . I'm sorry," she said again, uselessly.

"Fine. Fine. Whatever." Rejection flushed across his face. "I just figured you might want to have some actual fun. Be normal for a night. But I guess you just want to go off and wallow in your Oneness."

"That's not fair." And it stung like a wasp. "That's really not fair."

"It's what you're doing. What you always do. Because you think you're so important. You think you're better than everybody else."

On the next sting, deep and sharp, she lashed back. "I know I'm better than you. Right now, I know I'm a lot better than you."

She shoved him back and, tears burning bitter in her eyes, strode away.

"You kissed me back!" he called out.

"It won't happen again." She cast her tear-blurred eyes to the sky. "That's another vow."

She marched into the clearing. The candles lit through the day glimmered, and were charmed to flame till dawn. She wanted to snuff them out, just sweep a hand out and shut off their light, cocoon herself in the dark.

Because she knew she wasn't made for the soft and the sweet, but for battle and blood. The battles and blood she'd seen in the hot blue heart of the balefire. The battle raging around her while she rode Laoch through the clashing swords, the rain of arrows, the red spit of lightning. The blood on her face, on her sword still warm from those she'd killed.

And in the ash, in the dirty ash of the fire, she'd seen the rise of crows, heard them scream as they circled over the dead and dying.

She'd looked into the Midsummer balefire, and the pipes and drums of the feasting turned to beats of war. She'd looked, seen her future.

She went into the empty cottage and, for the first time in months, locked herself in her room. Curled on her bed, she cried herself dry.

Before dawn broke, she—a girl still shy of her fourteenth birthday—made her third vow of the night.

That those would be the last tears she shed over what was to come.

She didn't see a sign of Mick for a week, which was fine with her. Determined, she pushed Mallick to teach her more, give her more, test her more. By week's end she could make those demands in Spanish and Portuguese.

He knew something troubled her, but when he tried—perhaps clumsily, he admitted—to learn the trouble, she'd snapped shut. A locked box.

He could also admit her sudden, insatiable hunger for knowledge and skill exhausted him. So when she rode out on Grace or Laoch, he sighed with relief. And took a nap.

Because in the evenings, she peppered him with questions about battles he'd fought, battles he knew. Tugging, pulling, digging for every detail, debating until his mind blurred on why a battle was lost or won.

He knew she did the same with Minh, Thomas, the faerie warrior Yasmin. Not just of battles, but locations. Camps and settlements, numbers, containment facilities, internment camps.

He suspected she'd had an argument with Mick, as he hadn't seen the boy around the cottage, and a casual query about him had a heated Fallon snapping back with: *Why should I know?*

But Mick came around again, and Fallon's initial coolness toward him appeared to wear off. Though she rarely ran the woods with him as she had now that she spent more time with Mallick himself, or the elders from the clans and packs.

As summer slid away, he no longer held back during sword practice. And still she bested him nearly half the time.

She grew taller, her muscles sharper, leaner. She laughed rarely, and he found he missed the sound of it. And regretted, as they came to the close of their first year together, seeing the cool-eyed warrior consume the girl.

On her birthday, knowing his own lack of skill, he asked one of the elves who baked for a spice cake. He gifted Fallon with a wand he'd created himself from a branch of a rowan tree found on a long-ago journey to the Himalayas. He'd tipped it with a crystal of pure, clear quartz, carved into it symbols of power, then used three strikes of lightning to strengthen, imbue, and consecrate.

He'd made it for her a century before her birth.

"Mallick, it's beautiful." She lifted it, turned it in her hand to test it. "And strong. Thank you."

"It will serve you. You can practice with it by creating a cloaking spell. When we return."

"Return? Where are we going?"

"As it's the anniversary of your birth, I will take you to the rise over your farm so you can see your family."

Her face shuttered. "There's no need. They're safe, that's what matters. If you'd take me somewhere for my birthday?"

She rose, got one of the maps, spread it out. "Take me here."

Frowning, Mallick looked where she'd slapped her finger. "Cape Hatteras. This is North Carolina. Why?"

"Hatteras Village on the cape, specifically. Maybe I want to see the ocean. I never have. Maybe I want to walk on the beach."

"But this isn't why." Disappointed, he stared into her eyes. "You don't give me truth."

"It's not a lie." She shrugged. "I'd like to see the ocean and walk on the beach because I've never done either. But I want to go because this is one of the containment centers Minh knows of. It was, anyway. I want to see if it still is, see what the setup is, the security, the numbers."

He could refuse her. But he couldn't think of a reason to do so—and he knew that before long she wouldn't need him to astral project.

"Very well."

"Now?"

He put a hand on her shoulder. "Now."

CHAPTER FOURTEEN

S he stood on a beach—golden sand—and saw the ocean.

Vast, powerful, its greens melted into blues, waves rose, fell, spewing white froth like liquid lace. The sun, glorious in a cloudless bowl of sky, rained down on it to drop dancing points of light.

It took her breath.

She'd seen it in pictures, in books, on DVDs, but the reality of it swept all that aside. The sheer wonder of it blew through her. The sound of it, its booming, booming heartbeat, that throaty roar of constant movement, echoed inside her.

Overhead, seabirds winged and rode the current of air over water and sand.

She drew in its scent—one she'd never experienced—and let the sheer *life* of it wash over her in the quick wind that whipped at her shirt.

Unable to resist, she stepped forward. Water lapped over her boots as she crouched down to dip her fingers into the Atlantic. "Cool."

Then touched a finger to her tongue. "Salty. We could find ways to extract salt."

Even as her mind worked that problem, she picked up a little white shell. Then two more. She thought of Colin, and how he'd enjoy them for his treasure box.

Standing, she slipped them into her pocket. As she did, she caught the flash, a shimmer, a splash.

"A fish that big would feed the camps and packs altogether."

"Mermaid," Mallick corrected, "not fish."

"Mermaid."

"Or Merman. I didn't see the whole of it."

"You hear stories," Fallon said. "They live in the oceans?"

"And seas, bays, inlets, even rivers."

"Do they have warriors?"

"Fierce ones."

She nodded, filed it away, and turned.

She saw what had been houses above the beach, built on stilts. Time, wind, storms had taken roofs, windows. Porches hung drunkenly from buildings.

"They would have evacuated anyone who lived here, or taken them. They'd have taken the dead for burning or burial. But they'd have used the buildings, maintained them. For their own housing, storage, operations. But they're gone to ruin."

She walked up toward them as she spoke, found it a different matter to walk on sand. It pulled at her feet—a sensation that both amused and unnerved her.

"They chose this location, Minh had said, as they could control the single road leading in, and one that ends at the water. Ocean on one side, the sound on the other," she continued, using her hands to indicate direction, "and one road through a narrow line of land. They could control it, and it makes an isolated place for a prison. If someone escaped, where would they go? But they couldn't control the weather. Hurricanes, storms, and the erosion from them. Those who manned the prison would be as cut off in those storms as those they guarded."

He hadn't known of the place, Mallick thought. But she knew, because she'd asked, peppered others with questions, dug for details like a girl with a shovel.

"Was Minh here?"

"Once, he said, in the first weeks, when he still believed they protected, defended. He believed they brought people here to quarantine them until the cure came. But he learned that was a lie. Dunes," she said absently. "Sea oats? And those flowers, so many. Do you know them?"

"Blanketflowers."

She repeated it as they topped the dunes.

"There." She pointed, walked on. "The containment center. The prison."

Made of concrete and steel, it stood windowless across the sand-covered road. Guard towers reared up on all corners and sides, and she saw in one of them, at least one of them, some sort of weapon. One, she imagined, that would have spewed bullets with a terrible thunder. It, too, stood above the ground, built on steel pilings.

The large nest of some seabird made its home in another guard tower. A good post, she thought, with a fine vantage point, for bird or man.

Two stories of forbidding, cheerless gray, and she saw now the second level had some windows, steel-shuttered.

Around it rose a high fence, with signs that warned of fatal electric charges slapping, metal to metal. The gate, wide enough for one of the large trucks she saw inside, held tight, secured with chains.

"They abandoned it. The sand's over the wheel beds of the trucks, and there's rust from the water and the salt. There are places on the road I can feel underfoot that are impassable with the sand, and north, there? It's fallen in. Flooding maybe. They left it. Take me inside."

Recognizing the snap of impatience in her voice, she turned. "I'm sorry. I want to thank you for bringing me, and ask you to take me inside the building. I want to see inside."

"They're gone, Fallon, as you said. There's no life here any longer."

"I need to see."

He nodded. "Open the gate. You have the power. Consider," he added, as she took a step closer. "How you would approach the gate if there was life inside. If the enemy was inside."

She set aside the urge to simply fling out power, blast them open. Chains and locks, she mused, simple enough. But if the enemy was inside, she'd need something more subtle to bypass surveillance and security, the electronic locks, than a blast.

Then again, she'd learned strategies and tactics at her father's knee, and magicks at her mother's.

"First, I'd bespell the surveillance cameras. No point in letting the enemy know we're coming. No one manning them now, no power running them, but I'd . . . By the power alight in me, see only what I deem you see. To all of flesh and blood you're blind until this spell I do unwind.

"If I jammed it, the enemy would send someone to check. The chains and basic lock." She held her hands out, broke the links. "The electronics."

Now she walked closer, examined the gates. "If this was a real deal, we'd come at night. There would be sentries in the towers. Quickest solution: archers, simultaneous. If it's possible to limit casualties, simultaneous sleeping spells, but that's trickier. Then the gate—no, then the gate alarm."

"Good," he murmured.

"A technician could bypass or cut, but again, the quickest way."

She held out a fist, shot her fingers open. "It's already dead—no power—but that would do it. Then the gate."

She fisted both hands now, held them together, knuckles whitening. Slowly she drew them apart. The gate shuddered, opened a fraction, a fraction more.

She sucked in a breath. "Buried in the sand, heavy, resistant." Muscles trembled, sweat pearled on her forehead, but the gate opened a little more.

Frustration rippled through her, punched it. "Open, damn it!"

The gate ripped open, metal crashing, sand heaving.

"I guess that could've been quieter."

"Considerably. Next time you'd flow away the sand."

Recognizing her mistake, she puffed out her cheeks, blew out the air. "That would've been an idea. Anyway." She walked through the gate, across more sand, a kind of dry beach where trucks and equipment floated.

She studied the wide steel door. "Here, I would blast. Go in fast. I'd hope we had some inside intel, have a sense of the layout inside, but fast. There must be another door, maybe more. Back, sides. Same deal there. Go in fast, all directions. They'd be armed, so you have to neutralize—that's my dad's word—as many as possible as fast as possible, and shield the prisoners, get them out. That's the mission. Get as many people being held out and to safety as possible."

She looked at Mallick. "Can I blast it now?"

"Yes."

She wiggled her shoulders, rubbed her hands together. "Here's some birthday fun."

It came in a lightning force, hot and potent. And felt damn good. Stress she hadn't known she'd carried released in a single, brutal punch.

The steel doors blew open.

"Boom, boom!" A little giddy, she stepped in.

Without power, the building held dark, but the sunlight poured in through the doors. And the first body—the bones inside a scorched and tattered uniform—lay only a few feet from the entrance.

"Oh God. Oh God."

"Lights." Mallick gripped her hand. "With me. Lights."

She shuddered through it, joined her power with his to create a pale green glow.

In it she saw another door behind the remains, one of bars inside thick glass. Through it a security center, a guard station. And more, many more dead.

Skeletal remains slumped in chairs behind blank monitors. They spread on the concrete floor blackened by some ungodly fire.

Mallick released her hand, opened the barred door himself. He stepped through, turned to her when she didn't follow him.

Pale in the charmed light, he noted, with her eyes dark and shocked. Not just by the dead, not only, he knew, as he, too, could still scent the stink of dark magicks trapped inside for years.

He nearly took her hand again, took it to take her home again, away from the dead and the dark. But that was the weakness of his love for the child, not the duty of the chosen to the Savior.

"This you must face. War—and it was, is, and will be war—brings death. Death by man or magicks. In war you will cause death, by your sword, by your power, by your orders. To be just, to be wise, to be strong enough to bring death, you must face it, see its costs."

She trembled, but went through the door.

More doors, she thought. Dozens and dozens of steel doors lining the concrete walls. An open stairway leading to the second level and still more doors.

She made herself walk to one, though it felt more like swimming than walking. She opened the viewing slot, looked through the reinforced glass. No more than eight feet wide and deep, the windowless cell held a toilet bolted to the floor and a narrow bunk with the bones of whoever had curled tight on it.

Anger rose through shock, and she blew open the door, then another, another, so the crashing of metal to stone boomed and echoed. Some of the dead had been restrained to the bunks. Some had been children. All had been alone.

Rage shoved through anger and, on a furious cry, she threw out hands and power. More doors crashed open, some strongly enough to crack the steel.

"They're still trapped here. I can feel them." Her voice tore with outrage. "Can you feel them?"

"Yes. I can feel them."

She yanked the dog tags from a body on the floor, gripped them tight in her hand. "Show me," she commanded, shutting her eyes. "Show me."

She saw him, as he'd been.

"Sergeant Roland James Hardgrove, U.S. Army, attached to Operation Roundup. Commanding Officer Colonel David Charles Pickett. Age thirty-six. Married, two children."

Gripping the dog tags, she pushed.

"He would tell them they were taking them to safety. If met with resistance, the use of force, deadly force when warranted. Those were orders. A soldier follows orders. His team brought in the last group. Two men, three women, two minors. The boy, about eight, reminded him of his son, but he had orders. He'd completed the transfer, the paperwork, and was heading to the mess hall when he died.

"Orders. He followed orders."

She dropped the dog tags, walked to one of the scorched walls, laid her hands on it.

"Others will follow mine. I have to face death to order it, to send others to meet it, cause it. Then let me see. Let me see what turned light and life to death and dark."

"Fallon, you're not ready to—"

She snapped her head around. Her eyes, nearly black with power and fury, blazed. "On powers within, on powers without, I call. Show me now and show me all. If my duty brushes the dark, then the curtain I will part. And I will hear and feel and see. As I will, so mote it be."

Too much, Mallick thought, too much. But the die was cast.

Her body jerked, her head fell back, and her eyes went dark and blind with visions.

Voices screamed in her head, weeping, wailing, begging.

"Too many, too many. I can't hear. Oh God, so many."

Night. Though none in the cells knew day from night. They herded them in, already drugged with the food and water given out on the journey. So they shuffled, compliant, offered little resistance when they were examined, stripped, cataloged, given prison orange to wear. Most slept when led to their cells.

Some dreamed and cried out in sleep. Some pushed against the drugs pumped into them, day after day. And some, fighting, were restrained until another drug was pumped into them.

By category of MUNA—Manifestation of Unnatural Abilities—and date of containment, detainees were taken to the center's lab for testing.

Pushing herself, pushing her limits, Fallon merged her mind with the spirit of a girl, strapped to a table in a harshly lit room. Janis, a high school senior when the Doom struck. A cheerleader struggling with her chemistry grade.

He drew her blood, the blank-faced man in the white coat and white cap. He hooked her up to a machine, sticking little cold circles on her bare chest.

They'd taken her clothes, and it mortified her to lie naked under the lights, under his eyes and hands.

"Please. I want my mom. Where's my mom?"

They'd run together because her father died. Run because Janis grew wings, and her mom was afraid. Going to Grandma's house. They were just going to Grandma's, but Grandma wasn't there. They kept running.

And the soldiers came.

"Please," she said again, but the man who put needles into her, put the cold disks on her, said nothing.

She tried to turn her head, found she couldn't move. Had she been in an accident? Was she paralyzed? "Please," she said again. "Help me."

Then, she realized the words didn't make a sound. The words were only in her head, because she couldn't speak.

Couldn't speak, couldn't move. But she could see, she could feel. And when a tear slid down her cheek, the man dabbed the tear with a cotton stick, put the stick in a little jar. Labeled it.

"Brody, stimulant, on two."

A woman moved into her view, went to a machine, touched a dial.

Janis felt the quick electric shock through her body.

At the monitor, the woman rattled off numbers. Heart rate, blood pressure, respiration.

"Up to four," the man ordered.

Now the shock slapped, and she cried out in her head. Her wings flowed out with her instinct to flee, to fly away.

"Manifestation at level four. Let's clamp these down."

They hurt her, hurt her, hurt her wings.

Something inside her, through the drugs, remembered they'd hurt her before. Remembered her mother wasn't there. They'd taken her mother somewhere else.

The pain flooded her, as it had before, when he used the scalpel to slice off a piece of her wing. More tears fell, and this time the woman collected them.

"As before the wing section loses its luminescence when excised."

The man sealed the bloody bit of wing in a bag. Sealed it, labeled it. "We need hair with root, Brody. Ten samples from the head, ten from the pubis. Another urine sample. All samples sent to CUS by special courier."

"All?"

"This time. It has more when we need it."

He didn't smile, but something like satisfaction came over his face. With all her heart, Janis cursed him. Not for the pain, not anymore, but for that single look of satisfaction.

Then the fire washed in, black and brutal.

"No," Fallon murmured. "No, no, not from her. But from where, from what, from who? Show me."

Soldiers manned their posts. Three off duty ate in the mess hall— bean soup, mashed potatoes made from dehydrated flakes, hard rolls with their ration of margarine. Two more caught a smoke outside. Cigarettes went for five dollars each on the underground, but the army provided.

One swabbed out the cell of the detainee currently in the lab. The CO demanded every inch of the center be squared away, 24/7. With no other detainees scheduled for testing until morning, Private Coons planned to catch a little downtime with a DVD before he hit the bunk.

The CO sat in his office on level two, diligently reading reports. He had a picture of his family—wife, daughter, son, their spouses, his two grandchildren—on his desk.

His bitterness at their deaths by the virus burned continually inside him. His belief that those in cells below held responsibility was absolute.

In one of those cells a witch had gone mad. Abraham Burnbaum had once been a prominent neurologist, a prosperous man devoted to his work and his family. A man who gave back, used all his skill to save lives. Who'd enjoyed golf and sailing. Like the CO, he'd watched his family die, and none of his knowledge, his skills, his connections in the medical community had saved them.

Only he and the grandson named for him had survived. Little Abe with his quick, gurgling laugh, his passion for dinosaurs and absolute loyalty to Iron Man had survived and, like his grandfather, had begun to show abilities that the scientist in Burnbaum would have deemed nonsense.

For more than a year he'd kept the boy safe. Even when they'd had to leave the house in Alexandria, as the fighting came too close, he'd kept his boy safe. He'd made it an adventure. Hiking, hiding, fishing, making camp in the woods, or in a house already abandoned.

South, he'd taken the boy south. Warmer climates, longer growing season.

Then he'd made a mistake. He'd grown tired, careless, or just naive. He'd thought he could make a home for the boy in the little ramshackle house just over the North Carolina border. For a time he had, tucked away from the road.

But they'd come, the soldiers, sweeping in so fast he'd known escape wasn't possible. He could fight—he had a gun, he had the strange powers in him. But he feared for the boy.

"Abe." He'd pulled the boy into the kitchen. "Quick now. Into the hiding place."

"But, Granddad."

"Remember what we said." Abraham pulled up the door to the root cellar. "Remember what you promised."

"I don't want to—"

"You promised. Go down, and don't make a sound. No matter what. Don't come out, no matter what, until I come get you. Or until you know they're gone. And when you know they're gone, what do you do?"

"I stay quiet and I count to a hundred ten times."

"You don't start counting until you don't hear a sound." He nudged the boy down the ladder. "Hurry. Not a sound. I love you, kiddo."

"I love you, Granddad."

He shut the door, and as he'd practiced and practiced, he concealed the door. The handle melted from sight, not a seam showed.

They didn't knock or call for him to come out. They broke in, front and back doors, armed. Even as he started to put his hands up, one fired at him. Not a bullet, though it gave him pain. He staggered under the tranquilizer.

He heard their boots storming through the house, heard orders shouted to find the kid.

He came to, his mind muddled, in a small room. Restrained to a bunk, he struggled to think through the drug.

Little Abe. Had they found his little boy?

They could do whatever they wanted with him as long as Abe stayed safe.

They tortured him, using a paralytic while they ran their hideous tests. Sometimes he heard screaming, but it never lasted long. No one spoke to him except to interrogate, and after a few days, not even then.

He comforted himself he'd kept Abe safe. Let himself dream of that wonderful laugh, those mischievous eyes.

But then, the days, the weeks, the months of solitary captivity, the drugs, the brutal tests smothered all hope.

Was that Abe he heard screaming? Calling to him for help?

He screamed, and when they came in, he tried to fight, tried to find the magick through the drug. He sparked a fire, enough to singe one of his captors, enough to earn a beating until someone else snapped out an order.

They strapped him to the bunk again, poured more drugs into him, ran more tests.

They drove him mad and the madness drove him into the dark.

And the dark was sly.

He gave himself a seizure, just a small one, just enough to have them cut back the dose of the drugs. He showed them only compliance, even when they took him to the showers, hosed him down. Even when they tortured him.

All the while he gathered the dark around him, offered what he was to it, and heard its chortling laugh inside his head.

They would burn, all burn. Black fire, black crows circling, black smoke rising to blot out the sun.

He called on the dark, gave it words in his head he hadn't known. Saw it smile at him, heard its promises.

They would burn, all burn, and he would rise from the flames. Triumphant.

So when an agonized faerie cursed her tormentor, Abraham loosed all his hate, his rage, his madness, poured it out of himself in black flame. And they burned, all burned.

But the dark is sly as madness is, and swept him down with the rest.

Shaking, sweating, Fallon slid down the wall. "I saw. I saw. I'm sick. I'm going to be sick."

"Hush now." Mallick gathered her up. "Sleep now."

He took her under, took her away.

After he laid her on her bed, he lit white candles, set white sage to smoking, bathed her face. When she stirred, he urged a potion on her to ease the sickness and shock.

"I saw . . ." Could still see. Would always see. "I have to tell you."

"You did. You told me while you saw, while you heard, while you felt. You told me all of it. You need to rest. You pushed further than you should have. You weren't ready for so much."

"If I wasn't ready, I couldn't have done it."

"If you'd been fully ready, you wouldn't have gotten sick. That should settle now, and I'll make tea that will soothe the rest."

But she grabbed his hand. "He was a good man, Mallick. He was a good man. A doctor, a healer. He sacrificed himself to save his grandson. Then they wouldn't even tell him if they'd found the little boy, if the kid was okay. They wouldn't tell him. Like they wouldn't tell the girl—Janis—where her mother was. Why would they be that cruel?"

"To break the spirit. A broken spirit is more debilitating than a broken body."

"They broke his mind instead, and that's dangerous. They broke his mind, so he opened to the dark, and the dark heard him. Something dark heard him and . . ."

"Exploited him."

"Yeah, exploited. And lied to him, because he's as dead as the rest. Janis never hurt anyone, but I think when she cursed the lab guy, the one who hurt her, it gave whatever worked in Abraham more, even more. I think—there were so many voices I couldn't hear at first, so I had to push them back. But I think so many had broken, so many wanted to hit back, somehow, it all rose up, and when Abraham lit the fuse, it blew."

"It's possible. Very possible. Just as it's possible, with so many contained, there was already dark among the light. And that added more as well."

"Yeah, you're right." She closed her eyes a moment. "They had a hundred and forty-six people locked up. They had room for one-fifty. Some just died, others they sent somewhere else. But that night a hundred and forty-six. It was ten years ago. It happened ten years ago, March fourteenth, at nineteen hundred hours, twenty-seven minutes.

"We have to go back." She tightened her grip when he shook his head. "We have to tend to the dead. All of them, and we have to purify the ground."

"Yes, the dead should be tended, and their spirits released. A place of cruelty can be destroyed and the ground purified."

It made him proud she would think of it, she would know the importance of it.

"But not this day," he told her. "Tomorrow. They've waited this long. I'll speak to Minh, as he will want to go. Some of the others will."

"Tomorrow," she agreed. "But we won't destroy the building. It's well built and its location's good. We may need it one day."

He went to make her tea because she was weaker than she understood. The next time she wouldn't be, he thought. Already she'd shown a cooler head than he. What he'd seen and heard through her? He wanted to destroy all that stood on that spot.

But the warrior, the leader of warriors understood a war meant death. It also meant prisons.

"She'll never be a child again," he told himself as he added honey to the tea to mask the faint bitterness of the restorative. "Not after this day."

The day of her birth, he thought. Often the light could be just as sly and cruel as the dark.

He heard her moving about, though he wished she'd stay down for an hour more. Then he heard the shower. It banged a bit, the pipes, but it served. And she'd earned it.

He imagined she wanted to wash away the stink of the prison, the smear of death. And realized he wanted to do exactly the same.

He went out to walk to the stream. Once they were clean again, he'd take out the spice cake he'd had baked for her. Hope it pleased her.

Balance, he thought as he stripped. Some cake and tea, a quiet evening with no tasks for her.

A small way to balance out the ugliness of the day, and the sad duty they'd face on the morrow.

CHAPTER FIFTEEN

Winter followed fall and brought with it brutal cold, howling winds, and relentless snow. Despite it, Mallick pushed physical training. Battles, he told Fallon, didn't wait for balmy spring.

She learned to fight with a sword in one hand, a knife in the other. And when Mallick tripled himself in an illusion, how to fight multiple foes.

She died often, but she learned.

She rode Grace for pleasure, and Laoch for the thrill and the practice, as rider and mount must be one in battle.

Armed with a sword and a small shield she fought Mallick on horseback. Snow blew in sheets while the throaty wind whirled it, and again and again charmed steel rang against charmed steel.

The seasoned Gwydion charged, reared, pivoted with a fearlessness Fallon admired and respected. Laoch exceeded even that skill, Fallon knew, just as she knew her mount's disadvantage was his rider.

She'd get better.

Swords clashed, their ringing muffled in the curtain of snow. All the hours she'd wielded the sword, all the buckets of water she'd lifted, carried, had given her a sinewy strength. Despite the cold, exertion warmed her muscles. And with an eye and skill she hadn't possessed only a few months before, she slipped past Mallick's guard, struck his heart.

He only nodded. "Again," he said, this time conjuring the illusion of a battle raging around them. Warriors on horseback, on foot, arrows winging, fireballs blasting.

Gwydion charged, Mallick's sword flashed. But she was ready. She blocked him with the shield, and hammered at him while Laoch drove Gwydion back.

Despite the war cries, the screams of the dying, she heard Mallick's laboring breaths. And with her honed young strength struck blow after blow. Then swept out with her shield, striking to send him tumbling from his horse.

He landed in the trodden snow with a *thud*.

Grinning, she leaned forward against Laoch. "You gonna call 'uncle' this time? That's the third time in an hour I've—"

Her grin faded as he only lay, eyes closed.

"Oh shit!"

She leaped off her horse, dived to him. As she started to glide her hands over him, he opened his eyes, waved her off.

"Only winded."

"I'm sorry. I'm sorry. Are you sure you're not hurt? Let me see."

"I know if I'm hurt or not, and I'm not." He levered up to sitting. "You unhorsed me, but with your attack so focused on only one opponent, a half dozen could have struck from your flanks."

"No. Laoch would tell me."

Mallick's gaze shifted to the horse, who stood at his ease now. "Is that so?"

"Yeah. And I can sense—not everyone, not every time—but I can sense if one of your ghosts comes at me. Between us, we know. You can't always know. And you have to take out the primary foe. You taught me that. Take out the primary, take out the next."

He only grunted, but she heard approval in the sound. And fatigue.

"We should rub down the horses. They've been out in this over an hour," she said.

"They're strong, healthy creatures. And so am I. We'll go again."

But as he got up and started to remount, they heard the shouts.

Mick ran toward them, skimming over the snow at a speed that barely left a trace. His hair, coated with snow, flew behind him.

"You have to come!" he shouted. "You need to come."

Instantly, Fallon gripped the hilt of her sword. "What is it? An attack."

"No, no. Sick. People are sick. My dad—you have to come."

"Slower." Mallick stepped forward, put his hands on Mick's shoulders. "What sickness? How many?"

"A lot. It's fever and chills, and my father can't get his breath. Coughing. The teas and potions aren't working. You have to come."

"You don't look so good, either," Fallon pointed out.

"I'm okay. I'm—" Then he contradicted the claim by falling into a hacking, coughing fit. "My dad—"

"Come inside."

"No, I have to—"

"Inside," Mallick repeated. "We need medicines. You're feverish. Fallon, brew tea. Yarrow—"

"Yarrow, elderberry, peppermint. I know. Don't waste time," she told Mick, pulling him toward the cottage, signaling the horses to follow.

"Sit by the fire," she ordered Mick, setting it to blazing.

Ginger, she thought, thyme and honey. For the coughs. Licorice, echinacea, she added as she gathered the fever herbs.

She flashed a mug of water to boiling, added the herbs to steep. "Do you have enough blankets?"

"I think so." Shivering a little, he shot her a look of desperation. "We need to hurry."

"What about the shifters, the faeries?"

"The faeries have been trying to help, some of them are sick, too. The pack's good. At least they were."

"Drink this. I have to get more supplies. We have medicines in the workshop. Mallick's getting what we need, and I can get more from here and the greenhouse. We'll go as soon as we have what we need."

"Some of the elders are afraid it's like the Doom. They remember the Doom. They're afraid."

"It's not the Doom." Putting a hand on his forehead, she looked. "It's a virus, but it's pneumonia. You have it in one lung."

"What is that? What's 'pneumonia'?"

"It's not the Doom," she said briskly. "Drink that. I'll be back."

She raced up to the workshop. "Pneumonia," she said as Mallick filled two packs. "Viral."

He nodded. "Go to the greenhouse and gather—"

"I know what to get."

She dashed off. Her mother had helped heal three people with pneumonia in the village at home, and she'd watched. And Mallick had gone over this specific illness in her healing studies.

She filled another pack, ran back to the cottage just as Mallick came down the steps.

"We'll make more of what's needed at the elf camp. Take Mick on Laoch with you."

Once she'd mounted, she held out a hand for Mick. His hand, clammy and ungloved, shook in hers. "You need to hold on to me. We're going fast."

"I can hold on. Go. Go."

Snow flew as Laoch charged through it. When she felt Mick's grip around her waist held tight enough, she took Laoch up so he flew just above the snow, gaining speed as they weaved through trees. Mallick would fall behind, she knew, but she could begin to brew the teas.

The moment she crossed into the camp, Mick jumped off. Though he stumbled, staggered, he pushed himself to the hut he shared with his father.

"Anyone who's well," Fallon called out. "We need to brew teas."

Orelana, pale with exhaustion, added wood to a fire. "The teas haven't helped. We thought they were, they would, or we'd have sent for you sooner. It came on so quickly."

"These teas will have more, do more. We need to make poultices, and steam pots."

Around the central fire, she instructed Orelana and three others how to brew and mix, barely glancing around when Mallick rode in.

"The one who is most ill," Mallick demanded.

"My youngest. My youngest and Old Ned," Orelana called out, pointing to a hut. "Ned's granddaughter's caring for him. She's not ill. Minh is with the baby."

Mallick handed Fallon one of the packs. "You know what to do. I'll begin with Ned."

She took one of the pots, shouldered the pack, and then a second of her own. "Stay and help make more, Orelana. I know your hut."

"He's just a baby. He seemed better, then this morning . . . He's just a baby."

"Help make more."

Fallon hurried off. She could feel the sickness, feel the fevers raging so hot and high she thought it a wonder they didn't melt the snow.

She went into the hut where Minh sat on the edge of a cot, bathing the baby's face with a cloth. "He won't nurse. He's not a year old. He's only ten months old."

She knelt, ran her hands over the baby. Both lungs held fluid, and the fever spiked high. The eyes, glazed with fever, stared at nothing. Like a doll's.

"He needs to drink this tea, and this potion."

"He's not weaned. He—"

"But you'll help me," she said calmly, taking a dropper from her kit. "He's little, and he won't have to take much, but as much of the tea as you can manage. That first, Minh."

While Minh gave the tea to the baby, drop by drop, Fallon took a small pot from the kitchen, used the jug of water to fill it, added herbs, crushed crystals, drops of another potion.

"Now the potion I gave you. Four drops to start."

Minh struggled as the baby began to fret and fight.

"It has a bitter taste, but he has to swallow four drops."

Minh gathered up his son, and though his eyes watered, held the baby's arms down with one of his own, forced the drops down.

"Good, good. Heat the pot," Fallon murmured. "Water boil and steam rise." As the water bubbled, she picked up a cloth. "Is this clean?"

"Yes."

"He's not going to like it, but I'm going to cover his head with the cloth. You're going to hold his head over the steam. If he cries, that's okay. He'll be pulling the healing steam into his lungs. He'll cough. It might be bad. But you hold him."

"Will it hurt him?"

"The cough hurts." She took another cloth. "But he'll cough up the fluid, the sickness."

He coughed, he wailed, and tears slid down the soldier's face as Fallon caught the sickness in the cloth.

"Lay him down now."

"His breathing's better. Is it better?"

"Uh-huh." Once again, she laid hands on the baby. "Less fluid.

But . . ." She drew more out, into herself. Turned her head, coughed it out into the cloth. "He still has a fever, but not so high. Keep giving him the tea, and keep the poultice on his chest. I'm going to help some of the others, but I'll be back. We have to do all of this again."

"Again," Minh echoed, shut his eyes.

"It won't be as bad, it won't be, but we have to do it again. And maybe a third time. It's harder for the very young and the very old. He'll rest, and when he does, take the sick cloth to the pot I'll have boiling outside. It needs to be sanitized."

"I will. I will. Blessings on you, Fallon. Tell Orelana, tell his mother he's better."

"I will. More tea, Minh."

Like Mallick, she went from hut to hut, treating the oldest and youngest first. Those well enough continued to brew tea, mix potions.

When she went into Mick's hut, she saw Thomas shivering on his cot. He tried to lift himself when she came in, fell back with the violence of his coughing.

"You have to help," Mick said. "He had the tea. I got him the tea."

"Good. I brought more. Enough for both of you. Drink yours." Then she moved to Thomas, put an arm under him to help him sit up. "Drink."

When he'd managed a few sips, she set it aside, laid her hands on him. Like the baby, like several others, he held fluid in both lungs. "Two cups, Mick, two pots of water, four cloths."

"Okay."

While he gathered the items, she made the poultice. "You'll keep this on your chest. I'll leave medicine to renew it. Twice every day until your lungs are clear."

She poured potion into the cups, handed one to Mick. "Drink." And helped Thomas drink. "All. Every drop."

She doctored the water, set it to boil. "A cloth over your head, your head over the pot in the steam. Breathe in the steam. Use the second cloth to catch what you cough up."

"That's disgusting."

"It ain't pretty."

She continued on, patient after patient, then started over again. Just before dusk, she found Mallick sitting by the fire drinking a tankard of ale.

"I thought we would lose Old Ned," he told her. "But he's tough, and not ready to die."

"The baby—Minh and Orelana's baby—he's nursing."

"We'll leave them more tea and potion, and the mix for the steam. But I think the worst of it is behind. We'll visit tomorrow to be sure."

"We have to go to the faerie bower."

He nodded, drank more ale. "After I finish my ale. I sent a runner. It isn't as serious there, nor has it spread so wide. The shifter pack remains healthy. No sign of this there, but we'll leave them some preventatives."

He watched the fire a moment. "You did well today. You gave comfort and ease, very likely saved lives. And you did so with care and a cool head. Not once did I have to tell you what to do or how to do it."

"You already had. And my mother taught me."

"Not all you did or knew came from my teachings or your mother's. Cull out what they need until tomorrow, then we'll visit the bower to help, stop by the shifters' den. Then, by the gods, I want another ale, my supper, and my bed."

"It's contagious. You need to take a preventative potion. I'll take one if you say I have to, but I don't get sick."

"You're not immortal or invulnerable, but no, you're resistant to illness." He let out a sigh. "I, unfortunately, am not, so I'll take the preventative. I've never devised a way to make them taste less foul."

"Well, you just entrance yourself so you think it tastes like ale or wine or whatever. It doesn't, but you think it does and that's the same thing, right?"

He lowered the tankard, stared at her. "That's bloody brilliant, and it annoys me that in all my life I didn't think of it."

He took the preventative—two days running at Fallon's insistence. They made rounds at all the camps for a full week.

Mick came by at dawn, fully recovered, and brought her new pants—longer—and new boots—a size up.

"How'd you know I needed these?"

"I can see. Your pants are too short, and you keep fiddling with your boots."

"They're really nice. Soft, and strong. Thanks."

"I made them."

"You did?" She studied them again, the soft, soft brown leather, the sturdy soles. "I didn't know you could make boots."

"I'm an elf," he said dryly. "Anyway. Maybe I'll see you at the glade later. The pool's warm."

"Maybe."

He looked away a moment, over the white blanket of snow. "I was really scared about my dad. He's never been sick like that. I've never seen so many of us sick. You saved him—us—you and Mallick. I'm—we're all—really grateful. Old Ned's making boots for Mallick. He's nearly done, and he'll bring them himself. So. I'll see you later."

And with sickness, her friendship with Mick healed.

Through the winter, through the snow, in skies more often gray than blue, Fallon twice watched crows circling. Not close, by her estimation. Five miles off, maybe more.

But it told her that while she trained, while she learned, while she stayed safe, others fought and died.

Twice she asked Mallick to let her take Laoch and go closer. Just to observe. Just to see—and learn. Twice he'd refused her.

In March, when the winds blew and the buds of spring remained tantalizingly out of reach, she saw again, asked again. Heard refusal again.

The third time lit the fuse of her temper.

"How am I supposed to know when I only fight with you, with swords charmed not to harm? You can't beat me on horseback, and hardly ever otherwise. I can shoot an arrow farther than you and with more accuracy now. And with this?"

She flashed out her hands, sent the fire roaring, the candles flaming, the potion in the cauldron flying into the air and then spilling back in again.

"I'm as good as you."

"I remain your teacher, and you my student."

"Then let me learn what's happening in the world. All my life I've been protected. At the farm, now here."

"You're not ready."

"How do you know? I'll just all of a sudden *be* ready when I'm fifteen? I'm nearly fifteen anyway."

"Age isn't the line."

"What is? What is?"

"Open that door." He gestured to the locked cupboard.

She marched to it, tugged. Held her hand and her temper over the lock. "You locked it so I can't."

"No. When you can open it, ask me again. I'll work in peace now. Go, do something else, and do it somewhere else."

"Fine. I don't want to be around you, either."

She stomped away, stomped to her room. She didn't want to go outside in the continually crappy weather. She didn't want to ride or swim in the faerie pool. She didn't want to be there anymore.

She flopped down on her bed.

"I just want to see. I want to see, something else. Someone else. I want to see," she muttered again. "I want to see, I want to be. Free to begin what's asked of me. I need to start to play my part, to make my mark and hold back the dark."

She didn't intend to cast the spell. It just wound through her. She wasn't aware anything had changed even when she got up to pace and brood a little more.

Then she noticed the ball of crystal on her table. And saw it had cleared.

"I want to see," she repeated. "Now in this sphere my vision clear. I will see what I must see."

She saw it all, sharp and clear as life within the globe. Not what was or would be, but what had been.

She watched, even as her heart hammered, as she felt licks of fear cold on her back, she watched it all.

Knowing what came next, what must come, she strapped on her sword, shouldered her bow. Laying her hands over the crystal, she let it take her inside.

Mallick worked off his annoyance, and considerable insult. Or tried. But when Fallon came back to the workshop nearly two hours after what he thought of as her tantrum, he realized he hadn't worked off a thing.

"I'm not sorry," she began.

"Then there's no reason for you to interrupt my work."

"The crystal cleared for me."

He looked up then, looked at her. A little pale, he noted, and her eyes still full of visions. "And what did you see?"

"I saw New Hope. I saw the attack. I saw my uncle and his whore kill my birth father. I know their faces now. I know their faces. I saw my birth father shield my mother and me with his own body, his own life. I saw her grief and rage. And the killing wave of it. I was there."

"There?"

"I went into the crystal."

His first reaction, temper, took a great deal of will to hold back. "How?"

"It was open to me. I opened to it. I had to. I had a duty there. My mother ran, to save me and her friends. She ran, heavy with me inside her, alone, grieving, bloody. And she ran, hid, ran, evaded, and once dropped down exhausted, close to giving up. She told me I came to her then, and what I said, though she didn't know me. Didn't know I was her daughter. And what I said helped her go on. So I went in, and I went to her, and I said what needed to be said."

He walked over, poured wine for himself, then a little into a second glass. Added water to it, and gave it to her.

"You've seen now more than I've shown you. The crystal is yours. In it, with it, you'll see more."

"I followed her for a while, to make sure. She was so tired, her heart so broken, and so strong. Stronger than I ever knew. I saw that, and I saw the faces of the ones who killed my birth father. I didn't see if what she threw at them killed them. I know if they live, I will. I am their death. I swear it."

She walked back to the locked cupboard, tried again. It didn't budge. "I will open it."

"I trust you will, when it's time."

She drank the wine, frowned at the glass. "It's okay. When I go into the crystal, am I protected?"

"You are both here and there, and are vulnerable in both places."

"All right. I'm going for a ride. I need to clear my head."

When she left, he sat, no longer annoyed or insulted, and more afraid than he'd expected. She'd go into the crystal again, and now it was beyond him to stop her. This step was hers, as it had always been.

At fifteen, Duncan tolerated classes at the academy. He instructed more than he played the student, but attendance satisfied his mother and kept the heat off.

He worked in rotation on supply runs, scouting missions, hunting parties. When cornered, he took his turns in the community gardens, the trash and refuse committee, power and maintenance.

He knew first aid and could fill in as a medic.

He enjoyed weapons training, basketball, and heading out to the farm road on his bike. He liked hanging with his friends, messing around with Denzel, listening to Denzel rock it out on his guitar or kill it on the ball field.

He'd done considerably more than get his hands on interesting breasts, and enjoyed that, too. A lot.

That spring he began to help plan and organize rescue missions as well as joining the ranks.

He'd helped plan the one they prepared for tonight. As he and Flynn had captured the wounded Purity Warrior, brought him back to be questioned, he'd earned his spot.

"Better'n eighty miles out." Eddie looked at the map again. "Farther than we've ever tried one of these. A lot of road between here and there."

"And according to our guest, more than thirty being held, tortured, and up for execution." Will studied another map, one Arlys helped him create. "He says they've got about a hundred people—but only half of them soldiers. Built up walls here, barbed-wire fencing here, here, guards." He tapped the stick figures on the map. "Communication center here, in what was the town library, and prison here, in what was the local police station."

"Those are the primary targets," Duncan added, "after we neutralize the guards, get through the gate or through the fence. If we don't blow open the gate, or take out a piece of the wall, the fencing, we could end up cornered inside."

"Exactly right. And before we get there, we have to get through or around Raider camps scouting reports put here, here, here. So let's go over every step of it again. If anybody sees a hole, let's plug it."

As Duncan stepped out to join his squad, Denzel, hair in dozens of braids bunched back with a band, loped over.

"Can't you talk Will into letting me in on this? Come on, man."

"Can't do it, bro. You tanked weapons training again. And chem."

Denzel, already more than six feet of packed muscle, kicked at a stone. "Chem's bogus."

Duncan leaned back against his bike. "You need to study up." Never going to happen, Duncan thought, but he hated seeing Denzel's disappointment. "You got speed, agility. You just have to study up, and pick a weapon, practice."

"Kato's my weapon." With a grin, Denzel swiped the air with a panther claw.

"You got that. Look, you suck at chem, I suck at the guitar. I'll help you, you help me. Maybe we won't suck."

They'd tried it before with pitiful results on both sides, but they could try it again, Duncan decided.

"I'm up for that." Still he gave the trucks and bikes and weapons a wistful look.

"I gotta go."

"Take 'em out, take 'em down."

They bumped fists, and Denzel stepped back to the sidewalk to watch the warriors head out.

Duncan swung onto his bike, with Antonia riding behind him. The first days and nights of April remained pretty damn cold, but he wanted the agility and speed of his bike. Not that they'd speed through eighty miles, especially since parts of the best route still had old vehicles jammed on them.

Eddie drove Chuck's old Humvee—slow as it got, in Duncan's opinion, but it came in handy for busting through those rust buckets. Plus, they'd armored it, and it was a damn good weapon.

They left at night, calculating speed, miles, potential delays and detours, with plans to arrive for the raid an hour before dawn.

He saw his mom with Arlys, shot her a salute. Others stood outside to see the rescue party off. He saw the brothers he'd helped rescue, and Petra.

He sent Petra a quick grin. He knew she was stuck on him, but as pretty as she was, she struck him as just too young yet.

Give her another year maybe, and who knew.

"It's sticky," Tonia said in his ear.

"What?"

"The hero worship. It's so sticky it's going to clog your pores."

"Ah, give it a rest." He shot the bike forward and left New Hope behind.

They hit the first jam at mile thirty-two, and stopped while Eddie broke through the bottleneck. On her own bike, Maxie, one of the elves from Flynn's original party, pulled up beside Duncan, gestured east.

Flickers of fire through the dark, the haze of smoke rising.

"Raiders," Maxie said. "They burn for the fuck of it. We ought to send a team to drive them off."

Normally he'd have agreed with her, and volunteered to join in. But they had fifty miles to go.

"Probably be gone before we got there. Raiders usually set the fires after they've picked a place clean."

"Yeah." She looked ahead, revving the bike. "Like a shot at them though."

Maxie had purple hair with feathers pinned on the side. She was about three years older than he was and had seriously interesting breasts.

As they drove on, the possibility that he might talk her into getting naked with him kept him occupied for ten miles—and through another jam.

Stop and start, he thought, start and stop. He wanted to get there, get doing. Five miles out, when they stopped, he and Antonia would head northwest, with Maxie and Solo the shifter. Another team would peel off northeast. Duncan would take out the guards, then his primary task was the gate. Get it open, shoot some lightning— he'd gotten damn good at it—back to the building he could see on the map in his head. The armory.

Boom, bang, boom.

Sweep in. Tonia would head for the prison with her team; his team would head for the communication center. Most everybody still in bed, scrambling for weapons, half-dressed.

Guards, gate, armory, comms, he thought. They'd be in a world of hurt already.

They were fifteen miles out when their headlights swept over the girl on a white horse standing in the middle of the road.

She might have been a statue, spotlighted in the blue cast from the half-moon.

He knew her, Duncan thought as the party stopped. From dreams. He knew her from dreams, and the thought of it left him shaken and angry and thrilled.

"It's a trap," she called out. "They know you're coming."

He got off the bike, vibrating. Pleasure, temper, fascination all at once battering at him.

Did she know a dozen weapons were aimed at her? If she did, she didn't seem to care.

Will jumped out of his truck. "If you make a move for a weapon, it'll be a mistake."

"I'm not your enemy."

Eddie walked up beside Will. "Who the hell are you then? And where'd you get that horse?"

"We found each other." She dismounted, just flung a leg over and leaped down to stand with her hands out and up. "It's a trap," she repeated.

"Eddie, go down the line and tell everybody to hold."

"Eddie?" the girl repeated. Duncan watched her face, so serious, bloom with a smile. "Eddie Clawson. Where's Joe?"

"He's back at the . . . How do you know about Joe?"

"I know a lot of things about you. How Lana and Max found you, how you taught them about snow chains. You play the harmonica and come from Kentucky. I've seen where that is on maps."

"Listen, kid, you're going to have to . . ." Eddie walked forward as he spoke, then saw her eyes. "Oh my God. Oh sweet Jesus. You have his eyes."

"I know."

"You have your daddy's eyes." He ran the last few steps, threw his arms around her. "It's Max's kid. Max and Lana's kid."

"You were his friend. I'm your friend. I'm Fallon."

THE SWORD AND THE SHIELD

Men at some time are masters of their fates:
The fault, dear Brutus, is not in our stars,
But in ourselves, that we are underlings.

—*Julius Caesar* by William Shakespeare, Act I, Scene III

CHAPTER SIXTEEN

Hands on Fallon's shoulders, Eddie drew back, his eyes damp as he studied her face. "She gave you his name. You look like him, and her, too. Got the best of both. Your mom's okay?"

"She's very okay."

"I . . . I promised Max I'd look out for her, for you. I didn't."

"That's not true. You risked your life to try to get to them during the attack. But Max was dead, and she was already gone."

"Where is she?"

"I can't tell you. It's not time. I'm sorry, but she's safe."

"Okay. Okay." Eddie rubbed his hands over his face. "We'll get back to all that. But right now, you're what, fourteen? What are you doing out here by yourself? On that big-ass horse."

"Warning you. They know you're coming. They set a trap."

Will stepped forward. "Hold on, Eddie. And how do you know?" he asked Fallon.

"You're the leader?"

"Will Anderson."

"Your father's Bill, and he was with Eddie and the ones with him. They left you signs to follow, to New Hope. And you did. My mother told me about you, all of you. But I know about the trap because . . . I'm the daughter of Max Fallon and Lana Bingham. I am a child of the Tuatha de Danann. The man you found is a true believer. He let you capture him so he could give you false information, to lead you into a trap."

"He was half-dead." Duncan moved in.

He felt a pull, warm, slow, deep. He knew her. Knew her from dreams. But he'd been in on the capture, he'd seen the condition of the prisoner.

"A true believer," Fallon repeated. Her eyes latched on to his. "You're Duncan, and your twin with you is Antonia. Your gift is like mine, and you know—you *know* I'm telling you the truth. The prisoner's name is Patrick. Nigel Patrick, and he volunteered, to be shot, to be beaten, to be left where they knew you'd come to scout."

It rang like truth inside him, and still . . . "How did they know where we'd scout?"

"I can't tell you. I haven't been shown. But they're waiting for you. Five miles more. Twenty-five of their soldiers, armed. They've fortified the walls of their base with more. One of the men in charge is Lou Mercer. His brother was killed in the attack on New Hope, the attack that killed my birth father. Mercer wants your blood, even more than White and his circle want mine. For Mercer, this is personal."

"This is Max's kid," Eddie said. "She wouldn't lie."

"Trap or no trap, we can't leave those people in there," Duncan began.

"I'm here to help you." She took out a map, illuminated it with a brush of her hand. "Patrick told you the prison's here, but it's not.

It's here. The armory's here. And they have fuel tanks. Here. He told you about the main gate, but he didn't tell you about the one on the west side. It's guarded, but they expect you to come here. Their first line, here, twenty-five armed with automatic weapons, stationed on both sides of the road leading in. They'll catch you in cross fire, while a squad moves to your rear to cut off retreat. They've been stockpiling ammo for weeks now to prepare for this. Those who survived that first wave would be bottled in. Kill or capture. They want some of you alive, if possible."

"To torture, and execute."

She nodded at Will.

"They want most to capture either Duncan or Antonia. Both, if possible."

"Yeah?" Duncan cocked his head. "How do we rate?"

"Mercer hates all Uncannys, but he hates witches most. He hopes to use you, especially if he can use one of you to torment the other, as a way of getting through the security and taking New Hope as they failed to do before."

"Good luck with that."

"He doesn't know or understand you," Fallon said simply. "We have to move quickly now, otherwise they'll send scouts. You'll send some on foot from here, to get behind the first lines, break them. Then you pick them up as you hit the gates, one team to the main, one to the west."

"You're not in charge," Duncan pointed out.

The look she sent him now was as cool as the air. "I was born for this, or I wouldn't be here. I have a very strict teacher, and only this window of time to help you. You'll need to set up for your attack, and have your foot soldiers in place. I'll blow the fuel tanks."

"All by yourself?"

She sent Duncan a smile that edged toward a smirk. "I'll have

Laoch." And laid a hand on her horse's cheek. "You know what I am," she said to Eddie. "You know why my mother ran that day with my father's blood on her, her heart broken."

"Yeah, to protect you, and us. They wanted you dead. The wanted to kill The One."

"You're her friend. You're my friend."

"That's real nice," Duncan commented. "But how do you expect to get through? Just ride your horse up to the gate and knock?"

"No. When I blow the fuel tanks, when they're distracted, running around trying to deal with the explosions, can you do the rest?" she asked Will.

"Yeah. Yeah. We'll coordinate. Flynn, elves, and shifters on foot, to flank the first line."

"Good." Fallon approved. "Faster, quieter. You know my mother," she said to Flynn.

"And Max. We've waited a long time for you."

"The wait's almost over."

She listened as Will planned out the new attack, formed teams. And tried to keep her face impassive while her heart pounded, her blood ran hot and fast under her skin.

"You're sure about the locations?" Will asked. "Prison, armory, slave quarters?"

"I'm sure. Trust me."

"Looks like we're going to."

"Okay, I'm all for it, but this still hinges on one girl and a horse blowing up the fuel. How?" Duncan demanded.

In answer, Fallon swung onto Laoch's back, stroked a hand down his neck.

His horn slid out silver. His wings spread.

"Holy shit!" Eddie took one careful step back. "A flying unicorn. Kick my ass and call me Sally."

"An *alicorn*." Eyes bright, Tonia nudged her brother aside, and looking into Laoch's eyes, stroked him. "I've never seen one. Didn't know they really existed. He's so cool."

"They won't be looking up," Fallon pointed out. "And I'll"—she flipped open a hand, held a ball of fire—"hit the fuel tanks with a couple of these." She closed her hand, extinguished it. "You can trust my aim, too."

"Kid, you're all of that and a bag of chips." Eddie grinned at her. "Wait until I tell Fred."

"Queen Fred! My mother calls her that sometimes. She loves her."

"So do I."

"We have to move quickly. I only have an hour here."

"Wait. Can you get low enough to drop me by the prison?"

"Tonia."

Tonia waved Duncan back. "Prisoners are priority. She blows the tanks, swoops over, drops me? Everybody's running around. Any guards, I deal with. Get the prisoners out the west gate to the medics and transports. Can you get low enough to work it?"

Fallon nodded. "We'll get you there."

"Will?"

"Do you know how many guards are in the prison?"

Fallon closed her eyes. "I see two outside, one inside. A man and a woman outside, a man inside."

"Don't make the drop unless that goes down to two." Will nodded at Tonia. "You can handle two."

"Yeah, I can. I'm with her." She clasped her hand on Fallon's forearm for the boost up.

They both felt it, an instant connection, deep and strong in the blood.

Tonia swung on behind her. "Nice meeting you and all that."

"Same here."

"Let's do this. First teams, go." Will looked up at Tonia. "You fall off, your mother'll have my head on a platter."

"I've got this."

Now at Fallon. "Good luck. We'll move in when we hear the boom."

"Then get ready. This won't take long."

With that, Laoch bunched his powerful legs and rose up on a spread of silver wings.

"You think you've seen it all," Eddie murmured, "then you go and see something else."

"We're putting a hell of a lot of faith into that girl," Will mumbled.

"She is The One."

Will glanced over at Flynn, nodded. "Positions."

Duncan got back on his bike, but his gaze stayed glued to the horse and riders. He could feel his twin's joy—it shined as bold as those wings. And he felt something else, something he couldn't quite identify, from Fallon.

He'd think about it later, he told himself. Right now, he had work to do.

"This is amazing!" Tonia lifted her face to the wind. "We studied alicorns at the academy, but nobody'd ever actually seen one. Now I'm *on* one."

"He's wonderful. You're brave to think of the prisoners first."

"Do you know what the PWs do to them?"

"I've heard." And seen, Fallon thought, through the crystal. "You'll want to brace yourself. We're going to move fast now."

"I love fast."

Fast, Tonia discovered, was an understatement. She had to hold back the war whoop that rang inside her, and wondered as the wind battered, as the ground below sped by, if they blurred like an elf on full run.

"I see the ambush. I see them stationed just where you said. They'd have torn through us."

"Can you conjure fireballs?" Fallon asked.

"It takes me longer than it takes you, and I haven't managed one as big as the one you did. But my aim's awesome."

"We could hit the armory, after the fuel tanks, on the way to the prison. Not to destroy, but to block them from getting more weapons. Then your people can take what weapons you can, destroy the rest."

"That's good. Let's do that."

"Fuel first."

They skimmed over the wall, above the heads of guards and troops at the ready. She saw the prison, the armory, the houses. The scaffold.

And three tanker trucks of fuel.

"I hate blowing it. We could use the gas."

"It's a waste," Fallon agreed. "But the best way. Maybe the only way. Hold on."

Though she wasn't easily impressed with magicks, Tonia admired Fallon's speed—one, two, three fireballs the size of basketballs were hurled. And admired the accuracy as each hit the tanks.

They blew, bombs of fire and, hurtling shrapnel from the destroyed trucks, became an inferno. She saw flaming metal fly as the hot smell of gas smeared the air.

Fallon turned Laoch in a tight circle, then dived for the armory.

"We circle it with fire," she shouted as people scrambled, scattered in panic below. "All the way around so they can't get through. You can open your mind to the elf, Flynn?"

"Yeah."

"Let him know what we're doing so he can pass the word. I didn't think of it until we were in the air or I'd have told Will. Bring the fire, as much as you can."

Tonia dug deep, and with her body pressed to Fallon's, surprised herself by how quickly she produced a fireball. She measured the distance, chose her spot, flung the fire.

"Nice."

"I pitch for the New Hope Youth Baseball team. Flynn's on it," she added as Laoch swung to circle the building, and his riders built a wall of fire.

Over the roar of flames, more explosions, they heard gunfire.

"Get ready to jump," Fallon called out as they charged through the air. "I'll see you again."

"At the checkpoint."

"No, I can't stay. I'll help until I'm pulled back, but I'll see you again."

"Pulled back where?"

"Get ready." Fallon took Laoch into another dive. "No guards outside. The cowards ran. Jump! Good luck."

She saw Tonia land, notch an arrow, then break the door open with power.

Fallon took Laoch into a climb. She could feel the first hints of the pull. Only a little time left, she thought, studying the battle below to look for weaknesses to exploit, or to help plug. Duncan, with two others, swung his bike to a stop just outside her fire wall. She expected he could douse his sister's fire, but wasn't sure about her own. So she opened a door for him and his team, drawing the fire back enough to give them a path.

He glanced up, met her eyes, held them for a moment, just an instant, that seemed to spin out and out.

Then she and Laoch stood in the clearing facing Mallick. He held the crystal in his hands.

"Are you injured?"

"No." She slid off Laoch, ran her hands over him. The way the shrapnel had flown, exploded so high . . . But he didn't have a single scratch. "We're not hurt."

"Were you successful?"

"I caught them in time. Some of them knew my parents, so they believed me. The map you helped me draw, and showed me how to light it in the dark, helped. I followed the plan you approved, except . . ."

He lifted his brows. "Except?"

"Tonia asked to ride with me, to get to the prison faster. And together . . . I thought of it after we were in the air. We ringed the armory in fire so the enemy couldn't get more weapons. So the New Hope soldiers could take what they had time to take, then they'd destroy it."

He considered. "An acceptable amendment to our agreement." He wouldn't have known, he admitted. He wasn't permitted to see into the crystal.

"The rest is up to them, but they had the advantage. If I could've stayed a little longer—"

"One hour. We agreed. See to your horse, then come inside."

"I want to see. The crystal will show me."

"When you come inside. Laoch needs your attention."

"He was perfect, Mallick." Still pulsing from the journey, from the battle, the flight, she turned to nuzzle Laoch. "We were bound so tight. He knew, I knew, every move, every turn. You were right when you said Grace wasn't meant for battle. He is."

She led the horse away. You are, Mallick thought, and went inside to wait for her.

They would call it the Battle of Fire.

More than a rescue, Duncan thought as he sped home with Tonia behind him. They'd secured all the prisoners, freed more than twenty slaves, and added twelve semiauto long guns, twenty-two handguns, four boxes of grenades, a couple of sawed-off shotguns, and pounds of ammunition to their own stores.

What vehicles they hadn't disabled or destroyed they drove back to New Hope.

A rout, he thought, a frigging rout. What had nearly been a massacre had turned into one of the biggest victories of the New Hope Resistance.

"No way she just vanished into thin air."

Duncan rolled his eyes. Every few miles Tonia shouted some variety of that same statement in his ear.

"Certain way, because she did."

"She flew away."

"I told you she didn't. She was there, then she wasn't. She poofed."

"She wasn't astral projecting. I touched her. I was on the damn horse. She was there."

"She was there. Then she wasn't." How the hell had she done it? he wondered—as he did every few miles. He damn well wanted to figure it out and do it himself.

"There was something about her."

"Yeah, yeah. The One. The Savior. I'll give her the wicked cool horse and the firepower, but she looked like a regular girl witch to me."

"You didn't touch her. When I did? I felt this buzz, like in the blood. Not exactly like it is with you and me, but something. And I've been thinking about it since I've had time to think instead of fight. I was touching her—pressed to her on the horse—when I made the fire. I've never made it that fast, I've never made it that big. It just rolled, Duncan. I think, because of the contact. The physical contact."

"If she'd hung around we could've debriefed her. What was the frigging hurry?"

"She said—I forgot to tell you—something about she didn't have much time before she got pulled back. And no, she didn't say where or how or why. We were a little busy at the time."

Wind, cold and stiff, blew over them, but in it Duncan caught the scent of waking spring.

In his mind flashed an image of Fallon, face illuminated as she danced around a bonfire. A crown of white flowers over her dark hair.

"She wanted to stay."

"What?"

"Crap," he blurted; he hadn't meant to say it aloud. "She wanted to stay. It's something I felt from her. Yeah, there's a connection. I felt it when I looked up at her right before she went poof. She wanted to stay and fight, but . . . it wasn't time."

"One thing's for sure, if it hadn't been time for her to show up tonight, a lot of us, maybe most of us, wouldn't be heading home."

"How the hell did she know? That's my question."

"We've both had visions," Tonia reminded him.

"Have you ever had one so clear and detailed you could draw a damn map? A really accurate map."

He wanted that skill, too. Coveted it.

"It's like she'd been inside that base. She knew how many guards were posted at the prison, knew about the fuel tanks."

"And blew the hell out of them," Tonia added, full of cheer. "We're not The One, Dunc. She knows more because she is more."

To his mind, he would want more than an hour, no matter how successful, to be sure of that.

When they crossed into New Hope, Tonia went with the team to debrief, treat, and house those who'd been imprisoned or enslaved. He expected Hannah would spend most of the night at the clinic.

A lot they'd brought in were in bad shape.

He went with another team to transfer the confiscated weapons to their armory.

As Will went to interrogate Patrick, Duncan didn't expect to see him again until the next day. But in under an hour, Will came into the armory.

"Did that rat bastard confess?" Duncan demanded. "And what the hell do we do about him?"

"No, and we're going to bury him." Will paced the length of the room. "The son of a bitch. The son of a bitch hanged himself in his cell."

Eddie let out a sigh. "Well, hell, Will, maybe that's the best thing all around. Now we don't have to decide what to do about him. It's done."

"I needed to talk to him." Vibrating with frustration, Will pounded a fist into his palm. "I need to find out how they knew we'd scout just where we found him. How much more they know."

"They've worked with Dark Uncannys before," Eddie pointed out. "Those fuckers Eric and Allegra. We thought we'd killed them back in Pennsylvania, but they lived through it. Maybe they lived through what Lana hit them with after Max. Or they got another. Some of them have visions like Lana used to, some of ours do, too."

"Maybe." Will turned around, eyes cold in a weary face. "Or maybe we've got a spy."

"Well, Jesus, Will."

"We take people into the community. We're taking more right now. Some may stay, some may move on."

"We, you know, vet them pretty good."

"Another couple of hours out there, Patrick would've died the day we found him." Duncan worried at the germ of a thought. "Hannah told me, and she'd know. Rachel had to operate on him, and he had internal injuries on top of it. It's why I had a hard time believing the girl—Fallon—at first."

"True believer." Will nodded. "He wouldn't be the only one. We've seen the type before."

"They're half-crazy most of the time," Eddie pointed out. "We'd notice half-crazy."

"I'd like to think so." Will rubbed his hands over his face. "I don't know which to hope it is. Either way, we're going to have to take more precautions."

"We've already got magickal shields up, but we can add to them."
They'd work on that, Duncan thought. "If somebody working with
the PWs is already inside the shield, we have to figure out how they're
getting information out."

"Probably not a magickal. Yeah, they work with them now and
then," Eddie continued, "but mostly they don't. They hate their ever-
fucking guts. Sorry, Duncan."

"I hate theirs back, so we're good. Not that hard to get intel out,
is it? You volunteer for a hunting party, a scavenger detail, or scouting. Or one of the farms. You leave a message at some checkpoint."

"They have communications, too. We could have somebody with
a radio, transmitting information. Let's start there," Will decided.
"Add to the shields, start checking for transmissions, and I hate to
say it, but take a closer look at anybody who's come in and stayed in
the last six months. One of the slaves—maybe more than one—
could've been brainwashed, indoctrinated."

He walked to the window, stared out. "If Fallon hadn't warned
us . . . I'd've led us into a massacre."

"You don't take that on," Eddie began, and with considerable
heat.

"I took the job, I take it on. Now I'm going to bury the son of a
bitch I thought we'd broken down enough to give us information
on how to free slaves and prisoners."

"He did give it. I'm with Eddie on this, Will. He screwed with all
of us. We believed him because he told us the truth. Most of it. I'll
help you bury him."

"No, thanks, but Pinney and I will take care of it. It'll help Pinney.
He was sitting on Patrick. Just a precaution until we got back. Fell
asleep—no reason not to. Nobody figured the fucker for suicidal.
Woke up, went back to check the cell. Patrick's hanging by his bed-
sheet. Still warm, Pinney said. He cut him down, tried to bring him
back. Still warm, but gone."

"That's not on Pinney, either."

"No, Eddie, it's not on him, or anybody. Patrick made his choice, took his side. Just get this stuff locked up. You don't need to do a full inventory tonight. Just lock up, go home. I'll see you tomorrow."

"Will? I know it's a problem, thinking about how we almost got ambushed, and how that came to be. But we all got home. We did what we set out to do, and we all got home. You shouldn't forget that."

"I won't."

Eddie sighed again when Will went out. "I'm sure as shit glad I never had to be in charge. It carries a lot of weight. You're a soldier, that's hard enough, but it's a lot harder to be the one giving all the orders. So let's be good soldiers and follow orders. We'll lock up, go home. I want to tell Fred about Lana's girl."

As they stowed the rest for future inventory, Eddie elbow-poked Duncan. "Really pretty girl, huh?"

"Yeah, she was okay."

"Okay my ass. That girl is smoking."

"Jesus, Eddie, you're old enough to be her father."

Maybe it shocked a little to realize that was pure truth, but Eddie let it roll.

"Doesn't mean I don't have eyes. Smoking," he repeated. "You're not old enough to be her daddy, and you've got eyes."

"I've sort of got a girl."

"Yeah." Eddie locked up, pocketed the keys, waited for Duncan to add a protective layer. "Which one is it this week?"

On a quick laugh, Duncan shrugged. He'd moved on Cassie, drifted to Fawn, and now . . .

"Plenty to be serious about without getting serious about a girl."

"I hear that—at your age."

"And okay, she was hot. I don't know about smoking, but she hits the hot-o-meter."

"Got her daddy's eyes," Eddie added. "It sure meant a lot to me to see them in Max's girl. Get some sleep, dude, you earned it."

"You, too."

When he did sleep, finally slept hours later, Duncan dreamed of the girl with gray eyes, the girl on a white horse with silver wings. A girl who walked through a place so bright with light it hurt the eyes. And who took a sword, a shield from the fire that lit it like a thousand suns.

When she lifted them, she was the sun.

CHAPTER SEVENTEEN

Fallon fought Mallick and his ghost warriors. She took some illusionary hits—and they hurt. As her training time compressed, he decreed she would fight with pain.

She wouldn't bleed, but she would feel.

So when the sword of one of the ghosts laid a shallow groove on her left shoulder, she felt the hot flash of metal slicing flesh.

She fought on.

The first few times she'd fought with pain, the shock of a strike or slash had panicked her mind. And killed her. So she came to understand quickly why Mallick pushed for the progression.

A wound not only shocked, but weakened. He pushed her to train her mind and her body to fight through both.

Sweat ran down her face, and her right leg strained for balance against the pierce of Mallick's sword. But she defeated two of the four opponents, and battled brutally against Mallick and the remaining ghost.

She sensed her endurance flagging—the adrenaline would only carry her so far, so long. To end it, she hurled a fireball at the last ghost, dropped into a roll, then swept her sword at Mallick's legs.

When he dropped, she impaled him. And then she dropped down beside him.

"Everything hurts."

His breath in tatters, he nodded. "Yes."

Frowning, she looked over at him. His face, sweaty as her own, was considerably pale under the damp.

"You're fighting with pain, too? Why? I'm the one in training."

"When your sword strikes an opponent, they feel. So with this progress, I feel."

She rose, went to the well, pumped water into the ladle.

"Drink. There's no need for you to fight with pain, or to fight at all. Just use ghosts. And that way you can observe and evaluate."

Eyeing her over the ladle, he drank. "I'm able to fight, and fight with pain."

She had learned—and this had been an easy lesson—that her teacher had considerable pride.

" 'Able' is one thing, and you're plenty able. It's that you don't need to. In fact, if you watched instead of fighting, you'd be able to evaluate my skills, and my weaknesses, better."

He sipped again. "Are you protecting the old man, girl?"

"The old man drilled a hole in my right thigh." To prove her point, she rubbed at the throb. "I'm just being practical. We've gone up against each other day after day, so we know each other's techniques, rhythms, weak spots. Sure, there're some changeups, but mostly, if you feint left, I know to guard my right from a back sweep. And you lift your right shoulder, just a little, when you're going to go for the impale."

"Is that so?"

"Yeah." Because she did ache and throb, Fallon dropped down

again, lay flat on her back to watch puffy white clouds meander over the blue. "Odds are I won't fight many enemies I can read as well as you."

"Next we'll fight left-handed."

Her interest piqued, she propped up on an elbow. "Left-handed."

"There may come a time, and that will, as you said, change things up. But not today. Hand-to-hand, four opponents, no weapons."

"Right now?"

He handed her the ladle and the rest of the water in it. "Drink. Fight. I'll take your suggestion, and observe."

"I'm wounded from—"

"Another excellent suggestion," he said easily. "You've lost your sword in an earlier battle, and now face new foes in hand-to-hand."

"I'd still have my knife."

"Assume you don't for this lesson."

"My magicks?"

"They're always with you."

She gulped down the water, handed him the ladle as she got to her feet. She liked hand-to-hand well enough. Her father had taught her the basics of boxing, street fighting, karate. Mallick had expanded that with different forms of karate, kung fu, tae kwon do.

The katas he'd taught her, insisted she practice, appealed to her. She liked the fluid, deadly dance of them.

He conjured four ghosts, two male, two female. Fallon judged the smaller female as formidable. She looked both springy and fierce.

Even as they formed, she decided to try for the biggest male first. He looked solid, and brutal. He'd be strong, she judged, but likely lacked agility.

Before they could charge her, she charged them, pushed herself into a flying kick, and caught the biggest of them in the throat. Flipping back, she rolled, barely avoided a kick to her head. Whirled a wind to scatter them, and launched at the second female.

Watching, Mallick circled. Not yet, he thought, not quite yet did she have a true balance in her weapons—body, mind, magicks. But he found himself pleased with her progression.

And a great pride in her fearlessness.

She suffered blows—a fist glancing off her right cheek, a vicious kick to her left hip. But she'd learned to use the pain as well as the momentum.

When the smallest woman slid—speed and power—and took Fallon out at the legs, Fallon used that momentum to push up, kick out. And her aim proved true as her boots slammed hard in the remaining male's balls. As he dropped, she flung power at him, took him out.

Whirling, she spun into the smaller female, managed to catch the boot of the foot that kicked out, flung her hard at the remaining opponent.

The small one proved as agile as Fallon suspected, and sprang back on her hands, gained her feet. But she'd knocked the second woman back, buying some time. She took another kick, saw stars, heard them buzzing inside her head. Spinning again, fast enough to blur.

Back fist, back kick, side kick. Enough to take the ghost woman down. Then crush her hand under a bootheel.

Satisfaction proved short-lived as she flew back under a whip of power. Unprepared, she landed badly, bit back a cry as her ankle turned. She flung up her hand, met power with power.

Through a haze—she had hit her head—she saw the smaller woman leap toward her, a knife in her good hand.

Survival—instinct without thought—snapped in. She pulled power out, yanked in. The knife flew from her enemy's hand to hers, from her hand into the enemy's heart.

Furious, flooded with pain, she rose.

"Bitch," she said as power clashed with power. "You're done."

One hand out, pushing, pushing back against power, she cocked the other back, flung forward a blade of fire. It cut through the trembling air, hit its mark. The last of her opponents erupted in flames.

Fallon hobbled a few steps, gave it up, and sat on the ground. "I didn't know I could do that."

"We rarely know what we're capable of doing when cornered."

"You didn't tell me one of them would be a witch."

"Do you think you'll fight only those without magicks?"

"No, but . . . fair warning?"

"Battles and wars are never fair."

He moved to her, crouched down to lift her face.

"My vision's a little funny."

"Mmm. A mild concussion. Close your eyes, let me deal with it."

She did as he asked. "The ankle's bad. Left ankle. Not broken. Bad sprain."

"I'll see to it. Breathe slowly."

As the ringing in her ears eased, she could. Then caught it again as he moved to her ankle. Pain . . . a red haze, she thought. Look through the haze to the light. Her stomach wanted to heave so she imagined the sickness as a pool, calming, calming, smoothing, stilling.

His hand skimmed over her throbbing hip, then to her surprise gently over her face.

She opened her eyes, looked in his. "You always say a few visible bruises serve as a reminder to be faster, stronger, smarter the next time."

"I don't think you'll forget. How did you conjure the fire blade?"

"Anger." Since the healing left her sleepy, she brought up her knees, rested her cheek on them. "The little one had a knife. You said no weapons."

"She cheated, as will many you face. Stand now, test the ankle."

He helped her to her feet, watched her walk.

"A little sore," she told him, "but it doesn't hurt. I can take full weight."

"Blurred vision, sickness?"

"No, that's gone."

Satisfied, he nodded. "You'll have an hour free, then you'll mix six potions from memory, and two more of your own design. If you do well, the rest of the afternoon will be yours."

"After the potions, I want to use the crystal. I want to go to New York."

"I can't permit it."

Can't, won't, don't, she thought. For every yes she worked out of him, she got twenty no's.

"New York and D.C. are still at war, within. They still hold the largest population of Dark Uncannys. We'll have to take them back. How can I know, unless I see? Look, you always say, look and see."

"It's not yet time."

"Something else you always say," she argued.

"Because both are true. You will look, and you will see, when it's time."

She'd expected just this, and had her alternate ready. "It'll take me to before, like it did so I could see the Purity Warriors' plan to ambush the New Hope people. Let me go in, see the New York my mother knew and loved. Where she and my birth father found each other, lived."

"This is strategy. Ask for what you know will be denied, then ask for less in hopes it won't be."

"No, not exactly." Mostly, she had to admit, but not exactly. "I want to see the now. I want to go to New York, to D.C., to other places and see the now. But I figured I had a better shot at the before." She shrugged. "I guess that's the same thing."

"It's a well-worn strategy because it often works."

Hope bloomed. "Did it?"

"You'll find out after you've done the potions. Go. I'd like to work in the garden for this hour. In quiet."

"I'm going to take a shower. A long one."

It felt glorious, even if the pipes knocked and the water spat more than poured. The light beat of it eased remaining aches and twinges, and the faerie soap smelled like the glade—green, soft, quiet.

As she dressed she planned the rest of her day. She'd read for the rest of her remaining hour, she'd do the potion assignment. She wanted to work on one that created a mist, one that blinded the enemy to an approach.

Then, finally, she'd go into the crystal and see her mother's great city, as it had been. She'd see her parents together—surely Mallick knew that was her true goal. She wanted to see the people who'd made her together, to see the place where they'd lived together.

A lot to see in an hour, she thought. Mallick never allowed more than an hour. She'd make it enough.

Then, biding her time, she'd ask for another hour in another place. Until she asked to go to the first shield. The place she'd dreamed of with fields and woods and hills, and the circle of stones.

She glanced toward the globe. She wouldn't betray Mallick's trust. She wouldn't go in without his knowledge. But he'd never forbidden her from looking.

Walking to the globe, she laid a hand on it.

"Let me see, and only see. Here my mind, body, spirit stay while you with visions guide my way."

The crystal sparked clear and showed her in watery daylight what she'd seen under the light of a moon.

Green and gold the fields, overgrown now, and brambles grew thick. Dark-hided deer grazed. As it was now, she thought. The hills rolled up to the sky, thin light shimmered through the trees, but the land lay untended.

And the stones, gray in the gloom, circled blackened earth.

Even through the crystal she sensed a battle of powers, a push and pull, light against dark.

She heard the chatter of birds, the rush of wind through rough grass, and the echo of empty places.

Then the burned ground moved, pulsed, beat like a black heart. And the birds silenced under the stark cry of crows circling over the stones.

The woods went dark with the dark that came into it. It sent a fog snaking along the ground to slither around the stones.

From the dark, from the fog, she heard a voice murmur, "Mine."

It tugged at her, like a clawed hand. A grip that bit.

The voice, in the crystal, in her head, said, "Come."

Fear iced her blood. Talons pierced her skin, sharp pain, dark pleasure. She swayed a moment because something beat inside her now, hot, slippery. She shuddered with it, against it, confused, frightened. Excited.

If she went in, she'd know more, feel more, see more.

The ground beat faster, like her own blood. The call of the crows reached up to shrieks. And the light grew dimmer, dimmer, moving toward the dark.

Shocked, she yanked back, felt the pain as talons scored the back of her hand.

"No." She caught her breath. "No. I won't come to you. You won't keep what you've taken. Go back to hell."

Instinct, the same that had flung a blade of fire, had her washing light through the globe. The crows dropped lifeless to the ground; the dark rolled back with a hiss.

Fallon stepped back slowly, and saw Mallick, sword in hand, in her doorway.

"I didn't mean—"

"What did you do?" he demanded. "Did you go in?"

"No! No, I swear. I wanted to look, to see the place of the first shield. I dreamed of it, and I wanted to see it. It's deserted, but not dead. I felt the light and dark pushing at each other, the dark's stronger there now. And it came. I . . ."

She looked down at her hand, unmarked. "It spoke. And it had claws in my hand. And I felt . . ." She thought she knew, and the shame rolled through her. "It made me feel . . ."

"Yes, I understand." He sheathed his sword. "Seduction can be another weapon. You refused it, rebuked it. And destroyed its harbingers. Are you certain you didn't go in—not purposely, Fallon. Did it draw you in, even for a moment?"

"No. It's strong, but the crystal is mine. It can't take me where I don't want to go. I almost did, for a minute, want to. But I didn't. How did you know to come?"

"You called me, mind to mind. I'll always come when you call me."

"Can you call me?"

"I can."

"I'll always come when you do."

He laid a hand on her shoulder. "You did well. We'll have some food before we work."

"I could eat. And I'm ready to spend some time with potions instead of . . . Do you hear that?"

"What do you hear?"

"It's like . . . singing. Maybe the faeries are coming to see us, but—"

"It's not the faeries."

"No, it's not like that, exactly." It sang around her, sang inside her. "But it's beautiful."

She stepped out, and saying nothing, Mallick followed her across the small cottage, up to the workshop.

Like a thousand voices calling to her, but quiet and lovely, more welcome than demand.

The locked cupboard stood open, and light pulsed as the dark had pulsed from the defiled ground.

"Did you open it?" she asked him.

"No. You opened it."

"How?"

"By refuting the dark, by honor and by acceptance. Take what's yours, girl."

Heart fluttering, she stepped to the cupboard. Inside the light sat a thick book, its cover deeply carved with magickal symbols. The book sang, in harps and bells and voices that stirred her soul.

"It's mine?"

"It and all it holds, if you choose. Another turn on the path, Fallon Swift. It remains your choice."

Inside her, around her, through her, the song.

She stepped forward, flooded in light, and lifted the book.

"It should be heavy, but it's not."

It has weight, Mallick thought. So much weight.

"A girl will open the Book of Spells, the oracles say. And all within will be within the girl. She will know, and knowing will enter the Well of Light. There she will take up her sword and her shield, forged in the light, tempered by the fire. And so The One will rise."

Fallon opened the book.

The singing rang out, a thunderous chorus. A wind blew, warm and wild and tasting of earth and sea, flower and flesh as flames burned across the pages.

And wrote her name.

The force of power stole her breath. In her, around her, through her, of her.

Her head fell back, her eyes rolled up white as it flooded her. And still, she flung out her arms to take more.

She stood, tall and slim, legs braced, and drank in what was hers.

As on the night of her birth, lightning slashed across the sky, and the wind howled and whipped the trees.

The singing swelled, rose up ringing in the warm, whirling air. In the window overhead, the sky burst with light.

When the storm passed, when the voices stilled, she closed the book.

"It's . . . so much."

"Every spell ever written, ever conjured, ever cast, black or white, for good or ill, is within you. This knowledge and the weight of it is yours. This trust and the burden of it is yours. Others may open the book, but it will not speak to them."

"My father paid the price for me to stand here. There's always a price, I know that. But I've seen what the cost is for not paying the price, how much worse."

She set the book down, laid her hand on it. "It was your book first."

"No, never mine. I helped create it, and I've kept it safe a very long time. This has been my duty and my honor." He lay his hand over hers. "Will you go to the Well of Light, Fallon Swift?"

"Yes." She let out a long breath as she turned to the cupboard, the light. "Yes, but I left my sword downstairs."

Mallick stepped back, folded his hands. "You'll have no need for it."

Trusting him, trusting herself, she stepped to the cupboard. With a last glance at Mallick, she stepped inside.

And leaped.

Down and down through brilliant white light, within sheer white walls. The air rushed by her without sound.

She looked up where the light swirled above her—like water—and below where it gleamed.

She landed in a spread-legged lunge, a hand braced against the gleaming floor of the well. She felt the heartbeat pump with her own. Her blood and the living light.

When she stood, it flowed around her like the water, like the brush of hands, the flutter of wings.

She thought of the farm, her family, of riding Grace over the fields, of running through the woods. The hum of bees, the snap of laundry on the line. The years the light had protected her and those she loved.

She thought of Max Fallon, who'd sparked her life and given his own for it, and closed her hand over the symbols she wore that joined her fathers.

She thought of Mick and Twila and Thomas and all she'd come to know and care for.

She thought of great cities and deserted fields. Of the people in New Hope, and all like them who fought to survive and to build.

And she thought of Mallick, who'd given hundreds of years to bring her to where she stood.

Her choice, she thought, but they had all paved the way for it.

Bathed in brilliant light, she stared at the long trough of fire.

"Another leap. It's faith. They have faith in me. I have faith in them, and in the light."

She stepped to the flames.

Its heat bathed her skin; its light shined in her eyes.

She felt its breath.

"I make my choice, now hear my voice. In light and fire I make this vow, accepting what the gods endow. I am your daughter, child of wind and fire, of earth and water. With magicks bright I take up the fight. With this sword, with this shield, I will strike on battlefield."

She reached through the flames, gripped hilt, gripped strap, lifted the sword and the shield.

"They're mine," she voiced. "As the book is mine, as the owl, the wolf, the horse are mine. And I'm theirs."

She hefted the shield with its crest of the fivefold symbol, uniting the five elements with magicks. She thrust high the sword with the same symbol on its hilt.

It flashed, silver as Laoch's wings, and the flame that ran from hilt to point burned white.

In light and fire rose The One.

Mallick waited for her. He knew the moment she'd reached into the flame by the strike of lighting, the flaming candles.

And from the change within him. Now, his clock would tick again, his life cycle would begin again. He would know age. And for that alone, he blessed her.

He fetched the sheath he'd made for her long before her birth, laid it beside the book.

When she stepped out, the light dimmed behind her. But it blazed on her face, he thought, in her eyes.

He dropped to one knee.

"What? Don't!"

"I've waited hundreds of years for this moment. I will acknowledge it, so be quiet! I pledge my magicks, my sword, my life to you, Fallon Swift. I swear my allegiance to you, to The One."

"Okay, but get up. It makes me feel weird."

"Some things don't change." He got to his feet.

"You don't have to pledge what I already know." She glanced back at the cupboard, the softened light.

"The well, it's amazing. The light, it's really bright, but at the same time it's soft—like water. I guess that's why it's the Well of Light. And the fire—I could see the sword and shield in the flames, shining gold in them. But silver when I took them out. And they felt like mine."

"Because they are."

"It's just . . . Have you ever been there? In the Well of Light."

"Once, long ago, to place the sword and shield for you."

"You put them there," she whispered.

"I kept this scabbard for you."

"It's beautiful."

"Will you name your sword? It's a tradition," he said, "and one that adds power."

"Solas. Light."

"A good name. Will you let me mark it on the blade?"

She held it out to him and, touched by her faith, he laid a finger on the blade, engraved it with its name.

"Will you sit?"

"I feel like I could run ten miles." She paced around the room, turning the sword so the blade caught the sun. "And then another ten."

"Sit. Please."

She sat, seemed to vibrate.

"There is no more I can teach you."

She stopped admiring the sword to gape at him. "What?"

"You know more than I now. The knowledge is in you, and the power far beyond my own."

"But . . . What do we do now?"

"The last part of your time here I'll help you focus and hone what you have. We'll sort out all you've been given today."

"From the book, from the well."

"Yes. But you've opened the book, you've taken the sword and shield. I can't make you stay. I'm asking you to trust that I know you need the time we have left."

It struck her like an arrow from a bow. "You're saying I could go home now?"

"Yes. You've completed the quests, accepted your duties. You have the knowledge. You have skill."

"But you're saying, too, we still have work to do."

"Yes."

She rose again, wandered. "I want to go home. Sometimes I miss my family so much I can hardly breathe. I'll conjure up the smell of my mom's hair, or the way my dad's hand feels when he takes mine, my brothers' voices. Just to get through until I can breathe again. I want to go home so bad."

"It is your choice now."

"I want to go home," she repeated. "But I know these two years—almost two now—weren't just about training me and teaching me. That's a big part of it, but the other part—the side part of it—was to get me used to being away from them, from home."

He sat back. "This isn't knowledge gained from the book, but from good logic."

"You're big on logic. I'm not going to be able to stay on the farm, stay with them. I don't know where I'll have to go, how far, how long. But I'm going to be away from home, and them. These two years will make it easier. I'll miss them, but I won't miss them so I can't breathe. And the same for them, right? It'll be easier for them."

She sat again. "I know I'm not finished here. Not finished, and I need you to help me finish. So I'll stay, and we'll work for the rest of the time. But when I go home, I need some time to be home. To be with them. And there are things I need to do there, to start there. Before I have to leave home and them again, I need time with them."

"It's for you to say now, not for me."

"Then that's what I say. And there are things that need to be done, to protect them, when I have to leave again. When I have that time, and do what needs to be done, it'll be easier to leave again."

"Very well. For now, take Faol Ban and Taibhse on a hunt, or ride Laoch. Take your afternoon."

"I haven't done the potions."

"You've done other things."

"I'll do the potions." She rose, grinned. "It won't take me long."

"Arrogance."

"Confidence," she corrected, and got to work.

CHAPTER EIGHTEEN

Summer came and went with hot, bright days filled with study and practice. With fall's approach, hot days slapped against cool nights until the air went to war. In the distance funnel clouds swirled in skies purple as a bruise and fired stony pebbles of hail to tatter dying leaves.

The faeries murmured the war of wind, of ice and heat, served as a sign, as the time of The One's training approached its end, and the true battle of light against dark began.

Fallon called it science.

Still, when storms broke over the cottage, they broke with the fury of driving rain and snapping lightning, the bellow of thunder that echoed, echoed through the woods.

Fallon brought one herself, with a snapping fury of her own, when Mallick pushed her through three rounds of conflict, then criticized her form.

She stood on boots caked with mud on ground boggy from the

last rain and swiped the illusionary blood of the ghosts she'd defeated from her face.

"I beat them, all of them. Every time."

"You're wounded," Mallick pointed out, "because you were slow, and you were sloppy."

Her lungs burned, but that was nothing to the temper rising in her. "I'm standing. They're not."

As cool as she was hot—another clash and slap—he dismissed results, emphasized process. "Five times you lost your footing. Twice you failed to use your momentum and lost your advantage."

"Bullshit, bullshit, bullshit."

"Harsh language won't keep you alive on the battlefield, and only emphasizes your weaknesses."

"Fuck that, and you."

Enraged, insulted, she conjured three ghosts, battered at them. Blind to all but the need to strike back, she sliced, hacked, blasted power that erupted in flame while her temper boiled. With the boiling came the wind, and then the thunder.

Kill, she thought, riding her own rage. Kill them all.

And then the lightning, red as the blood spattered over her, slashed across the bubbling gray sky, fired in spears and pitchforks. As she decapitated the last ghost, a strike shot down and cleaved the tree where Taibhse often perched.

It exploded, shooting out sharp darts and daggers of wood and shredded leaves.

Drenched, muddy, stunned, she ran toward the blaze. "Oh God! Taibhse!"

"He was wise enough to keep his distance from your temper and stupidity."

She searched the sky, looking for the spread of white wings as the boiling clouds folded back into themselves. "He's all right? He's okay?"

"You'd know if he wasn't."

Trembling, she shoved her dripping hair out of her eyes. "I could've . . . I was so mad, but I didn't mean to—"

"'Mean to' is nothing. You endangered others, you destroyed a living thing out of pique. You misused your gift."

He didn't shout; she'd have preferred it. Instead his voice dripped with a disgust that crushed her.

Tears swam into her eyes. It hurt her stomach to hold them back, but she held them. She didn't deserve the comfort of tears.

"I'm sorry. I have no excuse. But—"

"'But' precedes an excuse."

She swallowed it, though it went down hard and bitter.

"Clean up your mess," he said, the words so cold she shivered. He walked away from her, closed the cottage door firmly behind him.

Sickened, shattered, she shut down the rain and walked to the smoldering remains of the tree. She watched smoke rise into the blue sky of summer, cooled the debris.

Slowly, laboriously, she gathered what could be used for firewood or kindling, carried load by load to stack. Her body ached—the ghosts had landed some hard blows—but the guilt hurt more. It took hours, as she wouldn't use magicks for this.

When it was done, she chose a twig, held it between her hands and offered her penance. She allowed the tears now, let them and her breath coat the twig to bring the roots. She spoke the words humbly as she planted it. Holding her hands over it, she called a quiet rain to tease out the first leaves.

"From what was taken new life begins. I ask forgiveness for my sins."

She picked up a charred stick, studied it, and began to create for herself a warning and a reminder.

Bruised, exhausted, her throat mad with thirst, she went inside. She wanted a shower, cup after cup of cool water, but she trudged up the stairs to the workshop.

Mallick sat working, a glass of wine at his elbow. He didn't spare her a glance.

"There's no excuse. I let pride take me over, and I used my anger to destroy. I harmed a living thing, and might have done worse because I . . . gave up control for temper. I had no control. I only wanted to kill, to prove you were wrong. You weren't wrong."

She needed him to know, to understand if not forgive. "I can use anger on the battlefield. I need to feel. Mallick, if I don't *feel*—anger, joy, sorrow, and everything else—I'm less. Feeling makes me stronger. But I know now, especially now, that without control, my power, my strength, my feelings are a weakness."

He capped a bottle of amber liquid, labeled it. "Then you learned a valuable lesson. Perhaps the most valuable."

"I didn't use magicks to clean up, but I did to bring life from part of the tree. To plant a new one, and ask for forgiveness."

He turned to her then, ready to give his own. And saw the carved wooden cuff on the wrist of her sword hand.

Amazed, appalled, he whirled to her. "You made yourself a *trinket*? You would use what you destroyed for your own adornment."

"No, no, not a trinket. A reminder."

She thrust out her arm.

He gripped it, another lecture on his tongue. Then studied the cuff.

It bore the fivefold symbol and the words *Solas don Saol*.

Light for Life.

"I'll shed blood. I'll take lives. I'll send people into battle or give them duties that may end their lives. If I accept that, I have to believe this. Light for life. To fight the war to end the war. And never, never to strike out without cause, without control, the way I did today. I'll wear this to remind me.

"I'm sorry. Can't you forgive me?"

He looked at her. A blackened eye, a badly scraped cheek in a face still so young. Youth couldn't be an excuse for her, but he'd allowed himself to forget it was a reason.

"We'll forgive each other."

"You didn't do anything."

"I let my own anger leave you untended. Healing is a gift, and I ignored my gift to punish you. Sit now, and let me tend to you as I should have."

In the morning, after a night of dreams, Fallon rose to bring in the tributes, and to leave her gifts. She smelled fall in the air, the spice and smoke of it. And she thought of home.

As she brewed tea she decided during her free time that day she'd go through the crystal and visit New York again. The one her mother had loved.

So many smells, she thought, so much color and movement. And noise! She'd already walked the sidewalks under the towering buildings, marveling at the wonders. Cars, so many cars making a constant thunder of sound. People, so many people, hurrying and dressed in such fine clothes. Windows filled with clothes and shoes and satchels and gems and gold and silver sparkling behind glass.

Food. Everywhere. In wagons, in windows, inside shops, even on the sidewalks. The smell of meat and flowers and gas and everything. Of humanity.

She'd watched a young Lana in her white jacket and cap cooking in a huge kitchen full of people and more noise, shouts, movement, steam, heat. It was wonderful.

She'd watched Max write in a room full of books and pictures. His fingers busy tapping letters—a keyboard, she knew a keyboard. And the letters, the words appeared like magick on the screen.

She'd go back, she decided, maybe to the day she'd watched them walk in a great green space, holding hands and laughing.

She wouldn't look, not today, at the now as she had, and Mallick with her. She wouldn't look through the crystal to the scorched buildings, the rubble of others, the filth and the blood. Today, she wouldn't have the screams in her head.

She let the tea steep while she walked out to gather eggs and feed the chickens.

Mallick already stood outside, beyond their little garden.

Before him, where the old tree had stood, where she'd planted the tiny sapling, rose another tree.

Full grown, its branches spread wide, curving up as if lifted toward the sky. Leaves, shaped like hearts, grew green and thick. As she walked toward it, she judged it would take three men, hands linked, to span its massive and glossy trunk.

"You enchanted the sapling." She studied it, smiling. "It's beautiful."

"I did nothing."

"Then how . . . I only enchanted a twig from the old tree, used tears and breath to call the roots, and a shower to bring out the first leaves. I didn't ask for it to grow and change. I was going to nurture it, and ask the faeries to look after it when I leave. Maybe the faeries—"

"No. This is from you and for you."

"I swear I didn't—"

He took her arm, tapped a finger on her bracelet. "*Solas don Saol.* Your light brought life, and this is a tree of life."

"A tree of life. There's more than one?"

"Yes. They're rare and special, but more than one. With this, you have given, and been given, a gift."

"It will bear fruit for nourishment and healing and comfort."

Mallick turned to her, folded his hands while the vision took her.

"Its roots embrace the goddess of earth. Its branches rise up to the sun god. Its leaves breathe life into the air, catch the rain. It will offer a home to birds, and their songs will sweeten this place for all time. It connects all things, the earth, the air, fire, water, magicks. What walks, what flies, what crawls join through it to the light."

She turned to him, took his hands, and in her eyes he saw more than visions. He saw the woman inside the girl.

"It is not for me, Mallick the Sorcerer, but for you. You will find rest and comfort here when your work is done. This is my gift, our gift, for your loyalty and your service and your sacrifice.

"And here." She lifted her hand. Fruit, like a deep rainbow, an array of jewels, swelled on the branches. "The fruits of life like the fruits of your devotion are come ripe at last."

She lowered her hand, breathed out. "It's yours. It's for you. I see now, what I asked. What I could ask because of you."

For a moment he couldn't speak, and had to fight to find his voice, to steady it. "I'm honored. It is a great gift. It blesses what has become my home."

"Is it? Home for you?"

"I'm content here, to live and to work when I'm not needed away."

And he'd rest there, he thought, in the earth, under the tree, when his time ended in this realm.

"Now there are eggs to gather and a cow to milk. When we've done what must be done today, you should begin to make your good-byes."

"Good-byes?" Surprise had her head jerking up. "We're leaving? But I've got more than three weeks left."

"Leaving will take time. Friends you've made here will want to fete you, make gifts. You should make gifts for those friends you're leaving here. But our time here is ending. This tree is not only a great gift but a sign. You are ready."

"You said just yesterday my form was sloppy and my defenses reckless."

"So they were. And still, you're ready. Get the eggs." He picked up the bucket he'd set aside, walked out to milk the cow.

"I'm going home," Fallon whispered. Then with a laugh, spun in circles. "I'm going home."

Mick proved the hardest. He sulked, picked fights, stomped off.

"Be patient," Mallick advised when she complained—again—about Mick's attitude. "It can be hard to leave. It's also hard to be left behind."

She didn't want to be patient; she wanted to punch him. Instead, she ignored him, as Mallick had been right about leaving taking time. There were parties and feasts and gifts. Last swims in the faerie pool, last races with the elves. And new revelations.

"If Mick keeps avoiding me, he's never going to see me run all the way to the top of the tallest tree in the woods. And I won't have to thank him for teaching me how to scale a tree in the first place."

"You will thank him for his help, and his friendship, when you see him."

"If I see him." It hurt her heart she might not. "I guess I'll thank him. I wouldn't be able to run up a trunk, flip, and dive from branches, if he hadn't shown me."

Mallick sighed. "Think, girl."

"About what?"

"Do you think such an ability can be taught to one who doesn't have it already in her?"

"Well, he showed me how to . . . and I can sort of boost with . . . Wait. Are you saying I have elfin blood? My mother doesn't. She never said my birth father did."

"Are you The One only for witches?"

"No, but—"

"You carry all in you, in your blood and spirit, and so you hold all."

"You mean I can run nearly as fast as some of the elves because I have . . . But the faeries? It's not like I have wings."

"You found their glade, swim in their pool. They come to you. You hear the voices of their smallest."

"Yeah but . . . I don't shift. Do I? Can I? If I can, why didn't you tell me, help train me, help me find my spirit animal?"

"Think." He sighed again. "You did find them."

"The quests? But I can't—" She broke off, understood. "I could— or will if I need—shift into those forms. But more, I can merge with them, all three, see through them. You did train me, in all of it. I just didn't know. It's why we came here, so I'd live close to the others, spend this time learning their ways, their people, their abilities. Free time, I called it." She rolled her eyes. "I was still in training."

"That doesn't diminish your enjoyment. Go now, find Mick. You know very well you can find him. Say your good-byes to him. We leave tomorrow."

"Tomorrow? You never said—"

"I just said."

"It's almost a week early. They won't be expecting me. Oh!" She beamed. "Oh, that's even better. I'll surprise them. Thank you."

She flung her arms around him. He let himself cup a hand to the back of her head as he thought, Yes, yes, it is hard to be left behind.

She didn't find Mick so much as lure him. She rode Laoch with Taibhse on her arm and Faol Ban pacing her, taking a meandering route to the faerie glade.

There, knowing his weaknesses, she set out a picnic of little cakes, fruit tarts, and sweet tea.

With the owl on a branch, the horse at his ease, she propped her head on the wolf as he curled behind her. And opened a book.

It didn't take long.

When she sensed him, she turned a page, picked up a cake to nibble. "I could share, I guess, but not if you're going to be mean."

"I don't care about your cakes. I came to swim." He stepped out of the trees, and in the green light kicked off his boots, pulled off his shirt, and dived into the pool in worn and baggy shorts.

"You don't own this place, you know. I was swimming here before you came, and I'll swim here after you go."

She turned another page. "I'll miss swimming here. I might even miss you, if you weren't such an ass."

"You're not going to miss anything or anybody. That's all bullshit."

He dived deep, and when he surfaced, she'd put the book aside. Sitting up, legs crossed, she met his angry eyes. "You know it's not, just like you know I have to go. I was always going to have to go. My family's waiting. And the rest, all the rest, but my family first. I miss them so much, but it was easier being away like this because you were my friend. You're still my friend even though you say mean things to me, things you know aren't true. Even though you're just stupid and we could've had the last couple weeks to hunt and swim and just be friends. Now that time's gone. Mallick says we're leaving tomorrow."

"Tomorrow." He launched himself out of the pool. "Why?"

"He says it's time. He says I'm ready. Don't go," she said quickly when she realized he was braced to run.

"You are. You don't care how I feel about it. You don't care how I feel about you."

"That's bullshit and you know it. I never had a real friend before you. My brothers, and some of the girls from the other farms, the village. But not a real friend, so I never had to say good-bye to one before. I want to go home, but it's hard to say good-bye. It's harder when my friend's mad at me for doing what I have to."

"Just because you have some magick sword . . ." He trailed off, tired and disgusted with his own venom. "Screw it." After muttering his new favorite phrase, he dropped down beside her. "I can fight. I will fight."

"I know."

"My dad says not yet. I said I could go with you, fight, but he says not yet. When?"

"I don't know. But I know I'll see you again. I know it."

He picked up a cake, frowned at it. Ate it. "I never felt about anybody the way I feel about you."

"You're my first real friend, and you're the first boy I ever kissed."

"But you don't want to kiss me again."

Going with instinct, she laid her hands on his cheeks, touched her lips to his. "You're going to kiss a lot of other girls after I leave."

"Probably."

Laughing, she jabbed a finger in his ribs. "But you'll still be my friend."

They sat quiet for a while, shoulder to shoulder, facing the pool.

"When it's time to fight," he began, "when I see you again, will you kiss me?"

"Probably."

Now he laughed, bumped his shoulder to hers.

"I made you something." She reached in her pack, took out the gift. She'd braided strips of leather together to form a wristband and attached protective stones.

"It's really nice."

"See, you wrap it around . . ." She put it on for him. "Then you just loop this. Like that."

"It's really nice." He let out a breath, dug in his pocket. "I made this for you."

He'd carved her face in the stone she'd taken from Laoch's hoof.

"I had to get my dad to help me a little, but—"

"It's wonderful. It's from Laoch, so it's especially wonderful. It really looks like me. Thanks." She turned her head, smiled at him. "Friends?"

He shrugged, picked up a tart. "I guess."

She packed. She'd take more home than she'd left with, but now she had two horses to help carry her things.

In less than two days, she thought as she carefully wrapped her crystal for travel, she'd be home. She slipped her shield into the protective cover the shifters had made for her, but strapped on her sword.

Two days on the road could mean Raiders or Purity Warriors or just the violent.

She whistled for Laoch, since he'd carry most of her things. Secured the first load to his back, went back for the rest. When she came out, she found Mallick waiting for her and holding Grace's reins.

"It took me longer. It's a lot. I've got this if you want to get your pack and bring Gwydion around."

"I won't need them."

"It's two days, but maybe . . . What?" Shock shoved her a full step back. "You're not coming with me?"

"I'll come with you, of course. I took you from your home, I'll see you get back to it. But I won't need my horse or a pack. It won't take two days."

Her heart leaped. "Now? Just like that? We're going to flash. I've never flashed that far."

"And so I go with you, to help, this last time."

She wanted to argue. She'd only just begun to have the skill to move from one place to another since she'd come back from the Well of Light. But she thought of flashing to the farm. Of seeing her mother's face in only minutes instead of days.

It filled her with joy and with nerves.

"Do you have everything?" Mallick asked her.

"Yeah, this is it. I just . . . Wow." She looked around, the clearing, the chickens, the garden, the tree, the cottage, the woods. "The elves will help you harvest the garden." Her stomach kept jumping. "And if you need help with the bees, the faeries—"

"Do you think me incapable? Infirm?" he interrupted.

"No, but I've been around for two years. You won't have my slave labor anymore." She mounted Grace, lifted her arm for Taibhse, waited until Faol Ban stood between the horses. "Are you sure about flashing? It's not just you and me like we've done before."

He slipped a hand in Grace's bridle. "Do the work, girl."

"Okay, okay." She drew in, drew it up, felt it stir in her. And a moment before she released the power, she saw Mick at the edge of the woods.

She lifted a hand in farewell, saw him lift his. And flashed.

To stand on the ridge over the farm.

She drank it in, the air, the view, the sounds. When she looked down at Mallick, her eyes gleamed with power and emotion. "I'm getting pretty good at it."

"You need more practice, but you did well enough."

"Dad's already in the field with the boys. Haying. Mom must be inside. Do you want to ride Laoch down?"

"I won't come down. Go to your family."

"You're not coming? But—"

"I've seen you home, and now I'll go back to mine. Go to your family."

"Wait, just— Mallick." She said it sharply, leaned down to grip his hand before he could leave her. "You're my family, too. You're family." She squeezed hard, then let him go. "Bright blessings on you."

"And on you, Fallon Swift." He touched a hand lightly to her knee, then stepped back. And was gone.

"We're going home." She steered Grace away from the ridge toward the farm road.

In the field Ethan looked over—God, he'd gotten big! He shouted something, waved his arms, and began to run. They all began to run.

In the kitchen Lana felt something shift, drop away, open. And on a sobbing breath, rushed outside. She watched her child, her beautiful child gallop down the road with a huge white owl on her arm, a white wolf running beside her, and a massive white horse keeping pace.

Lana ran, hair flying out of its pins, her heart swelling and pounding. When Fallon leaped from the horse and into her arms, the world that had been just out of focus for two long years snapped clear and clean again.

"Oh, my baby, my baby." She clamped around Fallon as if she'd vanish, swayed, wept.

"Mom." Fallon burrowed into her, all but buried her face in her mother's hair until Lana drew her back.

"Oh, oh, look at you! You're so tall, you're so beautiful. You cut your hair!" She ran her fingers through it, then over Fallon's face. "I love it. I love you. God, I missed you. I missed you every day."

Then Simon sprinted up, swept Fallon off her feet, swung her around and around. "There she is. There's my girl."

She laughed, chained her arms around his neck. "Dad." He smelled like the farm. He smelled like home.

"Jesus, you're gorgeous. What happened to your hair? I missed the hell out of you." He pulled Lana in, gripped them both tight, tight. "My girls," he murmured. "My beautiful girls."

With shouts and hoots, the boys swarmed in. Reluctantly Simon let Fallon go so her brothers could surround her.

Overwhelmed, almost dizzy with it, Fallon tried to hug everyone at once. They peppered her with questions—Colin in a voice she almost didn't recognize. A man's voice.

It reminded her they hadn't stayed still in her absence. They'd grown taller. Colin more solid, Travis suddenly gangly, Ethan no longer a baby.

Jem and Scout raced in, circled, pushed through to nuzzle in.

"The gang's all here." Fallon laughed. "Almost. Where are Harper and Lee?"

She saw it in Ethan's head droop before Lana spoke.

"They died this winter. I'm sorry, baby. They went together, in their sleep."

"Oh." It cut at her that she'd never see them again, that she hadn't been able to say good-bye.

"We buried them under the tree," Travis told her. "With Grandma and Granddad. You can visit them."

"I will." She looked around, the hills, the woods, the garden, the bees, the fields. "It looks the same. I'm so glad it looks the same."

"You don't."

She returned Colin's appraising look. "You, either."

"I hereby declare today a Swift Family Holiday," Simon announced. The boys cheered. "Guys, let's get Fallon's things inside, see to the horses. And where did you get that magnificent stallion? That's one hell of a horse."

"He's not exactly a horse." Ethan walked right up to Laoch. "He's more."

"He's more," Fallon agreed. "Do you want to see?"

She met Laoch's eyes. He tossed back his head. Revealed his horn, spread his wings.

"Son of a bitch," Simon managed, grinning as the boys moved in to touch.

"He won't hurt them." Anticipating her mother, Fallon took Lana's hand. "He'd never hurt what's mine. He's Laoch," she told her brothers.

"Where did you get him?" Ethan rubbed his cheek against Laoch's.

"It's a story."

"Does it include how you came by that white wolf and owl?" Simon wondered.

"Yeah."

"I sure want to hear it."

"You must be hungry. You can tell us your stories while you eat. Pancakes."

She didn't have the heart to tell her mother she wasn't hungry. Plus, her mother's pancakes could stir anyone's appetite.

"The men will take care of all this." Lana slipped an arm around Fallon's waist. As she led Fallon toward the house, Colin started to object.

Simon cut him off with a look. "Your mom needs a little time with her. You'll get plenty. Plus, it's not every day you get to handle a flying unicorn."

"Alicorn," Ethan told him. "He's an alicorn."

"Is that so? Well, let's unpack Fallon's alicorn, get him and Grace into the paddock—though a fence seems useless. Then we'll eat some pancakes."

Inside, Fallon wandered around the kitchen. She smelled yeast from the dough already rising in her mother's big white bowl, and the herbs in the pots on the windowsill.

"I was going to make a feast for your homecoming, and we were going to decorate—" Lana's voice broke. "Was he kind to you? Was Mallick kind to you?"

"Yes. Strict, and he could be hard, but he was kind, too. He taught me so much. He let me see you, all of you, in the fire once. He wasn't supposed to, but I was so homesick."

"I felt you, and it lifted my heart. The sword."

Laying a hand on its hilt, Fallon nodded.

"You opened the Book of Spells, went into the Well of Light." Turning away, Lana began to gather what she needed for pancakes.

"We'll talk about it, all of it, but I think for now, over pancakes, we'll talk of other things. Of your white triad, and—"

She broke off again when Fallon's arms came around her. "Don't worry. I'm home now."

For how long? Lana wondered, but closed her hand over her daughter's. "Yes, you're home now."

CHAPTER NINETEEN

She ate pancakes and realized just how much she'd missed her mother's cooking. She entertained her brothers with stories of quests and faerie glades. She told them about Mick and learning how to scale a tree like an elf.

For this time, this reunion around the kitchen table, she made two years of training sound like an adventure.

And fooled no one.

In the spirit of holiday, chores waited for later. She let her brothers take turns petting Faol Ban, who tolerated the gang of boys stoically. When she lifted her arm, the owl glided from the branch of the apple tree, came to her.

"He's Taibhse."

"Why'd you give him such a weird name? Why'd you give them all weird names?" Colin demanded.

"It means ghost, like Faol Ban means white wolf and Laoch means hero. It's Irish, and they came to me with their names."

"Why didn't you give them other names in English?" Colin challenged. "The only one around here who talks Irish is the old lady at Sisters Farm."

"I do, too," she stated matter-of-factly, and Colin didn't respond.

She'd missed her mother's cooking, Fallon thought, and weird as it was, she'd missed that suspicious, challenging look on Colin's face.

Travis touched his fingers lightly to the tip of the owl's wing.

"Would— Say his name again?" he asked.

"Taibhse."

"Would Taibhse come to me?"

"He might, but you'd need a falconer's glove. His talons."

"Fallon doesn't need a glove because he's hers." Ethan looked up at his sister. "Can we ride Laoch?"

"You want to fly?"

Lana, who'd been simply drinking in watching her kids, jerked, stepped forward. "I don't think so."

"I'd take them one at a time," Fallon told her. "Up with me. They'll be safe. I promise."

"Come on, babe." Simon gave Lana a wink. "I know I want a spin. I bet you do, too."

"Me first! I'm the oldest," Colin claimed.

"Ethan first," Fallon corrected. "He asked first." She whistled.

Laoch didn't need wings to fly over the paddock fence. He took it in one fluid leap.

Maybe Lana held her breath when her daughter launched into the golden saddle—and muttered a little prayer when Simon gave Ethan a boost up behind her—but she knew when she was outnumbered.

"Hold on to me," Fallon told Ethan.

Wings spread out; forelegs lifted. And Lana watched her girl and her youngest take to the air with Ethan's gut-deep laugh rolling.

Magnificent, she thought. Spellbinding. A sister giving her brother the thrill of his life, yes, but more. A warrior on her warhorse.

"She's the same," she told Simon. "But not the same."

"She's still ours. That'll never change."

They took the day for fun, for love. Accepting Colin's other challenges, Fallon scaled trees, dived from branches, executed flips.

With Travis she walked to the apple tree and the dogs' graves.

"It hurt Dad most," he told her. "They were his mom's. Ethan told Dad they had to go, the night they died. You know how he knows with animals and stuff."

"Yeah."

"Dad sat with them, even when they went to sleep, and sat when they went away, you know. It hurt him the most."

She put her arm around Travis's shoulders. "They were family, and his family first."

"They need to know the other stuff. The stuff you're not saying. I don't know what it all is. I can see more than before you left, but you can block better."

"And you know trying to see is rude."

He only shrugged. "Sometimes you gotta be rude. I know some's about the sword. Can I see it?"

She took it out of the sheath, and after only a brief hesitation let him hold it. "What's the word on it? Is it like . . . the sun?"

"Close. Light. Its name is Light. And none who would use the light for dark will lift it. As I took it from the fire, so will I raise it in battle, and the blood that stains it will be the blood of the beast and all who follow. And though it bring death, its blade shines clean. Light for life."

Travis handed her back the sword as she breathed out again. "You got spookier."

"Yeah. I know."

"Do we need to learn how to use swords?"

"Yeah. I'll teach you."

"Cool."

She'd hoped to put it off at least for a few days. To set aside the hard things and just be home. But Travis was right. Her parents needed to know. All she had to do was figure out how to tell them.

She stayed in the kitchen with Lana when the boys went out with Simon to feed the stock. And with the scent of the ham baking—her favorite—she helped prepare potatoes for roasting.

Surprise return notwithstanding, Lana would put on a feast.

"I did most of the cooking at the cottage. Mallick's a really terrible cook. It only took a couple of meals to realize you'd done me a big favor teaching me to cook. I got pretty good at it. Not as good as you, but pretty good."

"You were always pretty good at it."

"One of the faeries was a baker. She showed me how to make what she called Rainbow Cake. It's really good."

"You'll teach me the recipe?"

"We need a sprinkle of faerie dust—from the little ones. It's what adds the rainbow. I met Max Fallon."

"I never thought of using . . . What?"

Lana, chopping herbs, looked up. "Max? You had a vision?"

"No, Mom, not a vision. I met him. I talked to him, like I'm talking to you."

"He died, Fallon."

"I know. It was the first Samhain I was gone. It was, during the ritual, the first . . . rushing in of power, real power in me. I called him, I guess. I didn't realize it, not really. And that night, I snuck out to try to track the wolf, and I met him. My sire."

"Max." Carefully, Lana set the knife down, walked over to sit. "On Samhain, when the veil thins."

How her mother would feel, Fallon couldn't know. But it had to be said.

"He came to me. He loved you, Mom, and me. He's proud of you, and me. We walked together in the woods, and I took him to the faerie glade. We had the whole night to talk, for me to really know him."

Fallon went to Lana, knelt down, took her hands. "You need to know what he told me. You need to know he's happy, and he's grateful you found Simon."

"Oh, Fallon."

As tears fell on their joined hands, Fallon squeezed tighter. "He's grateful you found someone so good, so strong, someone you love and who loves you, and me. He's happy you—we—built a life and family."

"You had that time with him, and that—I can't even tell you what that means to me. You both got back something that was stolen. I loved him, Fallon. I see him when I look at you and love him. But—"

Fallon felt something release inside her because now she knew. She knew what her mother felt.

"You loved him, and love him, but Simon Swift is the love of your life. Not just your mate, your husband, not just the father of your children. The love of your life. I know it, feel it. I'm glad of it. I'm so glad."

"You're so grown-up. I missed so much, so many changes, so many firsts."

"I kissed a boy."

"Oh." Torn between laughter and tears, Lana cupped Fallon's face. "Mick, right?"

"How did you know?"

"Moms know. Was it lovely?"

"It was . . . nice. He's nice when he's not being a butt. Sort of like Colin. Huh, I just realized that. It was nice," she said again, "but he's not going to be the love of my life. I don't know that I'll have one of those anyway."

"Don't say that. Don't ever put up blocks to love. But," she added, "that kind of love can definitely wait a few years."

"I thought I was so grown-up."

"Don't contradict your mother when she's being contradictory."

Fallon laid her head on Lana's lap. "I have a lot more to tell you, to tell you and Dad." She eased back, stood. "But they're coming back."

"I don't hear them."

"It's probably the elf blood."

"What?"

"A lot to tell you," Fallon repeated.

Nobody, witch, faerie, elf, baked a ham like her mother. Nobody put on a celebration dinner to compare. They ate like kings, with candles flickering and the fire crackling.

She noted the pecking order in brotherworld hadn't changed. Colin still lorded it over the others with his firstborn-male status. Travis could still, when he wanted, level Colin with wit and words. Ethan remained sunny of nature.

When she caught herself wondering how she could help hone their individual strengths, shore up weaknesses for what was to come, she shoved the thoughts aside.

Not yet. Not yet.

She waited until after dinner, when the boys grumbled about kitchen duty.

"I want to check on the horses. Dad, maybe you'll come out with me."

"Sure. I'd like another look at that super steed of yours."

He took her hand as they walked in the cooling night from the house to the stables.

"What do you want to tell me?"

"I never could fool you. I have a lot, a lot to tell you and Mom together. But I already told her this, and I need to tell you. I met Max Fallon."

"How'd you manage that?"

The ease of the question, the simplicity and ease of it, relaxed her tensed muscles.

"You know, magicks, Samhain, ritual, stuff."

"Uh-huh."

"We had most of the night to walk and talk."

"Good." He opened the stable door. "That's good."

"You're not going to ask what we talked about, what he said to me?"

"Honey, he's your father."

"So are you."

"That's right." He grabbed her face, kissed her. "You got two for the price of one."

Just that simple, she thought. Just that simple with him. That was strength, she realized, knowing at that moment every man she met, any man she considered, would be measured by this one.

Any man, every man would have a high bar to scale.

She moved to the stall, to Grace, stroked the mare's head, offered one of the carrots in her pocket.

"You told me Max Fallon was a hero."

"He was."

"He said the same about you. He said you were a hero."

"I'm a farmer."

Tears shined in her eyes, but good ones. Loving ones. "You're my hero."

He drew her against him. "There can't be anything that means more to a father than hearing his daughter say that. Nothing tops it."

They walked to Laoch. "Must be twenty-two hands. Back in the day, I'd've pulled out my smartphone, got a video of you on him."

"You taught me to ride, to build with wood, to throw a ball, to block a punch, to love and respect the land, to be generous and not to take any bullshit."

"I didn't teach you that mouth."

"Sure you did."

He had to laugh. "Guilty."

She offered the second carrot to her father. "You give it to him."

"Here you go, big guy."

"I know Max Fallon now. I love him now, not just as a picture on a book or the words inside it. Not just from stories I've been told, but through the man. I know you. I know now everything you taught me mattered and helped me to be who I am. I know more of you, through the man you are, from being away.

"Max Fallon was my sire. You're Daddy. And I love you."

He held her close, held her tight. "You just found something to top it."

She knew her parents, their habits, doubted they'd changed. She waited until her brothers slept, until her parents assumed she did. Then she went out to the kitchen.

They sat, as she'd known they would after a momentous day, at the table, drinking wine and talking.

"Can't sleep? You must be overtired," Lana said, rising. "All the excitement after a long trip. Nearly two days' ride, you said. The cottage where you stayed. Let me get you something to help you rest."

"I'm not tired. It was over a day's ride to get there. We didn't ride back."

"Did you actually fly all that way on the stallion?"

She shook her head at Simon.

"This is a good place to start," she decided. "Even though it's the end instead of the beginning. Have you ever flashed?" she asked her mother.

"In what way?"

"Well, like . . ." She flicked her wrists, vanished, reappeared across the room.

"Oh my God," Lana managed while Simon let out a delighted laugh.

"Do it again."

"Simon."

"Come on, seriously. Do it again."

Lana pressed her fingers to her eyes. "I'm going to need more wine."

Obliging them both, Fallon flashed to the pantry, flashed back with the bottle. "I had some wine."

"Did you?" Lana asked, very coolly.

"Really watered down. Sort of medicinal. Anyway, I could teach you to flash."

"I've heard some can, but as I've never seen it myself, I thought it was just a legend."

"No, and I can teach you. You have more power than you use, and what you've used since . . . for a long time it's almost always been domestic or healing or growing. You have more than Max did because—"

"You grew in me."

"Yeah. So I can teach you that, and other things. Not everything," Fallon qualified, "but more things."

"You said something about elf blood before. What did you mean?"

"I have some of all. Mallick said that's part of the meaning of The One. Some of all in one. Me."

Simon decided more wine wouldn't hurt, and poured it. "Are you going to grow wings now?"

"I don't think so, but . . . maybe. I'll be able to shift when that comes into me."

"Into what?"

"The three I brought with me. All of them, Mallick said. I should go back to the beginning. We were attacked on the way to the cottage. Raiders."

She took them through the two years as best she could. The hard things she'd left out. She watched her father cover her mother's hand when she told them about going to the prison, what they found there, what they did there.

As time passed, Lana rose, brewed tea.

"Dad taught me the basics of hand-to-hand. You know more than you taught us. You didn't teach us because you thought we were too young. I'll need to keep up my training. I can bring the ghosts, but you could help teach the boys. And they'll need to know how to use a sword."

"Why a sword?" Simon asked.

"There are still plenty of guns, but they're not always easy to find now, and ammo's even harder. We can make it. But blades, arrows, fists, feet, they can and are just as lethal, and easier to come by. Some are already using them, even prefer the sword or the bow."

She told them what she'd seen in dreams. The man with the sword speaking to her from outside the circle of stones, how she'd seen that same place through the crystal.

"I can go into it, into the crystal, go to what I see in it. I'm there, and here, both. It's hard to explain."

"Not astral projection?" Lana asked.

"No, different. It's like a split, but I'm in both places. It's how I met the rescue party. How I met people from New Hope."

"You . . . New Hope?"

"Eddie," she told Lana. "Flynn. Others."

"You met Eddie." For a moment the worry cleared. "He's alive and he's well?"

"Both. He asked about you. I couldn't tell him where you are, not yet, but I could tell him you were okay. I met Duncan and Tonia."

"The twins." On a happy laugh, Lana pressed a hand to her heart. "Katie's twins? And Hannah?"

"Not yet."

"Oh God, Katie's babies. They're almost grown by now."

"They're warriors—I don't think Hannah is. Duncan drives a motorcycle and uses a sword. Tonia uses a bow. They're trained in other weaponry, but that's their preference."

"Katie must be . . . You didn't meet her?"

"She wasn't in the rescue party."

"Or Arlys or Fred, Rachel, Jonah?"

"Not them. Will Anderson. He leads them now."

"Will." Lana nodded. "Yes. Yes, I can see that."

"It was an ambush."

"What? Oh God. Was anyone hurt?"

"I saw through the crystal what the Purity Warriors had done, how they planned to lure the rescue party in, ambush them. I went to Mallick. He let me go through to warn them, and tell them how to turn the ambush into an ambush."

"You figured that out?" Simon asked.

"I've trained, and studied, and I had the advantage of seeing where the enemy had their lines, their positions, so I could plan and map it out."

"You could walk me through that sometime."

"I will. None of your friends were hurt, Mom. And they rescued people who were being tortured, enslaved, people who'd be executed."

"You're glossing it over." Lana folded her hands together. "You fought. You fought with them. I may have channeled my power into softer things, Fallon, and done what I could to build a safe life for my children, but I've been in the war. I've seen death and caused it. Don't think to wait until you have your father alone to say the rest."

Lana turned to Simon. "She walks us both through."

"You're right." Simon took Lana's hand, brushed his lips over it. "Your mom's right. Lay it out now."

"Okay. They had fuel tanks," she began.

She took them through it.

"They're strong soldiers, the people of New Hope. You'd like them, Dad."

"So your mom's always said."

"After the battle, after more training, after I saw the first shield through the crystal, and the dark there tried to draw me to it, that's when the Book of Spells called me."

The moon set before she finished telling them all of it.

"I probably left some things out, but not on purpose. I needed you to know everything because it's not right you don't. And not telling you makes it seem like I think you're weak, and you're not. I want time to just be home, like today. Just to be home. And to train and practice, to help you and the boys train and practice. Then . . . I'll know when I have to go. I'll know."

"Where will you go?" Lana reached for her hand.

"New Hope," Fallon and Simon said together.

Fallon smiled at him, nodded. "Yeah, New Hope. So much started and ended there. So much is waiting there. It's where I'll need to go."

"To New Hope," she said as her eyes deepened. "Where the light brought them, where the signs led them, where the blood of the sire stained the ground. There to raise an army, to forge the weapons against the dark. From there to the great cities, to the rubble and the ruin, across the seas, under the earth. Betrayal, blood, lies bear bitter fruit, and some will fall along the way. With the rise of magicks, the clash of the light and the dark, the worlds tremble."

Now Lana rose, took a small bottle from a cupboard. "Two drops," she said.

"I don't get queasy from visions anymore."

"Maybe not, but you don't usually have one after you've been up most of the night. Two drops. Stick out your tongue."

Though she mentally rolled her eyes, Fallon did as she was told. Lana leaned down, kissed the top of her head.

"I know what it's like when it comes on so fast and strong. Like being filled up and hulled out at the same time."

On a sigh, Fallon leaned into Lana, comforted by someone who knew, really knew.

"What works in us gives so much." Gently, Lana stroked Fallon's hair. "And demands so much. I haven't forgotten what it's like to feel that power surge inside me, or how to fight. How to use everything I have, everything I am to fight. Now, because I was given time and love, I have more to fight for."

"I didn't mean . . . I saw you, through the crystal. In New York, the life you had before, the way you had to leave it. And how strong you were going forward, always going forward. In the mountains, what you did there, faced there. I watched you fight for yourself and me and others, day after day, month after month. I saw that day in New Hope."

"I would have spared you that."

"Why?" Fallon pulled back, eyes fierce. "I saw people who'd begun to build something good, something bright and real. Honoring their dead, celebrating life. I saw the faces of those who came to kill me. I know those faces now. I saw my birth father give his life for you, for me, and saw you strike back."

"It was grief."

"It was *power*. Power—yours and mine. How many lives did you save that day? And how many more when you, with me inside you, with his blood on you, ran, alone? Left another place, another home you loved, friends who'd become family. You took his ring, for love. You took his gun. A woman thinks of the rings, but a warrior thinks of a weapon, Mom, and even in your grief and shock, you were a warrior."

"I had a child to protect."

"You did. Alone, hungry, scared, you kept going."

"I nearly gave up. You came to me."

"You wouldn't have given up. You never give up. I just gave you a boost when you needed one. I saw you come to the ridge above the farm, and I saw on your face something I hadn't since you ran. I saw hope. And . . ."

Fallon reached out, took Simon's hand. "I saw that hope realized in kindness, and the building of trust, and love. It's a lesson, that trust can build between strangers, but they have to take the first step, and that's faith."

"When did you get so smart?" Simon asked.

She squeezed his hand, looked straight into his eyes. "I saw you kill a man who gave you no choice, though you'd given him one. He wasn't your first, or your last. I come from warriors, my mother, my fathers. And from power and strength. From kindness. When I'm afraid I won't be good enough, brave enough, smart enough, I think of you, what you've taught me, and what I've seen through the crystal."

She rubbed her eyes and looked all at once like a young girl up far too late. "I wish none of what's outside the farm, what's coming, would touch the boys. But it will. You know more, the soldier knows more than you've told us—or told Mom—or taught us. I . . . watched the soldier, too, in the before, through the crystal."

It tore at him, more than a little, to know he looked into his daughter's eyes, and looked soldier to soldier. "You're going to take a few days," Simon told her. "Call it R and R. Then we'll start training them."

"You've had a long day," Lana said. "You should get some sleep now."

"I'm really tired."

"Yes, I see that. Go on to bed."

Nodding, half-asleep already, she hugged Lana, then Simon. "I'm so glad to be home."

Lana watched her go, listened to her feet on the stairs.

"Simon."

"We'll talk. We'll think, and we'll talk. But right now somebody else needs sleep. You're worn-out, babe, and I'm not far behind you."

"I've known. I've known since she was inside me, and I still keep running up against the wall of no. No, this is my baby."

"Join the club."

He got up, took her hand. "We're going to do what parents do."

"What's that?"

"Worry our asses off and do everything we know how to help her." They started for the stairs. "You think you can learn that flash deal? Because, hey, you could bring me a cold beer like that."

He snapped his fingers, making her laugh after a very long day.

CHAPTER TWENTY

She took a week, helped with the harvest, taught her mother how to make a Rainbow Cake. She went fishing with her brothers, hunting with Taibhse and Faol Ban.

At night she flew over the fields and hills on Laoch.

And though she was happy to be home, she missed Mallick, and the routine of work, training, practice, study. She missed Mick and all the others, and quiet times alone in the faerie glade.

But she spent her fifteenth birthday at home, with her family, and treasured every moment.

When the week ended, her brothers took to training like a game. It annoyed her down to the bone, but she took her cues from her father. After all, she told herself, he'd trained soldiers before, and raised children.

"It starts as a game," he told her. "They're kids."

"Colin's the same age I was when I went with Mallick. He sure as hell didn't let me treat it like a game."

"Colin isn't you. They'll learn, and more, they'll compete. With each other, and with you. Then they'll get better, then they'll get serious."

So through the fall and into the winter, it remained, for the most part, a game. She left Travis's and Ethan's magickal training to her mother, for now, and tolerated the complaints and malingering when she pushed them through assignments.

Reading, math, mapping.

They liked plotting battle strategies, and Travis particularly shined there.

When it came to the katas, the gymnastics, and sheer endurance, Ethan outpaced his older brothers as if born doing handsprings.

But when, during the wild and windy days of March, she introduced swords, Colin proved fierce, fast, and deadly.

Enough it irritated her a little when he mastered in days forms and techniques that had taken her weeks.

She took to working with him one-on-one, and though she killed him routinely, he made her work for it.

Her father proved a different matter. He'd spar with her, under strict rules. Blows would not land. He had his line in the sand, no matter how she argued.

He wouldn't hit his children.

She compromised with a quick shock for any strike, punch, kick. Even under the rules, she couldn't beat him without using magicks, and learned more and more.

The first time they used knives for combat—much to her brothers' delight—Simon did what he did whenever a blade was introduced.

He tested them on himself.

"They won't cut cloth, break flesh, or draw blood," she told him, as she did before every sword practice.

"Better safe than really, really sorry." He swiped his knife, then hers, over the back of his arm. "Okay." He handed her a knife, hilt first.

As they circled each other, the boys called out insults or encouragements. And Lana came outside. It gave her a jolt, as it always did, to see her husband, her child, facing off. Eyes flat and cold, bodies coiled.

Her heart leaped into her throat and stayed lodged there from the first swipe.

Simon lunged in, pivoting away as Fallon did the same so her vicious kick, her follow-up slice missed their marks.

A terrible dance that seemed to go on and on.

By tacit agreement, Fallon and Simon straightened, stepped back.

"Looks like a draw," Lana called out as the boys moaned and booed.

"You're good." Simon swiped sweat from his face.

"You, too."

Now he grinned. "I was holding back."

"Oh yeah? So was I."

"Okay then." He rolled his shoulders, moved into a fighting stance. "Don't."

"You, either."

They charged each other.

Horrible, horrible, Lana thought, the blows, the hacking, the swipes of blades. The jerks of their body as the shocks ran through at the illusionary strikes and cuts.

Then, with a speed that made the boys cheer, Simon swung around, caught Fallon from behind, and slit her throat.

"Better than good." Breath in rags, Fallon lowered to brace her hands on her thighs.

"You, too."

"Show me that move."

"Sure, but here's the thing. If these knives cut, I'd probably have been weak and woozy from blood loss. Adrenaline might've pushed me through, but you came damn close to severing a couple arteries. That's where you should focus if you can. Go for the brachial, the femoral, the jugular, and it's going to be over fast."

"I know, but the only way I could've gotten to them was to—"

She flicked her hand, jerked him back with a punch of power, then sliced a long line down his forearm. "Do that."

"Why didn't you do that?"

"First, I need the training. And more, I might be going up against someone with power, so I'd be pushing or blocking that while trying to get a debilitating or killing strike in. If the opponent didn't have power, magicks should be used only to save lives. If you have to take a life with magicks, you can't do it for convenience. You just— you just have to know."

He shook his head, and looked at her—warrior to warrior. "Here's what I know. You do what it takes to stay alive. Use what you need to use. Because if you're dead, the fight's over, and not just for you. For others under your command, others you won't be able to protect. Innocent lives shouldn't be lost because you played fair. Nothing's fair in a war."

He sheathed his knife, then caught her face in his hands, kissed her. "You wore me out, baby."

As he spoke, Lana appeared at his side, offered him a cold beer.

"Hey. Nice, thanks."

"We've been working on it. I think it's time for a break. And, Fallon, I could really use your help with something," Lana urged as she led her to the house and closed the door behind them.

"Your father doesn't understand," Lana began. "He knows using magicks to cause harm, and worse, is against what we are, but he also knows what it's like to fight for your life and for others."

"I get it. I do."

"It was hard for me and Max to use our gifts to harm. It should be hard. But, Fallon, your dad's right. He's right. If you, any of us, need to use our gift as a weapon, we use it. Not lightly, not for—as you said—convenience—but we use it. Whether or not it's power against power."

"I've already used it. I don't know how many lives I might have taken when I blew up those fuel tanks, and used magick to do it."

"How many did you save? Good soldiers, and innocents? You did what you had to do, and I know, I'm afraid, you'll have to do the same again and again."

"You can slip into the dark," Fallon said quietly.

"You won't. Your fathers didn't. I didn't. You won't."

"The more I train, the more I'm here . . . I thought, and told Mallick, I needed time to be home. I thought it was for me, just to be here after two years away. But it's more. I'm still learning. It's about training, all of us, and learning."

She paced away, back again. "I know people are out there, fighting, dying, suffering. And I'm here, still here. I thought when I took the sword and shield, I'd be ready. But it's been months, and I'm still here."

"It's not just about fighting for you."

"I know, I know, just like I know it's not time for me to go."

Restlessly, she walked from window to window.

"But there are people my age, younger, already fighting and I'm waiting to . . . lead," she realized. "I'm waiting instead of working toward that, toward leadership. The farms, the village, right here? I'm not leading. I'm not learning who'll fight, who has needed skills, or knowledge that can be used. We're not training beyond right here. I'm stupid."

"Don't insult me. I didn't raise any stupid children. You have your time, right here, and only here, with family. Training and teaching and practicing. If it's time now for you to do more, to begin with neighbors, that's what we'll do."

"If Dad goes with me. They'll listen to him. They know him better, and with me, they'll see a teenager."

Pleased, proud, Lana nodded. "You need to build trust."

"Yeah, and I will. I will. This is why I'm here."

"Why you're still here," Lana corrected. "You've begun what you needed to begin, and now it's time to begin something else. You *are* a teenager, Fallon. And you're impatient. Building trust, armies, movements takes time."

"Then I better get started. Tomorrow . . . Do you hear that?"

"What do you hear?"

"Voices. From . . ."

She followed them, with Lana behind her, to her room. To the crystal.

"Do you hear them?"

"I hear something now. It's not clear."

"Can you see?"

"It's indistinct."

"Take my hand."

It cleared for her.

Men, women, in trucks, on horseback, incredibly in tanks. Heavily armed, Lana noted, all in dark clothes with faces blackened against the glow of moonlight.

A night raid.

"Purity Warriors," Fallon told her. "And some Raiders. They're likely in this for the bounty as much as the killing. Maybe the PWs paid them to join for this."

"I know that road." Fear squeezed at Lana's throat. "It's going to take them straight into New Hope. God, that's one of the Mercers in the lead truck. He hasn't aged well, and that's a horrible scar on his face, but I know it's one of them."

"Lou Mercer. Don's already dead. And this one got that scar in the explosion, the fuel tanks. He's very pissed off. I have to go."

She turned, picked up the sword she'd left on for hand-to-hand.

"This is coming, it's yet to come, so there's time to warn them. Time for them to get ready."

"I'm going with you."

"I need you here. I still can't go through without the split. I need you to stay with what's here. I need Will. Will Anderson."

She put a hand over the globe, brought Will's image into her head. And into the globe.

"Oh God, it's Will!" Lana grabbed Fallon's arm, looked closer. "And Katie. That's Katie. Oh my God, look at them."

She saw the woman with dark curly hair—and the eyes she'd passed down to her son—sitting at a table with Will.

"Where are they?" Fallon demanded.

"I'm not sure, I . . . The kitchen, in the house where Katie and Rachel live. Or lived when I was there. And Jonah. He moved in with Rachel. They've painted it, but that's the kitchen. I can't hear what they're saying. I can't hear clearly."

"I have to go through." She turned to her mother. "I have to warn them what's coming. Two nights—it's in two nights. I know where the house is. You told me, and even if I didn't, the crystal would take me. But you have to stay here."

"Tell them . . . just tell them I saw them."

"I will. Stay here. Stay with me."

Once more she put her hands on the globe, and this time, put the image of the house, of the kitchen into her mind.

And she slipped through the crystal.

She smelled something burning just before she completed the split. She drew her sword as Duncan swung around with his.

Steel clashed bright to steel.

"That's a good way to get disemboweled." He lowered his sword but didn't sheath it.

"Don't you bother to look before you attack?"

"Defend," he corrected. "It's my house you just popped into."

"I'm looking for Will Anderson."

"He doesn't live here."

"I know he doesn't live here, but he was here. You're burning something."

"Damn it." He grabbed the skillet, and now with hands full, turned off the heat with a flick of his head.

"Don't blame me." Clearly, by the look in his eyes, he did. "It was burning when I got here."

"I like my grilled cheese crispy." He flopped it—one side certainly crispy, the other definitely blackened—onto a plate.

"Just tell me where to find Will so I . . . It's night."

"Yeah. It just likes to follow day."

When she gripped his arm, the urgency in her slammed into him. "What's the date? What day is it?"

"March twenty-ninth. Or thirtieth, technically, as it just hit midnight. What do you want?"

"Will."

"Well, you got me. Spill it," he began, then got a good look at her sword. Now he gripped her arm, and lifted it. "Light," he said, reading the engraving.

"How do you know what it means?"

"One of my instructors at the academy was visiting relatives in Boston when the Doom hit. He ended up here. He teaches Irish." His gaze, that deep, deep green, shifted from the sword to her face. "So The One answers the call, opens the Book of Spells and, taking all it gives, travels into the Well of Light. There, from the fire eternal she lifts the sword and the shield."

He let her go. "I get that right?"

"I don't have time for this. Where does Will live? Here, with your mother?"

"No. Jesus. Man, he's married and all that for, like, a million years."

"To who?" Fallon could've torn her hair out—or Duncan's. "My mother will want to know."

"Arlys."

"She'll be glad of it, but I can't get distracted. Are they in the house where Arlys lived? I know it."

"No, and you're not going to bother Will at midnight. He's worn-out and half-sick."

"He's sick? I can help."

"It's just a crap cold, and he's been treated. He needs sleep—that's from the healers—medical and magickal—so no-go on waking him up."

He got his plate, dropped it on the table, poured himself a short glass of milk. "You want?"

"No. I can't waste time."

"Then sit down and tell me what the fuck. I'll tell Will in the morning."

She could go back through the crystal, she calculated, bring Will's image back, try again. But not only did it seem impractical, she needed to accept there could be a reason she'd missed the mark.

So she sat.

"Night after tomorrow night, they'll attack. The group, or a splinter group of them, from the thwarted ambush."

"Mercer?"

"He's really, really pissed off. This isn't a sanctioned attack."

"He's gone rogue?"

"He was burned, badly, in the explosion that night. He's been stewing on this ever since. He lost status with Jeremiah White; he's been demoted. I can't get it all, and only got that because his hate's so huge. I didn't wait to try for more. I just know he has more than a hundred with him, and two squads of Raiders."

Duncan nodded, coolly calculating. "They've been known to hook up. They let the Raiders take some of the magickals for bounty. Dead or alive."

"They raided the armory—what was left of it—killed some of their own to do it. And they raided other settlements. They have a number of militarized weapons with them, and two tanks."

"Tanks? We could use a couple of tanks. Hold on, be right back." He started out, turned back. "Don't eat my sandwich."

"It's burnt."

"Don't eat it," he repeated.

She pushed up, paced. Midnight, she thought, hours past the time she'd aimed for. And now she was stuck in a kitchen that smelled of burned bread instead of talking to the leader.

Well, she could tell her mother they had access to cheese here, and that Katie's kitchen had walls the same color as the daffodils in a skinny bottle on the table.

And that Katie's son had very quick reflexes, even if he couldn't grill a sandwich.

He came back, dark jeans worn to gray at the knees, a black T-shirt, hair that had a touch of his mother's curl and fell shaggy over the back of the shirt.

He carried a roll of paper, pencils, a couple of hand-drawn maps.

Well drawn, she noted as he spread them on the table. One of New Hope, another of the area around the town proper.

"Okay." He sat, picked up the sandwich in one hand, bit in. "Show me. Which road are they using?"

She picked up one of the pencils, then stopped, narrowed her eyes at him. "Did you find out who told the Mercer group where you'd scout the day you found the wounded man?"

"No. We're keeping our eye on a couple of people. There's a woman who was part of a cult. Crazy bastards. She's still here—has a baby—but she keeps separate. She won't wear regular clothes. She might work with the PWs, even though they raided their camp and we saved her ass and plenty of others. Crazy bastards," he repeated.

"There are a couple of others. This guy who took a place about a mile out of town. Keeps to himself, big-time. He'll barter, but only with non-magickals. And there's Loony Lenny. He's just not right. Will's had to lock him up a few times since he wandered in. He just loses it. Otherwise he's quiet and a little spooky. Anyway, we're working on it. If we've got somebody who's part of the community working with the PWs, we'll dig them up eventually. Or they left already, and that's what most figure happened. People do move on."

"I don't want you to tell anyone who you don't trust completely. Who isn't part of the structure of command. Not friends, not anybody, not some girl you want to impress."

"You're a piece of work." He bit into the sandwich again. "I get you're going to—sooner or later—lead the forces of light against the forces of dark and all that. I'll be right there with you if and when, but right now? We've got a pretty good ear to the ground between Chuck and Arlys and the communication committee. We haven't heard anything about this attack you're talking about. But I figure you're not here to bullshit. I'm also going to bet my ass and half of yours, since there hasn't been a lot of talk about some girl warrior raising hell, I've clocked a lot more field time than you have.

"And one more? I don't need to blab and brag to impress girls. So show me where you saw them on the map, tell me what you know. You can even add in what you think."

She heard him, the cool logic in his words. And still she hesitated another moment. "There's something or someone *under* in this place. Something working under. Can't you feel it?"

He frowned, picked up his glass of milk. "Yeah, I can feel it. Yeah, it pisses me off I can't find it. I've tried. I can't find it. So you don't have to worry about me talking about this with anybody I don't know inside and out."

Fallon did a quick sketch on the roll of paper to coordinate with the maps. "This road."

"Straight onto Main Street? Bold."

"Mercer . . . He's angry and not a very smart person. He blames us—magickals—for everything that isn't the way he wants it to be. He's not a true believer like the one who sacrificed himself. He's a bigot, and only rose up the ranks through connections and his own cruelty. He likes to see us suffer. He likes to make anyone who helps or befriends magickals suffer. New Hope's his . . . you know about the Holy Grail?"

"Yeah, yeah. I read books, I've been to school. I've watched Monty Python."

"Who?"

"Too bad for you on that one," Duncan said over another bite of sandwich. "How do you know so much about Mercer?"

"I saw it in him. He doesn't have—what is it? A filter. He just doesn't. He thinks it, or feels it, it's his truth. We killed his brother, and years later, we humiliated him, disfigured him."

She frowned down at what Duncan sketched in the corner of the roll. "How do you know what Mercer looks like now?"

Duncan frowned at the sketch in turn. The thin face, the straggle of beard, the raw, rippled scarring that puckered the left side of his mouth and eye.

"I don't know. I'm getting it off you. I don't know how. Is it right?"

"Yes, it's right. You draw really well."

"It's something to do."

"Is reading people something you do?"

"Not usually like this." His gaze cut up to hers. "Vibes, you know how it is."

"One of my brothers reads people, but he understands and respects privacy."

"What can I say? It was pumping off you when you were talking about him. And I saw his face. How many?"

"More than a hundred. The tanks, about twenty trucks—some of them are the military trucks they sometimes use to transport prisoners. Ten on horseback, armed with swords. The Raiders on motorcycles."

As she spoke, Duncan scribbled notes.

"Horseback, swords, that's cleanup. They'll come in with the tanks first—after they send in a squad to take out our guards. That's what I'd do."

"That's what I'd do," she agreed. "So you'd want your line here, a mile out."

"A good mile. We're not going to let them get into town. Take out the tanks first."

They huddled over the paper, the maps, the plans for nearly an hour. Fallon figured Will and others would refine it further, but she'd given them all they needed.

"Not tomorrow night, but the night after. I'll watch," she told him. "If I'm needed, I'll come. But I don't think you'll need me. The Raiders don't have any loyalty to the PWs, and these PWs? Mercer's? They don't have any loyalty to anybody. They just want blood, and payback."

"Yeah, we'll handle it. Appreciate the heads-up. Again."

"Tell Will and your mother my mother saw them. She wants them to know she saw them."

"How does she see them? How do you watch?"

She started to smile, and when she did, it moved something inside him. Then the smile faded, and her eyes went dark with vision.

"Don't trust the fruit, the flowers. The fruit is black inside, the flowers hide the serpent's bite."

"What fruit, what flowers?"

"I don't know. Sorry." She dragged her hands through her hair because the vision, so short, so full of dark, made her head ache. "I have to go. I'll come back if you need me to."

"You went really pale. Do you want—"

She vanished.

"Never mind then. See you around."

Fallon came back through the crystal, back fully into herself, and fainted.

She woke on her bed with her mother clutching her hand.

"I'm okay. Just a little dizzy."

"I'm going to get you some water, and a restorative."

"Don't go. Give me a minute. How long was I gone?"

"Nearly two hours. Dear God, Fallon, nearly two hours, and you didn't split. The whole of you went through. I could only see little pieces, and only now and then. I couldn't see you."

"Too long, that's part of it. I've never stayed more than about an hour, and I . . . I pushed it too long, and I know better. You have to build it up. I'm sorry, you must've been so worried."

She brought Lana's hand to her cheek, soothed herself. "Right before I came back, I had this short, fast, really intense vision. It gave me a terrible headache."

"Nausea?"

"No, just the headache and a little dizziness."

"Let me see." Gently, Lana ran her hands over Lana's face, her head, rubbed at her temples. "Does it help?"

"A little. It feels so deep."

"I'm going to get what you need. Don't try to get up."

Lana flashed. All the training and practice with Fallon had paid off. Now sick worry added to her power and speed. She came back with a glass, water, a vial, and a white cloth.

"You'll drink this." She tapped pale blue drops into the water. "Three sips. Pause. Three sips, pause, and again a third time. Three by three," she ordered as she supported Fallon's head.

Fallon obeyed, felt the deepest layer of pain ease during the second dose. "Better."

"One more. Three by three. Where do you feel it?"

"Here." She touched her forehead. "But it's not bad now."

"Lie back, close your eyes." She laid the cloth, folded in threes, on Fallon's forehead. "What was the vision?"

"Poisoned fruit, flowers that weren't flowers but a serpent. I don't know if it was for me or Duncan. It was Duncan I talked to, not Will."

"I saw, when I could get a glimpse. I thought it must be Duncan. He has Katie's eyes. He's a very handsome boy."

"He's smart. A smart-ass, too." She opened her eyes. "Sorry."

"Close your eyes."

"He's smart," she repeated. "We worked out a plan. He'll take what I told him and what we worked out to Will in the morning. Will has a bad cold, and the healers said he had to sleep. Or Duncan said they did. I'll watch in case, but feel like they won't need me to help them this time. They're prepared. I told him to tell Will and Katie you saw them."

Her words began to slur as Lana glided her fingers over the cloth.

"Katie's kitchen has daffodil walls. She has daffodils on the table. Pretty. Duncan burned his sandwich, but he ate it anyway."

"That's good, that's fine. Sleep now, my baby. Sleep."

Lana stayed to make sure the sleep held, then went out to put the vial and cloth away. And did the only thing left to do.

She started dinner for her family.

JOURNEYS

Hope is like the sun, which,
as we journey toward it,
casts the shadow of our burden behind us.

—Samuel Smiles

CHAPTER TWENTY-ONE

Fallon thought she knew her father, all the ins and outs, the ups and downs of him. But she learned over the next weeks there were parts and pieces of him she'd never seen.

She'd known, of course, the people in the village, the neighbors on other farms, those who ran the mill, wove cloth, made music, made weapons, liked and respected him.

The village had its structure and systems. Though its positioning in the mountains, a fair distance from what had been cities and what had once been urban sprawl, made it of little interest to Raiders, bounty hunters, the PWs, even the fractured and struggling government, there had been incidents over the years.

She knew, too, her father had helped fight off those who wanted to steal or overtake, those who simply wanted to destroy for the sake of burning and blood. But, by and large, outsiders left them alone.

Those she knew from trips to barter, for schooling, to help with injuries or illnesses spent their days going about their business. Food needed to be put on tables, clothes on backs, boots on feet. Babies needed to be born and the dead buried.

She knew that for most she was simply Simon and Lana's daughter. A child. To begin to raise an army on her own doorstep, she needed her father to blaze the path.

He started with the farms, standing in fields or with his hands greasy helping repair equipment.

People listened to him. She saw that for herself when he held the first meeting, with about a dozen neighbors, at the farm.

"I grew up here," he would say. "Now my kids are growing up here. But the world I grew up in's gone. And the one, the only one my kids, your kids have ever known is nothing like before. Everyone here lost someone, to the Doom or the violence that came with it, and came after it. Some of you came here to escape that, to build a life in the world we've got left.

"We've been lucky," he continued. "We don't have a lot of trouble. That's mostly geography. We know by what we hear on the radio, or from people who pass through, even settle here, there are other places where people are trying to build a life. Some of them are lucky, some aren't."

There were some murmurs of agreement, but for the most part people remained quiet to hear what Simon Swift had to say.

"We can go on like we are, hoping for the best, hoping that bad luck passes us by. But we know better. We've lost people when that bad luck's come at us."

"We're better prepared now." Darlie Wertz, a rawboned woman with two teenage boys, gripped her hands together until her knuckles went white. "We don't want any trouble. Why go looking for it?"

Fallon knew Darlie had lost her whole family in the Doom, and she'd taken the boys in, made them her own. One, Charlie, bore the pentagram brand burned into his forehead.

"Darlie, not four months ago we had three people come through, one of them half-dead. They got caught in a raid not sixty miles from here."

"Sixty miles is a long way. It's not like it used to be."

"No, it's not like it used to be. I don't see it ever being the way it used to be."

You do. Fallon all but heard her father's thoughts, and the sympathy in them.

"Some years back I stood on my porch and killed a man." He kept talking in that steady way over the murmurs. "He didn't give me much choice as he, and the one with him, planned to take what was mine, and likely kill me for sport. But they came here, Purity Warriors, hunting Lana. Hunting the baby in her."

More rumblings, shifting, clearing of throats. "She'd had to run from a place where people, good people, were trying to build a life, a community."

Simon looked at Lana, nodded.

"We thought we were prepared," she said. "But we weren't. Not enough to stop them before they killed so many of us. I came here, like a lot of us, from somewhere else, but this is home. It's my home, and I want more than anything for my children to be safe and happy, to live my life with Simon right here. But they're not going to let us."

"You don't know that," Darlie began.

"Tell that to Macon Addams," Simon interrupted. "We buried him after the Raiders hit."

"Over three years ago."

"Raiders," Simon continued. "Purity Warriors, bounty hunters, rogue military, military following what passes for the government orders, holding people in camps and labs."

"Those are just rumors."

"You know they're not. We've all heard the stories from people who've come through. Some of us have stories of our own."

"I saw the inside of one of those rumors." Maddie Bates of Sisters Farm kept up with her knitting as she spoke. "Soldiers, some of them as scared of me as I was of them. And for some, fear made them hate. Six months for me, under the ground, being tested. If you tried to fight it, they used Tasers and worse on you. I didn't know what I had in me, not all of it, back then. But I found out, and I got away. They'll never put me underground again, or in one of their labs."

She looked up at Darlie. "You love your boys, I know you do. You want to tell me you wouldn't fight with all you had if those who put that mark on your Charlie came back for him?"

"They won't."

"Mom." Charlie put a hand on her arm. "She's scared, that's all. I was nine when they burned this onto me, and that was a year after soldiers—American soldiers—came in and took my mother away. She made me hide, so they didn't find me when they came and dragged her away."

He kept that comforting hand on his mother's arm. "We thought we were safe, too. We weren't hurting anyone, and we'd made a home, a small community of people who weren't hurting anyone. But they came."

"That was before, Charlie," Darlie insisted. "That was before."

"It was three years after the Doom, and they came for us. My dad was a marine, and he died in the Doom. He was proud to serve, too, but it was soldiers who dragged my mother away, three years after my dad died. I never saw her again. It was the PWs who caught me when I got away from the soldiers, and beat me and branded me. And would've hanged me like they did others if some locked up like me hadn't fought back. Some of them died fighting so some of us could get free.

"My dad was a marine," he said again, "and I know you were army, Mr. Swift. Just like I know if my dad was here, he'd say what you're saying. You're saying we've gotta learn to fight, gotta make an army.

Mom." He squeezed her arm when she let out a little sob. "You've gotta understand, my mother likely died protecting me, and I saw others die protecting me. And for ten years now you've protected me—eight years you've protected Paul."

He glanced at the young man who'd become his brother, got a nod.

"It's time we protected ourselves and you, and fight back." Charlie, an elf with straw-colored hair and a small, jagged scar under his left eye where a ring on a fist had torn the skin, looked now toward Fallon. "Do you have the sword and shield?"

As Fallon nodded, Darlie's voice cracked out.

"That's nonsense. I've told you and told you—"

"It's not." Paul, compact and quiet, a serious seventeen who always weighed his words, spoke. "Charlie and me, we love you a lot, but it's time you swallowed down what is instead of chewing on what you want."

"She's just a girl."

"She's my girl." Simon kept his eyes on Darlie's. He knew, and Fallon knew, he already had the others. "And I can wish all I want she was just a girl, and your boys were just boys. But that's not how it is, and it's never going to be how it is. We can put all that aside for now. It's a lot to swallow down. But what we can't put aside is we need to be ready and able and willing to fight for our families, our neighbors, our land, and the world we're going to make out of what we have."

"They used to call it boot camp." Maddie went on with her knitting. "I'd say you'd be a fine drill sergeant, Simon. My sisters and I, and Lana, I'm sure, will be happy to help with magickal training. Why don't you tell us how you want to set things up, Simon?"

He had a plan. Fallon realized he always had a plan.

Simon talked with the town elders, spoke with several others— former military—over a beer or a piece of pie.

He kept Fallon's connection minimal with most of the non-magickals. They had to get things started first, he explained, one step at a time.

He began, with other handpicked instructors, what he thought of as basic training. Ages sixteen and up. Always on a voluntary basis. For the younger children, he began the way he'd begun with his own. Calisthenics, sports, elemental self-defense.

He brought Fallon in, telling her the tactical way would be for her to straddle the line. Working with him, and working with her mother.

It appalled her to learn how many of the younger magickals had no training with their gifts, and how many of the older had either not explored theirs, or had let them go rusty.

Because, she understood, they wanted to believe as Darlie did. That they were and would remain safe, that their world was a kind of bubble that would never be penetrated from outside.

She understood also that her two years with Mallick had served her well. She knew how to train others, knew how to separate bullshit excuses from genuine concerns.

All through the spring, the blacksmith's anvil rang. It wasn't plowshares into swords—they needed to plow—but there was plenty of scrap metal, and a witch and alchemist who worked in the blistering heat of the forge to strengthen that metal.

Others melted metal to make bullets, and taught others how it was done.

Through the summer, into the fall, and to the first frost after her sixteenth birthday, Fallon taught and trained, conjured and brewed.

The soldier in her father watched her forge herself, as the smithy forged steel, into a weapon.

Sometimes with her father, sometimes with her mother—neither would let her go alone as yet—she flew on Laoch for supplies. Magickal and military.

But she went alone—what they didn't know wouldn't worry

them—through the crystal deep at night to study unfamiliar land, to walk places on her maps she considered strategic.

Once she'd slipped through to stand near the rubble of a memorial for a once-great president. Cloaked in darkness she listened to gunfire, explosions, watched a trio of small tornadoes whirl over the city spitting black lightning.

And the Dark Uncanny who winged by like bats.

Why, she wondered, did those who wanted to govern, who surely wanted to rebuild the city that had once held all those traditions and governance, strike and fear the magicks that would help them? It made no sense, it had no strategy.

How many of her kind had they locked away, had they "tested," tormented? Killed. Because they were different.

How did they justify hunting people down, even children?

And by doing so, they fought two wars—against the dark and the light—so their city, their capital remained a battleground.

While marauders roamed free, while violent cultists tortured and killed the innocent.

"This city is dead," she said aloud. She could taste it in the smoke. "It won't ever be what it was, what it might have been. And how much blood will fall because of people like you, people who fear and hate, when we rise up and fight back.

"And we will." She put a hand on the hilt of her sword. "We will."

She thought of her family, her neighbors, the sacrifice to come. Of New Hope, what courage and community could build—and lose.

"We will," she repeated.

She supposed it was because New Hope came formed in her mind that she went there back through the crystal instead of home again.

For the second time she and Duncan drew swords. And for a second time, as dark covered both, steel met steel.

And as it rang, light burst, flooded them both for two heartbeats.

He swore, eased back. "This is getting to be a habit."

Disoriented, a little dizzy, she struggled for dignity. "Maybe you're just always in the way. What are you doing out here?"

"Security detail. What are you doing out here?"

She wasn't entirely sure where here was, so evaded. "Just checking."

She could smell the woods, and now that her vision adjusted after that burst of light, see them beyond a thin trickle of snow.

The shadow of a building, other structures—greenhouses. And a garden with . . . winter cabbage, and kale she identified by scent.

Beyond it a cornfield rustling dry with the first winds of winter.

The community garden, she realized. The cornfield where her father died. Murdered.

She took a step toward it.

Duncan grabbed her arm. "Hold on."

It felt like the light, she thought, that blast when his hand gripped her. She shoved it off.

"I want to see."

She walked over a dusting of snow.

As she did, she could see it, feel it. High summer, bright sun, music, color, smoking grills, the garden thriving.

Gunfire, screams.

"Someone died here, just here." She looked down at the ground. "A woman, a witch, shielding a child."

"Twelve people died," Duncan told her. "Twelve of our people died, inside minutes. It only took minutes. Twenty-four wounded, some of those were kids."

She walked to the cornfield. "My father died here." Crouched down, laid her hand on the ground. "His brother and his brother's bitch. They rose up there." She pointed. "Wing tips scorched, but the edges like blades. A gift from the dark."

"They did blood sacrifices up in the mountains of PA—some bad shit. Eddie, Poe, and Kim were up there with your mother and father, and they've told us what went down. My father died in the Doom.

Mom put his name on the memorial tree." Duncan gestured toward it. "Your father's up there, too."

She looked toward the tree. The stars on it shimmered quietly in the thin snow. "Will you show me?"

He walked her over, picked out the star with MAX FALLON on it. "I don't know who put it up. I never thought to ask."

"It doesn't matter who. It matters you honor the dead."

"Is this why you're here? You wanted to see this."

"No." But she reached out, brushed her fingertips over the star with her father's name. "I didn't mean to come."

"Wires crossed?"

She looked at him in the shimmer of stars. He'd grown taller since she'd seen him last, and had a dark stubble over his cheeks. He hadn't bothered with a hat so the snow fell over his hair, as shaggy and unkempt as before.

He wasn't being an asshole, she thought, so she wouldn't be one, either.

"I guess so. I went to Washington, D.C."

"What? When? What's going on?"

"Just now. I mean to say: I went there, meant to go home, but I'd just thought about New Hope, and . . . I thought about why. Why, why, why?" She paced away. "Why are they trying to kill us, or lock us away? The Purity Warriors, they're vicious religious bigots—or they hide behind their version of God."

"White's version."

"And theirs, or they wouldn't follow him. Raiders, they are what they are. What they probably were before the Doom, or wanted to be. Bounty hunters, they want the reward, or just like the hunt. But the others. Why? Most of the world died horribly, and they waste time and lives hunting us down."

"They blame us."

"They're blind and stupid."

"Didn't say otherwise," he pointed out. "What did you see there? In D.C.?"

"Death. Death claiming more death. There's no heart beating there anymore. Do you know what I mean?"

"Yeah."

"Eventually we'll have to retake it, but its symbolism's finished." She turned back to him. "We're mobilizing at home. Training."

"About damn time."

"There are other places, not so different from here, from home. We'll need them. Did you find the traitor?"

"No. We haven't had any more trouble like that. We have to figure whoever it was left. But we're watching. They attacked, the PWs, like you said that night in the kitchen."

"I know. I watched."

"You were here?"

"No. You didn't need me."

"How did you get to D.C., then from there to here? Did you zip?" Her brow creased. " 'Zip'?"

"Yeah, like." He gripped her hand this time. She felt a quick rush, then they stood back at the edge of the gardens.

Her hand tingled in his.

"We call it flashing."

"Zip, flash, same deal." One that had taken him weeks of focused practice to learn, and weeks more to perfect. "Is that how?"

"No, it's different." She looked into his eyes. "I saw you in the moonlight walking from the trees through the fog toward a circle of stones. Toward the first shield. You told me I had to choose. You looked right at me through the dream and said I had to choose. I chose."

"I saw you standing in the moonlight, in the fog by the stone circle. You carried your sword. This one. Solas. And when you lifted it, the sky cracked open with lightning."

"What happens next?"

"I always come out of it. Wake up or come out of it. I never see. I've seen you on the battlefield, fought with you there. And . . . other things."

"What other things?"

"Hell."

He gave her hand one hard tug, and when her body bumped his, gripped her hair with his free hand, crushed his mouth to hers.

It was nothing like Mick, nothing soft and sweet and . . . nice.

This was hard and hot, and made her insides quake.

She could have struck him away—she would have if she'd thought of it. But everything churned and quivered and rocked.

The fingers of her hand on his shoulder dug in once as this connection, conflict, chaos that was nothing, nothing, nothing so gentle as the word *kiss* blew through her in a storm.

Then he drew her back as roughly as he'd drawn her in. His eyes burned into hers and didn't look particularly pleased.

"I just figured it. It half pisses me off."

"Let go or I'll make you let go."

"We could see who wins that battle, but"—he held his hands up, palms out, stepped back—"I guess you haven't had that dream yet."

"I don't dream about you." Lie, lie, lie.

"You just said you did."

"That's different." Everything felt different, and it more than half pissed her off. "You've got no right to grab me like that."

"You didn't say no. Didn't think it, either. A girl says or thinks no, that's no." He put a hand over her sword hand—just in case. Smiled at her. "Say no."

Instead she pushed him back, a little harder than she intended, and retreated through the crystal.

"Didn't say no that time, either," he mumbled. "Or think it."

He looked up as the light snow melted into light rain. "She's not my type!" he told the heavens. "So cut me a break."

He heard a distant rumble of thunder that sounded all too much like a laugh.

She didn't have time to think about boys or kissing. Part of her sensed that Duncan kissed more like a man than a boy—or at least some- one who'd done a lot of it.

It didn't matter. She had work, important work. Not only build- ing an army, brick by brick, but calculating just what to do once she had one.

She thought of D.C. often, pushed it aside, wound back to it. A dead city, but people lived in its ashes, and some who did lived locked away.

Prisoners, experiments, weapons.

Since the Doom, those who clung desperately to power or craved it had unleashed weapons. The magickal in killing lightning and burn- ing winds, and the bombs men made that turned cities to rubble.

The problem with bombs was they could be turned back on those who launched them. In her nighttime journeys, Fallon visited the cra- ters and ruins in Texas, California, Florida, Nevada.

The destructive power scorched her soul, but more, much more, the knowledge that humans would use such evil to destroy their own.

How many more waited to be woken to fly and fall?

Eradicating that power, that evil, had to be a priority.

"Even if you figured out how to disarm or destroy every bomb, every drone, and/or the capability to use them, globally," Simon told her over one of their late-night strategy sessions, "they'll build more."

"Then we eliminate them. It's too easy to kill when you're not look- ing your enemy in the eye. You don't see the child hiding under his bed when the flames take him. When black magicks fly, they seek to destroy. This isn't any different. We're asking people to fight with swords, small arms, their fists, and their powers when one of the enemies has the capability to turn them into dust with . . . technology. We find a way to destroy that technology. How do we thrive, Dad, after the battles, after all the blood and sacrifice and risk, if someone somewhere can kill thousands with a machine, with a code?"

She pushed up from the table, paced the kitchen, their usual meeting place. "It's man's magick—the atomic, the nuclear, the remote killing. And it's just as dark as a strike of black lightning or the shearing of wings, the hanging of children."

"Logistically, realistically, what you're talking about may be impossible."

"Did anyone believe, logistically, realistically, that it was possible for billions of people to die within weeks across the planet? That a shield broken in a circle of stones in a field in Scotland would kill so many and, because of the killings, change the world?"

"No. We weren't prepared."

Now we have to be, she thought. We have to be prepared.

"You and Mom insisted we study history, and we did. Wars, so many of them useless, waged for greed or twisted faith, and rebuilding from the rubble only to war again. But it changed, Dad, from spears and swords and arrows to guns, explosives to bombs. To weapons capable of wiping everything away. Oppenheimer was right: 'I am become death, the destroyer of worlds.' We didn't survive the Doom to let the rest fall. It's easier to destroy than to build. We'll find a way to make it harder, to take away the ability to kill masses."

"So if we, I don't know, turn bombs into flowers, we save the world with spears, arrows, and swords?"

"And tactics and courage and light." Idly, she rubbed a hand on the cuff she'd made from the tree. "You're thinking if we manage *that*, they'll build bombs again. They'll rebuild the cities, plant crops, make communities. And some will build bombs and weapons to kill masses again, and some of the some will do it believing it's for defense, for protection, a deterrent."

"Yeah. Still, it'll take a while."

She chewed over it, studied and considered methods from every angle she could devise. Every night now she went through the crystal. She stood on the tarmac of what had been O'Hare in Chicago. The tower that had guided the planes, gone. Planes in hangars, at gates, on runways, burned to husks. And the remains of bodies inside the husks, inside terminals, hangars, offices. No one had taken them out, buried, or burned them.

She walked the hallways of a small, rural hospital in Kansas, an empty school in Louisiana. She watched mustangs and elk, buffalo, red-tail deer run the plains in Montana.

She saw settlements as well, and farms, noted that most had regrouped, rebuilt in remote places.

Once she stood in a bunker deep inside a mountain. All the computers, the monitors, the controls lay dead and quiet. Her first instinct urged her to make certain they stayed that way because she recognized the place as not just for defense, but also capable of launching an attack.

But she'd learned, from her parents, from Mallick, from what lived inside her, to weigh instinct against cool blood. She didn't know enough, she decided as she wandered the counters, the buttons and switches and keyboards. What if by trying to eliminate she awakened?

Instead, she searched through, impressed that men could build so much so deep.

And as she had with every other place she'd traveled to, she marked the site on a map.

That night she dreamed.

She stood in the moonlight and fog at the circle of stones, studied the scorched and cracked ground within. A weight lay on her, in her, like lead.

"So many lost, so much death." Her voice flowed out across the empty fields to be whisked away by the wind. "Was it sacrifice so I could be? It's my blood that opened the door to the light and the dark."

"Our blood." Duncan stood beside her. Older, as he had been in that long-ago dream. "We're cousins, after all, if you go back a few centuries. Are you going to stand here and blame a young boy or the old man he became?"

"Your grandfather isn't to blame. What used him is. Why was it allowed? Why wasn't it stopped?"

"Why do you think questions always have answers?"

"Because they do."

"Answer this: Are we really standing here now, or is it another dream?"

"Both."

He grinned at her, took her hand. So much of the weight, so much, just fell away from her. "I'd rather be in bed with you than standing in the damn field debating the whys and philosophies."

"You kissed me in the snow."

"You didn't say no."

He kissed her now, under the moon, just as fierce and rough as he had in the thin snowfall.

White, she thought as she moved into him. White snow, white moon.

Then the crows screamed, a black circle overhead. And in the trees, in the rising fog, something dark as death stirred.

"It's time," Duncan said to her.

She nodded, drew her sword and, lifting it, burned the crows to ash. With him, she turned toward the trees and what waited.

"It's time," she agreed, and charged with him.

She woke, the candle she'd lit in sleep burning, the crystal shimmering clear. She picked up the teddy bear Ethan had kept for her faithfully, stroked it.

"It's time," she whispered, and rose to tell her family.

CHAPTER TWENTY-TWO

Fallon waited—animals had to be fed, eggs gathered, cows milked, stalls mucked and rebedded.

She helped with breakfast, and said nothing, as she realized she needed to speak to her parents first. Alone.

Knowing Travis, she kept her mind and her feelings shut down even as she took moments to study each of her brothers in turn.

Colin, tall and tough, shoveling in his food as he talked about sword practice. Not long before—yesterday, it seemed to her—he'd have been talking about going fishing or shooting baskets after lessons and work was done.

Travis, wily and wiry, taking his time with the meal, not planning a prank as he once would've been, but more likely thinking about shooting his bow or learning a new spell.

And Ethan, kind and wise, sneaking bacon into his pocket that he'd divide in two for the dogs. And nagging his father to let him ride a bigger, faster horse.

Not children anymore, Fallon thought. Potential soldiers, warriors in the making. Her making.

But still brothers who'd argue, interrupt, and show their hurt when she told them she had to go.

She exchanged a look with her mother, then her father—one she'd perfected that said she needed to talk without her brothers.

She waited. The table needed clearing, dishes needed washing. Being relieved of chores would cause suspicion, so the normal routine had to run. The normality bringing her both pain and comfort.

"I've got a couple of things I need to do around here before I go into the village," Simon announced. "You boys go ahead, saddle your horses, and ride in—straight there. No detours or screwing around," he added with a meaningful look at Colin. "I'll drop Fallon and your mom over at the Sisters and head in."

"Can I ride Thunder?"

"No," Simon told Ethan firmly. "You're on Pixie."

"Aw! Thunder wants me to ride him."

"Then he's going to be disappointed, too. You're not riding a stallion. Not yet. Argue and I can find chores around here for you, no problem."

"Jeez." But since both his brothers had already raced out, he gave up and ran after them.

"Can we sit down?"

Lana walked back to the table. When Simon sat with her, they gripped hands under the table.

"I have to go." She said it fast, shoving out the words she knew would hurt in hopes of lessening the pain.

"Are you sure?" Lana asked.

"I am. I'm sure. I'm sorry."

"When?"

She looked at Simon. "There are things I need, things I need to do before I leave."

"A week? Can you wait a week, two at the most?"

"I . . . Yeah." She'd expected more distress, and some argument about waiting months, not days. "I need to put together some supplies, and I want to plot out a route, and I thought you could both help me with that. I'll need to enlist more people on the way, start more training camps. I know the route I took with Mallick, and I'll start there. But I'll need to veer off to reach New Hope. And I want to hit as many places as I can on the way where I'll find people willing to fight."

"You won't go directly to New Hope?"

"No." She shook her head at Lana. "When I get there, I want to be able to tell them I have a thousand soldiers, magickal and non."

"That's a big number, baby," Simon commented.

"We have a hundred and sixty-eight here. There are a hundred more in the woods near Mallick's cottage. I'll get more. It may take a few months, but the weather's good. I want a thousand because it's a big number, and less won't have the same impact. I'll have them, and get to New Hope by the end of August."

"And then . . ." Lana stopped herself. "I'm pushing too far ahead. A week." She looked at Simon, got his nod.

"We'll be ready," he said.

"I'll get word back to you," Fallon continued. "Flash to you or come through the crystal. Or through the fire."

"I don't think you understand." With one hand still holding Simon's, Lana took Fallon's, joining them. "We're going with you."

"With me?" Genuinely stunned, Fallon gaped at them. "You can't."

"I made the trip from New Hope to here with you," Lana reminded her. "I'll make it back with you. We all will."

"Listen, just listen. I could be months on the road."

"Raising an army," Simon finished. "You could use some help with that. It happens we have some experience."

"The boys are too young."

"Ethan's the only one younger than you were when you left for two years," Lana reminded her.

"They've been training, and training hard. If I didn't think they could handle it, they wouldn't be going."

"They'll think of it as an adventure," Lana added. "Every one of them."

"But it won't be. Raiders cruise the roads. Purity Warriors hunt for Uncannys and for slaves. Outside this—this bubble, there are bounty hunters and military, and flat-out crazy people who'd put a knife in you for whatever's in your pack. It's not a damn adventure."

Lana leaned forward, eyes hot. "I was six months pregnant, alone, most often on foot, very often half-starved, and hunted outside this 'bubble' as you call it."

"Yes, but—"

"You're not alone in power and grit, Fallon. This man? This man," she repeated in a voice as hot as her eyes as she gripped Simon's hand. "He fought wars before you were born. He's protected us and our neighbors since the old world ended and this one began."

"I don't mean to say . . ." At that moment, when her mother looked fierce enough to lead an army herself, Fallon didn't know what she meant to say.

"What? Just what?" Lana demanded. "That we're too weak, too soft, too naive to face the realities of what's coming? We're not. We say our sons are ready. We say our daughter doesn't go alone, not this time. Not alone. And that's the end of it."

"I didn't mean to . . . The farm."

"It's not going anywhere." Simon left the heat to his wife, spoke easily. "We've talked this out and talked it through. The sisters and Jack Clanson and his people are going to look after things here. We'll take the horses because we'll need them, and the dogs because not taking them would break Ethan's heart. We'll take what the horses can carry, and be ready in a week. When your mother says that's the end of it, kid, that's the end of it."

Why hadn't she seen this? she wondered. In their eyes, through the crystal? She could just leave, be gone in . . . a flash. But they'd follow. And she'd have angered and hurt them.

"I never expected . . ."

"Adjust," Lana suggested.

"There's still training needed here."

"And people in place to deal with it," Simon finished. He rose, kissed her hard. "I'm going to head out, tell the people who need to know that we'll be leaving in a week. I imagine you and your mom have things to do here. Lana, if you want the truck to get to Sisters Farm later, I can leave it for you."

"We'll be fine on horses. We'll tell the boys tonight."

"That's the plan." He kissed his wife in turn, then left his women alone.

"I don't think you're weak, or soft."

Coolly now, Lana angled her head. "Just naive."

"No. Not exactly. It's just you, none of you have been very far from the farm in a long time. In a lot of ways it's worse than it was when you traveled here from New Hope."

"Safety and strength in numbers. Six together instead of one alone. We're a family. We go as a family."

"I couldn't stand if anything happened to any of you," Fallon admitted. "I'm afraid something will."

"I've watched my sons become men long, long before I want them to. I've known since before you were born what you'd be, and still it was, and is, so hard to let you be."

Reaching over, she covered Fallon's hand with hers. "But I've accepted all of it, because I have to. Now you, my precious girl, have to let the rest of us be what we are. I know before this is done, you'll

go without us. I know, before this is done, I'll watch my sons go without me. But not this time, Fallon. We go together."

Lana rose. "We should take inventory, make a priority list of what
we want to take with us. We'll get a start on that before we ride over
to the Sisters."

With a nod, Fallon got to her feet because, Savior aside, her father
was right. When her mother said that was the end of it, that was the
end of it.

The week stretched into two with the challenge of an entire family
setting out on horseback, on a long, potentially dangerous journey.
With no way of knowing when any would come back.

They considered the idea of taking the truck, a horse trailer—even
a wagon—and ultimately rejected it. They would, almost certainly,
have to travel off the roads as much as on them. Added to it, the logistics and time spent accessing fuel made the use of the truck too
complicated.

Horses might be slower, but Fallon wasn't in a hurry. Though she
still hoped to reach New Hope by the end of August, a few weeks
longer wouldn't matter.

The numbers she took with her mattered.

Lana insisted every inch, every corner of the house required scrubbing. Fallon saw that not only as pride, but a need to remind the
house, its spirits, its memories, that it was loved.

Simon walked the fields, went over equipment, feeding schedules,
the barn, silos, every outbuilding with those who'd serve as caretak-
ers. His version of scrubbing, Fallon thought.

As much as she wanted to go, as much as dreams pushed her to
begin, she took her parents' distractions as a way to pigeonhole each
of her brothers, one by one.

With Colin she played to his pride in being the oldest son and his protective instincts. She, and their parents, depended on him to look out for his younger brothers, and to show by his example the need to be careful and cautious, and to follow orders.

She appealed to Travis's intellect, slyness, and his gift. She knew he'd be smart, oh, she depended on it, as he knew as well as she that their brothers might do something foolish. So if he *felt* they might, she counted on him to distract them.

With Ethan, she had only to appeal to his heart. Their parents would worry, so she knew, could depend on, him listening carefully and helping them not worry as much. He'd also be her head scout, as animals often felt danger before people, and no one knew animals as well as he did.

She hoped that would keep them all in line at least for the first miles, but imagined she'd have to repeat the talks—and come up with new angles—regularly on the way to New Hope.

As the days passed she came to believe her parents had been right. More, she saw this as another choice, and the right choice, to go as a family.

And on a soft May morning with the leaves springing green, and the sun spreading its first gilded light over the hills, they headed south, as a family.

Her brothers chatted like magpies, and the dogs—nearly as young and just as excited—pranced. But Fallon saw tears glint in her mother's eyes as Lana looked back, one last time.

"It'll be where we left it, babe."

Lana looked at Simon, gave him a smile, and didn't look back again.

They rode through the first day with Taibhse soaring overhead. Her brothers never tired, nor did Faol Ban, and when the dogs did, Ethan took Scout up on his horse, and Simon took Jem.

They covered those first miles without incident, so Fallon nearly relaxed enough to enjoy her brothers' sheer wonder.

They'd never seen roads so plentiful or so wide, so many houses huddled together on what they considered one plot of land.

They'd never heard the wind whistle through the windows of abandoned cars or read signs that promised food and lodging up ahead.

Despite the broken windows and Raiders' graffiti on an old mini-mart—another new sight for her brothers—Travis began to weave a tale of a heroic battle.

Then they saw the remains, picked to the bone by time and carrion-eaters, hanging from what had been a flagpole.

She didn't object when her father rode to the remains, dismounted. The crank squeaked as he lowered the rope.

"Ethan, keep the dogs back. Colin, bring me the shovel."

Would she have ridden on? Fallon asked herself. Looked, pitied, but just ridden on past the dead rather than stop to do the human and the humane?

Here, she imagined Mallick would have told her, was another lesson to learn.

She dismounted, started to get the second shovel, but saw Colin already had. And with his father, her brother dug a grave for a dead stranger in the weedy strip of grass beside the pitted parking lot.

The wind flapped the rags of the flag on the pole and had the broken awning over the door of the mini-mart screeching metal to metal.

"He tried to run."

She looked sharply at Travis, saw it wasn't a story, but seeing.

"There's no need to look," she began, but he shot her a glittering glare.

"Somebody should. Somebody should know. He tried to run, but he wasn't fast enough. They took his boots and his pack, then they hanged him because he was too old to be of any use."

Fallon put a hand on his arm. It trembled under her touch, not from fear, she realized, but rage.

"We're going to stop them." He stared at her another moment. "We're going to stop them," he repeated, then turned into his mother and pressed his face to her shoulder.

Then he straightened his own shoulders, and walked over to help.

She watched Ethan pick flowering weeds, lay them on the grave. Whatever their father said as he lay a hand on Ethan's head had her youngest brother nodding.

"I was wrong," Fallon said to her mother. "I was wrong about them being too young for the journey. I'm asking them to train to fight, but I wasn't ready for them to see why. I was wrong."

To mark this turn on her path, she turned to the building, held out her hands, let the power rise up and out.

The skulls and crossbones, the ugly words faded. In their place she forged the fivefold symbol, and the words she'd carved into her bracelet. Into her reminder.

Solas don Saol

Late in the afternoon, she led them off the road into the trees where the map told her they'd find a stream. While they rested and watered the horses, she went to her father.

"There's a settlement about three miles southwest. I want to check it out while you wait here."

"Together, Fallon."

"It's just a precaution. I know they're not PWs, but I don't know if they're friendly."

"Didn't you figure that out during one of your midnight rambles?" When she said nothing, he tapped her chin with his finger. "We know where our children are. More or less."

They went together.

The settlement had once been a small mountain town that ran under a single steep mile from end to end. Before the Doom, the houses, two churches, a single bar, and a tiny general store had been home to less than two hundred people.

Now about eighty made the best of things. No community gardens or greenhouses, Fallon noted, but individual ones. No organized security, either, as she saw no posted guards. Just a few people who stepped out of houses or walked across sloping lawns with long guns.

She heard a baby cry, the mournful lowing of a cow, watched a young boy chase a hen who flapped wildly across the road.

From a distance she heard the quick crack of a bullet.

She looked to her father, knowing strangers would expect the man to take the lead.

"We're not looking for trouble," Simon began.

A man stepped forward, a little grimy around the edges despite the lack of beard and close-cropped hair. "What are you looking for?"

"Maybe a chance to stretch our legs for a bit. Simon Swift. My wife, Lana, our daughter, Fallon, our sons, Colin, Travis, and Ethan."

Smart, Fallon thought. The names made them people and a family.

"Don't have any supplies to spare."

"We're not looking for supplies, either. Are you in charge?"

"Don't need no in charge."

"Tim, don't be such an asshole." A woman moved up. Wide hips, rawboned face, a mass of graying hair. She wore jeans that carried as many patches as they did the original denim. "Mae Pickett," she said, and, resting her rifle on her shoulder, offered Simon a hand to shake. "This here's Tim Shelby. Where y'all from?"

"A few miles south of Cumberland."

"That so? I had a cousin lived up there. Bobby Morrison."

"Sorry. I don't think I know him."

"Well, he's likely dead now anyway, and always was an idiot. Those are some fine-looking horses." She held up her hand. "We don't steal from strangers here. We ain't got much to steal back."

"That works out nice for both of us," Simon said, making her laugh.

"You've got some poison ivy," Lana commented. Mae reached down to scrub at the rash that ranged angry from wrist to elbows on both arms.

"Yeah, driving me crazy. I didn't look before I reached."

"I've got something that will help."

But when Lana started to dismount, Fallon signaled her back. She got off Laoch, walked back to one of the packhorses, and dug out the balm.

She saw Mae's eyes cut down to the sword, but up again as she approached with the little jar. "It'll ease the itching," Fallon told her as she opened the jar, "give you relief, and start the healing."

She coated Mae's left arm.

"Praise Jesus, that works quick as a rabbit. First relief I've had in a week." She shifted her rifle, offered her gun arm. "I'm grateful."

Fallon offered the jar. "Put on another coat tonight. That should do it."

"Thank you kindly. What do I owe you?"

"Conversation."

Mae's eyebrows shot up. "That comes cheap enough. You a doctor, cutie?" Her lips curved as she asked, then sobered when she looked up at Lana. "You a doctor?"

"Healers."

"There's a boy lives right over there. About your middle boy's age, I'd say. He's been feeling poorly. Maybe you could take a look at him, maybe you got something to help him."

"I'd be happy to."

"Tim, you take Miss Lana on over to Sarah's place so she can see about Pete. Go on now, before I see if she can heal up your sour disposition. Mr. Swift, you can take your horses and boys right over that way, to the shade. We got that old well working a few years back.

The water's clean and cold. Nobody's going to bother your ladies. I promise you."

She turned to Fallon. "I owe you a conversation. That's my porch right there. We can sit a spell."

"I guess Mr. Shelby doesn't know you're in charge."

Mae let out a bark of laughter that ended on a hoot as she walked Fallon to her porch and the two spindly rockers on it. "He's not all the way wrong about no in charge. Mostly it's take care of your own first around here."

"More hands working together get more done."

"Won't say you're wrong, either. Me and Tim, we lived right here, went to school together. We're the only ones who didn't get sick when it came through. Came through so fast we didn't know we were dying until we were dead. Lost my husband, my ma and pa, too. Didn't have any kids, and I count that as a blessing now though it caused me grief in my younger days. I don't know if I could've lived burying a child. Anyway, that's past. You want conversation, so what do you want to talk about?"

"You don't have any Uncannys in your community."

"*Community*'s a stretch. We had a few come through, a few stay awhile. We don't have problems with them. There's a settlement of them about five miles on."

"I know. We're heading there next."

"We mind ours, they mind theirs." Mae lifted her wide shoulders. "We trade with them, and I can tell you, I was thinking of going to them about Pete. Boy's feverish and been running at both ends two days now. You one of them?"

"Yes."

"Your family?"

"My mother, two of my brothers."

"Then I'll be grateful again Pete's in good hands. He's a nice boy. Likes to help people. You didn't come for supplies, and there are lots of places to stretch your legs where nobody's going to hold a gun on you. Why'd you come?"

The woman had sharp eyes, Fallon thought, and from the way Tim had listened to her—from the way people with guns had melted away again—she was clearly respected if not technically in charge.

"Mrs. Pickett—"

"Mae."

"Mae, the Doom's finished, but the trouble isn't over."

"We don't get much of it here. Nothing worth stealing, too far off the road for Raiders to bother themselves. Government likely doesn't know or care we're here."

"They will. Do you have communications?"

As if it was just another lazy spring afternoon, Mae set her rocker creaking. "That we don't, unless you count somebody coming through with stories, but that doesn't happen often. Like I said, we're off the beaten path, and we're good with that. No communications, no electricity, no running water. We make do. Most of the young ones leave when they get your age or a bit older. Those who stay? They tend to have somebody they're taking care of. Sooner or later, there'll be nobody left but the ghosts."

"It doesn't have to be that way. You've got a good location." Strategic, Fallon thought. A good place for billeting troops. "There's a field going to waste over there that could be planted with crops. You've got houses that need repair. Electric lines waiting to be powered up."

"How we gonna manage all that, cutie? No plow, no tractor, no lumber, no electric company to throw the switch."

"I can help with that."

"That makes you damn handy." Those sharp eyes on Fallon's face, Mae drummed her index and middle fingers on the arm of the rickety chair. "What's the charge?"

"A trade. The use of some of the houses, one of the churches—or both if they're not in use. Some of the land. As a base."

"A base for what?"

"Soldiers. Training them, housing them, deploying them."

"Whose soldiers?"

"Mine."

Mae sat back, making the chair groan at the shifting weight. "You got soldiers?"

"Some, and I'll have more, because the trouble's not over. The next phase of it? It's just beginning. It'll swallow boys like Pete, and the little guy I saw chasing a chicken that should be in a coop so you don't have to hunt for the eggs or lose them to foxes. Have you seen the black lightning, ma'am?"

"In the distance."

"Crows circling, smoke rising?"

"In the distance."

"They'll come closer."

"Well, if you want to give me nightmares . . ." She trailed off, rose, walked to the end of the porch.

The owl had glided down to perch on a branch over the men in her family. The wolf trotted up to bump flanks with the dogs, and take water from the bowl Ethan set down for him.

"You see that big white owl?"

"Yes, he's mine. Taibhse. The wolf is Faol Ban."

"That horse got wings, girl? The white one you're riding?"

"When he wants them."

Slowly, Mae came back to sit. "I like conversations." Still, her voice came out raw before she cleared her throat. "I've had more than a few with some who live a few miles down. That's some sword you got there. A big sword for a young girl. How'd you get it?"

Fallon answered without hesitation. "In the Well of Light when I lifted it from the eternal fire, along with the shield."

Mae pressed her fingers to her eyes. "Sweet Baby Jesus. I've seen things, during the Doom, after, since, seen things my brain said my eyes were making up. But I saw them, and I know the whole world tilted like a table with a broken leg. It's never going back how it was."

"No, it's not going back. But it can, and it will, go forward. It's harder and slower to go forward if there's no in charge, and if people only mind their own."

"Some are happy enough just to stick in place."

"We buried a man on the way here, one we found hanging from a flagpole. He might've wanted to stick in place."

Mae let out a sigh. "There's a woman where you're heading next. Her name's Troy. First or last, I couldn't say, but that's what she goes by. She told me you were coming. She talked about you before, called you The One, and I didn't pay a lot of mind. That's her belief, and we oughta live and let. But the last time, not a week ago, I talked with her, she said you'd be coming to talk to me. You'd have a sword at your side. You'd ride a white horse, a winged horse. You'd have a white owl, a white wolf. She said you'd give me something I needed."

Mae looked down at her arms, let out a half laugh. "Damn rash is already clearing up. Said you'd ask me for something you needed."

"I'm asking. If you say yes—"

"If I don't?"

"We move on."

"Just like that?"

Fallon turned her head so their eyes met. "If we're meant to be free, if we believe that with all we are, why would I build an army by force to fight for freedom?"

"Plenty tried just that."

"And here we are," Fallon finished. "You'll make the choice. If you say yes, within six months I'll send some soldiers to you. To help you protect your community, help train any who want to be trained to fight or contribute. I could talk to your people."

"I'll talk to them. For some it'll take a lot of talking. For others, not as much. I have to think on it, and maybe have another conversation with Troy."

"You trust her."

"As much as anybody, more than most. I have to think on it," Mae repeated, "and let you know."

"All right." Fallon rose. "We'll stay the night with the Uncannys, if we're welcome."

"I expect you will be."

"If you haven't made up your mind by the time we leave tomorrow, I'll come back when you have, either way."

"How will you know?"

When Fallon just smiled, Mae shook her head.

The boy, Pete, had a stomach virus, and was well on the mend before they rode out. Out, into the thick woods and to a scatter of cabins where Troy waited.

Her curling mane of white-streaked black hair fell over her shoulders, framing a face the color of coffee beans. She had garden dirt on the knees of thin cotton pants, and a small spade in her hand.

Her eyes, dark as ebony, gleamed when they landed on Fallon's face. "Welcome. At long last, welcome."

As Mallick had done when she'd returned from the Well of Light, Troy went down on one knee.

"Please don't."

"Indulge me. We've waited so long. Welcome, mother, father, brothers." She rose, walked to Fallon, laid a hand on Laoch's head. "Welcome and bright blessings on you all."

Others came out, men, women, children, and as Troy had done, dropped to one knee.

"Do they think she's a queen?" Ethan whispered to his mother.

"Not a queen." Troy smiled at him. "But a witch and a warrior, and a promise. Come, please. We'll have food and wine. We'll tend to your animals."

When Fallon dismounted, Troy embraced her. "We're your army, and we'll help you raise more."

It wasn't always so simple and welcoming as that first day. Some wouldn't be convinced, some threatened.

Some, like the big, hulking leader of a band of two hundred she met on a sweltering day in June, laughed.

"We're doing fine here. Any bastards come around looking for trouble, they find it, and they don't come back."

"They will. In greater numbers."

"Save it, sister. We know how to handle ourselves, and nobody around here's going to fall in line behind some teenage witch. But you'll pay the fine for trespassing. One of the horses, and the supplies on its back."

Several dozen weapons lifted, aimed at her family. "That would make you thieves," Fallon said coolly. "I won't have thieves in my army."

"I don't see no army."

"Then see this." She swiped a hand through the air. Guns, knives, clubs turned red, burning the hands that held them. As people screamed, as weapons fell, she kept her eyes on the big man. "Nobody threatens my family." She didn't have to turn to know every member of her family now held a weapon of their own. She held up a hand.

"Wait. I'm about to make a bargain with . . . I didn't get your name."

"Fuck your bargain, little bitch."

"Not so little. Not as big as you, but not so little. Here's the deal. I fight you—you and me. If I lose, you get the horse and what he's carrying. If you lose, you and the rest here train when I say train, fight when I say fight."

She looked around. "Some of you know who I am, what I am. You've waited long enough. But I'll prove myself."

"I don't fight little girls. I don't fight damn witches who pull magick tricks out of their asses. And I don't fight when I've got that girl's daddy pointing a gun at my head."

"Fair fight. No magick—my word on it, and if I break my word, I'm disgraced in front of your people. And some of your people are like me. My father won't shoot anyone, none of my family will use a weapon against anyone who doesn't use one against us first."

As she spoke, she took off her sword, took out her knife, passed both to her father.

"Fallon."

"Trust me, or they won't. Fair fight, one-on-one." She turned back to the leader, let herself smirk to rile him up. "Do you agree to the terms I set?"

"I don't like fighting girls."

"When what's coming floods over you and yours, it won't matter what shape they wear. You were ready to steal from a girl, have your people pull weapons on a girl."

She turned the smirk into a sneer.

"Be man enough to fight one who's ready to fight you."

"You asked for it."

His face already red with insult, his mouth already twisted in a snarl reminded her of some raging bull. And rage was easily countered with cold tactics.

He charged—to knock her down, she realized. He honestly didn't want to strike her. Her advantage was that she didn't have the same sensibility regarding him.

She flipped back, to the side, so the momentum of his charge carried him through, had him stumbling.

Had several of his people laughing.

His face went redder. He charged again, she spun away. This time he skidded, tumbled, landed on his face.

"No magick!"

"It's not magick, it's training. I could train you, even though you're more bulk than muscle."

When he came at her again, she knew he expected her to spin or dodge. She did neither, but brought a boot up solidly between his legs. His face drained of all that burning color, and though she hated to hit a man on his way down, the point to prove was more important.

She knocked him flat with an uppercut that had her fist yelping, and her arm singing.

"You're down." She walked over to him while he wheezed. "Stay down. I'm better at this than you. You could be better. You will be better."

"Kicked me in the balls."

"The enemy would slice them off. I'm not the enemy." She went to her father, took her sword and, drawing it, held it up so the sunlight flashed on it like fire.

"I am The One, chosen to roll back the dark. And so I will. If you're afraid to fight, run, hide. But they'll still find you, root you out. Join me. Face them, fight them, and when the light burns the dark to ash, you'll be free."

She lowered the sword, looked down at the big man now sitting up, wiggling his aching jaw with his hand. "I won't hold you to the bargain. A warrior isn't something to be won in a wager."

He stared up at her. "You kicked me in the balls. And you damn near broke my jaw."

"Damn near broke my hand doing it." She offered the other. "Fallon Swift."

He got to his feet, winced. "John Little."

"Really? Like Robin Hood?"

He sighed. "Yeah. Son of a bitch. Why don't you just turn us all into zombies and make us fight for you?"

"My zombie spell's hit-and-miss."

He cracked the ghost of a smile. "Don't have one, do you?"

"Actually, I have something close enough, but I don't want anyone I'd have to make fight with me. With me, Mr. Little. Not for me."

"Calls me mister after she kicks me in the balls and breaks my jaw. I guess we ought to have a beer and talk this over."

"I'm not allowed to drink beer yet."

He stared at her. "Are you kidding me?" He looked toward her parents. "Are you fucking kidding me? She can fight a man twice—hell, three times her size, knock him flat, and she can't have a christing beer?"

"She's not old enough," Lana began, but Simon overruled her.

"Half. Half a beer. She put exes in his eyes, Lana. Half a beer."

Lana watched Simon and Fallon grin at each other, felt a hard tug of love. "Half."

As August dripped into September with unrelenting heat, Arlys Reid came out of the basement where she had what she called her studio in Chuck's cave. He lived there—always a basement dweller—with the equipment he'd brought with him from Hoboken and what he'd scavenged and built over the years.

Together, with a few hackers and IT nerds he'd groomed during those same years, they ran their communication underground. New Hope News—NHN—had gone from the broadsheets Arlys had hammered out on an ancient manual typewriter to a system of ham radio broadcasts and covert visual and Internet transmissions.

A long, long way from the anchor desk in New York she'd inherited thanks to the Doom, but to her mind more vital.

She dug up what could be dug, and continued to do what she'd done on that last fateful day at the anchor desk.

She told the truth.

She walked through the house where Jonah and Rachel raised their kids and out into the summer steam bath. She could dream of air-conditioning, but the mayor and the town council had deemed that use of power wasteful for anything but essential locations. And she had to agree.

So she'd go home to her oven of a house, turn on her stingy electric fan, and finish the final edit of the weekly *New Hope Bulletin*.

Maybe she'd walk over to the clinic first. She could use the hunt for another story as an excuse—and spend a few minutes inside one of the essential locations.

Teenagers ran along the sidewalk—Garrett's pack, Arlys noted. Some kids raced after them—Rachel's little boy Gabriel, Fred's Angel. The two of them had bonded like superglue.

And not far behind them Petra ran herd on Fred's toddler, Dillon, while she pushed the newest addition to Fred and Eddie's brood in a stroller.

Petra had proven herself an able and willing babysitter.

Petra, in shorts and a tank top, her dark blond hair in a bouncing ponytail, laughed at Dillon as he danced on his busy legs beside her.

It could've been a scene out of any small town. The teenage babysitter, the running kids and teens—all likely headed down to the park and gardens for one of the summer youth programs. People working in their own gardens, fussing with those bold summer colors and scents. Others sitting on porches with glasses of iced tea or lemonade.

You could think that, if you didn't consider the posted sentries, the group out even now on another scouting mission, the armory with so many weapons locked up tight.

Or the fact that most of the kids Petra's age spent two hours a day in combat training.

But this was the world they lived in, Arlys thought. And she had good reason to know it could be a whole lot worse.

She indulged herself, walked across the street to intercept Petra. She wanted to see the baby.

Dillon ran over to her, reached up those chubby arms, grinned a brilliant grin. "Up! Arls!"

"You bet." She hefted the toddler, snuggled, sniffed. Who'd have thought the ambitious reporter would find such a soft spot for babies?

"And look at your little sister!"

"Willow poops her pants and cries. I don't."

She had reason to know he still did both, but nodded sagely. "Because you're such a big boy. How are you, Petra?"

"Great, thanks. We're just heading down to the park. We were there earlier, but Dillon wanted to go see Mr. Anderson, so we took a walk."

"It's a hot day for it."

"We don't mind."

"We had popstickles."

"Popsicles," Petra corrected, "and that was supposed to be a secret."

"Secret sickles? Yum." Which explained Dillon's bright red tongue.

"I'd never had one before," Petra said. "They're really good. Mr. Anderson made them in these little molds and you eat them off sticks."

A first Popsicle at sixteenish (they didn't know for sure). That was also the world they lived in.

"I might go see Bill myself. I guess Mina wouldn't let you take Elijah to the park?"

"She won't go, and she's so nervous about him being away from her. She's a really good mom though."

"Mm-hmm." Arlys had a different opinion when a three-year-old boy wasn't allowed to play with others or go five feet from his mother's side.

But Mina, only a handful of years older than Petra, had been thoroughly indoctrinated by the cult.

"She never yells. It's just . . . she's still afraid. I guess she's always going to be afraid. And she . . ." Petra trailed off, pressed her lips together.

"Go ahead."

"She still thinks the master—and she still calls Javier that—is going to come back for her and Elijah. She prays for it every night. She's afraid to leave here, but that's because of Elijah. She knows he's safe here. She really loves him."

"Are you still comfortable living with her?"

"Oh sure. I know I don't have to, but Mina's nice, and I like being around Elijah a lot. And, well, she needs me, and I . . ."

"It's good to be needed."

"Yeah. I'm not allowed to use magick as long as I live with her, but I still don't want to anyway. It just makes me nervous, so it all works out."

"As long as you're happy there. I just wish she'd get out of the apartment more, let Elijah run around outside."

"She goes for walks at night." Flushing, Petra stopped herself. "Now I feel like I'm telling secrets on her."

"There's nothing wrong with taking a walk. Only at night?"

"When Elijah's asleep and she thinks I am. Sometimes she takes him, but mostly she just goes out by herself. Not for long, like an hour, even less."

Dillon squirmed, wriggled, so Arlys set him down.

"Wanna go to the park. See Mama."

"Okay, we're going. I should get him back. It was nice to see you."

Arlys waved them off, turned and studied the building where Petra lived with Mina and Elijah in an apartment over Bill Anderson's Bygones.

Just what did a woman still caught in the jaws of a cult do when she walked alone at night?

It was time to find out.

She walked up to Bygones.

What had once been a secondhand store with pseudo antiques and castoffs was now, thanks to Bill, an organized shop (though no money changed hands) stocked with the useful and the whimsical.

Kitchen tools and gadgets in one section, toys carefully cleaned and repaired in another. Tools, lamps, furniture, even some locally made art pieces, candles, oil lamps, brooms, mops, and other assortments filled shelves and old display cases.

Much of what scavenger parties brought back passed through Bill's hands for cleaning, repairing, inventorying.

Often a volunteer or two—generally kids—worked as assistants.

She found him, his glasses sliding down his nose, rewiring an amazingly ugly lamp.

She walked over to study it. "Why bother?"

"One man's trash." He shoved his glasses up, smiled at her. "Don't you look pretty today."

"What I look is sweaty, since I spent ten minutes outside in the steam bath we call air. I bet I'd cool off if I had a popstickle."

He laughed, his face, hewed and weathered by nearly eighty years, rolling into it. "Secret's out."

"How'd you come up with Popsicles?"

"Had some molds come through. It was our Cybil who came up with it more than me."

"Cybil?"

"She asked me what they were for, so I was telling her, and she wouldn't quit until we tried making some. Two of us sampled the first ones yesterday."

"And she didn't say a thing to her sweaty mother."

"My granddaughter knows how to keep a secret. We were going to make a bunch more, then take them on down to the kids at the summer program. I got another batch freezing now, but we've got some to sample. You want cherry, grape, or lemon?"

She had a flash of herself, eating a cup of lemon gelato at a street fair in New York. "You have lemon Popsicles?"

He winked at her, rose to go into the back. Her father-in-law didn't move as fast as he once had, and Arlys imagined he had some aches and pains. But he never complained.

He brought her back a small, frozen spear with a stick through it. An actual stick, she noted, with the bark peeled off.

"Sticks come back," he told Arlys as he handed it to her. "We spent a lot of time making them."

"Ingenious." She sampled. "Delicious!"

"Lemon juice, a little sweetener, water."

"It's the little things," she told him.

"You've got a look in your eye that tells me you didn't just come in to see me or snag a Popsicle."

"Right, as usual. I ran into Petra and Fred's two youngest. God, that baby is pretty. All that curly red hair. Anyway, I nudged Petra a little on Mina."

"You're good at nudging."

"I'm a professional."

"You are that. My son bagged himself a smart one." He gave her a pat before he sat again. "She'll talk to me a little—Mina. Every now and then I'll take up some toy that comes through. She'll take them for the boy, thank me, but she's not the sort who asks you to come on in and sit for a visit.

"Place is clean as a whistle though," he added as he fiddled with the lamp. "So's the little boy. What did Petra have to say?"

"Among other things, she told me Mina goes out at night. Do you know anything about that?"

"I've heard somebody going out the back way from up there. I thought it was Petra. Teenage girl, maybe going out to meet a boy, or some other girls, or just to get out."

He set his tools down. "Place is clean, like I said, but spare, too. Not much in it, and while she'll take things for the boy, she won't take any of the doodads for the apartment. Stuff for the walls, rugs, that sort of thing."

"Cult mentality," Arlys said.

"No question there. So I figured Petra was slipping out to have a little fun. And Denzel's got the moon eyes for her."

"Now why didn't I know that?"

"You're not the only professional nudger and snooper around here. So I figured it was Petra. Never crossed my mind Mina'd go out at night."

"Petra says sometimes she takes the baby, but she often leaves him sleeping and goes out on her own. She still keeps separate from all of us, Bill. She didn't come to the Fourth of July Memorial, or the Christmas party. I know she's let Rachel examine the baby, but Rachel has to go to her. She won't go to the clinic or the community kitchen, won't work in the gardens. Petra gets the food and supplies, does the bartering. I don't know how she'd manage without Petra running her errands and helping with the baby."

"She's not all the way right," Bill said simply. "She may not have been before she got tangled up with that cult. And the way things are, probably won't ever be all the way right."

"That's exactly my take, too."

"She's not the only one. We've got Lenny dancing naked down the street one day, and Fran Whiker digging up her backyard looking for buried treasure the next."

"You're not wrong."

"What did Rachel say about the little boy?"

"Healthy, clean, happy. It's the life he knows." But little boys grew up, Arlys thought, like her own Theo, who'd taken to archery like Robin Hood.

Or Denzel, with moon eyes for Petra.

"She's not breaking any laws or ordinances," Arlys continued, "and she does her sewing to barter—or for Petra to barter."

"But you don't trust her."

"I don't. I know Will doesn't. We haven't had any trouble since that near ambush, and the odds are whoever helped the PWs plan that is long gone."

"But," Bill finished.

"But. Lenny and Fran have issues, but they're part of the community. Mina just isn't. Refuses to be."

"I could slip out and follow her some night. See what she's up to."

"Let me talk to Will. I'll let him know what Petra told me, see what he thinks." She handed him back the stick, kissed his cheek. "Come to dinner tonight."

"I'll be there."

The two-way he kept on gave a squawk.

"Got a group coming in," the sentry announced. "Post One."

"Huh. Haven't had visitors in a while."

He plucked up the radio, and with Arlys, Bill walked to the door of the shop, out to the sidewalk.

Arlys used the flat of her hand to cut the glare as she looked up the street toward Post One.

She heard the horses before she saw them.

"No engines. On horseback."

Then she saw the girl on the white horse, short dark hair under a faded ball cap; a man, tan and lean, on a bay; a trio of boys. A couple of dogs, and . . . she knew a wolf when she saw one, but had never seen one as white as the horse. It distracted her before she scanned the group, looked at the woman.

A tumble of blond hair under a wide-brimmed hat.

It only took a moment, just a moment for her breath to catch, to catch and release. "Oh my God. Oh my God, it's Lana!"

Tears blurred her eyes as she took off running.

Lana swung off the horse with tears of her own as she ran to meet Arlys.

Lana let out a watery laugh as they met in a hard embrace. "Arlys."

"It's really you." Arlys drew back, laughed, then hugged Lana again. "It's really you."

"I'm so happy to see you. I'm so glad to be here. I missed you. I missed all of you, so much."

"You look wonderful. Oh, you really do. I should hate you for it."

"It's Bill. It's Bill." Lana threw out a hand for his as he hurried over.

"It's a good day. It's a fine day. I radioed down. You're going to have one hell of a welcome home party."

"These are your kids?" Arlys dashed tears away.

"My boys, Colin, Travis, Ethan. My husband, Simon. Simon Swift."

He dismounted. "Arlys Reid. I know your voice. It's nice to meet you."

"It's beyond nice to meet you." She held out a hand, laughed again. "Hell with it!" And threw her arms around him. "You brought her back."

"I don't know if I can claim credit for that." He looked up at Fallon.

"My daughter," Lana said. "Fallon. Fallon Swift."

"Fallon." Overcome, Arlys squeezed Lana's hand.

"You have a good place," Fallon said as she studied the street, the houses from Laoch's back. "Good security. The posts knew me from the night of the ambush, and one knew my mother."

"Fallon. Say hello."

At her mother's sigh, Fallon dismounted. "I'm sorry. Hello. I know your voice, too. You're doing a lot to help."

"We do what we can."

"We'll all do more."

Simon put an arm around Fallon's shoulders. "Not right yet. Is there a place we can rest and water the—"

He broke off because they were coming.

On bikes, in trucks, on horseback, on foot, on wing.

A damn parade, he thought, and it'd been a long time since he'd seen one.

One of those on wings—a mop of curly red hair and a baby in her arms—fluttered down in front of Lana.

"Queen Fred."

Laughing, the redhead shifted the baby—another red curly mop— to one arm, wrapped the other around Lana.

"You have a baby."

"I have five. This is Willow, the youngest. We have five, Eddie and me. Our oldest boy is Max."

"Oh. Oh." Lana dropped her forehead to Fred's. "You and Eddie. You and Eddie," Lana repeated.

"He was really slow about it, but I waited. I waited for you." She turned to Fallon, curtsied. "I waited for you."

Brakes squealed, a gangly man with shaggy straw-colored hair leaped out. His cap flew off as he came on the run.

He plucked Lana off her feet, swung her around, kissed her on the mouth, swung her again.

"Eddie. Eddie and Fred. Oh, Eddie. And Joe!" The old dog jumped out of the back of the truck, scrambled over for petting.

"We looked for you. Lana, we—Starr said—but we looked for you."

"I had to go." She rubbed Eddie's damp cheek with her hand. "And I got to where I needed to be. Eddie, this is Simon. This is my husband."

She needn't have worried, as Eddie shot out a hand, gripped Simon's, shook and shook and shook it. "I'm real glad to meet you. And to see you again," he said to Fallon. "And, hey, you got yourself three dudes on top of it. And . . . Shit, somebody else has themselves a wolf."

"Share." Will stepped forward, enfolded Lana. "Welcome back. Will Anderson," he said to Simon as they shook.

"Simon Swift."

"Your girl saved our bacon, not once but twice. Let's get these people out of the sun, and you'll have plenty of volunteers to get your horses settled in, if that's okay."

But Lana was pushing through the crowd. She'd spotted Rachel, Jonah. And Katie.

"Hey, you boys hungry?" Eddie called out and got a universal "yes" from the three boys.

"How about I take the boys here down to the community kitchen, get them some eats? We can take the horses down to the holding paddock on the other side of town, if that's okay."

"Sounds good." Simon put a hand on Fallon's arm. "Give your mom a little time."

Her dad was right, Fallon thought. Her mother needed time with the people who'd been, and were, so important in her life.

And things had to unfold a bit.

She helped her father, along with the boy named for her birth father, deal with the horses. The boy led them to the community kitchen, where her brothers had already eaten venison burgers and sweet potato fries and were now stuffing in large wedges of cherry pie.

Eddie sat across from them, just grinning.

"They got appetites. Hey, First Dude, go on back and tell Sal we got two more need some grub, and get some yourself."

"Solid." Max slapped his father's hand, sauntered off.

"I was just talking to Will a bit ago." Eddie rose to pour iced tea into glasses for them. "The thing is, the house where Lana used to live, ah, Will and Arlys have that now. And it wouldn't be big enough for all of you, not comfortable, especially with the dogs and horses. But there's a place near me and Fred? It's out just a bit. We're farming our place. Never thought I'd be a farmer, but there you go."

"I am. A farmer," Simon added.

"You could farm this place, if you wanted. It's got some land to it, and I'm not using all ours as yet anyway. But the house is good-sized. We'd get it cleaned up for you, and stock it up and all that. If it suits."

"We'd be grateful."

"No grateful about it. Lana's family and so are you. And Will's not lying about the bacon-saving. I don't mean no disrespect when I say Fallon's father? Max meant the world to me."

"He means a lot to all of us," Simon said. "We wouldn't have her without him."

"Ain't that the truth?" Eddie had to dash at his eyes that kept wanting to water up, just like the grin kept wanting to split his face in two.

"We could ride on out there after you get some food in you, see if it suits. I expect Katie's already sending out a committee to scrub the dust out and all that. Grass don't grow on Katie."

"Grass can grow on elves if they want." Ethan shoveled in the last bite of pie. "I guess she's not an elf."

"Nope, but we got plenty of them."

"Your wife's a faerie. She has red hair and pretty wings. What are you?"

"Just a regular dude."

Though she didn't care about the house itself, Fallon wanted to see the land and the positioning. The house turned out to be as big as Eddie said, and what her father called sprawling. She listened as the two men speculated about the big brown brick structure with porches (decks, they called them), and more glass than she'd have liked, which was probably built not long before the Doom, and by somebody with a lot of money and a desire for genial country living.

The boys, eager to claim bedrooms, ran right inside, and her mother, surely thinking of kitchens and practical space, went in after them.

Fallon walked the land. A nice, gentle rolling toward taller hills and mountains shadowed by distance. A winding, meandering creek cut through, a kind of natural boundary between the land here and the farm with its white frame and gray stone house where Eddie lived with his family.

She and her mother could and would add security and warning spells. But she saw a major advantage in the spread of green, the little copse of trees. They could install a training camp right here. She circled around as the men talked about converting a couple of fancy sheds into stables for the horses.

In the back she puzzled over the spread of flat stones, the canopy of slatted wood and madly twisting vines over a kitchen. Why would people build such a big house and put a kitchen outside?

She knew what the big hole in the ground beyond it had been. A swimming pool, now partially full of rainwater. Someone had maintained the gardens beyond that. She imagined Fred and some faerie friends were responsible.

"Oh God, a summer kitchen! As if the one inside isn't thrilling enough."

"Why did they need two?"

"Entertainment space," Lana said, simply glowing as she stepped out of glass doors. "They'd have parties out here, or just family meals during nice weather. It has seven bedrooms—including a second master on the lower level with its own side entry. You should take that, baby. I've already told Colin it goes to the oldest. Five and a half baths, a kitchen that brings tears to my eyes. Butler's pantry, sunroom. Oh, and look at that sweet gazebo. We'll have to deal with this pool, and I'll want to plant herbs and medicinals. There's not much furniture left, but we'll get more. I'm going to go help the cleaning team—they've already started."

"You love it."

"I love being back here, seeing people who matter so much to me. I love having enough space while we're here. And I won't lie," she added. "That kitchen makes me want to sing and dance."

She came out to slide an arm around Fallon's waist. "But I haven't forgotten why we're here."

"I really need to get back, talk to Will."

"I know. I talked to Katie, and we're going to meet at her house at seven. That gives us time to get some things organized here, clean up—the house and ourselves."

"Okay. Tonight's good. It's soon enough."

"This is a good place, Fallon, do you feel that? Not just New Hope, this place."

She hadn't let herself feel yet, but nodded.

"It'll be good for your dad and the boys while we're away from home. Living in town, for however long we're here? It would squeeze at them. And you, too, I think."

"There's another empty house." Fallon gestured across the roll of lawn, past the little copse of trees, to a two-story structure of cedar shakes that had gone sad and gray with time and weather. "It could be a barracks."

Lana might have sighed, but she nodded. "You want soldiers nearby. I imagine there are other houses in this area, too."

"We'll need some. And the land between this house and that. I know you and dad might look and see crops growing, but we need training camps. We need space for drilling, an obstacle course, archery."

Together they watched a herd of ten deer wander out of the trees to graze on the green.

"I can put in a kitchen garden. Eddie and Fred have their farm, we have the community gardens. We have the horses," Lana went on. "We can barter for some chickens. It'll be enough to keep your dad happy. In any case, I think he'll be more with you than the land for some time to come."

It pinched at her. "I'm sorry."

"No, no. No sorrys."

"It is a good place," Fallon said. "But we're outside the perimeter of New Hope security. We'll need to add some."

"We will. For now, let's get our things inside, and you should see your room. You have your own bath and sitting area."

"I have to go somewhere. Through the crystal. It won't take long."

She did like her room, the size, the privacy. The big heavy bed frame curved—her mother called it a sleigh bed. It didn't boast a mattress or bedding, but she had a bedroll until they found the rest. She liked having her own bath—holding both tub and a glass-walled shower five times the size of the one she'd helped build in Mallick's cottage.

She'd need a desk or workbench, so she could spread out her maps, plans, reports.

The sitting room had wide glass doors—did these people have no concern about security?—that led out to another spread of flat rocks.

The rest of the level held a family room, a home theater—terms her mother used that reminded Fallon what different worlds they came from—a bar, not for eating but for drinking.

As soon as she could slip away, she closed herself in her new room with the air still stale despite the breeze through the windows they'd opened, and took out her globe.

She slipped through, smelled the green, the earth, the thriving garden.

Mallick wore his big hat with the net as he worked with the bees.

She'd been away from him and here, she realized, nearly as long as she'd been with him. But she knew the music of the bubbling stream, the afternoon shadows, the scent of rosemary thriving in a patch of sunlight.

He turned, honey bucket in hand, saw her.

"Blessed be, Mallick the Sorcerer."

"Blessed be, Fallon Swift." He lifted the net as he walked toward her. "You're taller."

"Yeah, some, but I think I'm finished."

"There's tea already steeped. I'd be glad for a cup, a cool one, when I'm done with this."

She went inside, and since he'd take longer than she would, walked up to the workshop. The scents of dried herbs, crushed crystals, oils—and the overlaying tinge of magicks—were familiar.

Though she did wonder what he meant to do with the papery bat wings he had pinned to a board.

She went down, found cheese and bread, berries.

When he came in, she had the tea and a plate of food for him.

"You won't have bread and cheese?"

"I've eaten. In New Hope."

He sat, nodded. "I saw a star shoot across the sky last night, and the shower of light that rained from it. I should have expected you."

"And I should ask how you are, how our neighbors are."

"Well. All. And your family?"

"The same."

"We aren't ones for chatter, so as all are well, tell me why you've come."

"I have need for you, Mallick. For you, for Thomas and his people, for the faeries and shifters, the pixies and nymphs and all the rest. The waiting time's ended. The time of preparation's already begun. I need your help."

He ate in silence a moment. Did he think, she wondered, about his quiet life here? The bees, his garden, bat wings pinned to a board?

"I have been, am, always will be at your service. What do you need from me?"

"Your skills, your leadership, your gifts." She took out a map, spread it. "I need you here."

"What will I find there?"

"Recruits. Very raw, but willing. You'll speak first with a man named John Little."

CHAPTER TWENTY-THREE

Though Lana called it a meeting, it struck Fallon as more of a party. People crowded in the house, filled the air with voices and laughter. Wine filled glasses; party food filled plates.

Impatience crawled up her back like a spider.

But this was the core, she reminded herself. The first of the town structure—the council, the laws and rules and communications. She needed them all, as well as those who came from them.

Rachel and Jonah—medicals—and their oldest son with his mother's eyes, his father's build, struck her as prime for training.

Poe and Kim—scavenging and scouting—and their oldest daughter seemed sensible and solid.

Of course Eddie and Fred, and some of their brood carried magicks.

Flynn, an elf with no mate or children, as yet anyway. Scouting, scavenging, security.

Bill Anderson, supplies and wisdom.

Arlys and Will, communications, security. A son and a daughter, but she didn't know them or their potential as yet.

Chuck—no children or mate. Communications and technology.

Katie—organizer, town mayor. Her daughter Hannah another medical who gave off a calm, steady air, and a . . . goodness that reminded Fallon of Ethan.

Antonia—witch, archer, soldier. Already instructing, so that would be of use.

Then there was Duncan. She'd considered ignoring him, since he made her edgy, but that would make her reaction to him too important.

Instead, she acknowledged him with a kind of nod and shrug, and spoke to his sister. "You're Hannah, you're a healer."

"I try. I'm apprenticing with Rachel at the clinic."

"The building across the street. I need to see it."

"Anytime. I'll give you a tour. It's really great to meet you. My mom's so happy your mom's here. We all are. Do you like the house? It's really pretty, and you've got such good neighbors with Fred and Eddie and the kids."

"It's a good location, and the land will be useful."

"It has a home theater, doesn't it?" Duncan gestured with a beer. "And a house entertainment and security system. Too bad Chuck stripped all the goodies out."

"He'll make use of them. And my mother and I already added security. How many healers do you have?" Fallon asked Hannah.

"Rachel's accredited twenty-three. That's clinic and revolving staff, and field medics."

"That's a good number." For now. "How many do you train in archery?" she asked Tonia.

"Varies. We do practice courses and instructional. Adult and children—under sixteen." She bit into a little round of bread topped with a layer of thin meat, gestured with the rest of it while she spoke.

"Instructional's usually kids, unless we have a newcomer, and those are limited to groups of twelve. During the school year, I head two classes, three times a week. Summer, it's less, but we have summer programs."

"Why less in summer?"

"Two months off school," Duncan told her. "For one thing, it's too damn hot inside the academy or the civilian school for classes."

"You could cool the air."

He shrugged. "Kids need a break."

"But two months without training or structure—"

He shrugged again. "It's how we roll."

They'd have to roll differently.

"We should show you around," Tonia suggested. "The town, the academy, the armory, the clinic."

"Yes, I'd like to see how it's organized. I need to talk to Will."

"About what?"

She looked at Duncan. "About what's coming."

"You think we don't know?"

He did—she could see it on him, in him, but she eased back from that. From him. "I don't know what you know. I'm only sure of what I do."

She turned and walked toward Will.

"She's—what's the word?" Hannah wondered. "Formidable."

"She'd better be," Duncan muttered.

"She has to be," Tonia corrected.

Will glanced up as she stepped in front of him, and something in her eyes made him get to his feet.

"I'm sorry, I know this is a kind of celebration, but there are things I need to tell you, plans that have to be put in place."

"Okay. What do you say, Mayor?"

"I'd say we're calling this meeting to order, and Fallon has the floor."

She'd expected to talk to Will, not address the whole group at once.

"I . . . know that all of you are the reason New Hope exists. That it's grown and has structure. I know you're the reason so many have been saved from capture, from death. From all my mother's told me, and from what I've seen here, I know all of you not only fought to survive, but to build something strong and safe, a place where magick-als and non-magickals live and work together. It's why, I think, this is the center.

"There are other places like this, many not like this because they lack leadership and structure. And vision. Because they're afraid to look and to see. There's a reason all of you came here, why my mother and birth father came here, why he died here. A reason why I knew when the time came, I'd come here, with everyone who matters to me."

"The center of what?"

She turned to Jonah.

"Of war and peace, light and dark. Every choice you made brought you here. If you'd reached for the gun in your pocket instead of find-ing the strength and courage to help a woman who needed you, you wouldn't be here. And neither would the woman you love, your children, Katie, and hers. So, that one choice, light instead of dark. The same, the very same can be said of everyone here. This is the cen-ter and another shield."

These faces, Fallon thought, these people, her birth father had once looked at them, and trusted them.

"You're strong, all of you, strong. You'll need to be. Your children will need to be."

"I'm not going to dispute you've got something . . . extraordinary," Will began. "That extraordinary saved lives in this room twice. I was with your mom once when she had a vision, and that's stuck with me, so I'm not going to dispute you see things some of us don't. We've worked hard to make New Hope something solid and secure. We're willing to risk our lives to save others, and fight back against the ones who for whatever damn reason want to see us in the ground or in prisons or enslaved. But the fact is, there are only so many of us, we've only got so many resources. We can't take on the whole dark side of what's left of the world."

"And there's a lot of it." Chuck tugged on the short, pointed beard he sported. "Every time I turn around I dig up a little more. I've dug up some of those other places you were talking about. People trying to get their shit together. But some of it's hundreds of miles away, even thousands. We've got no way to get there to help or to fight."

"Then your magickals haven't plumbed deep enough, your technicians and mechanics haven't, either. Your leaders haven't fully considered that New Hope can still be swallowed by the dark."

"You just got here." Duncan moved forward. "You don't know what we've plumbed or done or think."

"You learned to flash," she retorted. "Have you learned to take someone with you? To take your bike or a horse? To take an army?"

She turned to her mother. "You left your friends, your security because you knew the ones who killed here would come back. For you, for me. You didn't consider they'd come back anyway. And they will."

"Eric and Allegra?"

"Them or others like them. They wait, too. Our coming here starts the clock again. But . . . From inside and out," she said as it swept through her, "the attack will come. From those boiled in the dark it will strike. The fruit and the flower," she said to Duncan. "The poison and the serpent. You are as I am, and the dark wants your blood, my blood, the blood of your sister. It will not have it! I have not come to see the blood of the Tuatha de Danann shed and another shield broken.

"I am an army." She stunned Duncan by gripping his hand, sending shock waves through him. "You are a sword shining. You an arrow in flight," she said as she gripped Tonia's. "We are the blood and the bone. We stand together for all who came before us, all who come after. Choose, you said to me, Duncan of the MacLeods, and I did. Now I say to you, choose."

She let them go, took a step back though her eyes still swam with visions. "We rise and fall on your choice."

"What choice?" he demanded.

"You'll know when you know." She rubbed at the headache in her temple, but shook her head when Lana started to rise. "No, it's okay. The point is, nowhere is safe—that's something all of you know already. What's been built can be destroyed. You said there aren't enough of us here, and you're right. We need more warriors, more leaders, more healers, and more technicians. I've gotten a start on that. I have sixteen hundred and forty-three recruits."

"Sorry?" Still a little dazed, Will held up a hand.

"She enlisted them on the way," Simon told him. "Settlement by settlement."

"Sixteen hundred," Will murmured.

"And forty-three. I have an accounting, separating the magickals with their skills, the non-magickals with theirs. I have maps. I can show you where some will train in place—but need supplies and equipment."

"And who's training them?"

She turned to Duncan again. "Mallick, who trained me, Thomas, an elf elder who leads a group near where I trained with Mallick. Troy, a witch who leads a group of magickals. A man named Boris, who was a soldier like my father. The others will come here when I send for them. We can train them in the fields by the house where we'll live for now."

"How many coming here?" Katie asked.

"For now, eight hundred and twenty."

"Eight . . . We don't have the facilities, that's double the population we're feeding and clothing and sheltering and schooling."

"More hands for planting and hunting," Fallon pointed out. "To build."

"We can expand at the farm," Eddie began, and Fred nodded.

"With a little help we could add another greenhouse, even double the crops. And Lana told me today she knows how to create the tropics we've been trying to do for years. We'll have sugar and coffee, cocoa beans, olives. Simon made an olive press. Olive oil."

"Poe and I've made it nearly two hundred miles out."

"One ninety-one," Poe confirmed, tapping Kim's knee.

"Fuel's the major issue," Kim said. "But there are places that haven't been scavenged where we could get fuel. You wipe out eighty, ninety percent of the world's population, it takes a really long time for the ones who're left to use up resources. It's the getting to them."

"It doesn't have to be." Flynn, who'd said nothing, absorbed everything, finally spoke. "If flashing's what I think it is."

"Physically transporting from one location to another in, well, a flash," Fallon told him.

"And you can take someone, more than one, with you?"

"Theoretically."

Flynn stood, offered a hand. "Show them."

"I haven't actually—"

"Show them," he repeated, taking Fallon's hand.

She felt it from him. Absolute faith. The kind she'd only felt from her family, Mallick and Thomas and a few others.

With that she took him with her to the gardens, a place she knew.

"Do you feel all right?"

"Fine. Elves are used to moving fast. Not that fast, but fast. One second before we go back. They'll need to talk."

"Yes, but—"

"They need to," he repeated. "It's the weight of responsibility, and the ones not like us will need a little longer. Some of them. I'm with you. I was with you before you were born. They'll be with you."

"My father told me about the first time he met you. In the market. The supermarket."

"Max? But . . ."

"I talked to him, one Samhain."

"Oh." Flynn smiled, no hesitation. "I'm glad, for both of you. We'd better get back. They'll freak."

When she flashed them back, Lupa was on his feet. He settled again when Flynn laid a hand on his head.

"Smooth ride" was all he said.

"How many can you take like that, and how far?" Will wanted to know.

"I'm not sure. It takes practice. My mother has the skill, so does Duncan."

Tonia raised a hand. "I can do it. I haven't tried it with a passenger. And you're right. Why haven't I? Why haven't we?"

"We don't know if a non-magickal can handle it," Duncan pointed out.

"If you need a guinea pig . . . " Poe started to his feet.

"I'd rather try it with a non-human first," Fallon said quickly. "A deer. But the point is, we should be able to travel farther and faster, find supplies, more recruits. We need more, so much more, and fully trained, fully armed, before we take back D.C."

"D.C.?" Arlys lowered her notepad. "You want to take the fight to D.C.?"

"In time. But it's need, not want."

"Hold on. You said it was a dead city."

"It is." Struggling not to bristle at another interruption, Fallon turned to Duncan. "But they cling to it, the government, the Dark Uncanny. Its symbolism, its history, the broken power structure.

While they fight each other, they want us dead or captured. They want to rule over the rest. It's one of the centers, and one we have to take from them, purify. New York is another, but we're not ready."

She lifted her hands as she turned back to the main group. "We're not ready. I don't know when we will be. And there are others, more remote places. Underground, some deserted, some where they hold Uncannys. Some where bombs wait for the spark."

"We've talked countless times about that last one." Because it made her stomach clench, Katie lifted a bottle of faerie wine, topped off her glass. "They used a bomb on Chicago three years ago, another on Dallas two years before. Both were disasters. But that won't stop some maniac from using one again. Or cutting loose with the nukes."

"We'll eliminate them. It has to be a priority. It'll take time, and even with training, it's a risk. But it has to be done before we surge on D.C."

"How do you eliminate bombs?" Katie demanded. "How do you find them in the first place, not just here but all over the world?"

Duncan sat on the arm of her chair, ran a hand down her arm to soothe her. "Magick. Locator spells. Flash a team to the location. Disarm."

"Not disarm," Fallon corrected. "What's disarmed can be armed again. Eliminate. I thought about just transforming, but even a strong spell can be broken."

"Yeah, that's a point. Poofing them? Tricky."

"I'm working on it."

"You could use some help," Tonia pointed out. "Duncan and I will help work on it."

"Excuse me," Katie said, "while I try not to have a stroke at the idea of teenagers working on 'poofing' nuclear weapons."

Tonia came to sit on the other arm of her mother's chair, and Hannah to stand behind it.

"Well, the first thing is to find supplies, housing, and everything else another eight hundred people will need." Hannah laid a hand on Katie's shoulder. "Maybe we just start there."

Fallon decided the meeting/party/debate had gone as well as she could expect. She'd had nearly four months' experience in trying to convince people to do what she needed them to do. It didn't just take time, she thought, but projecting confidence, and a willingness to compromise on small details.

She discovered someone had brought her a mattress and some sheets, a pillow, a blanket. She'd have to find out who to thank.

No desk yet or worktable, so she prepared to sit on the floor, spread out her maps. But she heard someone moving around in the family room.

Stepping out, she found Colin pacing and poking.

"What are you doing?"

"Just looking around. It's a pretty cool house. Maybe you can figure out how to get the home theater thing to work."

"There's no whatever it is to run it."

"There's you and Mom."

"Maybe. Maybe," she said again, calculating. "I can work something—for a trade."

"What do you want?"

Since his last growth spurt he stood eye to eye with her. It occurred to her—with a little annoyance—he'd end up taller than her before much longer.

"I want you to help train the non-magickals, sixteen and under."

"Kids?" He scoffed from his great age of fifteen.

"They'll look up to you, and want to impress you. You're good with a sword, you're good with your fists. You're an expert at bullying and cajoling two younger brothers."

"I want to fight, not babysit."

"It's not babysitting. If a boy or girl of twelve isn't trained, isn't taught how to defend, how to fight, when to run, when to strike, they'll die in what's coming. Some will die anyway. Help me so more don't die."

"I guess."

"You'd be in charge," she said, knowing him. And smiled. "You'd be president."

He gave a snort. "Maybe. Sure. But the home theater?"

"I'll work on it."

"Deal. I'm going to get something to eat. Mom sure is crazy about the kitchen up there. When we get back to the farm, I bet she talks Dad into fiddling with ours."

She went to her room, shut the door. Sitting on the floor, she spread out her maps, began to plot the best routes arrowing out of New Hope.

She felt the ripple in the air, surged to her feet. Since her sword stood across the room, she raised her fists. And Duncan flashed across from her.

"You can't come into my bedroom uninvited."

"Didn't know it was your bedroom." He glanced around. "Big space, big bed, and not much else. Anyway."

"I'm busy. Go away."

"We need to talk. You, me, and Tonia need to talk, but we'll start here. That vision you had back at my place. Damn fruit and flowers again."

Because it worried her, she pushed her temper back a notch. "I don't know what it means. If I did, I'd tell you because it's important."

"I get that." Hands in pockets, he wandered her space, into the L that formed the sitting area, and back again. "I've chosen, haven't I? I've chosen to fight. What else is there?"

"I don't know that, either."

"Visions are a pain in the ass. Half the time they only tell you half the story, so that's only a damn quarter of things. You got a headache from yours."

"It happens sometimes, when they're really strong. It doesn't last long."

"I used to get dizzy from mine. I had some of you."

He glanced back at her, then stopped pacing and turned with her maps between them. "It wasn't just dreaming. My mother says when I was a baby—Tonia, too, sometimes—I'd get really happy and excited if your mother came around. Because you came around, you know, in there. I knew you, before you were born. And the bitch of it is, I half remember it. Not just her telling me."

"The three of us, you said. Tonia and me, the MacLeod blood."

She didn't have to notch her temper down now. It simply drained. "It wasn't his fault, your grandfather."

"I know that. MacLeod blood, back to the Tuatha de Danann. I accept that, okay? I'll fight with you. We'll figure out how to find nukes and things that go *boom*, get rid of them. We'll figure out how to take D.C. I'll help find more recruits, I'll help train them. I'll help scout, scavenge, plot, plan, and whatever the hell else."

"But?"

"But we spread out on rescues. If people are underground, in cages, in labs, we get them the hell out. You didn't say anything about that."

"Because I thought it was understood. Rescue operations need specific training. I have notes on that." Shoving her fingers through her hair, she looked around, trying to remember where she'd put them.

"Never mind the notes. They can wait. I just wanted to make sure we were on the same page."

"If we're not fighting for people, what are we fighting for?"

"Some people fight for power."

"That's not why I'm doing this."

"Well, you've got more than most already." He held up a hand when he saw the fire light in her eyes. "Just needling you. Didn't I just say I knew you?"

"Then you should know I don't like being needled."

"Who says I don't?" He looked down at the maps. "What are you working on?"

"I wanted to plot out some routes, for supplies, for recruits. I've seen some settlements. I have a crystal."

He glanced over where she'd set it on a little table. "Handy."

"And rescues," she added. "I know places where people are held. Some have to wait until we have more soldiers and arms, but some we could take."

"I'll help you." He sat on the floor. After a moment, she sat with him.

"You could show me where you and your people have been, where you've scouted, where we can eliminate. I'm most interested in south and west. We came from the north. From here." She touched the map where she'd marked the farm. "Traveled along here, looped there, and then here. But I've never been south or west of those points. Except here."

She tapped Cape Hatteras on the map.

"What's there?"

"A prison, for those like us—empty now. When we need it, we'll use it. But for now, I need to know places you know that I don't."

"Yeah, I can show you. I knew you were here."

She looked up to find his eyes on her.

"Before I saw you, I knew. I felt you. It's like a rush in the blood. What do you make of that?"

"Shared ancestry."

"I share even closer with my mother. I don't always know when she's around. Not every single time with Tonia, either, and we lived damn close for nine months. But with you? There's that rush."

His eyes were a deep, deep green, like the shadows in faerie-land. She wanted to look away from them, but didn't want to show weakness.

"I don't know how you feel or why."

"How about this then? How do I know you've got a weak spot for Rainbow Cake when I'm not even sure what the hell that is? Or that you like to read, in front of a fire or under a tree? That you like to build things with your hands? How do I know that?"

She knew he liked to listen to music. He had a friend, a shifter named Denzel, he thought of as a brother. She knew his favorite gift was a box filled with pencils and paints a man named Austin had given him.

Austin—not his father, but someone who had, for a short time, stood as one for him.

She didn't want to know these small, intimate things about him. Or for him to know hers.

"Those aren't important things."

"I think they are. I think there's a reason I know those things. I'm not sure I'm going to like the reason, or you are, either."

Just as her heart started to hammer, he looked down at the map. "Okay, so here, picked clean."

Over the next few days, she built things with her hands. With scavenged and salvaged supplies, she and her father worked with various teams to repair and expand two houses that would serve as barracks. Other teams worked on readying more to house families, children. Some would camp, so trailers, tents, RVs formed groups outside what would become the training area.

With Simon she cut and soldered angle iron to form frames for solar panels. They'd done the same years before for the farm and several neighbors, but New Hope had hit a treasure trove of solar cells, hauled them out, used them, stored them.

She'd learned New Hope had volunteers for everything, something they'd implemented from the start. Rotating teams scouted outlying houses, and those abandoned, fallen into disrepair, or damaged beyond any practical repair were stripped of everything useful.

Wood, nails, pipes, hinges, tiles, shingles, windows, window glass, doors, wiring. Another team sorted, inventoried, and stored everything in a barn next to their feed and grain operation.

She checked the caulking on another frame, glanced around at the hive of activity. Some built the ropes course or hauled in old tires for the obstacle course, built the climbing wall while others framed in what would be the expanded kitchen and mess hall.

An army had to eat.

She knew her mother was off with Fred and some others working on the first stages of the complicated spell to create a tropical area. Her brothers remained in town at the summer program with Colin, who, no matter how he tried to deadpan it, was relishing his role as instructor.

She glanced over at the laughter rising over the sounds of hammers and saws, frowned as Duncan did a slow somersault off the roof, then floated back up with a stack of completed panels.

Inside himself, Simon sighed. He knew when a guy was showing off for a girl, and was pretty sure he spotted more than a spark of interest under Fallon's frown.

As if war and survival weren't enough to worry about, now he had a boy sniffing around his baby.

They finished the next run of panels, and not to be outdone, Fallon floated them up to Duncan and his crew. Simon took off his cap, swiped the sweat off his face, then jaw-pointed to an oncoming van.

Bill Anderson climbed out from the driver's side, and a pretty girl with dark blond hair slipped out the other door.

"Hot day for this," Bill called out, and set his hands on his hips to study the progress. "You're sure getting it done. We brought out some wild boar barbecue, coleslaw, and other eats from the community kitchen. Got a couple vats of cold tea and more water."

"You're the man," Simon told him.

"Got someplace we can set this up?"

"We'll make someplace."

A couple of salvaged doors on sawhorses served as workers swarmed. Fallon headed for the creek to wash up and nearly ran into the girl carrying a box of rolls probably baked that morning.

"Sorry, ah—I don't remember your name."

"We actually haven't met. I'm Petra."

"Fallon."

"I know. Everybody . . . knows."

"I'll take that, honey." Bill grabbed the box from her.

"You're doing this for soldiers." Pink flushed Petra's cheeks as she spoke. "You're going to lead them."

"Do you have a problem with that?"

"No, but. No. I don't want to fight," she said quickly, gripping her hands together. "I don't want to be a soldier. I take care of children. I can help make food. I don't want to fight."

Won't. Coward.

Fallon heard the words in her head, glanced toward a woman with short brown hair. Starr, she remembered, an elf who said very little.

Starr simply shrugged, shot Petra a look of contempt, then walked away with a plate of food to a solitary spot away from the rest.

"I'm not going to force anyone to fight."

"I just thought . . . I wasn't sure—"

"What would you do if one of the kids you were taking care of was attacked?"

"I—I'd try to protect them, get them away. They're only children."

"Hey, Petra."

"Tonia." Instantly, Petra relaxed and smiled. "I didn't know you were here."

"Helping build an obstacle course for training. Can't wait to try it out. You know, Fallon, I've got some ideas for another course for magickals. Uncanny Falls." She laughed. "Add in some magickal traps and puzzles."

"I like it."

"You treat it like a game," Petra said in a soft voice, then flushed deeper. "I'm sorry. I'm sorry. I need to—" She hurried away.

"I want to wash up before I eat," Fallon said, giving Tonia a long, direct look.

"Oh. Yeah, good idea."

They walked together to the lazy creek.

"What's up?" Tonia asked.

"I don't know Petra or why Starr dislikes her. It helps to know."

"I don't know that Starr likes anybody. And that's not fair. She's just not sociable. She fights, she works as hard as anybody. She hangs with Flynn mostly—no sparks there."

" 'Sparks'?"

"Romantic, sexual. They're sort of like brother and sister. Anyway, what I know about her is mostly second- and thirdhand. She was a kid, about twelve maybe. PWs caught her and her mother. Raped and tortured both of them. The mom saw a chance to get Starr away, talked to her the way elves can." Tonia tapped her temple. "Made her promise to run and hide, and then caused a commotion so Starr could. They hanged her mother while she was hiding, and she couldn't do anything to stop it. So she fights, she works, but she's just never been really part of the community. Keeps to herself."

"And Petra?"

"A rescue a few years back. She'd been taken in by a cult, her and her father. Sick cult, anti-magick magickals, led by some whack. The women all had to submit, you know, sex, have babies."

"They were forced?"

"Brainwashed, so it's the same thing. Some of them were just kids, like Petra."

"She was forced?"

"Yeah. She's steadied up pretty well considering. She lives with another woman and her kid we rescued from the cult. The rescue was ugly," Tonia added. "The PWs attacked, we attacked the PWs. A lot of people died. Her father was one of them. They torched him right in front of her."

"It should make her want to fight."

"Well, I guess you can say Starr and Petra had different, you know, scars from a similar experience."

"What is she? I didn't get a sense."

"She blocks it. A witch. She won't use magick, either. They made her afraid of it. I think she knows better in her head, but they made her see it as evil, as dark, so she's afraid of her own gift."

Fallon nodded. "There are others like that."

"Duncan and I made a little progress for a while, but, since it freaked her so much to explore her powers, we didn't push. And, well, she started sort of getting this crush on Duncan, and he backed way, way off. She's too young, you know? Not in years but how she is. He won't touch that."

Fallon glanced back. "Does she still . . ."

Tonia shrugged. "Maybe a little, but she's sort of hooked with Denzel. You met him, right?"

"Duncan's friend, shifter. He's helping with the solar panels."

"Friends since baby time," Tonia added. "I'm pretty sure Duncan gave Denzel a nudge toward Petra."

"Magickally?" Fallon demanded, ready to condemn that kind of interference or influence.

"No, hell no. That's outside the lines. He just talked Denzel into making a move Denzel wanted to make anyway. Worked out. So that's all to circle around to how Starr doesn't much like Petra. She doesn't respect Petra because she won't train, won't even take basic self-defense or go out to scavenge or scout. This is about as far out of town as she'll go, and that's only because Fred and Eddie and their kids are out here, and she's nuts for their kids. Kids in general."

Now she knew the stories, Fallon thought. And understood how Petra—who wouldn't fight—could be useful.

"The younger ones need people willing to take care of them, to keep them safe while the rest of us fight."

"She's good with them, patient and, you know, responsible without being a hard-ass. I'm surprised she didn't have some kid hanging on her today, but I'm betting she wanted to come out and see you. Get a sense of you."

"Now she has. Thanks, Tonia. It helps to know."

Knowledge, Fallon thought as she washed her hands, cooled her face with creek water, was always valuable.

She might have thought the sexual, romantic, and personality quirks simply confused what needed doing with drama, but knowing about them would help her lead.

CHAPTER TWENTY-FOUR

Within two weeks, busy, rotating teams completed work on the base and barracks, and Fallon asked for another meeting. This time she requested New Hope's leaders come to the house her mother had already made a home with her kitchen garden, her pots of herbs and bottles of flowers, with the scent of freshly baked bread and honey cakes.

She asked specifically for Duncan, Tonia, Starr, and, though she knew it grieved her mother a little, Colin to be included.

She stood in what her mother called the great room with food and drink on the wide kitchen counter and the furniture volunteers had brought in already arranged.

"I first want to thank everyone for all they've done to complete the barracks so quickly. Most who worked on the barracks and the courses don't know me, but they gave their time, contributed supplies because the people in this room asked them to. Now I'm going to ask all of you to keep anything we talk about here tonight confidential. Um . . ."

When she looked at Arlys, busy taking notes, Arlys glanced up. "Off the record?"

"Yeah. At least until things are in motion."

"Off the record until what things are in motion?"

Take a chance, Fallon told herself. Her mother trusted Arlys absolutely.

"I'll be sending for the recruits. The more who know they're coming, where they're coming from, the less security they have."

"Scouts and supply teams are going to catch wind of them," Jonah pointed out.

"Not until they get closer. At that point we can send people out to help ensure their safe arrival. I have some names for that detail. Poe and Kim, Flynn, Starr, ah, Maggie Rydell. If you have other or different suggestions, I'd appreciate the input. Some of the recruits are really raw, won't have serious training. Some are coming as families, with young kids."

"All right. Off the record," Arlys agreed. "Until."

"Okay. I'm asking that Colin continue to work with the younger recruits, but there'll be too many for him to handle when the new ones get here, so I'd like suggestions on that."

"Denzel." Duncan said immediately. "He's good with kids, and he's better in theory than execution."

"I agree with that," Will put in. "Bryar and Aaron have plenty of experience with instructing. What about the other bases?"

"I'll wait for Mallick, Thomas, Troy, Boris to tell me if they need more instructors. If they do, are there any in New Hope who are qualified and would be willing to travel, to spend months away? Maybe longer?"

"I can give you a list of names." Katie looked at Arlys, got a nod. "Those who don't have families, or who'd be willing to take their families outside of New Hope. I'm going to be straight with you, Fallon. There's some concern in the community that you'll just order people to train or fight or uproot to one of the other locations."

She'd seen the looks, heard some whispers. She'd sensed some fear. "Hannah doesn't fight."

"I—I take combat training," Hannah began.

"You're a healer, not a soldier. You have a skill, a calling. Why would I push a sword into your hand?"

"She's pretty decent with a bow," Tonia put in. "You're better with a tourniquet," she said to Hannah.

"And others are better at providing food, at building, at caring for children, at making weapons rather than using them. Or with . . ." Fallon waved a hand toward Chuck. "Technology."

Chuck tapped his chest with his thumbs. "I'm that guy."

"Why would I demand anyone fight? That doesn't accomplish anything but resentment. Why would I demand someone uproot their life, or the lives of family?" Frustrated, she paused, looked inward. "I haven't proven myself yet."

"Change comes hard," Arlys pointed out. "We found that out when we first introduced rules and laws, and the town council. We're bigger now than we were, so you're going to get some pushback, proven or not. You're so young," she added. "That's already a problem for some. Among the Uncannys, there's more unification. But even there."

"People get complacent." Bill patted his hands on his knees. "We've got a kind of routine around here, and anything that changes it gets some worked up. Hell, a few years after we got settled here and voted on mandatory recycling, composting? You'd've thought, for some, we'd instituted indentured servitude. But we got through it, and now it's just the way it is. Not everybody's happy right now you're bringing so many people in."

"Plenty of complaints coming in," Katie confirmed. "A lot of rumors. You can leave handling that to me and the town council for now."

"If we have more soldiers, Hannah can focus on healing, someone like Petra can concentrate on child tending. A cook like . . ." She searched for the name.

"Sal," Eddie provided.

"Yeah, her. She can cook, and so on. But more? Those who complain and push against change ignore what happened to the world that was, and learn nothing from it. They forget, choose to forget, what happened here on July Fourth, and those who died that day, they take for granted those who risk their lives to rescue others, to fight back against destroying everything you've built."

Katie nodded. "You're not wrong, but some won't want to hear it said just that bluntly. And it's hard, Fallon, it's brutal for a parent to accept their child, whether that child came from them or came to them, is training for war. Hard for some of them to accept a child is going to lead them."

She held up a hand. "Don't say you're not a child. I'm aware, as is everyone in this room. But you're young, and you'll find pockets of people who'll see you as a child."

"They won't, after I prove myself."

"You said that before," Lana chimed in. "What do you mean by prove yourself?"

"It starts tonight. I'm sorry. I'm sorry. I am your child, and I know the sacrifices both of you've made already."

Simon took Lana's hand, linked fingers. "What are you going to do tonight?"

"I'm going to eliminate some nuclear weapons."

"For God's sake, Fallon."

"I know where and how. Mom, the Book of Spells is in me. I know how. This is necessary, and it's a show of power, of strength, of commitment to the light. We'll start with five locations tonight."

" 'We'?"

She glanced toward Duncan and Tonia, then back to Katie. "I'm sorry. I need them."

"Whatever your powers, you're three teenagers going up against nuclear weapons. We need to find an expert, someone with experience on nuclear weapons, on disarming—"

"I said before, we won't disarm, but eliminate. They'll cease to be."

"Radiation poisoning—"

"Mom." Duncan cut her off, gently, before addressing Fallon. "Magick's still a science. You can't eliminate matter without replacing it. Magick 101."

"But you can alter the matter."

"An alchemy spell?" Intrigued, Duncan hooked his thumbs in his front pockets, considered. "Now you're talking postgrad work."

"They'll cease to be and become something else, something harmless, and we destroy the harmless. We'll also eliminate the means to launch them, or fire them."

"Wait, wait." Chuck waved a hand. "Computers, electronics, components. Oh, baby, and the data in them. We can use those. You can't just change them into daisies or puppies. Take me along, I can shut them down, then we need to bring them back. Jesus Christ, what I could do with . . . Sorry, ladies, but it gets me hot."

"You could tell us what's most useful, what to bring back—and we could transport some of it to the other bases. Would you help set up communication centers outside New Hope?"

"I'm your man. I got a couple people I'd want with me once we have the goods. In fact, you'd save time if you spread us out. They're not as good as me, but, seriously, who is?"

"You're in," Fallon said. "Mom, he'll need an energy tonic. Poe and I found out—"

"Boy, did we," Poe confirmed.

"Flashing's draining and disorienting for non-magickals," Fallon finished.

"Ton . . . holy shit." Grin spreading, Chuck did a chair boogie. "This is freaking awesome."

"Prepare for a head rush," Poe warned him.

"You need me, too."

Will's jaw dropped as he turned to Arlys. "Why? Come on."

"On-site reporting. With my own eyes. People trust me, Will, to tell the truth. People here and wherever we can broadcast. Fallon's right, this is a huge show of power—and intent. Will, this is what I do, just like you go out, take on Raiders, PWs. You need to do this, Fallon, but you also need people to know and believe you have."

"Yes, you're right. But some of what we do will have to be kept out. Like the details of the spell itself."

"Off the record. Absolutely agreed. Make that tonic a double, Lana. Chuck and I will split it."

"On the road again." He winked at her.

"I'll get the tonic." Pale, Lana rose. "You've calculated the risks?"

"I promise you."

"You've calculated the risks," Lana repeated, "factoring in that without you, the dark wins?"

"I promise you."

"I need to go to the office, get a couple things. Video recorder, which will be off," Arlys assured Fallon, "during your spell, and whenever else you say."

"I need a few things myself. Give me a lift?" Chuck asked.

"I'm walking you out." Will pushed to his feet. He had some things to say to his wife.

"I need to talk to Duncan and Tonia for a minute." Fallon gestured toward the back, then walked all the way through and out onto the patio.

"You could have mentioned we'd be on a mission tonight," Duncan began.

"I wanted it contained."

"You think we'd go blabbing about something like this?" Tonia snapped.

"No, but the sooner we can go after the words are said, the fewer who know they've been said, the better. I have what we'll need in my pack, but I wasn't expecting to take a couple of civilians or bring anything back but some supplies and weapons. The computer equipment—I see how valuable it'll be, but it's a challenge. It's going to take more time, more power."

"A couple more witches? Your mother?"

"No." Fallon shook her head. "It has to be the three of us. That's something I know. The logistics are more complicated now, but it's doable. The spell itself? I need to pass it from me into you for it to work. All three of us have to know, and you have to understand that knowledge will be in you not only tonight but always."

"How's that done?" Duncan asked her. " 'From,' 'into,' that doesn't sound like talking it through."

"Through the blood. Here and now." She drew out her knife. "Blood to blood, power to power, light to light. You have to be sure, because—"

"Blah blah blah, blood magicks, serious shit, blah blah. Let's do it." Duncan held out a hand. "And get this party started."

Tonia mirrored his gesture. "What he said."

"It is serious shit," Fallon replied. "Both hands, for all." She scored her own palms first, then his, then Tonia's. "Hands clasped." She gripped Duncan's, Tonia's, breathed in.

"A circle of three, a circle of trust, grant knowledge from me to do what we must. We are your children," she said as their blood mixed and heated and glowed. "We are what was written. One, two, three, three, two, one, with knowledge shared the dark is undone. Through the blood this gift from me, and as I will, so mote it be."

It came with a jolt, through the gut, the heart, the mind. For a moment, Duncan swore his blood burned with light. Then it banked, quiet and calm. And he knew.

"It's so damn simple. Once you know, it's so damn simple."

"Logical," Tonia agreed. "On the other hand? I feel like I just stuck my finger in a live electric socket. Is my hair doing the Einstein?"

"It does half the time anyway," Duncan said.

"It looks fine. We should go back in. The sooner we start, the better."

"Hold on." Duncan still had Fallon's hand, and yeah, his tingled. His whole body tingled. "Are you going to tell us where we're going? Tell them?"

"Only the first place. It's too far away to matter. Nevada."

It took time. She had to show Will precisely where on the map she intended to go, work out where they'd transport the computer equipment, the weapons, and other supplies.

And she had to hope her mother's tonic would prevent the civilians from having too extreme a reaction.

"You're sure it's empty?" Simon pressed. "No holdovers inside? No military? No booby traps?"

"I've been there, through the crystal and otherwise. It's been empty for years. Some remains," she added, glancing at the civilians. "I should've told you."

"We've seen remains before. Don't worry." Arlys gave Will a quick, hard kiss. "I'll be back with the biggest scoop ever."

"Take hands," Fallon ordered. "Breathe. It'll be fast," she said and, with a glance at Duncan and Tonia, flashed.

"They're going to be fine." Hannah slipped an arm around her mother, then one around Lana. "Just fine."

"Beam me the fuck down, Scotty." Swaying some, Chuck tried to catch the breath the flash had stolen. He could've sworn his eyes jiggled in their sockets. "Okay, hot stuff?"

"Am I all here?" Arlys wondered as the floor rocked under her feet like a ship in high seas. "I feel all here."

"Every smoking bit of you. Hell of a ride, kids. Hell of a ride. And oh, oh, come to Papa!"

He rushed toward the monitors and equipment.

"I thought here first," Fallon said. "So he can tell us what we should take back."

"Can I have all of it? Can I, can I?"

"Just the essentials this time."

"Let me get this on record." Arlys switched on her camera. "What else is here?"

"It's a kind of plant," Fallon explained. "For weapons storage, testing, maintenance. There are supplies—MREs, uniforms, medicine—though most of that is probably outdated. But medical supplies and equipment I think the clinic would be glad to have. The warheads have to come first. Can you work here?" she asked Chuck.

"I got this."

"The warheads are several levels below. There's an elevator. You can't take another flash so soon, Arlys, so we'll go down in that."

"Is there power? You're adding the light. I know magickal light."

"No power. It died long ago. But I can make the elevator run."

They went down several levels in what Arlys tried not to think of as a big steel box running on witchcraft.

She followed Fallon, who apparently knew just where she was going, through another warren, running the camera and a commentary as she went.

Then stopped in her tracks as she saw, through thick glass, the warheads. "Oh my God."

"You can record them, but you have to stay here. And when we go in, you'll turn off the camera."

"Yes."

"I'll tell you when you can turn it back on."

"Okay."

"You need to turn it off now."

With Duncan and Tonia, Fallon flashed. And with her heart in her throat, Arlys watched the three of them face down destruction.

She recorded nothing. But she didn't forget.

She'd seen circles cast before, and had seen and felt the power that could rise from them, in them, around them. But this was more, more because even through that thick glass she felt the pulse of it, saw the air stir. Candles lit and words spoken she couldn't hear.

The three of them levitated as if they were one entity, and there, Arlys thought, was a stunning beauty in it.

Liquid, the palest of pale blues, poured from a cup that somehow spilled into the moving air, then vanished. Dirt, light as tropical sand, flung from a hand that scattered and disappeared. Wind circling, the three who stirred it rising and rising. Light glowing, brighter, brighter.

Something burst, white and bright. It struck her eyes like a laser, and she waited for annihilation.

But it quieted to the palest of pale blues.

Her breath caught when each of them drew a knife, scored their palms, let their blood drip. Clasping hands, they lowered again, and lifting those joined hands high . . .

The warheads shimmered, sheened, became sheer, shining glass. Inside she saw whatever had been in them, the death they carried, was now dead itself.

She knew the Oppenheimer quote, and now thought of her lede. *I am become the death of death, savior of worlds.*

They brought their hands down with a power that made the floor beneath her shake.

The glass shattered into countless harmless pieces.

Fallon, flushed with power, eyes alive with it, turned, nodded at Arlys.

With a hand that trembled a bit, Aryls recorded.

The next day after a long night, Arlys sat with Lana on the front porch of her home. A home that years before Lana had shared with Max.

"It's been a while since we've done this." As the long day after the long night edged toward evening, she took her first sip of wine. "I know it must seem odd to you."

"It doesn't. It really doesn't. I'd always hoped you and Will would get together. Now here you are, raising a family. So much has changed, so much hasn't. And one thing I know hasn't is your reporter's instincts and sensibilities. It's hard for you to hold this story."

"Teenage Triad Nukes the Nukes. Everything I've seen, Lana, everything from those first days in New York? Nothing compares. And holding it, yeah, it sticks. But I understand weighing the greater good over the public's right to know. Fallon wants the recruits here, and those at other bases secured, before I break the story. It can wait a few days."

She took another sip. "And though, at the time, it galled me when they just dumped us off after their first strike, I can understand that, too. Chuck and I were added weight—not even considering all the equipment they brought back."

"They wouldn't let me go, let me help. Even after they brought you back. Even understanding why on some level—Fallon's absolute insistence it had to be only the three of them—I felt so damn helpless."

"You said they didn't get back until just before dawn. Horrible night for you, for Katie."

"Simon and I pretended we weren't worried, then gave that up. Paced, prayed. Can I just add Hannah is a rock."

"She is," Arlys agreed. "She always has been."

"I can see leaning on that rock, and I guess Simon and I are going to have to get used to the pacing and praying."

"Here's a change. We're mothers now, having to face sending our children into war. Will and I talked seriously about not having kids. We're realists. New Hope is a good community, but it's not the world, and we understood we'd have to fight to keep the community, and eventually the world. Did we want to bring children into that? And then . . . Well, if you can't have hope in a town named for it, where?"

"You have beautiful children."

"I do." She took Lana's hand. "So do you. Simon's just terrific, Lana. I wanted to say that here on the porch that used to be yours and Max's. I can see how much you love him, and more, how much he loves you, the boys, Fallon."

"He went with me early this morning to the memorial tree, to Max's star. He's such a good man, Arlys."

"I know it. So I'm hoping I'm doing the right thing." She reached in her pocket, took out a flash drive. "I've gone back and forth the last couple weeks about giving this to you. It's Max's."

"The book he was working on."

"Yeah, and a kind of journal, random thoughts and observations. We hoped we'd find you, then when we didn't, we hoped you'd find your way back even though Starr told Flynn what you'd said. Will and I decided we'd take the house, and I found this. I put it away, held on to it in case I ever got the chance to give it to you."

"This means so much." Lana took the drive, closed her hand around it. "So much, Arlys. I'll give it to Fallon. It should be hers."

"I was afraid it would make you sad."

"No. It reminds me he had hope, too. He was writing again. It reminds me what he did, what I did, to protect the child we'd made together. And what Simon did to protect her, right from the start. It reminds me giving up is never an option."

———

Every night Fallon traveled with Duncan and Antonia to repeat the spell. On the third night, they traveled throughout Russia, on the fifth, Asia.

They told no one.

Fallon updated her maps, plotted locations. She believed once they'd eliminated the worst of man-made destruction, they could move on.

During the day she worked with organizing and housing arriving recruits. She found Katie invaluable with her capacity for creating lists, spreadsheets, organizing data, and her innate ability to welcome strangers with warmth.

"They need to start training."

Katie sat at a picnic table outside the barracks working on a laptop. People milled around; children played with dogs. Two of those dogs were Jem and Scout.

"They need to start training," Fallon repeated. "They need structure, discipline."

"Yes, I know." Katie continued working without looking up. "But right now they're not soldiers, or a lot of them aren't. They're adjusting to a new place. And we're working to ensure there's adequate housing, supplies. Rachel and her team are still doing medical evaluations. We have over four hundred of the eight hundred plus you expect."

"I know all you've done, are doing." But a storm's coming, Fallon thought. Something big and dark, and soon. Still the crystal wouldn't clear for her, wouldn't show her.

She sat, waited for Katie to look up.

"With the data you've collected, I know how many we have with medical training, with specific skills, with battle experience, with families."

Katie folded her hands to show she listened. "You'd already collected most of that."

"But not all, not as detailed. People talk to you. They don't just tell you they were a surgical resident before. They also tell you they liked to garden as a hobby or paint or they have a child with an aptitude for building. They tell you what they hope for, what they're afraid of. I'm learning from you how to see the whole, and not just the pieces I need to fit the whole."

Katie sat back. "But they need to train."

"It needs to start. I've asked my dad to take charge of this base. He has the experience. He'll need help, others who can train, make decisions, lead."

"Poe," Katie said immediately, and Fallon smiled.

"I agree."

"I know you said Maggie, and she's a good choice. There's Deborah Harniss. USMC. She was a JAG lawyer. She's a shifter, and I think she'd be willing to work at one of the other bases."

"I don't know her, but if she comes from you, I'd like to ask her, or have you ask her."

"I will, and I'll have her come speak with you."

"We need two cooks, a supply officer, a communication officer. From your list and mine, we have those inside the recruits."

"And using people from inside and out helps them blend, take some ownership."

Working with someone who knew how to run things helped smooth the road, Fallon thought.

"For blending, I'd like some of the recruits—experienced for now—to join your supply runs, scavenger and scouting missions. Hunting parties."

"Give me the names, where you want them. We'll work them into the rotation."

"Thanks."

Katie shook her head. "I want none of this to be necessary because I can remember a time when it wasn't. You can't. My children can't. So I'm going to do everything I can to work toward a time when it won't be necessary again. Isn't that what you and Duncan and Tonia are doing every night? No, they didn't tell me," she said when Fallon's face shuttered. "I know they've been gone, just like I know they're exhausted and starving every morning. Just like I know your parents know. And they probably feel, as I do, frustrated none of you trust us enough to talk to us."

"It's not that. Oh, I'm so bad at this. It's not trust. We knew you'd worry."

"And you actually think we don't or won't by being kept in the dark?"

"I'm really bad at this," Fallon repeated. "I'm sorry. Yes, we've been continuing what we began the night we took Arlys and Chuck. We've stockpiled supplies and equipment. We should be done in another week, maybe ten days. The ICBMs don't take as much power to eliminate, but—"

"ICBMs." Katie sighed.

"Intercontinental ballistic missiles."

"You know, I don't think I ever knew what that acronym stood for. I'm going to do what mothers do and give you some very direct advice. Talk to your parents."

"I will. I'm sorry."

"I'm going to accept that on a condition. Take the night off. The three of you need to, let's say, recharge. I know my kids, honey, and I can see it in you, too. You're running close to empty. You need to take a break."

She wanted to push forward, push, push until it was done. Everything felt so urgent. But she saw the logic in the R and R. "We'll take tonight off."

"Good. You're forgiven."

It wasn't as quick and easy with her parents. She wanted to talk to them both at once, and without the boys around. Though now that she considered things, she imagined Travis had felt what they'd been doing.

She had to wait until after dinner, after chores, after Ethan, bubbling, left for his sleepover with his new best friend Max.

She eased into it, discussing first the people chosen to work with Simon, the suggestions for other bases, asking her mother to initially supervise the cooks and meals at the barracks.

Stalling, she admitted, and ashamed she hadn't let herself see the worry in her parents' eyes.

"I want to start off saying I'm sorry. I'm sorry I didn't tell you what Duncan, Tonia, and I have been doing. It's my fault, all of it, because I made it a provision we keep the mission secret."

"You put a lot of worry weight on your mom, Fallon."

"I know it. I put more weight on by convincing myself I was doing the opposite. But—"

Lana shook her head. "Don't qualify. Just don't. I've known what you are to the world, some of what you'd face since before you were born. So has your father. We raised you, however hard it was for us, so you'd be strong and able to pick up that sword and shield. Deceiving us, keeping us out of what you do? It demeans that. It demeans us."

Really, really bad at it, Fallon thought again. She'd get better.

"Mom. There's no one in the world I need more than the two of you, no one I trust more, no one I love more. I'm going to make mistakes, and I know when I do they can have terrible consequences. That scares me more than anything. I should've told you, that's respect. I won't make that mistake again."

Something cold crawled up her spine, had her shifting.

"What is it?" Lana demanded.

"I don't know. Something . . . Probably guilt, but—" She looked up, saw nothing but stars and a hanging white moon.

"It might be you're a little worn-out," Simon suggested. "Keeping this secret, bouncing and flashing all over the country turning bombs into broken glass." His eyes narrowed on her face. "What'd I get wrong there?"

"It's just we've been alternating sites in the U.S. with sites overseas. Like, ah, Russia, Asia, Europe."

"You've been to Russia?" Simon broke out in a grin.

"You flashed to Russia?" Lana's reaction wasn't a grin. "For God's sake, Fallon. What if you'd lost the connection on the way, dropped into the damn ocean? What if . . . and this is exactly why you didn't tell us. Exactly."

She closed her eyes, drew in a breath. "My mistake, and I'll try not to make it again."

But Fallon felt that chill a second time, and something pushing, pushing to get in, to open.

"Do you feel that?" It squeezed at her heart, twisted in her belly. "Do you feel that?"

"What?" Even as Lana reached for her she sprang up from where she'd sat on the porch.

"Something's coming."

She heard the engine, saw the headlight. Laid a hand on the hilt of her sword. Then relaxed it again. "It's Duncan's bike. It's Tonia on Duncan's bike."

She waited.

Something's happened. Something's happening. Something's coming. Something's here.

Tonia stopped the bike, turned it off. "Hey. Ah . . ."

She got off, walked to the porch. "Anyway, Duncan said he'd already talked to both of you."

"Duncan?" Fallon repeated.

"Yeah, he tracked me down at the barracks."

"And came to talk to me at the community kitchen. I got flowers," Lana added. "Come up, sit down."

"He's such a suck-up." Tonia offered a wan smile. "I don't have any flowers, but I'm just as sorry as he is. Apologies, sincerely."

"It's my fault. I made it a condition."

"Condition's bull." Tonia shrugged as she came up the porch steps. "We agreed with you. We know it, you know it. We were all wrong. And don't try to hog my apology."

"Let's call it a clean slate." Simon glanced at Fallon and his easy smile slipped away. "You okay, baby?"

"Can you feel it? Can you hear it? Crows circling, wings slicing. The fruit and the flowers. Dark masked by innocence. Blood of the blood, bone of the bone. Can you feel it?"

"I can now." Tonia, a hand on Fallon's arm, went pale as the moon. "I can now. Oh God, oh Jesus. Duncan."

They flashed together.

"What the hell!"

"Something's coming."

Simon rounded on Lana, grabbed her hand. "Don't even think about going without me. Let me get the rifle, a sidearm."

"Hurry." She ran inside with him, shouted for Colin. Pounded up the stairs for the knife she'd carried out of New Hope.

Colin rushed out of his room, sword in hand.

"Get Travis."

"I'm here. What is it?"

"I'm not sure. Go to Fred's, tell her something's coming. Something's coming to New Hope. Tell Eddie to come, tell him to get everyone he can." Lana spun to Colin, took his shoulders in her hands. "Stay with the children."

"Mom—"

"Stay with them, listen to me. Listen. If this gets through us . . . Keep the children safe, Colin."

"I will." He looked at Travis. "We will."

"I love you." She sprinted downstairs, grabbed Simon's hand. "I love you," she said again, and flashed.

CHAPTER TWENTY-FIVE

Since they were taking a night off to recharge before hitting the next sites on Fallon's list, Duncan wandered down toward the community gardens and park. Some of his friends talked about hanging out, playing some music.

He hadn't had much of a chance to do either, or even think about getting his hands on his girl of the moment, Carlee Jentz. Trouble was, he admitted, he hadn't much missed getting his hands on Carlee. They'd hung together most of August, into September, but now as October came calling . . .

He liked her fine—a lot, really. She was just the sort of girl he liked getting his hands on.

Curvy, fun, uncomplicated.

He just needed to unwind, he decided. Fallon kept him wound up, in all sorts of ways.

He liked her fine, too, and holy hell they did good work together. He respected how she got things done. Dealing with the bombs, building an army. He admired her skill with a sword. He'd watched her one night before they'd met for the mission. He'd sat on the roof of the barracks, just to chill, and out she'd come, sword in hand.

She'd conjured three opponents, took them on at the same time. Took them out.

He looked forward to testing his skills against hers in practice one of these days.

But the fact was, she wasn't anywhere near curvy, she wasn't a hell of a lot of fun, and she was seriously complicated.

He didn't know why he wanted to get his hands on her, wanted them on her more than he wanted them on Carlee. Or anybody else.

Maybe it was the power connection, or the blood connection. Maybe it was just that she was different from anyone he'd ever known. Whatever the reason, he knew thinking about her—that way—made him itchy.

So he'd stop thinking about her that way, and for tonight, at all. He'd hang out in the park, listen to music, watch Denzel smoke his guitar.

Denzel handled a guitar—a banjo, even a violin—like he'd been born to play, just like he handled any sort of ball. God knew he handled them better than he did any kind of weapon.

He needed to spend more time with Denzel, improving his skills, tightening up his form. And convincing his friend to focus his talents in some other area. He was never going to be a warrior.

Maybe he'd enlist Petra on that mission, since Denzel was gone, gone, gone over her, and Petra seemed good and stuck on him.

As if thinking about her conjured her, he heard Petra call his name. Turned. Smiling, she walked toward him carrying a box.

"Heading down to the park?" he asked.

"Yeah. I'm meeting Denzel. Is Tonia coming?"

"She'll be around. She had something to do first."

"I've hardly seen her lately."

"Lots going on right now."

"I know. All those new people." It put a cloud in her eyes. "Anyway. I hope Hannah comes, too."

She'd latched on to his sisters from the first, Duncan thought. "I think she's already there. Stalwick's bringing his keyboard, and they're hanging a lot lately."

"Oh, he's really good! I like music. I like it so much. And it's a perfect night, isn't it? Cool, but not cold, all the stars, the moon. Just so perfect."

"Yeah." But he felt something, a chill, a twist. Looking up he half expected to see clouds swirl over the moon and stars. "Nothing like music outdoors, and we won't get that much longer."

"I can hear them. They're already playing. Do I look okay?" She stopped, fussed a hand over her hair the way girls did. "Mina really doesn't like mirrors in the apartment, so I only have a little one in my room."

"Yeah, you look good."

She beamed at him, almost bobbled the box.

"Whatcha got there? Smells sweet."

"It should. Cupcakes. I worked in the community kitchen today, and got permission to make cupcakes for tonight."

"I was in there today. Didn't see you."

"You must've come in during one of my breaks. Here, try one. I really hope I did them right."

"They look right." He glanced in the box at the swirling peaks of white frosting sprinkled with color and texture. "Fancy. What kind?"

"I think they're from one of Mrs. Swift's recipes. Yellow cake with a raspberry filling and whipped cream icing garnished with wild violets."

He lifted his eyes to hers—big, innocent blue. A shy, hopeful smile. "Fruit and flowers," he said.

"That's right. I hope they taste as good as they look."

She held the box out, stood smiling with the faerie lights of the park and gardens glowing at her back, with music winding through the air. With the moon, full and white, showering over her.

He took the box and, for an instant, just a finger snap, saw the dark glee in her eyes.

Keeping his eyes on hers, Duncan flipped the box over. The pretty cupcakes hit the ground, and oily black oozed out while the bits of violets turned to tiny, slithering snakes.

Petra laughed. "Now look what you've done."

"Hey, Dunc! You trying to make time with my girl?"

The sound of Denzel's voice turned his blood cold. "Stay back! Get everybody out."

"What the what, man?"

As Petra laughed again, Duncan struck out.

She moved fast, faster than he'd prepared for. And had Denzel as a shield in front of her, had a thin black blade pressed to his heart.

"I can't move." Denzel choked the words out. "Dunc, I can't move. Petra?"

"Let him go. You're not interested in him."

"But you are, and that's enough. Now if you'd fallen for me, as planned, I wouldn't have had to put up with him. Wasn't I pretty enough for you, *Dunc*? Sweet enough? Helpless enough?"

"This is because I didn't go for you?"

"Oh, please. You're just a means to an end. You and your idiot sisters."

The music still played, voices still sang. Had she put up some sort of barrier, or were they still just far enough away?

How could he use it?

"Right from the start then. But this isn't from the cult shit. You got black magick going—it stinks up the air." In the hope of keeping her focused only on him, Duncan flicked his fingers, shot light, burned the slithering snakes, the oozing poison to ash. "Yeah, that's a smell. So it's not from the cult."

"Another means to an end. I spent almost two weeks in that sty."

" 'Weeks'?"

"Your power's so pale and weak you can't do mind illusion? Anyone who survived the attack would swear I'd been there nearly two years. Even two weeks was disgusting. Of course, I did take little breaks, have little bits of fun. The man you watched burn—and wasn't that a lovely light?—only thought he was my father because I made him think it. Just as I arranged for your pitiful rescue group and the PWs to attack that night."

"Got wasted." Denzel's head lolled. "How many beers we slam, bro?"

In the park someone shouted, someone screamed. And the music cut off. Petra swept a hand back and sent people flying, tumbling in a tidal wave of wind.

"Duncan." Denzel's eyes blurred. "Too much beer. Gotta go home, man."

"I hate to be interrupted." Petra tapped a finger to Denzel's lips, seared them together. "Don't you? And I've held this in for so long."

He could fix it, Duncan thought, he could fix Denzel once he got him clear. But everything he'd tried hadn't touched that thin, black blade.

"The rescue was a setup, to get you into New Hope. You set up the ambush, too."

"You're not a complete moron."

"Didn't work."

Her smile widened. "Didn't it?"

Yes, it had, he realized. Of course it had.

"Fallon. You wanted to draw out The One."

"Not a complete moron. It took her long enough to get here. I've had to live with that pious bitch all this time, run around after a bunch of brats. That's over now, and so's the pious bitch. I didn't have time to finish off the brat. I had cupcakes to deliver. Oh, and just a quick stop on the way. Carlee won't be joining in the fun tonight. Or ever."

He felt it like a blow to the gut. "Why?"

"You liked her better than me."

She lifted a hand. The clouds he'd imagined rolled over the stars, smothered the moon.

Crows circled, screaming.

Denzel moaned.

"God, I'm bored with him."

With a flick of her hand, she broke his neck, and Denzel slid bonelessly to the ground.

On a cry of rage, of grief, sword flashing, Duncan leaped forward.

Petra threw up her arms, swooped high on wings. One black, one white, just as one side of her hair faded to midnight, the other to moon pale.

"Did you feel it coming?" she shouted as she hurled fire and power at Duncan. "Did you feel the storm coming?"

He slapped her weapons and power away with his sword as Fallon and Tonia flashed beside him.

"I *am* the storm!" Fallon hurled her own fire.

Petra tucked her wings, dived under the flames, then speared again. "At last. Hello, cousin."

Lightning, black, glistening, tore through the sky, struck the ground. Grass, green with summer, flamed, and the whirl of wind swept the fire toward the playground, the gardens, the memorial tree.

Even as the gazebo erupted, shooting hunks and spears of wood, Fallon brought the rain. Smoke billowed from the smolder, hazed the air.

"You spoil my fun." Petra slapped away a trio of arrows Tonia loosed. "Mummy! They're so mean to me."

Suddenly Allegra appeared, pale hair streaming, white wings spread. "There, there, precious." With a laugh, she stroked a finger down her daughter's cheek.

"Can we kill them now? Can we?"

"Of course, my treasure. But we want them to suffer first, don't we? There must be pain, and blood. On their suffering, on their screams, we feed."

Allegra snatched the arrow aimed at her heart out of the air, hurled it back. Tonia dodged it, but not the vicious fist of power that flung her up and back.

With a delighted giggle, Petra tossed balls of fire as Tonia lay crumpled and dazed. Duncan leaped to shield his sister, slamming the balls with his sword, ignoring the shocking burn as one slipped by, grazed his side.

"I'm okay, I'm okay." Swiping blood from her mouth, her nose, Tonia shoved to her feet. "Just woke me up, that's all. I'm a distraction. Fallon."

She stood alone now, face lifted, sword sheathed.

"Do you feel their pain, whelp?"

"I do. And I see beneath your mask. Your beauty's false." She stared into Allegra's eyes, streamed vision with power.

And watched the flowing hair dissolve to a straggle, watched it recede to leave part of the scarred scalp exposed even as one of the crystalline-blue eyes drooped, the cheek puckered. The pure white wings blackened and frayed.

Enraged, Allegra pounded lightning, flame, wind. And Fallon saw tears of humiliation spill from the ruined eyes.

"My father did that to you," Fallon shouted. "And my mother. So now your face reveals your heart. Ugly and twisted. But I'll end you."

"At your six!" Duncan shouted as he enflamed his sword, deflected the attack.

"I know," Fallon murmured, and whirled as Eric flew at her back.

She'd been waiting for him. Waiting, she knew, since before her first breath.

She drew her sword, struck, sliced through the edges of his left wing. The shock sent him careening to the ground, the force like the thunder that boomed overhead.

"Hold them off me."

She wanted to see his face, his true face. And the bubbling thirst for vengeance burned in her blood. "You took his life, your brother's life, for power and greed. I'll take yours."

He rolled away from the strike of her sword, flew up, wavering where Allegra folded him in a wing.

His true face, Fallon thought. Like raw meat, one eye gone, his lips seared and drawn back by scarring.

She heard others coming, fast. Heard the shouts as Petra, hissing like a snake, flung fire, toothy black darts.

When her parents flashed a few feet away, Fallon's heart stuttered.

"Get back! Get away from this."

In the chaos of smoke and flame, of clashing magicks, gunfire and calls for help, she pivoted in front of her parents.

"You did this to me!" Allegra screamed down at Lana.

"I did, and I can do it again."

"Not yet, not yet." Fallon saw it, that wild red haze of power, saw it in the way her mother's hair streamed back in her own storm. "Not yet.

"Taibhse! *Ionsaí!*"

The owl exploded out of the sky, a white streak through the dark. With talons and beak he tore through the crows, sent mangled bodies falling.

"Faol Ban! *Garda!*"

The wolf charged through the smoke, fangs gleaming, to stand in front of Lana and Simon.

"Laoch!" Through the haze, he galloped to her, and she thrust her sword toward the boiling sky. "*Eitilt!*" As he rose, wings spreading, she leaped on his back.

"Not alone." Lana pushed that fury, barely banked, toward Allegra. "Duncan, not alone. I can help, from here. Please."

"Tonia?"

"I'm good." She lifted her bow. "I've got this. Arrows!" she shouted.
"I need more arrows."

Trusting his sister, and hoping like hell he could hit a moving target, Duncan flashed.

He nearly overshot as Fallon wheeled the horse to the left, and
slammed hard into her back.

"Goddamn it!"

"Sorry. Blame your mom. Later. You want your uncle, let's go get
the bastard. But Petra's mine. Do you hear me? She's mine."

Vengeance. She heard it bubbling in him as it did in her. Did it
strengthen or weaken?

They rode through a rain of fire, slicing spears of lightning, into
heat that boiled the air. She blocked attacks with her shield, deflected
with her sword. And would have taken a hard hit if Duncan hadn't
slapped a bolt away.

They hit the edge of her mother's fury, and Duncan hissed out of
breath at the toothy, red flood. "Shit. Push through it! Just push
through it."

But it shifted away.

"It's my mother's power."

"It still fucking bites. Move in."

"I know what I'm doing."

They circled the three, striking power to power. Whirlwinds spun,
spinning flames she met with fists of ice, sweeps of driving rain.

And Fallon's mind cleared just enough of her own fury for her to see.

They flanked their child. Shielded her. Took strikes for her.

Loved her.

"Can you talk to Tonia? Mind to mind?"

"A little, sometimes. Not like elves. We need to draw them away
from the park, from town."

"No. Do it now, call Tonia. Do it with me—I have elfin blood.
Tell her to train everything on Petra. Everything she has. On Petra."

Duncan fought to open himself, felt a blaze of black lightning scorch by an inch from his face. Sweat dripped into his eyes, his side pulsed with pain, but he felt the click of connection.

A glance below showed him Tonia looking up, and notching another arrow. And to his horror, Hannah on the smoldering grass using her body as a shield over one of the wounded.

"On Petra," Fallon told him. "Concentrate on Petra. Everybody! Everything!"

The barrage was brutal. Arrows flaming, fire shooting from sword strikes, bullets winging. And the thrust and push of light against dark that rocked sky and earth.

They shielded her, losing the force of attack in defense. Blocking missiles and magicks in panic while Petra, Fallon thought—coolheaded now—laughed.

Not just a twisted heart, not just a twisted gift. A twisted mind.

"Hey, *cousin!*" Fallon shouted it, putting a taunt in her voice. "I guess you don't want to play, since you're hiding behind Mommy and Daddy."

Allegra threw a bolt that stuck Fallon's shield with enough power to shoot shock into her shoulder.

"Maybe you're just shy." Drawing in, Fallon punched with the shield to thrust the bolt back.

Understanding now, Duncan filled his shout with contempt. "She's not worth it. Cowardly little bitch. Weird-looking, too. Let's just finish this and go have a beer."

"I'll kill you both!"

Face clenched in fury, Petra swung clear of her mother's wings. She flung fire, bolts, angry power with her eyes—one blue, one black—mad with rage.

Fallon blocked, blocked. "Wait," she said to Duncan. "Wait."

And when she raised her sword, shot light through it as bright as the charging horse, Eric screamed.

He flew in a gale of wind, shoved his daughter away, and took the blade.

Fallon's strike cleaved off his wing, scorched across his chest, burned down to his belly.

As he fell, and with Allegra's shriek shaking the air, she took Laoch into a dive.

"Now. Mom! Now!"

She saw her mother's full power—old grief locked with new—love joined unbreakably with love. The red haze roiled, rolled. Allegra wrapped herself around Petra, shot high as the killing edge clawed at her.

Mother of Darkness, Fallon thought. And Mother of Light.

"Let it go. Mom, let it go. Help me clear the air. Duncan! I have to see."

"They're gone."

Still, she urged Laoch into a climb, searching.

"Are you hurt?" she asked Duncan as she scanned the sky, as she saw the first stars blink back through the thinning haze.

"Not much. Not as much as they are. We need to go down."

When Eric fell on the edge of the cornfield, Simon left Lana's side. He knew the sounds of a battlefield—the cries of the wounded, the calls for medics. He knew the stench of it—smoke and blood and death.

Just as he knew death when he looked it in the eye.

Eric, what was left of him, still breathed, but it was short and bubbling bloody froth. No medic, no magick, would save him.

"You're done. Maybe you'll live long enough for my women, my incredible women, to say what they have to say to you."

"Who—" Eric wheezed, coughed up blood. "Who are you?"

"I'm the man who brought The One into the world. She came into my hands." Sidearm aimed, steady, Simon glanced over briefly as Fallon brought the horse to earth, leaped off, ran toward him.

Then he saw sweat mix with the blood on Eric's face, saw the shaking hand form a black dagger. As Eric lifted it to throw, Simon put a bullet into him.

"That was for Max Fallon, you son of a bitch."

Breathless, Fallon looked down, saw the dagger dissolve into muddy ash, the single eye glaze as it stared up at her.

"I wanted to be the one who ended him."

"You did."

Fallon shook her head, sheathed her sword, took Simon's hands. "No, you did." Then her mother's as Lana ran to her. "You did. It was always meant to be you. Not standing in for my father, because you are my father. Standing for the man he betrayed, the brother he killed."

"You're hurt."

Fallon glanced down at herself. Some cuts, some burns. "Not really, but others are." She turned to her mother. "I underestimated you."

"You're not the only one," Simon agreed.

"I won't do that again."

"Right with you."

"You'll help with the wounded."

"Yes. You first. I'm your mother," Lana said when Fallon started to object. "You first."

While her mother tended her, she studied Eric and found the rage that had driven her ebbed just like the burning under her mother's touch.

"He'll be enflamed with spell fire, and the ashes salted and taken away to barren land to be buried with the head of a snake, the fang of a jackal, the head of a crow."

She looked at Lana. "You hurt her again."

"Not enough. They'll come back."

"They'll come back, but this time we don't run."

"No, we're done with that. Go on." She touched Fallon's cheek. "People need to see you. I'll help the medics, and your father will deal with that." She looked down at Eric.

"Yeah, I will."

When Fallon moved off, Lana turned into Simon. "Max died here, right here where Eric fell. Fallon's sword sent him here, and you finished it. Right here, Simon. Max tried to stop him. I tried. You and Fallon did. It matters, I think, it was you and Fallon."

"It's done." He kissed her. "Go help patch people up. I'm going to get a couple of guys to help me move him more into the open, and we'll keep a guard on him until we can do what Fallon wants done with him."

It relieved Fallon to see familiar faces as she moved across what had, for the second time, become a field of battle. She saw the wisdom in Fred and some of the other faeries recharging the earth where it had been struck and scorched, and people gathering up the ruined remains of the gazebo.

Some wept, and there should always be tears over blood, but most dealt with what needed to be done with a grim determination.

She stopped Hannah.

"Can you tell me how bad it is? Dead, wounded?"

"A lot of gashes and burns, and shock. Some serious injuries." She pressed her fingers to her eyes. "Starr's one. She took a hard hit, but she's fighting treatment. She panics if they touch her. I know Flynn's trying, but he's hurt, too. And—and Tonia."

Fallon gripped Hannah's arm, hard. "How bad?"

"Rachel says second- and third-degree burns, probably a concussion, whiplash. I'm not sure. Mom made her go to the clinic. She couldn't make Duncan go, and he's hurt, too."

Fallon looked to where he sat, his arm around a woman who held Duncan's dead friend. Who rocked, who keened.

"Denzel . . . her son . . . I loved him. We all loved him. And I heard Duncan tell Will to check on Carlee, and on Mina and her little boy. That Petra—oh God—that she said she'd killed Carlee and Mina. I have to go, they need me."

"I'll come to the clinic. I can help. I'll be there."

First she went to Duncan. He didn't look at her, just held the grieving mother, kept his eyes on his friend's face. But he jerked away when Fallon laid a hand on his wounded side.

"Leave it alone."

"You're more help uninjured." Despite him, she pressed her hand against him, slid her power in. Searing, she thought, and deeper than she'd realized. She had to clamp her teeth on the shock of the burn, kept them clamped until it eased and she could breathe clear again.

"Rachel will want to have a look at you," she said, and rose, began her walk to the clinic.

Scores injured, she saw as she went in. Some huddled in chairs with their wounds, others lay on gurneys. Some wept, some moaned, some just sat with eyes glazed in shock.

Her mother, hair pinned up, worked with other healers. She stopped by a girl she recognized as one of Tonia's friends. April, a faerie, who shivered with shock under a blanket.

"It's not bad. They said it's not bad. Do you know where Barkly is? I was with Barkly."

"I'll find out. Look at me. April, see me."

"It's not bad."

"It'll be better." Cuts, burns, shock, the system jolt of a lightning strike only feet away. She soothed it, closed the little gashes, healed the burns.

"My mom's probably looking for me, worried. And Barkly."

"Your mom'll find you. Sleep now."

Fallon sent her into a light, healing sleep, moved on.

She found Flynn in one of the exam rooms with Lupa at his feet. Flynn had blood on his face, on his shirt, raw burns on both hands. And still he pleaded with Starr.

"You have to let them help you. They can't help you if they don't touch you. You know these people, Starr."

"I knew Petra."

There was a wildness in her that was pain, Fallon knew, and delirium. Her body shook from the burns that covered her arms, her legs, and dripped with what Fallon scented as infection already setting in.

A graze on her face oozed blood.

"You know me." Fallon closed the door behind her, stepped to the gurney. "I've come to ask your forgiveness. I thought you might have been the one who betrayed us."

"I know. Don't touch me."

"I was wrong. I had you come to the meeting to see if things we spoke of, things we did, would be passed on. I set a trap for you, and I was wrong."

"I'd never betray you."

"I know. Forgive me. Show me forgiveness by letting me help you. I have need for the brave and the true. You're both. Without help you'll die, and I'll lose a warrior and a light. Flynn will lose a friend and a sister. Look at me, Starr."

"She'll fight a trance," Flynn told her.

"She won't fight me. Do you see me?" she asked Starr. "I see you. You see the light in me. I see the light in you. Trust what you fought for. Trust me as I trust you."

She took her deep. "Get my mother, or another powerful healer. Tell her the burns are infected. She'll know what to bring. Where's Rachel?"

"Surgery."

"Get my mother if you can, and have someone tend to you."

"After Starr. I'll get your mother."

She began, and the pain turned her legs to water. She had to stop and start again, stop and start. She had the power, Fallon thought, but her experience remained limited.

Pale, drenched in sweat, she looked over as her mother came in with a tray of magickal supplies.

"Too much," Lana said sharply. "Ease back, right now."

"I think she's dying."

"It won't help you to die with her. Slowly, Fallon. Layer by layer."

Lana set the tray down, glided hands, light as clouds, over Starr. "We have to let the poison out. We need the athame, the cup, the healing powder. Watch."

She drew the knife Fallon gave her over a seeping burn, caught the drainage in the cup. Then another, and another.

"Salt it, pour it out, wash and purify the cup. Next, we heal slowly, layer by layer, use the healing powder, and do it all again, and again, until she's cleared of infection."

They worked for more than two hours, and most of it under Flynn's watchful eye.

Finally Lana mopped her face, laid a hand on Starr's forehead. "She's cool again."

"She won't die?"

Lana turned to Flynn. "She should have died. Anyone without her iron will would have died. She'll have scars, inside and out. We can only heal so much. But she'll live, and she'll need someone she trusts to coat the burns we couldn't heal through with a balm I'll give you. Twice a day. Can you do that?"

"Yeah, she'll let me. She might let Fred. She'll let you now," he said to Fallon. "She ran straight into a fireball. It would've taken out at least six, but she ran straight into it."

"Do you know how many dead, how many wounded?" Fallon asked him.

"Nine dead on the field, another two touch and go. Wounded? Fifty, sixty. It would've been worse if it hadn't been for you, Duncan, Tonia. You," he said to Lana, "and your man. It would've been worse if the recruits you brought in hadn't come swarming to fight."

Flynn looked over at Lana, smiled a little. "Your son rallied them. Colin. That's the word anyway. I'll stay with her until she wakes up."

"She won't wake till morning," Lana told him, and he shrugged.

"I've got nothing else to do."

Fallon left the clinic, walked back to the field. The faeries had done their work, greening the grass, healing the trees. She imagined the non-magickals would do theirs as well, rebuilding the gazebo, the playground.

Symbols, she thought. They would not stop building, surviving, fighting, living.

She walked to Eric's body and the two guards. "I'll deal with this now."

"Your father and Will, they said we should help you with him."

"I need to do it alone."

She waited until they left her. "The choices you made brought you here. I swear on my life over your death, your woman and what you made between you will end as you did. Not for vengeance. For justice."

From where he sat in the shadows with his grief, Duncan watched her call the fire, spread it over the body at her feet. He heard the words she spoke, but only understood some of the Irish.

Fire of light. Body and soul.

She took handfuls of salt from a pouch, spread it over the ashes, drizzled liquid over it that squirmed, then stilled. With fingers curling through the air, she brought what remained of Eric Fallon up and into a box. She sealed it with a finger, with a line of light.

Slipping the box into the pouch, she called her horse, her wolf, her owl. Then lifting her sword toward the moon, vanished.

He thought he saw, as he sat in the shadows, light streak across the sky, send a shower of stars like rain.

The One rides to honor her blood, to protect the light, he thought as he got to his feet.

And so, until the end, would he.

EPILOGUE

Exhausted from the battle, from the healing, from the travel and the ritual, Fallon tended her horse, and freed her owl and wolf to hunt.

She wanted her bed, and nothing else. No questions, no comfort. No dreams.

Tomorrow, she'd speak to Colin, tell him her pride in his quick thinking, in his willingness to stay back with Travis and Ethan and protect the children.

Tomorrow she'd talk to the recruits, visit the wounded, speak to the loved ones of the dead.

Tomorrow she would plan and plot, but tonight, she only wanted sleep.

She went in the side entrance, forced herself into the shower to wash away the blood, the grime, the stench of battle, the smoke of spells.

She came out of the bath, intending on falling into bed. Duncan sat sprawled in the single chair she'd put in her sitting area. That was jolt enough, but the second was remembering she wore nothing but skin.

She hurled a curse at him, and embarrassed herself only more by the instinctive move to cover herself with arms and hands.

"Get out."

"I didn't come to catch you naked. It's a nice bonus, but it's not on me you're not wearing anything. I need to talk to you."

"I don't want to talk to you or anyone tonight. I'm tired. I'm naked. Go away. If my father catches you in here, he'll knock you senseless."

"I'll risk it." Duncan flicked a hand at the dresser, yanking open drawers. "Put something on if it bothers you so much. I've seen naked girls before. You barely qualify."

He closed his eyes, held up a hand as a ripple of pain moved over her face. "I'm sorry for that. No call for that. Get dressed, would you? I'll wait outside."

He walked out, wandered. He wondered if they'd put water in the pool. He wondered why people wanted a kitchen outside. He wondered why he couldn't have stayed away until he had better control of himself.

He heard her come out, kept looking up at the sky. "I was still in the park when you dealt with your uncle's body."

"Don't call him that."

"You're right. Where did you take the ashes?"

"Away. Far. Where his whore and his bitch won't find them, won't find solace in mourning him."

"Good enough." He turned, saw she'd put on a T-shirt, cotton pants, was barefoot. "I brought her here. She set it up so Tonia and me, we'd be the ones to bring her to New Hope. She bragged about it, after . . . She had cupcakes."

"Cupcakes?"

"Raspberry and wild violet. Fruit and flowers. She offered me one, and then I knew. All the time she's been here, I didn't see the dark in her."

"Did you look?"

"Not really, not especially. I bought it. I helped save a traumatized kid. I'm a hero."

"I looked. In her, in Starr."

"Starr?"

"I saw almost nothing in either. Both block. Tonight, I could in Starr, could see she blocks rage and grief and fear. It wasn't until tonight I saw what was in Petra."

"You've had days. I've had years."

"Just you?" She arched both eyebrows. "Is that because you're a hero?"

"Kiss ass. If you hadn't warned me about the damn cupcakes, the fruit and the flowers, I'd have taken one. Poison and black snakes. I'd be dead because a pretty girl baked me a goddamn cupcake."

He looked older, she realized. Closer to the man at the circle of stones than the boy on a motorcycle.

"I don't think so. I think before you took it, you'd have seen."

"Well, we'll never know, will we? I didn't take her out on the spot. She had more than I bargained for, and that was stupid. Stupid."

"Maybe, but she was prepared and you weren't. She was someone you helped, someone you thought needed help."

"I didn't move fast enough, hard enough, so she got Denzel. Then I could only think of making her let him go, keeping it between us. She snapped his neck while I stood there. Snapped his neck like you'd break a stick in two."

Grief soaked his words. "He didn't mean anything. He was harmless."

"She killed him to hurt you, to damage you."

Fury slapped back. "You think I don't know that?"

His grief nearly flattened her, and opened something inside her that made her step to him, made her put her arms around him. "I'm sorry. I'm sorry about your friend."

Duncan stiffened against the comfort, then dropped into it. "He never hurt anyone. Lots of big talk about being a warrior, but he never hurt anyone. It wasn't in him. And she killed him like he was nothing. She killed Carlee. Her father found her in her room with her throat slit. She killed Carlee because we . . . shit."

"You loved her. I'm so sorry."

"No, no, not . . . We just got together sometimes. She was as harmless as Denzel. She wasn't a threat. She killed Mina, and would have killed Bill Anderson, but he was over at Will's. He wasn't home when she went into his place and wrecked it. Why did she do all that? They didn't matter. I mattered, you mattered, Tonia mattered."

She started to draw back, but he was holding on now, so she gave it another minute. "You didn't look straight into her."

He pulled back. "Fuck that. What's that mean?"

"You saw evil. You saw the dark and the vicious. You didn't see the product of the two who made her."

"One black wing, one white, the weird hair and eyes. I get it."

"You didn't see those as symbols. You didn't see that the dark in her, merging from them, is twisted. It's . . . flawed."

"You're saying she's crazy."

"I'm saying she's crazy."

He paced away. "Well, that . . . makes perfect sense."

"She's sly with it, a rabid fox. And they're patient, Duncan, really patient. All these years they waited, plotting, planning. They sent their child to . . . infiltrate."

"She could've done a lot more damage once she was in. She could've done more than plan an ambush."

"She probably did. Little things. An illness, an accident. When we look, we're going to find the place she held her rituals. We'll purify it. We hurt them, as my father did in the mountains, as my mother did on that same field. They'll take time, again. And so will we. Petra's father died for her. She won't forget it. I know. They loved."

"That's not love."

"It is. As real as any. Parent for child, child for parent, mate for mate. They loved. Now they're grieving, and they're hurt."

"So are we." Sticking his hands in his pockets, he looked up at the stars. "She liked killing. I saw that when she killed Denzel."

"It gives her joy, causing death and pain. I . . . understand that better now. I felt, for a moment, I felt joy when I put my sword in Eric. I never want to feel that again."

"I got that," he murmured. "I get that."

"We wanted revenge, both of us, so there was chaos. People fought, but there was chaos. There won't be the next time. We'll get more soldiers, make more, and we'll have leadership instead of chaos."

She let out a breath. "I failed."

"Bullshit."

"I failed because I went with impulse and anger." Remembering, she rubbed a hand over the cuff on her sword hand. "I wanted Eric's blood on my hands, and I got it, but I forgot strategy, tactics."

"Not altogether."

"Mostly then. You had my back. So, thanks."

"I guess we're even there."

"How's the side?" When he shrugged, she made an impatient gesture. "Lift up the shirt."

"It's fine, but maybe you want to see some skin, since I saw so much of yours."

"Don't be a dick." She laid a hand on his side, palm to skin. "Still some heat." She cooled it, remembering her mother's advice. Slowly. Layer by layer.

"There. Is Tonia—"

He grabbed her as he had before, yanked her to him. "I need this," he said before his mouth took hers.

She knew need, and it confused her. She wanted, didn't want. Her blood beat so fast, so fast, she heard it in her head like tribal drums.

Her mind ordered her to pull away, but she gripped his hair, let out a sound of shocked pleasure as his tongue swept hot over hers.

He had visions of a windswept cliff over a boiling sea—and her. Of a forest so green the air tasted of it, and her, always her. A circle of stones under a sky red as blood, and her calling the thunder.

Of a bed in the moonlight, bathed in it, and her under him, moving, moving, moving, her eyes like storm clouds.

Visions swam and swirled through him until, dizzy with them, he drew back.

"Did you see that? Do you feel that?"

"I don't know. I don't know. I can't think. I have to think. I can't do this." Storm-cloud eyes met his. "I don't know how to do this."

"I could walk you through it, but . . ." He turned, paced away, decided the best place for his hands was his pockets. "I think I need some space. I need to take some space, some time. And I need some distance from you. I guess you need it from me."

"I can't be distracted by—"

"Shut up." He strode back to her, and the air seemed to quake and sizzle around him. "I really don't like being called a distraction, so just shut up a minute. Which one of the bases could use me as an instructor? I'm good at it. It'll be hard for Mom, but she'll deal. I can help recruit from wherever that is. I can scout and report and help train.

"And take that space, take that distance."

It stunned her, worried her how much she wanted to insist he was needed here. How much she didn't want him to go. "You'd help most with Mallick. They're so raw there." And there he could train and be trained, she realized.

"Okay, I'll go there. A couple of days, and I'll go there. How long are you figuring, at this point, before we try for D.C.?"

"Two years, minimum. We'll need to—"

"Two years," he interrupted. "I can do that. That was your sentence, right? Two years. But I can flash back, report. That'll make it easier for Mom to get used to it."

He stood in the moonlight a few paces from her. "I'll come back, and I'll come back for you. You've got a couple years to think about that."

"We have a war to wage and win, Duncan. Everything, just everything depends on it."

"We have lives to live, or what's the point? I'll help you build and train your army, Fallon. I'll fight with and for you. And I'll come for you."

He smiled. "You still didn't say no," he said before he vanished.

Alone, Fallon stood where she was. Two years, she thought. So much could happen. Lives lost, lives saved. When she thought of two years, she had to think strategically, not emotionally.

He stirred too many emotions.

Space and distance, that would be good for all.

She had an army to lead, battles to plan, magicks to make.

Two years, a blink of an eye, an eternity? Whatever it was, it started in the morning.

She went inside, lay on the bed without bothering to undress. For the good of all, she'd send him away. Would either of them be the same when he came back?

Half-asleep, she lifted a hand to light her candle.

And in dreams saw it guiding his way, her way, as they traveled their own paths.

Was it love? Was it need? Was it duty?

Could all three find a way to be one?

Outside, the moon swam in the star-filled sky. This storm had passed. The next had already begun to gather.

Stockton & Billingham College

Stockton
LIBRARY
Techni

T022830

27000

780.9

22. [
-7.
19
2ᴬ
25.

Technical College